RAG and BONE

RAG and BONE

A Billy Boyle World War II Mystery

James R. Benn

Published by Soho Press, Inc.
853 Broadway
New York, NY 10003

Library of Congress Cataloging-in-Publication Data

Benn, James R.
Rag and bone / James Benn.
p. cm.
ISBN 978-1-56947-849-3
1. Boyle, Billy (Fictitious character)—Fiction.
2.Russians—England—Fiction. 3. World War,
1939-1945—England—London—Fiction.
4. Katyn Massacre, Katyn, Russia, 1940—Fiction. I. Title.
PS3602.E6644R34 2010
813'.6—dc22
2010021610

10 9 8 7 6 5 4 3 2 1

For Debbie

Wine comes in at the mouth
And love comes in at the eye;
That's all we shall know for truth
Before we grow old and die.
I lift the glass to my mouth,
I look at you, and I sigh.

William Butler Yeats

Now that my ladder's gone
I must lie down where all the ladders start
In the foul rag and bone shop of the heart.

"The Circus Animals' Desertion"
William Butler Yeats

CHAPTER ∙ ONE

Naples, Italy
Late December 1943

EVERYONE WAS HAPPY. The sky was a vibrant, vivid blue, clear in every direction. The breeze out of the north felt crisp and cool at our backs. Sunlight warmed our faces as it cast long, thin shadows across the gray decks of the destroyer. I stood close to Diana, our hands clasped discreetly amid the folds of my flapping trench coat. We were on duty with the boss, but this was light duty, an excursion out of Naples harbor to the island of Capri, twenty miles due south. Nobody was paying us any mind, so we stood together at the rail, close, touching when we could, making believe it was a holiday outing. Diana and I had been through a lot, separately and together, the terrible and the wonderful. For the last two days we'd enjoyed each other's company as never before, as if all the burdens and terrors of the past had decided to take a holiday as well. We were together, neither of us in danger, and we had time alone. Nights, as well as days.

I heard Kay Summersby laugh. She and the general were huddled in the lee of the deck gun, sheltered from the wind. He leaned in to speak to her, their heads touching. She laughed again and laid her hand on his arm briefly, before she glanced at the naval officers grouped around them. It was a passel of navy brass, all shiny braid, big grins, and ready with a light whenever Uncle Ike pulled a cigarette from the pack in his coat pocket. They reminded me of doormen at the Copley Plaza the week before Christmas.

I could tell Uncle Ike was happy. He looked relaxed, and his smile was natural, not the posed face he used for politicians and photographers. Hell, he had just been told by the president of the United States himself that he'd been picked as Supreme Commander of the Allied Expeditionary Force. Uncle Ike had been expecting to be sent back home, or to watch the big show from the Mediterranean. Instead, he'd beat out his own boss, General Marshall, and gotten the top job, along with a handshake from FDR. Add blue skies and a beautiful woman to the mix and you had all the wartime happiness any man could handle. This was his last day in Italy, and he'd wanted to see the famous Isle of Capri, which he had ordered turned into a rest center for combat troops on leave. He'd made this cruise into a treat for the HQ staff, his family of secretaries and aides who worked long hours, seven days a week, keeping the paperwork, and the war, moving along.

Kay was happy, too. She'd just received her orders to accompany the general to London, along with most of his core staff. Not that anyone thought she wouldn't, but she'd been on pins and needles for a while, especially when odds were that he was headed back to the States. Kay, a British citizen, would have been left behind. When he got the Supreme Commander job, I'd almost asked Uncle Ike if Aunt Mamie would move to London, but fortunately thought better of it. He was my relative, of a distant sort, but he was also the highest-ranking general this side of the Charles River, and I was a dime-a-dozen lieutenant. And I liked Kay, whatever was going on between them. Maybe nothing, maybe something. Who was I to judge? There was a war on.

I sneaked a kiss, tasting the salt from the sea spray on Diana's lips. Kay saw us and raised her eyebrows in mock horror. Diana laughed, and put her arm through mine, as loose strands of her golden hair caressed my face. We were in love, Diana Seaton and I. It had been rocky for a while, but right now we were walking on air. I had a week's leave, and it would be ten days before she departed for wherever the Special Operations Executive was sending her. It seemed like we had forever.

"Look," Diana said, pointing to Mount Vesuvius off the port bow. "Smoke."

"That's all we need," I said. The night before, a thin trail of lava had snaked down the mountain. The locals said it happened all the time, and there was nothing to worry about, unless the mountain exploded. Then worrying would be of little help, so why bother? I felt the same way about the war, so I understood.

"Let's hike up there, Billy," Diana said. "I want to see the crater."

I leaned in to whisper to her. "Diana, in ten days you'll be jumping out of an airplane. How about we take it easy until then?"

"I never said anything about an airplane, Billy Boyle," she said, jabbing her elbow into my ribs. "You're not afraid of a dormant volcano, are you? Or of being beat to the top by a woman?"

"That thing belches molten lava! But you're probably in better shape than I am, I'll admit it. I haven't had much to do since Ireland, while you've been busy with training exercises."

"I promise to go slowly. We'll pack some food in the morning, and have a picnic."

"On a volcano."

"It does sum things up fairly well."

I didn't argue the point. I was happy, too. Yesterday Uncle Ike had pinned the silver bars of a first lieutenant on me, along with the Purple Heart for a wounded arm that still ached. It was a step up from a second louie, finally. He'd apologized for taking so long, explaining that he didn't want headquarters staff getting more than their fair share of promotions. I didn't quibble, even though Purple Hearts are pretty rare around typewriters and filing cabinets. Now I was looking forward to celebrating the new year with Diana in Naples, wearing my best Class A uniform, silver bars polished and sparkling in the candlelight of the fanciest restaurant I could get us into.

I watched Diana gaze at the smoldering, distant mountain and wished there could be a medal for her. She wore a British uniform without any insignia, and few people would ever learn how she'd served. I knew about her first mission, since we'd stumbled into each other in Algiers. But this time, there wasn't much to go on. Of course, she wouldn't tell me a thing, but I had noticed her practicing her Italian, speaking with any Neapolitan who would spend time with her. Since most were starving, the extra rations she passed around insured a steady stream of chatterboxes. So I figured Italy, somewhere north of the Volturno River, which left a lot of territory—all in German hands—where the British might want to plant a spy.

"It's Rome, isn't it?" I asked, keeping up the playful banter.

We'd almost called it quits over her working with the Special Operations Executive, until I decided it was crazy to lose her *because* I was worried about losing her. I'd taken a bullet through the arm not too long ago, and that brush with death made me think things over. Maybe we would both survive this war, maybe one of us, perhaps neither. So why not make the best of the time we had together? I'd decided if the choice was to be happy or be miserable, why not go for happy? If either of us ended up dead, at least we'd have had our day in the sun. And today it was as if happiness were contagious. Smiles all around, a beautiful day, nothing to worry about for the moment, if you ignored the fitful plumes of smoke rising from the volcano off the port bow.

"You're the detective, you figure it out," she said, jabbing her finger at my chest.

"Italian lessons, that's a major clue."

"We are *in* Italy, Billy. You know I enjoy languages. What better place?"

"Hmm. OK, let me think." I studied her, trying to summon up any hint of an unusual remark or interest. The wind freshened, and she held her collar up, shielding her face. I followed her to the bow. Fine mist blew into our faces as the destroyer cut through the calm, pale blue waters. Diana turned away from the spray, leaning against me, pressing her body against mine. I put my arms around her, thinking of last night and the night before in her room at the Hotel Vesuvio. It was difficult not to caress her, kiss her lips again, envelop her as droplets of water cascaded over us. I resisted, and returned to the guessing game at hand.

Church. She'd gone to church with me on Sunday. I had written my mother, telling her I went to Mass whenever I could. Knowing she'd ask about it in her next letter, I made sure to go at least once in Naples. Diana came too, which surprised me. She's not Catholic, not even close. Church of England, minor aristocracy, stiff upper lip. Everything the Boyles are not. We yell, holler, cross ourselves, curse God, and beg the saints for forgiveness. Diana had asked me about confession, communion, being an altar boy, and all the other rituals of the Catholic faith as practiced at the Cathedral of the Holy Cross in Boston.

"Turn around," I said. She did, her service cap pulled down tight on her forehead, her stiff wool collar held against her cheeks as protection against the wind. It was a familiar look, her face framed by a uniform.

"Who was that nun you were talking with after Mass? When you left me with that gasbag colonel, remember?"

"Sister Justina? She's from Brindisi, as it turned out. She knew about the twelfth-century mosaics in the cathedral there. We had a nice chat."

"Oh," I said. Diana had been to Brindisi several times. The SOE had a station there. It was a good location, easy access by sea and air to Yugoslavia, Greece, Crete, and Italy north of our lines. It was also the seat of Italian government, at least the one now allied with us. "How was her English?"

"Poor. We spoke Italian. Why?"

"No reason, just curious. Could you understand her? I thought they spoke some sort of dialect down there."

"Salentino, I believe it's called. Yes, it sounded a bit different, probably much like the Sicilian you've heard. But anyone who speaks Italian can understand it, even if the words sound a bit different. Why the sudden interest?"

"I'm interested in whatever you're interested in."

"I'm interested in climbing Mount Vesuvius with you, and enjoying the whole week ahead of us."

"Me, too," I said, keeping my thoughts to myself. I wanted nothing more than to spend the few days ahead with Diana, climbing volcanoes if need be. But another part of me couldn't stop trying to figure out what she was up to, and I wasn't smart enough to listen to that distant, small voice in the back of my mind, telling me to leave well enough alone.

I didn't. Brindisi was well south of our lines, a safe place for an SOE agent to claim to be from. It made sense that Diana would want to pick up some local dialect, to solidify her cover. Her Italian was fluent, but it was classroom Italian, and she'd want to sound like a native when she spoke it. It was only when I saw her face framed as it would be in a nun's habit that her trip to church with me made sense. She was going as a nun, a sister from Brindisi. Maybe she'd even taken the name Justina, if they hadn't picked one out for her yet. There were nuns all over Italy, but there was only one place the SOE was likely to send an agent disguised as one.

"The Vatican," I whispered to her. "You're going as a nun."

Her eyes widened for a moment, and then anger narrowed them. She moved away from me, gripping the rail with both hands. Her knuckles went white.

"It isn't a game, Billy. You should know that."

"You said I should figure it out, Diana."

"Yes, let's see how smart Billy Boyle is. That's what it's all about, isn't it?" With that, she stalked off, heading into a gaggle of naval officers, surrounding herself with them, sealing me off behind a wall of white hats and gold braid.

I'd gotten it wrong. Well, I'd gotten it *right*, but that was the problem. It wasn't a guessing game, it was life or death. And something beyond that for Diana. It was what she needed to do to prove herself worthy of living. So many people had died around her that she needed to face death all over again to understand why it hadn't taken her. I shouldn't have cheapened that with my guess. But I had to know where she was going, in case she needed me. Knowing might allow me to pretend, at least to myself, that I could protect her. Things got complicated when it came to women; I wasn't good at complicated.

I walked back toward the bridge, where the newly promoted Colonel Sam Harding was installed, monitoring radio traffic from headquarters at Caserta, in case a communication needed the general's attention. Harding was another one of the joyous crowd today, having received his promotion along with me yesterday. He was now a lieutenant colonel, and I knew he was happy about it because he hadn't frowned once all day. That was riotous joy for Sam Harding, regular army, West Pointer, and my immediate boss.

Before I came to the bridge, I joined Uncle Ike and Kay as the destroyer changed course to starboard and the craggy white cliffs of Capri came into view. The sun sparkled on the dolomite rock formations and the villas dotting the beaches and hills. Kay pointed to one of the largest homes, blinding white with an orange roof, remarking on its stark beauty.

"Whose villa is that?" Uncle Ike asked of a naval aide at his side.

"Why, that's your villa, General," the aide said. "Captain Butcher assigned it to you."

The general lost his smile. He stepped away from Kay and pointed to an even larger villa. "And that one?"

"General Spaatz, sir."

"Damn it, that's not my villa! And that's not General Spaatz's villa!" Uncle Ike exploded, turning on the naval aide and forcing him back a step. His face was red with anger. "None of those will belong to any general as long as I'm boss around here. This is supposed to be a rest center for combat men, not a playground for the brass."

"All the other villas on Capri have been requisitioned by the Army Air Force, sir, orders of General Spaatz. General Clark reserved Sorrento for army officers."

"And what does that leave for the GIs coming off the line? The gutters of Naples, goddamn it?"

"Yes, sir. I mean no, sir," the navy officer said, backpedaling as fast as he could. He looked like he'd enjoyed spilling the dirt on air force and army brass, but both barrels of Uncle Ike's anger were still pointed at him.

"Kay!" Uncle Ike barked sharply. "Get ahold of Captain Butcher. Tell him to contact General Spaatz immediately and clear his officers out of there. His action was contrary to my policy. It must cease at once."

"Yes, General," Kay said. "I can call him at Caserta when we get back—"

"Now, damn it. Right now!" Kay stood alone, the clutch of officers staring at her, each thankful he'd kept his mouth shut. No one offered the general a light. Kay lifted a hand to her mouth, for a second. Then she was all business again, the general's faithful secretary off to do his bidding.

The deck became quiet. Uncle Ike drew on his cigarette as if it might calm him. He exhaled a long plume of blue smoke into the wind and caught my eye. "William, sometimes you'd be surprised how hard it is to get something done, no matter how much authority you have. Jesus Christ on the mountain, you'd think it would be common sense to give the fighting men a decent place to rest up."

"Yes, sir," I said, moving to his side. We watched the magnificent coastline drift by. Sometimes my job was to be someone Uncle Ike could blow off steam with. We were actually related to Aunt Mamie through my mother's family. But he was an older guy, and when we were in private, sometimes I'd call him Uncle Ike. Today wasn't one of those days. He flicked his butt into the water and turned up his collar. Colonel Harding climbed down from the bridge and joined us. If he'd taken in any of the drama on deck, he didn't show it.

"General," Harding said, handing him a teletype. "Message from London."

Uncle Ike read it and glanced at Harding. "Confirmed?"

"Yes, sir."

"William, we are going to have to send you on to London ahead of schedule. Colonel Harding will give you the details." With that, Uncle Ike went to the bow and stood alone.

"Colonel, I have a week's leave—"

"Consider it canceled. Sorry, I know you and Miss Seaton had plans, but—"

"I know. There's a war on. I've heard." Harding let that pass.

"A Soviet officer has been found murdered in London. Red Air Force Captain Gennady Egorov. Except we have reason to believe he was actually a senior lieutenant of state security. With the NKVD."

"Is that their secret police?"

"They call it the People's Commissariat for Internal Affairs, but the answer is yes."

"What was he doing in London?"

"Getting a bullet in the back of the head. This may involve the Poles. See Lieutenant Kazimierz as soon as you can and find out what he knows. You leave as soon as we dock in Naples."

I hadn't seen Kaz in a couple of months, since he was called back to London from his liaison duties by the Polish Government in Exile. Once I got over missing my leave and saying good-bye to Diana, I'd be glad to see him. A couple of majors were vying to impress her. She'd watched Harding bring the message and observed the expression on my face. Now she brushed by the two majors and embraced me, oblivious to the spit-and-polish brass all around us. Her fingers pulled at the fabric of my coat as she pressed her face against mine. We didn't speak, we didn't have to; neither of us had words to match the touch of warm skin in the cold air.

Everyone had been so happy.

CHAPTER · TWO

"WELCOME BACK TO the Dorchester, Lieutenant Boyle."

"It's good to be back . . . Walter, isn't it? I'm sorry, but I've been gone more than a year."

"Yes, sir. Walter it is. This is yours." He handed me a room key. It was for Kaz's suite.

"How did you know I was coming?"

"I didn't, sir. Lieutenant Kazimierz left instructions that a key be left for your use. He furnished the staff with a photograph so they would recognize you. I did not find it necessary, since I recall your first visit here."

"Thanks. Is he in?"

"No, but the lieutenant asked to be informed of your arrival. I will telephone the Rubens Hotel and let him know."

"He's at another hotel?"

"The Free Polish government is headquartered there. It is a fine hotel, of course, but as you know Lieutenant Kazimierz prefers the Dorchester."

I knew that, and I knew the reason why. I thanked Walter and took the elevator up, remembering my first day in London, and my first sight of the Dorchester. I had been nervous, and working hard not to let it show. Walter had thanked me for coming, and it took me a moment to realize he hadn't meant to the hotel. A year ago, things had looked darker than they did now. Back then, Italy was still in the war, and along with the Vichy French, the Axis had held all of North Africa. Now Italy had been knocked out, we'd cleared North Africa, and were slowly working our way to Rome. The sandbags were still stacked in front of the hotel, but they seemed to be from another era. It had been months since a bomb had fallen on London. The Germans weren't exactly on the run, but now neither were we.

I unlocked the door and stood for a moment in the hallway. The wood paneling glowed in sunlight streaming through the windows, and sparkling colors refracted from the prisms of the crystal chandelier. It was quite a place for a kid from South Boston to bunk in. It was the only home Kaz had now, and it was filled with ghosts. His parents had visited him in England before the war, when he had been a student. They'd celebrated Christmas 1938 in this very room, the last time they'd all been together. Now everyone but Kaz was dead. When I got here in 1942, Daphne Seaton, Diana's sister, had been living with him. She'd been killed soon after that. Then I moved in, after Kaz gave up caring if he lived or died. We'd stuck together, through North Africa and Sicily, until the Polish Government in Exile called him back to London.

His father had been wise enough to deposit his considerable fortune in Swiss banks before the Germans invaded Poland, which allowed Kaz to keep this suite permanently available. His family had been rich, really rich, and he was actually a baron of some sort. Lieutenant Baron Piotr Augustus Kazimierz. It was only his connections that got him a military commission in the first place, since he had a bad heart, poor eyesight, and a physique like the kid who got sand kicked in his face at the beach. Uncle Ike had taken him on as a translator, since he understood most European languages. Turned out, Kaz was as good with a gun as he was with paperwork, and there had been times I was damned glad of it.

I'd missed him, and as I emptied my duffel bag, I thought I should head right over to the Rubens Hotel, which wasn't far. It was still early afternoon, and he probably couldn't get away until late. But then I took off my shoes and lay down to rest my eyes for a minute. It had been a long trip, first waiting for a flight out of Naples, then cooling my heels in Casablanca for a day before the roundabout flight to avoid German fighter planes. New Year's Eve had come and gone, toasted with a bottle of bourbon passed hand to hand while we bounced around inside the fuselage of a C-54 transport twenty thousand feet above the Atlantic Ocean. A catnap seemed to be in order.

I heard a noise, and lifted one eyelid. The room was darker than it had been a minute ago. The noise came again, a muted *thump*. I got up quietly and dug out my .45 automatic from the duffel bag, found a magazine, and loaded as I listened to heavy, labored breathing. It sounded like a quiet struggle, or someone searching for something. Occasional grunts and rasping gasps carried in the still, darkened room. I glanced at the clock. I'd been out cold for three hours.

I pushed my door open with the muzzle of the automatic. The hinges creaked, and I froze. There was no one in the living room. The glow of sunset lit the park outside, and the sounds of traffic drifted up from the street. I felt my palms go sweaty and my heart slamming against my chest. A crack of light showed at the door to Kaz's bedroom, and I edged around the furniture toward it. Another grunt, this one louder and more anguished. There was no time to lose. I kicked the door and spun sideways, presenting the narrowest target I could, pistol leveled, cupped in my left hand, exactly as Dad had taught me. "Don't give them any advantage, and take even the smallest for yourself. And be ready to pull the trigger." I was.

I didn't. Instead I stared into Kaz's wide eyes as he lifted a dumbbell in each hand, then let them down slowly. His teeth were clenched and his neck muscles tightened as he began again.

"You . . . looked . . . like . . . you needed . . . to sleep," he said, as he finished a final repetition and set the dumbbells down on the plush carpet. *Thump*.

"Kaz?" It was all I could say. He was in his skivvies, and there were ropy muscles on his arms. Not massive, beefy biceps, but real muscle where before there had been skin and bone. And I swear he actually had a chest that broadened above his rib cage, instead of caving in on it.

"Who did you expect, Betty Grable?" He took off his horn-rimmed glasses and wiped sweat out of his eyes. Kaz was a skinny guy, but now he was packing some muscle onto his frame. I could tell he was enjoying this exhibition. "One minute, Billy, and I will be done."

He dropped and did twenty push-ups. The last few were pretty shaky, and I figured he had gone beyond his usual quota to impress me. It worked.

"What gives, Kaz?" I said as I collapsed into a chair. "You turning yourself into a pug?" Kaz liked American slang, and I was sure I hadn't taught him this one.

"A dog?" He toweled himself off and sat on the edge of the bed. "That can't be right."

"A boxer, or maybe somebody good with his fists."

"Ah, pug. Excellent," he said, savoring the new word. "It is good to see you, Billy."

"Same here, Kaz. Are you sure you should be doing this? With your heart condition?"

"Billy, after seriously considering the alternatives, I have decided life is to be lived. Fully." He got up and took a drink of water, setting the glass down hard, the noise clear and sharp. It fit the new Kaz before me. In his eyes I saw the first acknowledgment of his penchant for taunting death. He looked in the mirror on the table next to me, his gaze lingering there. He touched his scar absentmindedly, drawing his finger from his eye down his cheek, tracing it as if it were a map to lost fortune.

"In this war, one must be strong," he said, moving away from the mirror. "I have decided to strengthen myself. There once was room for a weak, studious man in the world I used to know. That is why my father decided I should come to England to study, that a quiet life with books would be the best for me. But he is gone, and so is that studious boy, who lived for words. I believe that is why I was careless of my own life, because I felt so adrift from everything. Family, country, and finally even the woman I loved."

"I think about Daphne all the time," I said. "I half expect her to walk through that door."

"Yes, I know," Kaz said. He sat on the bed again, unable to keep his gaze from the entrance to the room. He was sad, but didn't look as hopeless as he once had. "Daphne is gone, my family is gone, all dead, everything ruined by this war. Even my face."

We sat for a while in the quiet, the rumble of traffic a faint reminder of the great city around us. The sun was setting, and Kaz stood to draw the curtains. All over London, people were doing the same, shutting in the light, trying to live with the blackout and the threat of death, the reality of it.

After a minute of silence I said, "You were never that good-looking in the first place."

Kaz laughed. "Billy, that is one reason why I missed you! You remind me not to take things too seriously."

"Glad to help, buddy. It's good to see you smile. So you're lifting weights, doing push-ups, what else?"

"The army won't let me train, because they know of my heart condition. So I do what I can here. I've started to jump rope, which is very challenging. And I walk in the park at a fast pace, whenever I have time. The only thing I have left—besides you, my good friend—is the hope of a return to my country when the war is over. It will take more than scholars to accomplish that, I believe."

I glanced at the pile of books on Kaz's nightstand. He hadn't exactly given up on his studies; there were several tomes in foreign languages among the foot-high stack of books and reports. With whatever the Polish Government in Exile had him doing, and his workout routine, I doubted he'd been having any fun.

"Why don't we both get cleaned up and go out? We can catch up over dinner."

"We can go down to the dining room or have room service bring something up if you're too tired."

"No, I want to stretch my legs and take a look around."

"Very well. You'll see London has changed since you were last here. There hasn't been a Luftwaffe raid in months."

I washed up, got into my Class A uniform, and showed off my first lieutenant's bars to Kaz. He pretended to be impressed, but he was a baron, so I shouldn't have expected much. As usual, he managed to outdo me in his hand-tailored dress uniform, making me look like a rumpled bumpkin. I rubbed my shoes on the back of my pants leg, hoping for the ghost of a shine.

We left the Dorchester amid greetings and tips of the hat. The main door was held open. Kaz was popular with the staff, not because of his status as a permanent guest, but due to his reason for staying there. Everyone knew the story of his family, and took pride in his dedication to the memory of their home away from home. It made everyone feel special to be associated with that. It was part of Kaz's charm, and the shared suffering of the war that he embodied. It was as if, having failed to protect Poland, this little bit of England had decided to protect Kaz as best it could.

We walked through Berkeley Square, and I felt the return of the easy familiarity Kaz and I had shared, here and in Algiers. The square was swarming with GIs, sailors, and the occasional English soldier. Most were Yanks, laughing loudly, whistling at the few young women out on their own, living life, killing time. Generally, when we passed a group of them, they ignored us, but every now and then one guy would salute, and we'd have to respond.

"If it wasn't for the extra pay and better food, I'd hate being an officer," I said.

"You wouldn't be a very good enlisted man either, Billy. Tell me, how is Diana? Have you seen her lately?"

I told him about our little boat ride to the Isle of Capri. It had been two days ago, but already it felt like forever.

"Is her mission on?" Kaz asked in a whisper.

"Yeah. I think it's the Vatican," I said, lowering my voice as well. I don't know whom I expected to overhear us, but I couldn't help it. I told Kaz about my brilliant guesswork, and Diana's reaction.

"Sometimes, I think for a smart detective, you are quite stupid."

"Geez, Kaz," I said, steamed at the remark. But then I thought about it, and found it hard to debate the point. "I do always seem to put my foot in it with Diana. We're OK, though. I think."

"Good. Women seem difficult to understand for Americans. Or perhaps you understand American women better than others?" Even in the dark of the blackout, I could see Kaz smiling.

"Yeah, I got them nailed, no problem. Hey, watch out." We'd turned onto Regent Street, where the sidewalk was blocked by a neat stack of bricks. The pile was shoulder-high, and stretched along the road, broken every ten feet or so by a narrow passage to the vacant lot beyond. The smell of smoke and dust lay thick upon them. Beyond the bricks was a gaping hole where a building had once stood.

"The remains of homes and shops," Kaz said. "Everything but the bricks bombed and burned away. All this once held life." He trailed his fingers along the bricks, and I found I had to touch them as well. They were rough to the touch, and the smell of years of London's coal smoke, the grit of collapsed buildings, and the soot from raging fires lingered on my hand. The odor of the Blitz. We passed another long row of empty spaces and more of the tidy piles of bricks salvaged from the rubble. Some of the lots had been cleared and planted with gardens. It was a warm December, at least by Boston standards, and I wondered if they had any winter crops still in the ground. I remembered my mother saying she liked to keep parsnips in the garden past the first frost since it made them sweeter, and suddenly I could see her hands cradling the good china, placing a steaming bowl of mashed parsnips on the table at Thanksgiving.

"Billy, we are here," Kaz said, standing by the restaurant door. I had walked several paces on.

"Sorry," I said. "Daydreaming." I followed Kaz into Bertorelli's, where of course the headwaiter knew him. I tried to shake off the visions of home but they stayed with me, an insistent ache I couldn't dismiss. I had been away almost two years now, and I'd begun to wonder how long it would be before I returned.

I followed Kaz to the table. It was in a back corner, chairs arranged so they both faced the room. The place held about a dozen tables, with a small bar up front. It was almost full. Uniforms of blue, brown, and khaki draped most of the customers, male and female. The few folks in civilian clothes looked dowdy compared to everyone else. Clothes were rationed, as well as food, and the fashionable thing to do was to wear the oldest suit you had, to show you were doing your bit. Except for more wear and tear, that hadn't changed since I'd last been in London.

"Backs to the wall?" I asked. "Are you expecting trouble, Kaz?"

"You've taught me to be observant, Billy. Remember when you told me I should start noticing more than women and artwork when I enter a room?"

"Yes, I do. Seems like a long time ago."

"Yes. In many ways, it was. I've learned that it is wise to be in a position to observe things, and one cannot do that facing a wall."

"True," I said, wondering if there was anything else to it. Kaz's eyes swept the room, checking each table. I did the same, and found nothing but the usual assortment of brass, dames, and civilians. "Are you looking for someone?"

"No. Just looking at faces, checking the exits," he said with a sly grin. There was a new strength in Kaz's face, a hard determination where before there had been wryness disguising a great hurt. But there was something else, something he was holding back.

Our waiter appeared, who seemed to be an old friend of his. Kaz chose the fillets of beef for us both, and selected a red wine that sounded expensive.

"To obtain a really good meal in London is still possible, but one must be ingenious," he said in a low voice after the waiter left. "The government has prohibited charging any more than five shillings for a meal, to contain the black market. It makes it difficult to get some things, like a decent cut of beef, but if one orders a good bottle with it, the beef miraculously improves."

"Everyone's got an angle," I said. "And I'm glad you worked this one out. The last thing I had to eat was a cheese sandwich that had been made in Gibraltar."

Kaz laughed and crossed his legs, leaning back in his chair. I heard a faint, soft *clunk* and looked for the source. There was a lump in one of the lower front pockets of Kaz's uniform jacket, and when he moved it had hit the side of the chair.

"Are you carrying, Kaz?"

"Just a precaution."

"A precaution? In London? What kind of peashooter do you have there anyway?"

"A Colt .32-caliber automatic. I understand it is a model favored by American gangsters for its ease of concealment. I read that Al Capone always carries one in his jacket pocket."

"Kaz," I said, leaning over the table. "What is going on? Don't give me that gangster riff, and tell me what the hell you need a piece for to go out to a London restaurant." The waiter brought the wine, and Kaz went through his tasting ritual, acting like nothing was wrong.

"Welcome back to England, Billy," Kaz said, raising his glass in a toast.

"Cheers," I said, watching his eyes. We drank, and I set my glass down. "Spill."

"It is difficult to explain," he began. "You have heard of the Polish officers found in the Katyn Forest, yes?"

"Yeah, that was back in the spring, right?"

"April. The Germans broadcast the news that the bodies of ten thousand Polish officers had been found in mass graves deep inside the Katyn Forest, in Russia. Outside of Smolensk, to be precise. They had just taken that area, and the local peasants told them where to look."

"I remember. It was in the newspapers. The Russians said it was Nazi propaganda, that the Germans had captured those officers when they invaded. It would be just like the Nazis to kill their prisoners and blame it on us."

"Us?"

"The Allies. Us. The good guys."

"Yes, well, remember that Poland was attacked by both Germany and Russia. That's what started this war. It is not so easy for Poles to think of Russia as an ally."

"That doesn't explain why you're making like Al Capone."

"Billy, we know it was the Russians. We have evidence that they murdered thousands of Polish officers, professors, and priests in 1940 while they were at peace with Germany. But the British government has sided with the Russians and their story of a German massacre, since it is easier than facing the truth. Your government has been silent, which is just as bad."

"What kind of evidence?"

"Mountains of it. I can tell you the whole story later. For now, please understand that this is very dangerous. No one wants to hear the truth, since it may break the Allies' alliance. Poland is being sacrificed, once again."

"And you don't like the idea of being sacrificed."

"No. Neither did General Sikorski. You know what happened to him." It had been big news. Four months ago, General Wladyslaw Sikorski, prime minister of the Polish Government in Exile and head of Polish military forces, had died in a plane crash.

"Yeah. It was an accident. His plane crashed after taking off from Gibraltar, right?"

"Correct about Gibraltar. But what you don't know, because the news was suppressed, is that a military aircraft carrying the Soviet ambassador and other officials was parked next to Sikorski's plane before he took off. No explanation has been given for the crash, even though the pilot survived." Kaz cocked an eyebrow, full of meaning.

"Wait, why would the Russians kill Sikorski?"

"Because he was the leader of a free Polish government, and he insisted upon making known the truth about the Katyn Forest murders. Which made him a very inconvenient leader, for all parties concerned. Gibraltar is a British base, of course." He took a long drink of wine and set the glass down, hard. Tiny spots of red appeared on the white tablecloth.

"Kaz, have you gone crazy?" I tried to keep my voice in a whisper. "Are you saying the British worked with the Russians to assassinate General Sikorski?"

"What could I be thinking? The British government condoning murder? I must sound like an Irishman. A crazy Irish rebel." He lifted his glass and drank again, a satisfied smile curling around the rim of the glass.

"Are you in danger?"

"It is war, Billy. I am fighting for my country."

"What exactly does the Polish Government in Exile have you doing anyway?"

"Investigating the Katyn Forest Massacre. So we may reveal the truth about it."

"And that means you need to carry a gun? In London?"

"General Sikorski probably thought his plane was safe from sabotage in Gibraltar."

I didn't know what to say. I did know what not to say: that I was in London to investigate the murder of a lone Russian. The fillets of beef came, and I tried to concentrate on eating and not think about the knot in my gut. I didn't like keeping a secret from Kaz, but I had a bad feeling about our reunion. He sounded like he was on a collision course with the Brits. And I knew that Uncle Ike valued unity among the Allies above all else. Kaz and his Polish pals were aiming to throw a monkey wrench into the workings of the alliance.

But that wasn't what had my guts in a twist.

It was that, deep down in my Irish heart, I knew Kaz was right to keep his automatic close at hand.

CHAPTER THREE

KAZ WAS ON the couch, the London *Times* scattered on the floor, drinking coffee and munching on toast from a room-service cart. He had a towel around his neck and looked like he'd been working out. Again. I pulled my bathrobe on and shuffled my way toward the aroma of coffee.

"Good morning, Billy. I thought about waking you to join me in calisthenics, but decided you needed a good sleep."

"Kaz, it's barely seven o'clock," I said as I poured myself a cup and sat down. "What's the news?"

"Heavy RAF and American bomber raids on Berlin. General Clark is approaching Monte Cassino, which overlooks the road to Rome. The Russians took Kiev, and held it against a German counterattack."

"All good news."

"Billy, Kiev is roughly two hundred miles from the Polish border. We are still eight miles south of Rome. Do you know what that means?"

"No, not before I've had my coffee, I don't."

"It means the Russians will take all of Poland before the British and Americans even get close to Germany."

"I thought we called that liberating Poland," I said, gulping the hot, black joe.

"I call it trading a Nazi master for a Communist master. The Nazis are the more bloodthirsty of the two, but neither will let Poland be free. And isn't that what started this whole war? We were the first to be attacked, and Poles have been fighting ever since. In Italy, here with the

RAF, and with the underground in Poland itself. I sometimes wonder what we are fighting for. Or who will fight for us, once the war is over and the Soviets occupy my country."

"Would you go back after the war if the Russians ran the place?" I asked.

"Billy, I know what the Russians did to Polish officers. I think they would take even less kindly to Poles who had worn British uniforms. It would be a death sentence."

"Isn't that kind of harsh?"

"Harsh? I don't think you understand, Billy, I don't think you understand at all."

"I don't doubt you, Kaz. It's just that General Eisenhower has been pounding Allied unity into our heads for so long, I have trouble criticizing the Russians. Hell, I even have trouble criticizing the Brits these days. And after all the propaganda stunts the Krauts have pulled, I have a hard time believing they're aboveboard about the Katyn slaughter."

"I know they are not to be trusted. I don't mean to put you in a difficult position, Billy, but after what I've seen and learned, I've begun to question things. Everything has changed, hasn't it?"

"Yeah." I chewed toast and washed it down with coffee. "And it's only getting started."

"I must get to work," Kaz said, standing up. "Can you come by and visit today? Perhaps I can show you the evidence I've been gathering. It may help to explain things."

"You don't have to explain yourself, Kaz," I said.

"Thank you, Billy. But do come to the Rubens Hotel. It's off Buckingham Gate, immediately south of the palace. Ask for me at the desk and they'll take you up."

"I'm busy this morning, Kaz, but I'll try to stop by this afternoon."

"Are you going to Norfolk House? It's a short walk from there to the hotel."

"Yeah, I have to check in, scout out the arrangements." Norfolk House was in St. James's Square, a stone's throw from Piccadilly Circus. It was going to be Uncle Ike's new headquarters.

"Is Major Harding here yet? Is Big Mike coming with you?"

"I forgot to tell you, it's Colonel Harding now. And yes, Big Mike will be here with him, maybe tomorrow." Corporal Mike Miecznikowski was an MP who had joined up with us after Sicily, where he'd gotten in hot water for helping me out. He was a former Detroit cop, and as the nickname implied, a really large former Detroit cop. He was handy to have around, and I wondered what his take on this Polish stuff might be.

"Why did they send you ahead?"

"I didn't have anything to do," I lied.

"Well, I'm glad you're here. I didn't mean to unload all my troubles on you, but it is good to have a friend to talk to."

"It is, Kaz," I said as he left to dress, glad he wasn't watching me as I felt my face flush with betrayal. I sat alone, drinking the remains of my coffee, thinking how right he was and how guilty I felt at not being straight with him. I decided to come clean that afternoon, and get it out in the open. But first, I had an appointment at New Scotland Yard.

THE RAIN FELL in fat, slow drops, as if it couldn't make up its mind, and it fit my mood. I pulled up the collar of my trench coat and set off from the Dorchester toward Westminster. It would be a straight shot on Park Lane, alongside Hyde Park, past Buckingham Palace, then down Birdcage Walk to Big Ben and Parliament. But I decided to reacquaint myself with the side streets of London. It had been a while, and I was in town to find a murderer. Backstreets and alleys might be useful.

I walked a few blocks through Mayfair, filled with neat, low brick buildings. Varnished doors with polished brass fixtures stood like sentries along the street. A few automobiles purred through the neighborhood, all shiny, low, and expensive. It was quiet, the kind of city quiet that money gets you. Black umbrellas hid faces from me, but I could've guessed: thin lips, narrow noses, bored eyes, all the marks of good breeding and high culture. It wasn't my part of town.

The clouds finally cut loose and I ducked into a shop doorway, shaking myself like a soggy dog. In a minute the rain was gone and I headed south on Curzon Street to Half Moon, which I knew would take me across Piccadilly. On Curzon, where a row of houses should have been, there was nothing but stacked rubble. On either side of the cleared area, the buildings were boarded up and deserted. The rising trail of smoke and fire had left its trace around every window and door. Sooty black, each looked like the dark hand of death had marked that room, that family, for destruction.

I'd always liked Boston after a rain. It made everything seem clean, no matter how dirty it had been. London was different. There was too much to wash away, even in the posh part of town. The gritty smell of coal smoke stuck in my nostrils, and the foul smell of burnt wood and charred family possessions rose from the brickwork. Rain always revived the memory of a fire, coaxing its odor out of blackened wood and scorched earth. The bricks were precisely stacked, cleaned of concrete, ready to be put up again, to form parts of new houses that would always smell a bit odd when it rained.

I went through St. James's Square, eyeing Norfolk House, which stood in one corner, my future home away from home. It was taller than most neighboring buildings, seven stories. The windows started out large on the bottom floors, nearly vanishing into a series of tiny gables jutting out of the slanted slate roof. I guessed one of those would be mine, if I had a window at all.

I scooted around St. James's Park, passing by the sandbagged War Rooms, where Churchill himself was probably growling into his special telephone, the hotline to the White House. Minutes later, I'd walked past Westminster Abbey, Parliament, Big Ben, the vaunted heart of the British Empire. Big Ben struck the quarter hour, the great bell still astounding me with its clear, deep tones. I'd heard it through static on news broadcasts hundreds of times, but when I heard it here, I thought of Edward R. Murrow reporting during the Blitz. We'd all gather around the radio, and the house would go quiet as we waited for his words.

This . . . is London.

I shivered. The damn place still gave me goose bumps. Or maybe it was the memory of Southie that it stirred up. I stood on the Embankment, watching the Thames flow dark and murky beneath me. For a moment, it was South Bay, and I was back walking a beat in the old neighborhood. But that seemed like so long ago, far more than barely two years. I tried to shake off the homesick blues, but it was getting harder as time passed.

Crossing the street, I craned my neck to take in the turreted white-and-red-brick headquarters of the London Metropolitan Police. New Scotland Yard. I went in and asked at the duty desk for Detective Inspector Horace Scutt. A uniformed constable showed me to the Criminal Investigations Department. Plainclothes. I walked into a room where any cop in the States would feel at home. Desks pushed together in the center, filing cabinets against the walls. A large city map on a bulletin board. Heavy black telephones ringing, and the low buzz of conversation, tinged with sharp frustration. The only difference was the tangy odor of stale tea leaves instead of coffee grounds.

"Excuse me," I said, interrupting a detective who was perched on a desk, talking to an older man. The old fellow didn't look like a suspect, more like a victim. His white hair was tousled, his cheek bruised, and dark brown stains on the front of his shirt marked where he'd bled. "Sorry, but I'm looking for Inspector Scutt?"

"Well, you've found him, lad. Now what do you want with him?" the older man asked.

"You're Horace Scutt?" I tried to keep the surprise out of my voice. He looked ancient. Pure white hair and mustache, dark bags under his eyes, and the evidence of a beating added up to something other than a Scotland Yard detective. "Inspector Scutt?"

"Some days I wonder that myself. What's your business here?"

The younger detective flashed a grin, but it wasn't the friendly type. More like the kind you wear watching someone slip on a banana peel.

"Lieutenant Billy Boyle, Inspector. I was told to see you about the murder of Gennady Egorov, a Soviet Air Force captain."

"Yes, we had a chap from the Home Office come by and instruct us to cooperate with you. So we must. Have a seat, Lieutenant, and we'll go over the file with you." Scutt nodded to the other detective, who went to gather the files.

"You have a rough night, Inspector?"

"Not as rough as it could have been. Half a dozen young ruffians escaped from the remand home at Wallington, then broke into the Home Guard armory at Upper Norwood. Got away with a couple of Sten guns and more ammunition than any sane man would want to carry around. Lucky for us, they fell out over who should have the guns and who were to be the ammo carriers."

"Looks like they didn't go down easy."

"The young ones never do, Lieutenant, not if they've had a taste of incarceration."

"If you don't mind me saying, Inspector, aren't you a bit too senior to be running around after armed kids?"

"I do mind, Lieutenant. Cosgrove told us we must cooperate with you, but that doesn't mean I need to take any guff, now does it?"

"No, sir. Sorry, no offense intended," I said. Scutt looked ready to jump out of his chair and go a couple of rounds. "Did you say Cosgrove? Big guy, big mustache? Stuffed shirt?"

"I'd say that fits the man," Scutt said.

"He's a major. MI5." Military Intelligence, Section 5, was the British Secret Service, responsible for counterintelligence and security.

"I said he was no civil servant, guv," the other detective said. "Didn't I?"

"So you did, lad. Now, Lieutenant, what is your involvement with MI5?"

"As little as possible, sir. I had no idea Major Cosgrove would be in touch with you. I'm on General Eisenhower's staff, and he asked me to look into this for him."

"Not the worst answer you could've given. Go on."

"I was a detective myself, Inspector. In Boston, before the war."

"A bit on the young side for a detective, I'd say."

"I made the grade just before Pearl Harbor. I'd been on the force for a while, but I didn't spend much time celebrating my promotion. Next thing I knew, I was working for General Eisenhower."

"Well, Lieutenant Boyle, we won't hold Cosgrove against you, unless you give us reason to."

"All I need to do is review the case, and let the general know if there's any possibility of trouble with the Russians. I won't get in your way, I promise."

"Possibility of trouble with the Russians? Did you hear that, Flack?"

"Quite the joker he is, guv."

"I guess there's trouble with the Russians," I said, wishing I hadn't sounded like a naive colonial.

"You'll find out, soon enough. DS Flack will go over the details of the case with you. I'm going to get some fresh clothes and a few hours' sleep. No rest for the wicked or the young, Flack." Scutt rose with an agility that surprised me, given his age if not his injuries.

"Roy Flack," the younger detective said, extending his hand. "Detective Sergeant."

"Glad to meet you, Roy. As I said, I don't want to be a pain. I know what we'd think in Boston if the FBI told us to cooperate with a stranger."

"You'd think he was a troublemaker, looking either to claim the glory for himself if things go well or to find a scapegoat if they don't."

"You've given this some thought."

"We've been handed a hot one, all right, and I don't much like the idea of some Yank second-guessing our every move." Flack leaned forward in his seat, his eyes narrowing as he studied me. All I could see were dark brown pupils, two little pebbles of suspicion. "So tell me the truth. Why are you here?"

"Is this why Scutt left? So you could give me the third degree?"

"Detective Inspector Scutt left because we've been chasing those buggers for thirty-six hours straight. I can hardly keep up with the man myself, so I have no patience left, especially for an American spy."

"General Eisenhower recently sent an American officer home because he called another officer on the staff a British son of a bitch. If he'd called him a plain SOB, he'd still be working for Ike. Instead, he's on a slow boat home in disgrace."

"All right, Lieutenant Boyle, I will rephrase. I don't want any son of a bitch second-guessing or spying on us. Is that clear?"

"I'm not a spy. I don't even think I'm a son of a bitch." We stared at each other, the usual territorial cop's pissing contest in full swing.

"Maybe not," Flack said, leaning back in his chair, releasing some of the tension from his furrowed brow. "Why does General Eisenhower care about a dead Russian in London? Last the newspapers said, Eisenhower was still in Italy."

"Who am I to argue with the press?" I raised an eyebrow, trying to signal knowledge that wasn't yet public. Plenty of military types knew about Uncle Ike's promotion, but the official announcement was being handled at levels even higher than his.

"Oh. For the big show? Really?" Flack pursed his lips, giving the idea a try.

"Really," I said. "But you didn't hear it from me."

"All right then," Flack said. "For the sake of Allied unity, here goes. First, meet Captain Gennady Egorov of the Soviet Air Force." Flack tossed four photographs onto the desk. The first was a picture of a man lying facedown, his hands tied behind his back. It looked like the kind of string you use to wrap parcels, but lots of it. He was dressed in a military-style overcoat, and there was dark splotch on the back of his head. The second was a close-up of the head. The entrance wound from a bullet was clearly visible, a hole dead center at the back of his skull. The third picture had been taken from several steps away. It showed the body lying between two stacks of bricks, like the ones I'd seen at cleared bomb sites. The final photograph was of his face, contorted by the effect of the bullet, but not so much as to disguise his features. Blond hair, a faint mustache, thin lips, and prominent cheekbones. Maybe a good-looking guy, or maybe short of that. His eyes were open, dull with death.

"Where was he found?"

"In Shoreditch. Near Spitalfields Market. In a tunnel of bricks. Do you know London?"

"I was stationed here a while ago. That's over by St. Paul's?"

"Close by, but east of there. Directly north from the Tower, if you've time to play the tourist. Kids found him in the morning, when they came out of the Underground shelter."

"You mean the subway—the Tube? People still sleep down there?"

"Not in the numbers they used to. Back in the Blitz, we had nearly two hundred thousand people sleeping in the Underground stations. Nowhere near that now, of course, but I'd say there's two or three thousand every night."

"Why? There hasn't been a raid in months."

"Well, you've got to have a permit to sleep in the shelters. Some are afraid if they stop going down, they'll lose their permit. I guess they figure Adolf's not quite done with us, so they're taking no chances. And a few are just plain afraid, can't sleep aboveground, worrying about the Luftwaffe. Others are bombed out and still got no place to go. They all have their reasons. Liverpool Street Station, the one in Shoreditch, it's one of the biggest."

"You think he was killed during the night?"

"The doc says so. Between midnight and two o'clock. Most likely he was shot right there. Soil on his pants and overcoat matches the ground. You could see the bits of red brick on his knees, from when he knelt."

"When was this exactly?"

"Five nights ago. Friday night, or Saturday morning, I should say."

"Have you recovered the bullet?"

"Dr. Mullins barely got it out of his skull before a delegation from the Soviet Embassy showed up. Protested at our lack of respect for the dead comrade, and took him away. Anyway, the bullet looked like a .32 caliber. It was a mess, like a dumdum bullet, perhaps a homemade one."

You could make your own dumdum slug by taking a hacksaw and cutting an *X* on the top of the bullet. That way it would fragment on impact and cause horrible internal injuries.

"The killer must have been close. Those slugs aren't very accurate. No one saw or heard anything?"

"Not a soul. The idea of those stacks of bricks is to keep them close for the rebuilding. Problem is, no one's rebuilt anything yet, and they're a warren in which all sorts of mischief goes on. Prostitutes, gangs, drunks, they all end up using them. Found one with a tin-roof add-on overhead, all nice and snug."

"So either he was forced in there or was meeting somebody where he didn't want to be seen."

"I don't think he was forced. Neither his watch nor wallet had been taken. Close to ten quid on him."

"That would rule out any prostitutes or gangs I know. A drunk would be more likely to bash his skull in with a brick. Who does that leave?"

"The first thing we looked at was political extremists. Fortunately, all the Fascist sympathizers have been put in custody or sent away. It doesn't have the look of a political assassination. No note, nothing to give credit to an anti-Communist cause."

"You said some kids found him?"

"Yes. Bunch of them, ten to twelve years old. They'd left the shelter ahead of their parents, and were playing in the cleared areas. Those bricks are a great attraction for the lads. One of them was running pell-mell when he tripped over a boot, which proved to be attached to Captain Egorov. The boys came out screaming to a constable, saying they'd found a dead Nazi. They didn't recognize the uniform, and jumped to the most exciting conclusion."

"Are there many Soviet officers in London?"

"Apparently there are. I'd never seen one myself, but there are a number at the Soviet Embassy, others working with British Lend-Lease, and some with temporary military missions. Egorov was part of a Red Air

Force contingent conducting some sort of joint meetings with your Eighth Air Force. Beyond that fact, we were told in no uncertain terms it's all top secret." Lend-Lease was FDR's brainchild, a swap of arms in exchange for military bases on British soil. Most of the weaponry went to England, some to the Soviet Union.

"Who did you ask?"

"We went through the proper channels. Up to the home secretary, requesting clearance to talk with Egorov's counterparts in your air force. Basically, we were told to stuff it."

"What about the Russians?"

"Have you ever dealt with the Russians, Lieutenant Boyle?"

"I know a good Russian bakery in Roxbury."

"And I know a nice Russian lady who gives piano lessons. But our Soviet friends refuse to answer any questions. Refuse to even talk to us. Except to say that when English workers establish a Marxist state, all crime will vanish along with private property. But until that day, we should find the gangsters who killed Captain Egorov and avenge his death."

"With no help from them."

"Or from the Americans. Until now, that is."

"I don't know how much help I can be, Detective."

"Well, I'd say an officer on General Eisenhower's staff, who has Colonel Blimp from MI5 smoothing the way for him, might be able to open some doors." Flack relaxed, leaning back in his chair, arms folded across his chest. Daring me to say no.

"Eighth Air Force doors, you mean."

"What a grand idea, Lieutenant! Glad to have you with us."

"I'll try. It might have to wait a few days, until my boss gets here. A colonel will make more of an impression."

"Captain Egorov is in no hurry. Anything else you need to know?"

"Yes. Did you search the boys who found him?"

"Search them? What for? I told you Egorov still had his valuables."

"From the point of view of a thief. What about from the point of view of a young boy who thinks he found a dead Nazi?" Flack was quiet, and I could see his mind turning the idea over. I had a hunch that a killing like this, an execution, had to come with a message. I wasn't certain, but if there had been one, it could be hidden in some kid's sock drawer, if he'd thought it was a souvenir swiped from a dead Kraut.

"All right, Lieutenant Boyle. That's not a bad idea. I'll talk to the parents while you talk with your air force chaps. Anything else?"

"Yeah. A couple of things," I said. Scutt and Flack had responded to me no differently than my dad would have to any outsider back at the Boston PD. They were suspicious, and I couldn't blame them. So I thought it wouldn't hurt to tell them what Harding had told me, to show them I had something more to offer than half-baked ideas. "It's likely that Captain Gennady Egorov was not really an air force officer. My information is that he was NKVD. Secret police."

"If that's true, it answers something that's been bothering me. The Russians don't let their people go out alone; they're always in groups. He must have been one of their watchers."

"So who was he watching?"

"Someone who found the workers' paradise lacking in some way?"

"That would be my bet," I said. Flack nodded in agreement as he removed a pack of Gold Flake cigarettes from his pocket. He offered me one and I declined. As he lit up, I wondered why I didn't tell him about Colonel Harding's other suspicion, that this might have something to do with the Poles. And with the Katyn Forest. I didn't even want to think about Kaz's pistol, his .32-caliber pocket automatic.

CHAPTER · FOUR

I TOOK BIRDCAGE Walk, the leafless trees lining the road, stark and bare against the sky. Big Ben tolled at my back, and ahead of me was Buckingham Palace, with its white facade gleaming even in the dull, gray light. These were grand sights, but all they did was reinforce what my gut was telling me—that an empire doesn't back down from tough decisions. If the Poles threatened the coalition, that would threaten victory, and if I knew anything about the Brits, they didn't like losing. Not that their American cousins liked it much either.

So maybe Kaz was right about General Sikorski, maybe it hadn't been an accident. Maybe it was the Russians, or the British, or both working together to solve a common problem. But that was pure conjecture on his part. Me, I needed proof, and some link to the dead Russian. Otherwise, it wasn't any of my business.

Or was it? Had Kaz gone off the deep end and started killing Russians? It was too fantastic to be true. First, he wouldn't have known Egorov was NKVD. And even if he had, Kaz was too smart to carry around a pistol that matched a slug found in Egorov's skull. No, it didn't make sense. Best to forget about it, and not mention the coincidence to anyone. But I did need to talk to Kaz and tell him what I was up to. I was meeting him for lunch at the Rubens Hotel, and it would be the perfect time. I turned left at the palace as the wind gusted, swirling leaves around my feet, pushing me toward the hotel.

I signed in at a desk manned by a sergeant wearing Poland's red shoulder patch on his British Army uniform. He made a call, then sent me up to the third floor. At the head of the stairs were a couple of guards, both with Sten guns hung from their shoulders. I gave them my name and they looked me over like bodyguards while I wondered what a couple of bursts from those Sten guns would do to the woodwork.

"Billy, come in," Kaz said from an open set of double doors. "*On jest z mna,*" he said to the guards.

"*Tak, pan,*" one of the guards said as he patted me down before letting me proceed.

"Kaz, you've been watching too many gangster movies."

"Standard precautions, Billy. No exceptions."

He led me into a sitting room with a table for four laid out. It was a pretty fancy room—high ceilings, big fireplace, and a soft, deep carpet. Two guys in British Army dress uniforms. Severe creases in their tailored trousers. Red shoulder patches with *Poland* emblazoned across them. Big smiles. I looked at Kaz, but he avoided my gaze. Instead, he took my arm and guided me toward the two officers.

"Billy, allow me to introduce Major Stefan Horak. He is my superior. And his aide, Captain Valerian Radecki."

"Welcome, Lieutenant Boyle," Horak said, shaking my hand. Radecki made a little bow. "How is your uncle?"

"Fine, sir. How is yours?"

"I pray he is well, but I have no idea," Horak said, his eyebrows knitted in confusion. He looked at Kaz, then back at me. "Your uncle is somewhat more famous, is he not?" Horak spoke near-perfect English, with only a slight accent, but I could tell he was unsure of the conversation, which suited me fine. I wasn't sure I liked it either.

"Not really, not outside of Boston, anyway." Horak and Radecki stared at each other, then at me, then at Kaz, doubt gaining over cordiality.

"Billy," Kaz said, his voice hissing between clenched teeth. "Major Horak is not inquiring after your uncle Daniel. He means your *other* uncle."

"Oh, him! Sure, he's fine. Well, nice to meet you both," I said, nodding to the two officers. "We won't keep you from your lunch. Ready, Kaz?"

"Billy, don't do this," Kaz whispered.

"Lieutenant Boyle," Captain Radecki said, limping between Kaz and me, grasping the edge of a table to steady himself. "Let me apologize. When the baron told us he was lunching with you today, we prevailed upon him to include us. The least we could do was to provide the meal." He gestured to the table, which was set with polished silver, bone china, and cut crystal. His nails were manicured, his jet black hair slicked back, and he sported a neatly trimmed pencil mustache. He oozed self-confidence in spite of his limp, and I thought it might be bad for Kaz if I didn't play along. Guys like that liked to get their way. I wasn't feeling too charitable toward Kaz for setting me up, but I wasn't quite ready to throw him to the wolves.

"Sure, Captain. I don't mind." Major Horak lost his worried look, and we all sat.

"General Eisenhower will be in London soon, we understand?" Horak said nonchalantly as he unfolded his cloth napkin. I did the same and thought it was big enough for a flag of surrender.

"I saw him a couple of days ago, in Naples," I said, avoiding the question. "Who told you he'd be here?"

"One hears things," Horak said, making a dismissive gesture with one hand as he made a point of not looking at Kaz. He had a broad, expressive face, unlike Radecki, who would have been a much better poker player. Horak was forty or so, his brown hair falling untidily over his forehead. He played with his knife, turning it over in his hand as he spoke. "London runs on gossip and spies. Not German spies, mind you, but we all spy on each other. The British, French, Poles, Russians, Belgians, everyone except you Americans, I think. You are too direct for spying and gossip, yes?"

"One hears things," I answered. "And sometimes one does not, even from his friends." It was my turn not to look at Kaz.

"Everyone is saying General Eisenhower is to command the invasion," Radecki said, lighting a cigarette as he held his bad leg straight. "We thought it would be your General Marshall."

"Was that the gossip?" I asked, watching Radecki do a French inhale, his eyelids flickering against the smoke. He ignored me.

"Almost a certainty, we were told," Horak said. "But then again, some of our sources were English, and they thought it should be Montgomery. But it had to be an American, don't you think? It has become an American war, with all the troops, ships, planes, and armor coming from America."

"Polish troops are fighting in Italy," I said. "Along with the British and French. Even the Italians are fighting with us now. It's not a purely American war."

"No matter," Radecki said. "It will be an American general. No European general could see beyond his own borders, except to covet what lies beyond." He crushed his cigarette out, and no one else spoke. White-coated waiters entered, filling the silence with the clatter of serving dishes and wine bottles. We ate well. Grilled lamb, dumplings, mushrooms. Washed down with a chilled white wine, something French I couldn't pronounce. Topped off with an ice-cold glass of Polish vodka. I drank it down, feeling the alcohol warm my gut and stab at my brain. Then I waited. I watched Horak lean back and nod, ever so slightly, to Radecki.

"We thought it important, Lieutenant Boyle—"

"Call me Billy, Captain. Everyone does." I pushed my empty glass toward the bottle and Horak poured. Half a glass. I guess they needed me half sober.

"Very well—Billy—as I was saying, we thought it important to fully inform you of the situation concerning the Katyn Forest Massacre. The Americans, until now, have been silent on the matter, unlike the British. Or the Russians."

"What do you mean, until now?"

"It is not yet public knowledge, but an American colonel, attached as a liaison to the Polish Army in the Mediterranean, drafted a report for General George Strong, your chief of U.S. Army Intelligence. He interviewed Poles who had been released by the Russians, reviewed evidence collected by the Red Cross, and submitted his report. It said all the evidence pointed to the Russians as the executioners of nearly twenty thousand Polish officers, at the Katyn Forest and other locations as well."

"I didn't know that," I said. I drank some more.

"Lieutenant Colonel Henry Szymanski," Horak said. "I met him in Egypt. A fine officer. But his career is over."

"Why?" I asked, conscious of a slur creeping into my voice.

"Several days ago the War Department in Washington officially charged him with an anti-Soviet bias, and informed his superiors of such. They may as well publicly have called him a liar."

"Poor bastard," I said.

"It is unfortunate, yes," Radecki said. "Which is why we wish to provide you with details, so at least some other American officers will be fully informed."

"And you choose me because my uncle is General Eisenhower, and I'm on his staff?" My tongue felt thick, and I had to focus on getting Uncle Ike's four-syllable last name out right.

"Because Lieutenant Kazimierz trusts you," Horak said. "And we would be fools not to take notice of your connection with the esteemed general. And you would be a fool to think your friend brought you here under false pretenses. He speaks well of you, and this luncheon was entirely my idea."

"OK," I said. "How about a cup of coffee, and then you fill me in?" We moved to a pair of sofas facing each other by the fireplace. Radecki brought a file and sat across from me, kneading his thigh.

"War wound?" I asked as the coffee was poured.

"I wish it had been," Radecki said with a wry smile. "It was a tram accident, in Bucharest. The bone was not set properly, but I had no time to go back to the hospital. I had a freighter to catch in Constanta, on the Black Sea. Otherwise I would have been trapped in Romania."

"It looks painful," I said.

"It is. I fell again, hurrying on the stairs recently, and aggravated it. My doctor has prescribed laudanum, which I take only when I cannot sleep. They say they can reset the bone, but it would be a long convalescence. After the war, perhaps."

"Captain Radecki knows I rely on him," Horak said. "With so few experienced officers, he is worth more with a bad leg than ten junior officers." He gave a nod to Radecki to begin.

"I am sure you know the basics, Billy," Radecki said. "But, to summarize, in September 1939 the Germans attacked Poland, the beginning of this war. England declared war on Germany, but could do nothing to aid us. The Russians, who had a nonaggression pact with Nazi Germany, then invaded our nation from the east. The Russians and Germans divided Poland between them."

"I know," I said. "It was a raw deal." I drank the hot coffee, remembering the newspaper headlines at the time. There had been rumors of peace, with the most optimistic, or naive, thinking that with the two big powers in eastern Europe in cahoots, it might end quickly. I guess if a few small countries had to take it on the chin, that didn't bother some people much.

"Indeed. The Russians took a quarter of a million Polish troops prisoner. They released many of the lower ranks, and turned thousands over to the Germans. Ultimately, they were left with forty thousand. Officers from all services, plus many professionals who had been arrested. Physicians, clergymen, teachers, judges, and so on."

"Wait a minute," I said. "If the Russians and Germans were taking everyone prisoner, how did so many Poles make it out? How did you two end up here, if you don't mind my asking?"

"The border with Romania was open," Horak said. "Many of us crossed the border after the fighting, before either side had firm control. My unit was in the Carpathian Mountains, south of Krakow. After the Russians and German forces met, some of us made it on foot into Romania. From there, we went to France, where Polish forces were reorganizing."

"I also went through Romania, paying bribes to get a ship on the Black Sea to take me to Palestine," Radecki said. "The Germans were putting pressure on Romania, which was then neutral, to intern all Polish nationals. The escape route did not last long."

"Meanwhile," Kaz said, "the Russians were trying to convince their Polish prisoners of the virtues of Communism. We know they spent a lot of time in the camps interrogating everyone, trying to find converts."

"There were very, very few," Radecki said. "Perhaps that sealed their fate. For months, letters had been going to families back in Poland. In April 1940, the letters stopped. Mail that had been sent to prisoners was returned. Thousands of parcels and envelopes came back to Poland 'Addressee unknown.'"

"Apparently the decision had been made to eliminate any future threat to Soviet domination of Poland," Horak said. "Stalin did not foresee the Nazi invasion of Russia, and thought the Polish officers were an unnecessary surplus. So they were eliminated."

"But in June 1941, the Nazis did invade Russia," Radecki said. "Suddenly, the remaining Polish prisoners, mostly enlisted men, were needed to fight Germans. Stalin kept the few tame Poles to form a Polish unit within the Russian Army, and let all the others go. They came from 138 camps. A center at Buzul'uk was set up to take in the released prisoners and send them on to the British in the Mediterranean."

"General Wladyslaw Anders was in charge, Billy. You may have met him in Italy."

"Yes, I did. He's commander of the Second Polish Corps."

"Right," said Radecki. "One of the first things Anders discovered was that he had practically no senior officers. He was one of sixteen generals captured by the Russians, but only one other general was accounted for. According to our estimates, we were missing, from one camp alone, one hundred colonels, three hundred majors, one thousand captains, twenty-five hundred lieutenants, and hundreds of cadets, doctors, teachers, engineers, and so on."

"This was the camp at Kozielsk," Kaz said. "These were the victims who were shot in the back of the head and buried in mass graves. There were thousands of others, killed in other locations."

"But the Germans found the graves from Kozielsk?"

"Yes. In the Katyn Forest, outside of Smolensk. In April of last year, the locals told them what had happened. They unearthed the bodies, and revealed the crime to the world."

"But the Nazis," Radecki said, "being murderers themselves, were not believed by many. Not the press, certainly. But we knew that, for once, they told the truth. We asked the Red Cross to investigate, and for this crime, Stalin cut off relations with the Polish Government in Exile."

"And formed his own puppet regime," put in Horak.

"So where does all this leave us?" I asked.

"For now, we will go on fighting wherever we can. But we must prove Russian guilt beyond all doubt, so that when Germany is defeated, we can go home to a free country, not one dominated by the Soviet Union," Horak said.

Radecki opened the file and tossed a stack of photographs on the table between us. An open pit with layers of bodies, the army greatcoats and boots marking each man an officer. Close-ups. A neat hole in the back of each head. Hands tied behind the back with rough twine.

"Is this how they were all killed? Hands tied, and a bullet in the back of the head, I mean."

"For the most part, yes. Reports from the Red Cross indicated that some had their hands tied with barbed wire. There were some with stab wounds from bayonets, but those were in the minority, likely those who resisted at the last minute," Radecki said, lighting another cigarette. "It appears they were driven into the woods, then forced to walk to the pits. Each man saw, and heard, what was done to those who went before him."

It was a horrible vision, but what I was seeing was not a forest outside of Smolensk. It was a London neighborhood near the Liverpool Street Tube Station, where a dead Russian was found, his hands bound behind his back with string, and a single bullet hole to the back of the head. I looked at Kaz and wondered.

"It is a terrible sight, isn't it?" Radecki asked.

"Can you be certain this wasn't done by the Germans and then blamed on the Russians, as a propaganda ploy?"

"Yes, we are certain, and so is the International Red Cross. The bodies were all heavily clothed, which points to the date of the killings as being April of 1940, when the temperature was still quite cold. The Russian story is that the Germans captured the Poles in August 1941, when they were performing roadwork as part of a labor detail. The clothing does not make sense for hot, dusty summer work."

"And there is the matter of the letters," Horak said. "Both the letters that were returned, and the fact that many letters and other documents were recovered with the bodies. None had a date after April 1940."

"This is a Russian crime, Billy. A mass murder. And no one wants to hear about it," Kaz said. "The British government worries that a split over this might move the Russians to make a separate peace with the Germans. They are quite willing to let us die to defend England, but they will not seek justice for our murdered dead."

"Look at this," Radecki said, handing me a memo on the stationery of His Majesty's Government. It was from Anthony Eden, British foreign secretary, to Winston Churchill, on the Katyn revelations. One line stood out: *His Majesty's Government have used their best efforts not to allow these German maneuvers to have even the semblance of success.*

"What does that mean?" I asked.

"The best efforts of a government in peril often bring out the worst they are capable of," Radecki said as he took the memo back. "It means that the British will never reveal that the Russians were responsible for the executions. It is not in their interest."

"How did you get this letter?"

"Remember, London is a city of spies."

"I will," I said, looking Radecki in the eye, and wondering if he went out armed, and what caliber his weapon was. "Do you think the American government will listen to you if the British won't?"

"We hope so. We hear that General Eisenhower is a fair man."

"Major Horak," I said, appealing to the ranking officer present. "If there is one thing the general values above all, it is Allied unity. Fair or not, I don't see him risking that, no matter how strong your evidence. You could argue it was all circumstantial. A clever plot by the Nazis to divide the Allies. There are no living witnesses, except Russians."

"That is not quite the case, Lieutenant Boyle. There is someone we would like you to meet." He nodded, and Radecki and Kaz left the room. "There is a witness. Lieutenant Kazimierz will bring him in. It is best if Captain Radecki is not present. He may make him somewhat nervous."

"Why?"

"The ordeal has been difficult, and he would prefer to not speak of it. Radecki had rather insisted, and the poor fellow suffered a setback, so we kept them apart for a while. Then we tried again, and their relationship improved greatly, but still, there is no need for a crowd. Our guest does have a nervous disposition. Ah, here they are!" The door opened, and Kaz entered the room with a young man. Kaz had his arm around him, and I wasn't sure if it was to keep him from falling over or running away. His eyes flitted around the room, as if he was searching for an unknown threat. Kaz whispered something to him and he relaxed as they drew nearer.

"Tad, this is my friend, the American I told you about. Billy, this is Tadeusz Tucholski."

"Glad to meet you," I said, standing and extending my hand. Tadeusz flinched.

"It's all right," Horak said in a calming voice. "We are all good friends here."

"Yes, yes, sir," Tadeusz said. "Sorry." He and Kaz sat on the couch together. Tadeusz was dressed in the same uniform with the Poland shoulder patch, but he wore no indication of rank or other insignia. He looked maybe twenty, but it was hard to tell. His face was thin and pale, and his dark eyes seemed to bulge out of their sockets. He rubbed his hands together, rubbed them on his pants, then together again. He studied them for a minute, and then spoke without moving his eyes off them.

"They want me to tell you, to tell you what I saw. I don't want to, but I will. I know it is important." The words came out in a rush, the rapidity of his speech at odds with the stillness of his body.

"If you want to," I said. "Do you want some coffee?"

"Coffee?" He sounded like it was the oddest question he'd ever heard. "Yes, please." I poured a cup from the silver coffee service and put it down in front of him. I filled my cup and held it, wisps of steam drifting above it. I took a sip, and it was still warm.

"I was a cadet," Tadeusz began. "When the Russians came, I was a cadet, in training to become an officer, you understand? In a special school for cadets."

"Yes, I understand," I said. He spoke English well, though with a heavy accent.

"They took us prisoner. It was terrible. At first, they put all of us in the basement of a building. They left us there for three days. No food, no bathroom. A little water, nothing else. Do you understand?"

"Yes."

"Good. Three days, over one hundred cadets. In a dark basement. Do you understand?" He took the cup and saucer in his hands. They trembled, and the china made a clattering, clinking sound as he spilled coffee into the saucer. Kaz took it from him gently and touched his arm.

"Then we spent two days and two nights in railcars. There was bread and water. It was bad, but not as bad as the basement. There was fresh air, and we had something to eat. Do you understand?" He raised his voice, the question insistent.

"Yes, I do. It wasn't as bad."

"No, and then they marched us to the camp. There were showers, and barracks. Soup for dinner. We thought the worst of it was over. They let us write home. They questioned us, each of us, alone. They seemed to know a great deal about us, what our parents did, what youth groups we belonged to. There were many rumors, always about going to Romania. They were going to send us there any day. But that day never came."

"What happened next?" Kaz prompted him.

"They came for me one morning. I thought it would be more of the same. More questions about school, the other cadets, and about Marxism. They wanted us to believe in Marx and Stalin, but no one listened. I thought it was going to be more of the same. But they beat me. A big NKVD sergeant, he started beating me while an officer sat in a chair and watched. No one said anything. Then they threw me out into the snow.

The next day, they came for me again. This time the officer sat at a table. He had a confession for me to sign. It was in Russian, and he told me it was my confession about spying for the Germans."

"But you were just a kid," I said.

"They said my father was a spy. He had been to Berlin, for business meetings. He was an architect, so it was normal for him to travel. I tried to explain, but they said we were all spies, all capitalists, my father, mother, and little sister, we were all enemies of the people. He told me my father had confessed, and showed me a piece of paper with his signature. It was his, I recognized it. I knew they had forced him, I knew he was not a spy, not an enemy of anyone. He was an architect, do you understand?"

"Yes."

"Good. They told me it was important for you to understand. I wouldn't talk about it otherwise. It's too painful."

"You don't have to, you know."

"Yes, I must, it is my duty. I did not sign. They told me they would be lenient with my mother and sister if I signed. But I was smarter than that. I knew that if my mother and sister had confessed, they would have shown me their signatures. But they hadn't. They beat me. They put me in solitary confinement. But I didn't sign."

"Good for you."

"Perhaps, but I am not sure. One day the officer who interrogated me was gone. They stopped coming for me. Spring came, and then one day they announced we would be leaving the camp. Romania, we thought. Finally. They took us out in small groups, marching out the main gate, everyone in good spirits. The most senior officers went first. I was in one of the last groups. We marched to a train. NKVD guards stood along the road and prodded us with bayonets, forcing us into railcars, like the ones that had brought us to the camp. It was springtime, but it was cold, very cold. We wore everything we owned." Tadeusz shivered and rubbed his hands together. "Someone realized we were not traveling south toward Romania. I didn't know what to think. The train stopped and they had buses and trucks back right up to the cars. They shoved us in, packed us in tight, so we almost couldn't breathe. When the truck finally stopped, they hauled us out and tied our hands behind our backs. No one knew what was going on, and the guards cursed at us, kicked us, hit men with their rifle butts. They marched us into the woods, on a muddy road, still screaming at us to hurry, hurry. I began to hear popping noises, like fire-crackers, lots of firecrackers. The noise would start up and then stop, start and stop. More guards came, with pistols in their hands. One had blood on his sleeve. I was scared, but there was no time to do anything, nowhere to go, it was all shouts and *pop pop pop*, I couldn't think. There were NKVD officers standing around with clipboards and lists of names. They took a group of ten men in front of me and pushed them up and over a hill. I heard the shots, and then they came for us, bayonets sticking into our backs. They were calling us Polish pigs, telling us to hurry, hurry, or they'd shoot us right there. I fell at the top of the hill when I saw what was there. A huge pit, and it was full of bodies. I remember thinking it was astounding that so many of us had run to our deaths like that. I saw four men kneeling and a Russian walk behind them, bang, bang, bang, bang, and they all tumbled into the pit. There were men in the pit—Russian prisoners, they looked like, not Poles—stacking the bodies. One row of heads in one direction, the next row feet in that direction. It was so unbelievable that I was no longer afraid. I sat on the ground while madness went on around me. I don't know why they left me there, although it was only a minute or so. I saw men pushed up the hill, saw pistols being reloaded, saw more bodies fall. It was mechanical, like a killing factory, except we were in the woods, on a beautiful, clear spring day. I see every moment of that minute, over and over again, every day. Every hour. Every night. Do you understand?"

"Yes," I whispered. "How . . . " I didn't have to finish, the question was obvious.

"The NKVD officer, the one who had questioned me. He was there, and he had a list of names. There were six of us. You see, he'd had appendicitis. He was in hospital, and hadn't finished his interrogations. He was angry that we'd been sent to the forest with the others, since he needed to produce confessions. Well, a dead man can't confess, can he? He had a guard detail, and they beat us, but that was nothing. They put us into a Tshorni Voron and drove us to the NKVD prison in Smolensk."

"A what?"

"Tshorni Voron, Black Raven in Russian. A special NKVD bus for transporting prisoners. Locked compartments on either side, just big enough for one person to squat. You can't stand, can't sit. When you see the Black Raven, you see death itself."

"But you didn't die."

"No, I didn't," Tadeusz said mournfully. "They sent four of us to Lubyanka, the main NKVD prison in Moscow. I never saw any of the others again. I never saw the NKVD officer again. Nobody came for me; they just fed me and kept me in a cell. They didn't even beat me. I think they forgot about me, or lost my file, or perhaps the NKVD man was denounced and he was in the cell next to mine, I have no idea. One day, a guard came and gave me extra food and clean clothes. The next day, they put me in a truck with ten other Poles. I don't talk to anyone, I don't trust them. But they put us on a train, a real train, not in a railcar, but in a car with real seats. We got off in Buzul'uk, and there were Poles everywhere. They tell us the Nazis invaded Russia, and now the Russians want us to fight the Germans. But I trust no one. They send us through Persia, to Palestine, and the British give us uniforms, and food, and everyone asks about the camps. But I say nothing. Do you understand?"

"You don't speak, because if you did, you'd have to tell the story," I said.

"Yes! Yes, you do understand. I did not speak at all, not one word, not in Buzul'uk, not in Persia, or Palestine, or Egypt. Not on the ship, not in London, until I came here. Not until I met Piotr and got to know him. He is a good man. Then I decided to speak, for Piotr. But it is not easy, you understand. Can I go now?"

"Yes," Kaz said. "That was very helpful. I will take you back to your room now."

"Thank you, Piotr." He held on to Kaz's arm and didn't look back.

"A drink, Lieutenant Boyle?" Major Horak asked.

"No, no thanks. Tell Kaz I'll see him later, OK?"

"Certainly." Horak made no effort to persuade me to do or say anything. He knew that Tadeusz's story would either work or it wouldn't, and if that poor boy couldn't convince me to take action, nothing would.

I left the room. It wasn't that I didn't want another drink. It was that I wanted to drink alone, and wash away the image of that pit, and what men could so willingly do to each other. That, and the thought of what somebody had done to one Russian right here in London.

I felt a little tipsy as I walked down the stairs and out into the street. I wasn't exactly drunk from all the wine and vodka, but I took care of that as fast as I could when I got to the bar at the Dorchester.

CHAPTER ▪ FIVE

I COULDN'T TELL if we were walking through heavy fog or light rain, and I didn't much care. Kaz had shaken me conscious a half hour ago, presenting me with aspirin and hot coffee, the only things I wanted more than to be left alone. I knew we had to talk, and I also knew fresh air would be good for my hangover. I pulled on a wool cap, grabbed my Parsons jacket, and followed Kaz into Hyde Park. It was just after dawn, not that there was a trace of sun.

"Can you walk a little faster, Billy?"

"Sure, no problem," I said, picking up the pace as we double-timed along Rotten Row, the now seldom-used horse track that ran along the south edge of the park. I felt like my head might burst, but I didn't want Kaz to think I wasn't up to it.

"I wanted to tell you I was sorry about yesterday. I had only mentioned to Major Horak that morning that we would be meeting for lunch. He insisted, and you know senior officers like to get their way." Kaz pumped his arms energetically, like a chicken trying to take flight. He might've looked funny, but he wasn't out of breath.

"But you'd told them about me," I said, huffing and blowing air. "About . . . Uncle Ike . . . and all that."

"Yes, it was only natural to tell them. We've been working together for some time, Billy. Of course I would tell them about my friend. Are you all right?"

"Maybe . . . Slow down . . . a bit, OK?" I stopped, leaned over, and rested my hands on my knees, praying I wouldn't throw up. The moment passed, and we moved on, a quick pace, but nothing torrid. Jesse Owens had nothing to worry about.

"How long has Tadeusz been with you?" I asked, as soon as I could get a full sentence out.

"About six weeks. He had been in and out of hospitals and clinics. At first they believed he was mute, but one of his doctors thought otherwise. We knew he was Polish, and that he had come from Buzul'uk, but that was all. I was asked to speak with him because I can speak Russian, Ukrainian, and a little Romanian."

"Of course," I said. Kaz had been a student of languages at Oxford before the war and a translator at Uncle Ike's first headquarters when I met him. "He responded to you?"

"Not at first. When I spoke Russian he became agitated, and would not look at me. From that point on, I spoke only Polish, telling him about myself, and where I was from, just making conversation, to put him at ease. Once I mentioned Radymno, a small town in the Carpathian Mountains I had visited. He spoke, in a clear voice, telling me he had lived there."

"And then he told you about Katyn?"

"Not right away. It was clear there was something he was afraid of, and Major Horak thought he might know something. We took him to the hotel to help him feel safe, but he did not react well to Captain Radecki."

"I imagine few people do."

"He does his job in the best way he can. And he and Tadeusz seem to get along better now. When Tadeusz first came to us, he was quite agitated, and it was some time before he calmed down and let everything out. He talked as he did with you, in a stream, a torrent of memory. He is quite helpless to stop once he starts. Then he goes into a depression. He will sleep most of the day today, and not speak to anyone, not even me, tomorrow."

"It's amazing he got this far."

"I don't know if he can survive," Kaz said as we walked through Kensington Gardens. Fog shrouded the Round Pond, the damp creeping into my bones. I picked up the pace as best I could, the throb in my head keeping beat with my steps.

"Was he wounded?" I asked, but I didn't think Kaz was talking about a physical injury.

"He tried to kill himself last week. He kept a knife from his dinner tray and had it to his throat when I came into his room."

"How did you stop him?"

"I told him someone very important was going to come and listen to what he had to say, and that he had to remain alive to tell what he had seen."

"You don't mean—"

"Yes, Billy. He took the knife from his throat in order to tell you his story."

I didn't like it. I didn't like anyone putting off death just to meet me. I was bound to be a letdown. I didn't like keeping a secret from Kaz, and I didn't like being suspicious of him. I didn't like how I knew I wasn't going to tell a soul at Scotland Yard about Kaz and his pocket automatic, and I didn't want to be responsible for carrying a Polish cause to Uncle Ike's doorstep. I sure as hell didn't like my head pounding and my stomach feeling like a rat had curled up and died in it. I felt cold sweat at the small of my back, my face went prickly, and I went to my knees, bowing to the pond, heaving coffee-flavored bile on the royal grass, as my head spun from the effect of last night's alcohol and today's guilt.

I felt Kaz's hand on my back, patting it like you'd do with a crying baby. He helped me up as soon as I was sure I had nothing left to give, and steadied me as we walked, slowly now, around the pond, past the statue of Peter Pan that seemed oddly out of place and still timeless, in the midst of London at war.

"Do you feel better, Billy?" Kaz asked.

I didn't, and I wanted to come clean with him, but a small voice whispered inside my head, telling me he was a suspect. I argued with the small voice, and finally we agreed he was a *potential* suspect, which was something different, but it still meant I should play my cards facedown.

"Yeah, I'm fine. Keep me away from vodka for a while, OK?"

"OK, Billy."

We walked through the clearing mist, a cold breeze blowing at our backs. The sky revealed itself, sullen and gray, heavy with the promise of rain. I liked being with Kaz in these early hours, even with a hangover, even with my doubts. He was a friend, someone I could count on to back me up, no questions asked. I silently vowed to do the same for him, until whatever was between us became too powerful for anything I did to matter.

A POT OF coffee, a bath, and a couple of hours later I was at Norfolk House, trying not to think about vodka and half-mad Poles. I needed a jeep and a map to get me to High Wycombe, where the Eighth Air Force was headquartered. Someone there should know what Soviet Air Force officers were doing in London. I asked at the duty officer's desk where the chief of staff's office was.

"I'd stay away from there if I was you, Lieutenant," the sergeant at the desk said after giving me directions. "That new guy, Eisenhower's chief of staff, he got here yesterday, and no one's come out of there with a smile on his face."

"That's Beetle for you," I said. General Walter Bedell Smith, known as Beetle, was Uncle Ike's man through and through. No-nonsense, a face like a bulldog, and a personality to match. He didn't have much patience for those who didn't pull their weight and then some. Actually, he didn't have a drop of patience in his body, which is why I tried to steer clear of him at all times.

I made my way up the stairs and down a long hallway, while the sounds of typewriters and teletypes echoed against the black-and-white tiles. Clerks, secretaries, and junior officers scurried about, eyes cast down, mouths hanging open in fatigue, or dread. Beetle had already made his mark. Fortunately, before I needed to stand at attention under his scrutiny, I heard a couple of familiar voices.

"How the hell am I supposed to know where they are? Sir?"

"You packed them, Big Mike, and you brought them to the plane."

"Yeah, but I didn't fly the goddamn plane here, and I didn't unload the goddamn plane, now did I? Sir?"

I stood in a doorway, watching Lieutenant Colonel Samuel Harding pawing through boxes of files while Big Mike stood with his hands on his hips, shaking his head sadly.

"Colonel, I'm telling you I looked everywhere. They ain't here."

"Then goddamn it, Big Mike, find them." Harding tossed piles of folders on a table, looking for some paperwork that was probably destined to sit gathering dust in a file folder until the next war came along. I thought about backing up and getting the hell out, but Big Mike saw me.

"Billy! I mean, Lieutenant. Good to see you. Come in, we're getting set up here. Nice place, huh?"

Big Mike was big. So big, I was surprised he could find a uniform to fit into. Six feet plus, and about as broad in the shoulders. Big, beefy arms. He was a brother officer in civilian life. Somewhere, there was a piece of paper that designated me as part of General Eisenhower's Office of Special Investigations. Me, Kaz before the Poles called him back, Diana when she was detached from the SOE, and Big Mike. Colonel Harding kept an eye on us. We didn't have a plaque on the door, and you wouldn't find us on any Army Table of Organization, and Uncle Ike thought it was best that way. When he needed us, it was to get things done quietly. Like with the dead Russian. When he didn't, Harding always had a job waiting. He was in Intelligence, specializing in relations with our Allies. It made for interesting work.

"Yeah, Big Mike. Reminds me of city hall. Colonel," I said, nodding my head toward Harding. You were supposed to stand to attention and salute when reporting for duty, but I thought Harding might be steamed enough at losing his precious files that he wouldn't care. I hated saluting.

"You look like hell, Boyle. Have you been on a bender for the last couple of days?"

"No sir, Colonel. I've been on the case. I had to keep up with some Polish officers making toasts last night. All in the line of duty."

"Polish *wódka*?" Big Mike asked, a grin spreading across his face. "With Kaz?"

"Yes," I said, my stomach turning at the memory. Big Mike was angling for an invite to a repeat performance. He and Kaz were quite a combination. A big American Polack working stiff and a small, thin, aristocratic Polish baron, who, for some reason, had hit it off. But I wasn't in the mood for another bout with the bottle.

"You have anything to report, Boyle? Anything other than your level of alcohol consumption?" As usual, Harding was short-tempered. I was beginning to think I should have saluted.

"I've met with the Scotland Yard detectives on the case. I need to get up to High Wycombe, Eighth Air Force HQ, and find out what the Russian Air Force officers are up to. Can I get a jeep, and maybe Big Mike to drive me up there?"

"You'd do me a favor to get him out of here. Then maybe I can find half the stuff we shipped from Algiers. Go."

Big Mike didn't waste any time grabbing his jacket and cap.

CHAPTER ▪ SIX

THERE WERE NO road maps to be had, but there was a wall map of greater London posted in a back room where drivers and staff could get a hot cup of coffee. Uxbridge, Denham, Beaconsfield, High Wycombe. About thirty miles west of London. I guessed there would still be no road signs, but you could pretty much follow the main roads from one village to the next.

A staff car would have been nice, but all a lieutenant could hope for was a jeep with a canvas top. We took Kensington Road to Uxbridge Road, which naturally enough got us to Uxbridge. On the western outskirts of London, the bomb damage was not as extensive, but it hadn't been cleaned up as well. We passed a row of damaged houses, some collapsed and others with open rooms, their bathtubs, chairs, dressers, and tables on display like a giant's dollhouse. Some pictures still hung perfectly level, and I saw one easy chair at the edge of the floor, where the front of the building had been torn away, the lamp next to it a sentinel of normalcy in a catastrophically altered world. Past Uxbridge the city turned to country, and military traffic dominated the road. No civilian vehicles, only British and American trucks, jeeps, staff cars, all snarled in traffic jams at every village center, then thinning out on the narrow country roads.

The sky had cleared, leaving only scattered clouds to drift over the landscape. A faint, distant drone turned into a steadily growing, ground-shaking *thrum* of high-powered engines. We pulled over and got out, gawkers on a country lane as Flying Fortresses climbed and circled, forming up into a mass of bombers, hundreds of them, the highest trailing white contrails as they headed for their target. The deafening roar turned again to a dull, faraway noise, finally leaving us in silence, except for the scurry of tires on pavement.

"Jesus Christ, I ain't never seen so many airplanes," Big Mike said. "Not all at once, anyway."

"Me either," I said, but I didn't feel much like talking. The procession of B-17s had left me feeling odd. Out of step. Hundreds of men and machines were off on a mission, and what was I doing? Talking to people, asking questions about other people who were already dead. It seemed a waste of time, when so many others were going to be killed in a few hours. I used to think that every death mattered, especially those who could've made it through the war alive. Now, I wasn't so sure. Captain Gennady Egorov was dead and gone, and nothing I could do would bring him back. Those boys in the B-17s, they were alive now, but plenty weren't going to make it home, never mind whoever was at the receiving end of their bomb loads. Feeling the vibration of the passing bombers, hearing the thunder of engines, seeing their gleaming white contrails, I felt the enormity of this war. The willingness to accept loss of life and limb, to witness planes burst into flame and fall to the earth. In the wake of such mass, intentional killing, it seemed disconcerting to place so much emphasis on a single bullet that had pierced a single skull. Here I stood by the side of the road, on my way to ask questions about one dead Russian. There they went, off to deal death and maybe draw a dead man's hand themselves.

Maybe I thought too much about this stuff. Maybe it was better to follow orders and do the job, whatever it was.

"Let's go, Billy," Big Mike said, his glance lingering on my face. I wondered what he saw.

"Sure," I said, climbing into the jeep. The army seemed to be making a soldier of me, regardless of my attempts to prevent it. Or maybe it was the hangover. Whichever, it was the first time the thought of following orders had ever seemed comforting, and that bothered me.

"What exactly are we looking for?" Big Mike asked after we had a few more miles under our wheels.

"Russians," I said, and filled him in on my assignment and what I'd learned from Scotland Yard. I showed him the photo of Gennady Egorov. Kaz and his pistol I kept to myself.

The road to High Wycombe paralleled the River Wye, which was more of a stream, as it meandered by fields, wooded groves, and low rolling hills. Luckily, the U.S. Army Air Force didn't stint on road signs, and as soon as we entered High Wycombe we followed posted signs up a short hill, and took a long gravel drive to an imposing gray granite three-story building sprawled across tree-lined grounds. Twin turrets rose from the corners, making the place look more like a medieval fortress than the headquarters of a modern air force. A church, stuck onto the end of the building, looked like an afterthought.

Big Mike came in with me and peeled off to find a mess hall, saying he was hungry. That was pretty much a normal state for him, except for about a half hour after each meal. But he was also going to gather information, scuttlebutt from other noncoms. I went to the duty desk and asked where the XO's office was. In any unit, the executive officer was the guy who had to know everything. No sense asking for the commanding officer, he probably wouldn't bother with a lieutenant from outside his command. The XO would be different; he'd want to know why I was here asking questions.

I signed in and was sent up to the top floor, my feet fitting the worn grooves in the stone stairs, as thousands of others had done. Officers, clerks, WACs, and occasional RAF personnel swept around me in purposeful motion. Looking for the XO's office, I passed an open doorway, the sign above it marked OPERATIONS. A private was affixing another sign below that, freshly painted letters spelling out that this was home to Colonel Dawson. The name was familiar, and I figured it was worth a shot.

"Is that Bull Dawson, by any chance?" I asked the private.

"No idea, Lieutenant. I just paint 'em. They come and go and I change the names. Ask inside."

In the outer office, a sergeant sat at a desk typing with two fingers. The door to the inner office was open, but I couldn't see inside. The sergeant didn't look up. With so much brass around, my silver bars didn't carry much weight.

"Help you, Lieutenant?" He didn't stop typing.

"Colonel Dawson," I said, crooking my thumb in the direction of the inner office. "Bull Dawson, by any chance? Fresh from Northern Ireland?"

"Who the hell wants to know?" A voice boomed out.

"That answer your question, Lieutenant?" *Click clack.* His lack of interest was formidable, so an answer wasn't needed.

"How's the shoulder, Bull?" I said, entering his office. It was large, with two map tables and one large wall map, pieces of string marking the distance from airfields in England to targets in France, Germany, and beyond. Bull was standing at the wall map, removing pins, letting strands of red string drop to the floor.

"Billy Boyle! Goddamn, I thought you were back in Algiers. The shoulder still hurts when it rains, which is most of the time." Bull shook my hand, enveloping mine in his big, beefy grasp. We'd met in Northern Ireland, and there had been gunfire involved. Bull had taken one in the shoulder, but it hadn't kept him from getting me off the island on the q.t.

"They still got you flying a desk, Colonel?" Bull Dawson wasn't much for protocol, and wouldn't mind my calling him Bull. But I'd never met an officer who didn't like being given his rank.

"Yeah, they found something more useful for me to do than scheduling transport planes in and out of Northern Ireland. Got my orders three days ago, just getting settled in. No missions yet, but that'll come. What brings you here, Billy?"

"I came in a few days ago myself, ahead of General Eisenhower. I'm investigating the death of a Soviet Air Force officer, Captain Gennady Egorov. Got himself shot in London."

"Someone here involved?" Bull said, gesturing for me to sit down in one of the two armchairs in front of his desk. He took the other.

"Not as far as I know. I heard that he'd been involved in some sort of liaison role with the Eighth. Thought I'd check it out, see if anyone knew him."

"We don't have any Russians here, Billy," Bull said, lighting a cigarette with a Zippo. "English, a few Canadians; the rest are all American. What would a Russian be doing here anyway?"

"Good question. What about Poles? Any of them stationed here?"

"No, but I did meet a few of them from the RAF 303 Squadron. The Kosciuszko Squadron, they call themselves. Highest kill rate in the Battle of Britain, a real wild bunch of fliers. They're stationed over in Ruislip, ten or twelve miles from here. But that was a social occasion. Invite to the new American brass to dine in their mess, that sort of thing. Why?"

"No reason, Bull. Occupational hazard of a detective. Once you start asking questions, you can't stop. Is there anyone who's been here a while, who might know about any Soviet personnel visiting?"

"Let me ask our G-2. Intelligence ought to know about people show-ing up in funny uniforms, right?"

"Sounds good, if you're not too busy," I said.

"Billy, you and I have been through the real thing. I'm never too busy for former aircrew, even a ground pounder like you. Now you wait here. This will go a lot faster if I don't bring a stranger, you understand?"

"Sure, Bull." He slapped me on the knee as he left. I got up and stretched my legs, tired after the jeep ride and perhaps last night's drink-ing. I looked out the window in time to see four fighter planes arcing across the sky, but they were too high for me to make them out. I looked at the maps on the table, one of France, the other Germany. Papers and files covered each of them, and I didn't want to be shot as a spy in case the G-2 officer came back with Bull, so I left them alone.

The wall map ranged from Northern Ireland and Scotland in the north to Sicily in the south, and all the way to Moscow in the east. Red string from Italy went up past Rome, with others going into Romania and Poland. Strands from England crisscrossed each other, some headed deep into Germany, others along the coast of France. Not hard to guess what they were up to.

I picked up the strings that Bull had let drop to the floor. Three of them, all longer than any of the others. What had they pointed to? An ashtray on a table held colored pins, and it was easy to see former targets on the continent by the pinholes they had left. But where had the long pieces of string led? I let my fingers run across the map at about the right distance from England. Beyond Poland and Romania, the paper was unscarred. Until my fingertips found two tiny pinholes, deep into Russia, about midway between Moscow and the Black Sea. Right next to Mirgorod and Poltava, in the Ukraine. I held up a piece of string, and it reached perfectly from a number of bases north of London. What the hell was going on? Those weren't targets; the bases were well behind the Russian lines.

I heard Bull's voice in the outer office and stuffed the string into my pocket as I stepped away from the map.

"Billy, there's a problem. Come with me, right now."

"What . . ."

"Never mind, Lieutenant. Now!" He turned and checked the hallway in each direction as his sergeant continued with his typing, oblivious to the cloak-and-dagger drama. The phone rang and Bull nodded to him.

He picked it up and told whoever was on the other end that Bull had me in his office, safe behind closed doors. He hung up and winked at me before he went back to his typing. Bull grabbed my arm and I followed him to a rear staircase.

"What's going on?" I asked as we descended the narrow metal steps.

"I thought I'd be able to help you, Billy, I really did. But you sure stepped into it this time. As soon as I mentioned you were looking for Russians, that goddamn major was on the phone to the MPs."

"You said there weren't any Russians here," I said as we stopped at a second-floor doorway.

"There aren't. I wasn't lying to you. But there is something brewing, all top secret, and I thought they might let you in on it, given your connections. But they didn't give me a chance to explain, so I thought it would be best to get you out of Dodge. Again. You're a lot of fun to have around, you know that?"

"I'm my own barrel of monkeys. What about your sergeant?"

"He's been with me for a year. He's solid, don't worry about him. You come here alone?"

"No, I had a driver. He went to find the mess hall."

"Christ. Tell you what, I'll get him and tell him to hustle out to the main gate. You go out the back door, right down those stairs, and take off before they notice we're not in my office. Hank will keep them talking a while longer. Drive back on the main road in ten minutes and pick up your driver. How will I know him?"

"He's a corporal, and guaranteed he's the biggest guy in the room."

"OK, get going. I'll look you up in London, at Norfolk House, right?"

"Yeah, and I'm quartered at the Dorchester. Bull, you said you didn't lie to me. So there are no Russians here?"

"I haven't seen any. Can't say anything else. Now get the hell out of here."

I did. I walked around the back of the building like I owned the place. Started up the jeep as a couple of snowdrops double-timed across the lawn. The MPs in their bobbing white helmets, looking just like the little flowers. I had to admire Bull for trying, but it would've been better all around if I'd just stayed in bed today.

Ten minutes later I picked up Big Mike and gunned the jeep, putting distance between us and trouble. I had a feeling it was going to catch up.

"Looks like the air force doesn't much like you, Billy."

"Pretty much par for the course. Bull found you all right?"

"Yeah. Decent guy for an officer. No offense intended."

"None taken. You get any coffee?"

"Yeah, along with a couple of baloney sandwiches. Not much for a growing boy. But I did have a nice chat with a corporal who apparently hadn't gotten the order to imprison anyone asking about Russians."

"What did this corporal say?"

"That they don't come here no more. On account of security."

"But they've been here? Was he sure they were Russians?" I asked, checking the rearview mirror. No one in pursuit. Yet.

"Yeah, five or six of them. And she was a WAC corporal. She said she knew a little Russian from her grandmother and spoke to one of them. She recognized the uniforms, too. You know those shoulder boards they wear? Plus a couple of them had a big red star above their pocket, some kinda medal."

"Would she recognize any of them if she saw them again?"

"I thought you might want to know that, so I asked her. She said yes, she'd recognize two of them. The guy she talked to and the guy who told her to get lost."

"In English?"

"Yep, she said he spoke good English. Took the other officer by the arm and herded him back into the group. She said the one she talked to spoke perfect English, no trace of an accent."

"Sounds like they had a NKVD minder."

"That's their secret police, right?"

"Yeah. Like the one who ended up dead a few nights ago," I said as I slowed.

"Billy, what the hell are you doing?" Big Mike said, gripping the dashboard as I took the jeep into a hard turn.

"Going to pay your WAC corporal a visit. What's her name?"

"Estelle. Estelle Gordon. But why are you going back there? They'll be on the lookout for you."

"No, they won't. I got away. The last thing they'd expect is for me to turn up again."

"They got pretty solid thinking on their side, Billy."

"Yeah, but they're not looking for you. I know where the back door is. Stay in front of me and I'm all set."

"Sure, that'll be a breeze. You going to show Estelle that photo?"

"That's the idea."

"Great," Big Mike said. "I show up with a lieutenant on the lam showing off a picture of a guy minus the back of his head. I'm sure Estelle will want to see me again."

"You didn't waste any time in there, did you?"

"Hell, no. I had to talk to somebody, didn't I? I picked the noncom who looked the smartest and had the best legs. Just happened to be all in one package."

CORPORAL ESTELLE GORDON worked in the logistics office. We got in easily. People always tended to look at Big Mike, which meant that any normal person around him was invisible. I sat across from her, shielded from the rest of the G-4 staff by a row of filing cabinets. She did look intelligent, her quick eyes darting between Big Mike and me as he introduced us. Her eyes were large and brown, the kind of eyes a guy could get lost in. But she was all business with me, straight backed, her hands folded on the desk in front of her.

"Lieutenant Boyle, I'm not sure I shouldn't call the MPs. Aren't they looking for you?" She smiled, but it was the kind of smile reserved for naughty children and mischievous lieutenants.

"It's all a misunderstanding, Corporal. I only need a minute of your time. I want to know what you can tell me about the Russian officer who broke up your conversation with the other Russian. Would you recognize him if I showed you a picture?"

"Why, Lieutenant?" Her hands were still folded, but one finger tapped against her knuckles. She was interested.

"Because a Russian officer was murdered, in London. I need to know if he was one of your Russians."

"How many Russians are there in England, Lieutenant Boyle? I wouldn't think they'd be so hard to keep track of."

"Listen, Corporal Gordon, this is a murder investigation. I'd appreciate an answer."

"If it was murder, why aren't the MPs asking?"

"Because they're busy looking for me. Do you know how to actually *answer* a question?"

"Yes, I do. See?"

"Estelle," I said, leaning closer to her. "Are you under orders not to talk about the Russians?"

"If such an order had come down since you gave the MPs the slip, I wouldn't be able to answer that question, would I, Lieutenant Boyle?"

"See, I told you she was smart," Big Mike said. He was leaning against the filing cabinets, keeping watch and threatening to crush them. Estelle rewarded him with a smile. A nice one.

"OK," I said. "I'm not going to ask you anything. But I am going to show you a photograph. I'm sorry, but it's not pretty."

"The dead . . . individual?" Estelle asked.

"Yes."

"And you'd like to know if I recognize this person, regardless of nationality?"

"Exactly," I said, glad to have finally figured out how to play this game. I placed the picture of Gennady Egorov's face on her desk.

"That's the bastard who told me to get lost," she said. "He wasn't very nice about it either."

"Somebody wasn't nice to him either."

"Hey, it wasn't me," Estelle said, raising her arms in mock surrender. "I haven't had a pass to London in weeks. Although I am due one in a couple of days." This was followed by a wink in Big Mike's direction.

"When was this, exactly?"

"Oh, I'd say about two weeks ago," Estelle said, checking her calendar. "Just short of that, actually. It was the same day we had a big meeting with Fighter Command, so I remember. Twelve days ago. When was he killed?"

"Six days ago. Last Friday night," I said. "Did you see him again?"

"Yes, one more time, but I kept my distance. It was two days later, when they all came here again, along with three officers from the Royal Navy."

"The Royal Navy? Why?"

"No idea, Lieutenant. And I'm not asking. I want to get to London, not Leavenworth."

CHAPTER ■ SEVEN

BIG MIKE DROPPED me off at New Scotland Yard, after bending my ear about Estelle. Apparently he'd done a very thorough interrogation, and had ended up with a date for Saturday night. He wanted to show her London in style, and quizzed me on the best restaurants. I told him to talk to Kaz about that. As he drove off in the direction of the Rubens Hotel, I gazed at the Thames, thinking of all the happy couples making the most of a weekend pass, and all the lonely people, pining for the dead and the living. Big Mike was lucky, with someone new and exciting to look forward to. For guys like Kaz, there were only memories, some good, some bad. Either way, the past had bricked up a wall around them, and it would be damned hard for anyone to bust through it.

I had to count myself lucky, but in a distant, someday sort of way. Diana might never return from her mission. But she could, and that had to be enough to get me through the night. That, and the memories of our last nights in Naples, with room service and wine, clean sheets and a soft bed. I could see Diana in her dressing gown, her arms around my neck, as we danced in her room to the sound of a band drifting up from the piazza. The memory was heaven, except for the possibility that it would be my last of her. I almost envied Kaz his certainty, but I knew it was because I hadn't paid the price he had for it. I focused on that dressing gown, shimmering and silky in the moonlight, praying that this memory would serve until we could make new ones.

The wind howled up the river, casting a damp chill along the banks. To the south, I could see streams of contrails, heavy bombers making their way back to bases north and west of London. Were they the same groups we'd seen this morning? The formations were more ragged now, individual aircraft flying behind the others. The drone from their engines was faint, a distant mechanical sound you could easily ignore, unless you thought about the shot-up boys inside, especially in those last, low, limping bombers. The sound stayed with me as I entered the Met and took the stairs to CID. I let the clatter of footsteps and conversation work their way into my brain and bring me back.

"Tell us again," I heard Detective Sergeant Flack say. He was leaning against Detective Inspector Scutt's desk. He and Scutt were staring at a young boy, maybe ten years old, seated on a 'ard-back wooden chair. The kid twisted around to look up at his father. I knew it was his father because he stood with his arms folded in the way a father does when he finds his kid in trouble with the cops. Tight across his chest, and a scowl on his face. The kid's eyes were wide, and his lower lip quivered a bit. Flack gave me a quick nod and I moved closer.

"Speak when yer spoken to, lad. And look to the sergeant there, not me!"

"It was like I told you," the boy said. "I found 'im, but it was Tommy who ran off ta call the rozzers and I didn't want 'im claiming all the credit. I figured if I got a medal or somethin' offa the dead Jerry, they'd know who found 'im. Thought there might be a reward. Is there a reward?"

"Your reward, young man," said Scutt, "shall be the knowledge you served the Crown by telling the truth."

"Oh," he said, in a small voice.

"Where did you find the map exactly?" Scutt said.

"All folded up, inside 'is cap, it was. I was gonna take the cap, but I thought the map might be important, so I took it 'ome to work it out as best I could."

"What did you work out then?" Flack said. I moved closer and saw a road map unfolded on Scutt's desk.

"They're bringing somethin' right into London, from up north. Nazi commandos, maybe? The road is marked clear as day, right to the palace, all the way from the country. I been up there, when we was evacuated. I 'ated it. Too quiet, with sheep and whatnot roaming about. I was glad ta get back."

"Alfred, please do us a favor. The next time you find a map that might direct German commandos to Buckingham Palace, please bring it to me," Scutt said. "And the victim was not a German, he was a Russian officer."

"Oh," said Alfred, taking in this new information, nodding his head as if he were a connoisseur of dead foreign officers.

"Sorry for the trouble, guv," his father said. "Ever since his mum was killed, I've had a hard time keeping my eye on him. I'm a docker, and we get double shifts as often as not. Not so bad now that they ain't bombing us, but it's 'ard enough. The boy didn't mean any 'arm by it."

"The Blitz?" Scutt asked, standing to look the man in the eye.

"Aye. October 1940 it was. Alfred was up north. I came 'ome after a big raid, fires burning all around. Could 'ardly see. Thought the smoke had got to my eyes when I couldn't find our 'ouse. The whole street was gone. Gone."

"Can we go now?" Alfred asked, sounding older than a kid still in short pants. He stood and took his father's hand.

"There's nothing else you can tell us, Alfred?" Flack said. "Nothing else you saw, or took with you? Even something small?"

"No, and I ain't lyin'."

"Had you ever seen this man before?" I asked. Alfred and his father turned, surprised to find me standing behind them.

"A Yank!" Alfred said. "Got any chewing gum?"

"Alfred!" His father gave him a light cuff on the ear. "Show some respect."

"That's OK," I said.

"I don't mean for you, I mean for the lad 'imself. Ain't right to go begging."

"I didn't look at 'is face," Alfred said, rubbing his ear and chancing a glance at his father. "There was blood and stuff everywhere, and 'is face was to the ground. I didn't want to touch it, know what I mean?"

"I do. Take a look at this photograph. Recognize him?" I laid the picture of Egorov on the desk. Alfred and his father leaned in to study it.

"Well, 'e don't look so good, but that's the fellow what asked about Chapman outside the Tube," the father said. "I'd appreciate it if you didn't mention Alfred in connection with that, nor my name neither."

"Is that 'im who's dead?" Alfred asked.

"Yes."

"Couldn't 'ave been Chapman then, right, Dad?"

"True, boy. You're right there."

"Why not?" I asked.

"Too quick, a bullet to the 'ead," Alfred's father said. "Ain't Chapman's style. Now, if you gentleman are done with us, we'll get 'ome."

"Yes, thank you for your cooperation," said Scutt. "And we won't mention your names and Chapman's in the same breath."

"I appreciate it, Inspector. Wouldn't do to get on Chapman's bad side, not down in the shelter."

"Where's home?" I asked, following them out. "Where did you go after being bombed out?"

"Moved in with my sister and her 'usband, down on Threadneedle Street. But we spend nights in the shelter. Don't want to take a chance with the boy here."

"But there hasn't been a raid in months."

"True. But the Jerries are a long way from beat, and they'll be back. If we give up our place now, we won't 'ave it when it's needed most. So down we go, every night."

"Along with this guy Chapman?"

"Listen to my advice. Stay away from 'im. You'll find nothing but trouble if you don't. Let's go, Alfred." The two shuffled off, the father's arm draped over his son's shoulder.

"Good idea you had, Boyle," Flack said when I returned. "The boy was holding something back, and as soon as his father came home, he gave it up."

"What does it mean?" I asked, tracing the line drawn on the map, from Stowmarket in Suffolk through Chelmsford and into London. It lazily terminated in the area of Buckingham Palace.

"It was the lad's imagination that concluded it led to the palace, as you can see," Scutt said. "But it does end near the Soviet Embassy. It starts outside of Stowmarket, where the Russians purchase much of their foodstuff from the local farms. Pigs, beef, whatever is in season. As diplomats, they are not subject to rationing, and can buy what they wish direct from farms, for their fancy dinners."

"Egorov was selling information," I said. "To this Chapman?"

"I wouldn't put it past him. We've had lorries hit all over London. Liquor, clothing, even bread. A load of food for an embassy would be worth a fortune on the black market."

"Is that the business Chapman is in?"

"Oh no," Scutt said in mock horror. "Archibald Chapman is a perfectly respectable contractor. Building, renovating, that sort of thing. Plenty of work these days, putting London back together."

"But he didn't lack for work before the war," Flack said. "Since his competition had a habit of disappearing."

"I know the type," I said. "Did you find any other evidence on Egorov's body? Anything in his billfold?"

"No," Scutt said. "A few pound notes, pictures of a young woman and a baby. His identity papers, nothing else. We cataloged everything, but that Russian captain took it all. What was his name, Flack?"

"Kiril Sidorov," Flack said, consulting his notebook. "Red Air Force captain. Came in here with a couple of fellows with arms the size of ham hocks, took all the evidence, such as it was, along with the late Captain Egorov. I asked him if we could search Egorov's quarters in the embassy, and he just laughed."

"Smooth chap," Scutt said. "Not all bluster and blather. Spoke decent English, and apologized for interfering with our investigation. He didn't mean it, but it showed good manners, which the few Bolsheviks I've met lacked."

"Here's the bullet," Flack said, opening an envelope. A misshapen slug rolled out onto the map, tumbling to a halt north of London Bridge. "You can see the filing marks, what's left of them."

I picked up the bullet. The sides were peeled back, torn away when the crisscross indentations had met the skull bone, turning a deadly round into a destructive missile. I could see the remnants of the file markings. The size was about right for a .32 caliber.

"No way to identify the caliber, is there?" I asked, trying to keep the hope out of my voice.

"Not in a courtroom, but I'd bet a month's wages we're looking for a .32," said Scutt, taking the bullet from my hand and squinting at it. "Wouldn't you say, Lieutenant Boyle?"

"Hard to say. Maybe, yeah. But the pistol could be at the bottom of the Thames by now. We need to focus on why someone wanted Egorov dead."

"Indeed," Scutt said. I hardly heard him, as I was thinking about the best place to drop Kaz's sidearm in the river.

"I've been up to Eighth Air Force HQ," I said.

"What did you learn?" Flack said.

"That Russians have been there, and that it's unhealthy to ask questions about them. I had a pack of MPs looking for me. I'd be in the stockade now if a guy I knew hadn't helped me get out ahead of them."

"Can this guy, as you call him, be of assistance?" Scutt asked.

"Maybe. He's a colonel, but he's OK. He said he'd try and get in touch. Meanwhile, I think I'll pay Chapman a visit."

"Watch your step with that one," Flack said. "He's as liable to slit your throat as to say good evening. He likes the blade, he does. His right-hand man is his son, Topper. Not as flashy as the old man, but smart. Archie sent him to the best schools, trying to put a shine on the family name. Topper knows how to dress and talk so you'd think him a banker, but don't let him fool you."

"I try never to turn my back on a banker."

CHAPTER • EIGHT

WALTER SIGNALED ME from his post at the front desk when I returned to the Dorchester, and handed me a message from Kaz. It said he'd be working late at Polish headquarters and would stay the night at the Rubens Hotel. I tried to call him from the room, but I couldn't get through. Lieutenant Kazimierz was unavailable, in conference, and would be all night. It sounded like something big was brewing. Maybe it had to do with the Russians and Katyn Forest, maybe not. There was plenty else going on in this war. Polish troops were fighting in Italy, and the whole Polish underground movement was coordinated from London, plus the Polish RAF squadrons were only an hour's drive away. But all that paled in comparison to the atrocity at Katyn. Every Pole who fought on our side was a volunteer, risking his life for his country. Death was a tragedy among them, but not unexpected, not avoidable. The Poles at Katyn were prisoners of war, murdered by our own Allies. They'd been helpless, and their deaths were as unnecessary as they were cruel. It was murder, and I had come to hate murder all the more because of the war. There was enough killing to go around. The thousands shot in the head by the Russians and thrown into pits should not have died that way. It was wrong, so wrong that it made my gut ache. So wrong that I could understand the need for revenge, the absolute necessity of it.

I set down the receiver and stared at the telephone. Kaz was my friend, but it was time to start acting like a cop. At least a cop who knew how to dispose of incriminating evidence. He probably had the .32 with him, but I had to look. I went through his desk, rifled his bureau drawers, then moved on to his clothes, patting down jacket pockets. Nothing. I pulled down boxes from the closet shelf, and one fell open. Letters spilled out. They were from Daphne. The postmarks went back to early 1940, when they'd first met, here in the dining room of the Dorchester, as bombs fell on Hyde Park. There were notes as well as letters, probably from when she'd moved in with him. Her handwriting flowed over the paper, a river of words that Kaz would never hear again, even if he read them a thousand times.

I felt like a lowlife. I put everything back, and wished I was still in Naples, hiking up a volcano with Diana. I couldn't betray Kaz, but I wasn't sure I could protect him either. It was the same with Diana. I'd learned I couldn't talk her out of volunteering with the SOE, that she needed to do her bit, as she liked to say. She needed to risk her life, to prove to herself she deserved it. I couldn't stop her, and I couldn't protect her from the risk of death either. I cared for both Kaz and Diana, more than any-one this side of Southie, and fear curled up inside me as I thought of the worst of what might be in store for them.

I pulled the heavy curtains shut, pausing to watch the last of the afternoon light bathe the park in a soft glow. Vehicles crawled along Park Lane, tiny beams of light seeping onto the roadway through blackout slits. London had never felt so lonely. Everyone was going somewhere. Home, to dinner, back to the barracks, maybe down to the shelters. Those things that passed for a normal life these days. Friends and family, small talk, even if it was on a subway platform. Me, I was in a high-class hotel, rummaging through my best friend's possessions, spilling letters from his dead lover onto the floor. Welcome to my war. I poured a drink from the bar Kaz kept stocked with Irish whiskey, just for me. Here's to you, pal.

It went down smoothly, but I still felt a twinge of that morning's hangover. I shouldn't have drunk so much vodka the night before, and I shouldn't have any more tonight, I told myself as I poured one more. But then I thought, hell, if I'm looking to steal Kaz's pistol, I might as well drink all his whiskey, too.

Daphne's letters made me realize how long it had been since I'd writ-ten one myself. I pulled some stationery from the writing desk—heavy, creamy paper with *The Dorchester* in elegant script across the top. I could sneak it into the airmail bag at headquarters, instead of using the Victory Mail forms. Mom would get a kick out of the hotel stationery. I switched on the desk lamp and set down my drink, the heavy crystal settling on the polished cherrywood with a satisfying clunk. It was a high-class sound, the kind of sound that said a lot of money had gone into the furniture, glassware, and booze. A rich man's sound, the echo of privilege and place. But right then I'd have preferred the sound of a beer glass going down on a coaster at Kirby's Tavern in South Boston. Soft and quiet. Comfortable.

I started off the letter with the obvious news that I was back in London. I asked about my kid brother, Danny, who had just started college under the Army Specialized Training Program. He'd turned eighteen and would have been drafted but for the ASTP, which was an army deal to insure a supply of well-educated officer candidates in case the war dragged on longer than they expected. It sort of satisfied Danny, who got to wear a uniform and march around campus. He was a smart kid—I mean a really smart kid—straight As and all that. It was a cinch for him to get in, and I hoped it would keep him safe until the shooting died down.

Then I had to write about what I was up to. I couldn't tell them anything about Diana, on account of her being British, since I didn't want a written lecture on the evils of associating with the English. Or about dead Poles in a Russian forest, a dead Russian in bombed-out London, Kaz and his possible murder weapon, getting drunk on vodka last night, being chased by MPs at High Wycombe, or drinking too much whiskey tonight. I almost wrote about young Alfred finding the body and thinking it was a German, but that was too depressing. It was a short letter, and I fell asleep on the couch, a spilled drink soaking the carpet and the vision of motherless Alfred leading his father by the hand worming its way into my dreams.

IN THE MORNING I called Kaz, who was still not available. Then I called room service, which mercifully was. I wolfed down toast and jam, and then washed that down with hot coffee until the cobwebs cleared. I told myself no booze today, but I knew that morning promises had a way of giving in to evening temptations. I wanted to talk to Kaz, but until I could, I needed to work this case some more. There were two visits I had to make. One was to the Russian who had come to claim Egorov's body. Kiril Sidorov, captain in Stalin's air force, or so he claimed. He was certainly NKVD, charged with cleaning up an embarrassing murder of a

Soviet officer gone bad, tempted by the degenerate English criminal class. The other was to Archibald Chapman, one of those degenerate English criminals. Sidorov was first on the list, since degenerates generally slept in, while secret police never sleep.

It was a cold, clear day. I'd dressed in my heavy wool brown pants and the chocolate brown wool shirt I'd picked up in Naples before coming north. With my light khaki tie, it made me look like a gangster, which was why I had chosen it for today. The Russians probably thought all Americans were gangsters, so why not go along? I set my garrison cap at a smart angle, put on my mackinaw with the warm wool collar, and added a scarf and leather gloves. It felt like winter in Boston on a sunny day with the breeze howling up the Charles River. The Soviet Embassy was on the other side of Kensington Palace, where the lesser royals had to make do, and the wind gusted over the open park grounds. It was a swanky area, not the kind of place you'd find many Bolsheviks among the neighbors, but even a Red ambassador had to put on a good show.

Walking to Kensington Palace Gardens was a little like walking up Beacon Hill, except the English had more room to spread out than the Boston Brahmins had. I found the Soviet Embassy, which wasn't hard, given the big bloodred flag snapping in the breeze, the yellow hammer and sickle vanishing and reappearing in the silken folds as the banner waved in the wind. The building was a two-story, ornate structure, beige brickwork bordered by gleaming white trim and elegantly carved cornices. Two sentries stood at the ironwork gate, dressed in Soviet Army greatcoats. I asked to see Captain Kiril Sidorov, and they opened the gate without asking a question or speaking a word. I wondered what you had to do in their army to get embassy duty in London. It must have seemed like springtime in paradise, compared to the Russian front.

Inside the main entrance was a small room. It was painted a stark white, with one door, a desk, and two chairs. A man in a baggy dark suit sat at a desk and, without looking up, started asking me a series of questions as a bigger guy in an even baggier suit searched me. Neither of them had spent their spare time shopping in London, that was for sure. Who was I, whom did I want to see, for what purpose, who was my superior officer, and finally, what was my civilian occupation.

I used Harding's name, holding Uncle Ike in reserve in case things got dicey. I told them I wanted to speak to Captain Sidorov in connection with the murder of Captain Gennady Egorov.

"The assassination of Captain Egorov," the smaller dark suit stated, waiting for the answer to the last question. It didn't seem worth debating the difference. He had a thin face, with a thick mustache that looked out of place over pale, pursed lips. He spoke English carefully, considering each word as he strung them together in a series of harsh consonants.

"Why does it matter what I did in civilian life?" I asked. I wondered if his mustache was an imitation of Joe Stalin's.

"It will assist us in determining if you are an enemy of the people. We do not want provocateurs causing trouble for our comrades."

"Aren't we all on the same side, comrade?"

"We must be vigilant in the class struggle, as well as in the struggle against Fascism, especially in this decadent city. Your civilian occupation, please?"

"Have you guys seen *Ninotchka* yet?"

"We have no one here by that name." Busy writing in his notebook, he still hadn't looked me in the eye. The big guy stood with his arms folded, a bored look on his broad, dull face. His neck was thick and his knuckles were decorated with scar tissue. I wondered what his civilian occupation had been.

"No, the film," I said. "With Greta Garbo."

"Western films are a frivolous waste of time. We have our own Russian motion pictures brought in for entertainment. Perhaps Captain Sidorov will invite you to see one. Your civilian occupation?"

"Police detective. Friend and protector of the people."

"Hmm." He wrote some more, and finally looked at me. I sensed he was weighing the obvious benefit of a detective working on the assassination of Comrade Egorov against my being a lackey of the ruling class. We had our fair share of Communist sympathizers in Boston, especially over in Cambridge, where the most ardent of them usually came from the richest families. I wasn't exactly a fan of the moneyed crowd and politicians who ran things, but it seemed to me the Reds had as many bosses as any factory hand, and less of a chance of quitting than any textile worker in New England.

"Very well, Lieutenant Boyle. I will inform Captain Sidorov you wish to see him. Be seated."

I sat. Big Suit stood and looked out the window as the thin guy picked up a telephone and spoke in Russian. He set down the receiver as Big Suit cracked his knuckles, then refolded his arms. It was a cozy little scene. Big Suit leaned over to get a better view out the window, and I could see the outline of an automatic pistol in his waistband. I bet the thin guy kept his in a desk drawer. The guards outside were window dressing; this was the real security, or at least the main line of defense.

After twenty minutes, a young woman in a Red Army uniform came to my rescue. She wore a brown high-collar shirt, yellow shoulder boards, a wide leather belt, and a row of medals lying at a pleasing angle on the curve of her breast. She smiled and crooked her finger at me. I followed, happily, leaving the white room and dark suits behind. She wordlessly led me up a flight of stairs and through a set of double doors, which she closed behind me.

A Russian Air Force officer came forward, hand outstretched. "Lieutenant William Boyle, I greet you in the name of the Union of Soviet Socialist Republics. Captain Kiril Sidorov, at your service."

His steel blue uniform was well tailored, suiting his slim frame. The light blue collar tabs and piping matched his eyes perfectly, and his leather belt gleamed. He'd definitely paid a visit to Savile Row, just as many American officers had, to get a bespoke—tailored—uniform. I wondered what his comrades thought of it, but then I noticed one of his red ribbons held a medal with Lenin's face on it, and the other a gold star. That probably gave him some leeway.

"Pleased to meet a hero of the Soviet Union, Captain. The Order of Lenin, too. You must have been in the thick of it."

"Pay no attention to these baubles, Lieutenant Boyle. The real heroes are at the front, not in comfortable London rooms." Sidorov pointed to a pair of chairs facing the fireplace, where embers glowed, giving off a welcome heat. He shoveled more coal from a bucket, rubbing his hands together over the fire. He wore his clothes well, remembering to lift his trousers at the knees as he took his seat. Sandy-colored hair fell over his forehead, and he brushed it back in what seemed to be a habitual gesture.

"You speak English perfectly," I said, glancing around the room. At the far end, a balding, stout middle-aged man sat at a desk, working on a pile of papers and files. A cigarette protruded from the corner of his mouth as he sucked in smoke and exhaled, not breaking stride with the paperwork he was shuffling through.

"Thank you. I was taught by a former Oxford professor who came to the Soviet Union to be part of the glorious international struggle. He imparted his accent as well as his intellect," Sidorov said as he caught my look at the other man in the room. "Do not mind Sergei. We do not meet alone with westerners. Sergei was available, although he speaks English poorly. Still, it allows us to follow the rules laid down by our security people."

"To protect you against provocateurs," I said.

"I see you have been lectured by our reception committee. They are sometimes overenthusiastic, but these precautions are necessary, believe me. The revolution has enemies beyond the Nazis. Czarists and other émigré groups are based here in London, and none of them wish us well. But never mind about our security procedures. Tell me how I can help you."

"General Eisenhower asked me to look into the death of Captain Egorov," I said, avoiding the distinction between murder and assassination. "He's also concerned about security, and wanted to be certain there was no further trouble."

"You work for General Eisenhower?"

"Yes, I'm on his staff."

"Please excuse me, Lieutenant Boyle, if I fail to be impressed by a mere lieutenant detailed to this investigation. It does not signal true concern on the part of our American Allies." Sidorov smiled, almost apologetically. He looked half serious and half amused at the lines he had to speak. He wasn't what I had expected. He was stern, but not harsh. He spoke the jargon of Communism naturally, but lightly, as if we were all in on the joke. It occurred to me that the Soviets picked their personnel for foreign posts very carefully, and that his casual veneer of nonchalance was well practiced. Possibly dangerous.

"I was a police detective before the war," I said, "and General Eisenhower is my uncle, which should indicate his personal interest in this case. He wishes this to be handled discreetly."

"All within the family," Sidorov said slyly, with an exaggerated lift of the eyebrow. He offered me a cigarette, and I declined. He lit up a Woodbine, flashing a lighter that sparkled silver before it vanished into the folds of his jacket. "Very well. What have you discovered in your investigation?"

"That Gennady Egorov was forced to his knees in the ruins of a bombed-out building near Spitalfields Market in Shoreditch, not far from the Liverpool Street Tube Station. That he got a bullet in the back of the head. That he may have been selling information to a criminal named Archibald Chapman, about deliveries of food to your embassy."

"Really? All that in two days? Remarkable, Lieutenant Boyle. Although the first two items you would learn within five minutes of being briefed at Scotland Yard. The third item, though, that is more impressive." He drew on his Woodbine and exhaled a plume of blue smoke toward the ceiling.

"That's not all."

"What? Have you apprehended this criminal? Chapman?"

"No. But I now know that you must be aware of why Egorov was in Shoreditch, a fair distance from here, late at night. Either that, or you're complicit in his assassination." I saw Sergei lift his head from his paperwork. His English probably wasn't all that bad. "And I know that you were expecting me."

"Yes, yes. I knew I made a mistake when I said two days. Stupid of me, of course. And you assume since we do not meet westerners alone that either I knew Gennady had gone out by himself, or someone from the embassy was with him, possibly his killer."

"So you've been spying on me?" I said, not wanting to skip over that part so lightly.

"Don't be melodramatic, Lieutenant Boyle," Sidorov said, flicking his cigarette into the fire. "We simply stay informed of the comings and goings of those we are involved with. It is common practice in London. Everyone spies on everyone else, and then we all smile and go to meetings together, dine and drink, toast to victory over the common foe, and then collect information on each other from our informants. Quite possibly the same informants. So, yes, I knew you had arrived and your assignment. It seemed obvious that your next step would be to come here."

"All right. Tell me what Egorov was doing in Shoreditch."

"I cannot, because I do not know. Even the most dedicated Soviet officer may succumb to desire, Lieutenant Boyle. Perhaps it was a woman?"

"I see you have women here," I said.

"True, but often the forbidden is more tempting. Who knows?"

"Don't you keep track of people going out as well as coming in?"

"Yes," Sidorov said, nodding his head. "But sometimes there are

circumstances . . . the gathering of information is a delicate matter. . . ."
He waved his hand in a dismissive fashion, as if he couldn't think of the
words but that any simpleton should be able to figure it out.

"You mean NKVD officers masquerading as Soviet Air Force officers
can come and go as they please."

"Yes, exactly," Sidorov said, slapping his hand on the arm of his chair.
"That is the gist of it." He grinned like a schoolboy. "It makes solving a
murder that much more difficult. Who watches the watchers, yes?"

"It's been my experience that someone is always watching. They may
not understand what they've seen, but sooner or later you can find someone who had their eyes wide open when everyone else was asleep."

"That, Lieutenant Boyle, is a great truth. A sad one, perhaps, but very
true. Everything is seen; there are no secrets." We sat quietly and watched
the glow of the coal fire for a minute. Sidorov spoke to Sergei in Russian,
and Sergei made a phone call. Within a couple of minutes, a tray with
hot tea was brought in. The tea was poured into glasses set in brass hold-
ers, and Sidorov added sugar to both before handing me mine.

"Tea, prepared the Russian way, not the English style," he said.

"What's the difference?" I said after a hot sip.

"Well, we don't ruin it with milk. And we prepare the tea in a concen-
trated form first, then boiling water is added. It enhances the flavor."

"It's good," I said. It was, but I wasn't about to debate tea. "We threw
English tea into the harbor, during our revolution."

"In Boston, yes?"

"Yes. That's my home. What about you?"

"Vyazma. It is west of Moscow. I have not been home for a long time."

"Your family is there?"

"No, my wife and daughter live in Moscow. She works for the
Propaganda Ministry. Vyazma is on the approach to Moscow. It was occupied by the Germans for two years. We retook it last March. Vyazma once
had a population of over sixty thousand. We found exactly 617 alive."

"I'm sorry."

"As am I. It makes all this attention to the death of one man almost
ludicrous, does it not?"

"Another great truth, Captain Sidorov. Even in the midst of war,
murder is unacceptable."

"Yes," Sidorov said slowly, almost reluctant to grant the point. "Tell me, what did you find that links Gennady to this criminal—what did you call him—Chapman?"

"Archibald Chapman. Seems to be the local crime boss, in Shoreditch, anyway. The kid who found Captain Egorov was going to pinch his cap as a souvenir. He found a map folded up inside and took that instead. It showed the route between your embassy and the farms up north you buy supplies from."

"Scotland Yard didn't mention any map," Sidorov said, frowning.

"I thought it might be worth pressing the kid on it, so they brought him back in, with his father."

"That was smart, Lieutenant Boyle."

"Even a blind squirrel manages to find a few acorns now and then," I said. Sergei laughed, and I decided his English was excellent. Sidorov smiled over his glass of tea.

"We did have a large truckload of supplies hijacked on the road to London last week," he said. "Beef, lamb, and a large quantity of whiskey. We thought it due to the rampant criminal activity associated with a decadent imperialist society. Now it appears one of our own had a hand in it."

"But what would Captain Egorov get out of it? If he was paid off, how would he get the money home? Wouldn't a large quantity of English pounds raise suspicions when he returned to the Soviet Union?"

"Yes, but he was not a stupid man. He could convert them to jewels, perhaps, and sell them for rubles in Moscow, or trade them for what he desired."

"Or maybe he didn't plan on going back."

"Comrade Egorov may have been tempted by the lure of easy money, Lieutenant, but he was not a traitor, not to the motherland, nor to his family."

"There would be reprisals?" I asked.

"That is a ridiculous word," Sidorov snapped. "We have laws in the Soviet Union. Article 58 of the criminal code makes any kind of counter-revolutionary activity punishable, including the nonreporting of crimes by others. The usual sentence is six months' imprisonment in a labor camp."

"Six months in Siberia seems like a very long time."

"Well, what should we do? Send them to the Crimea for the sunshine? But this has nothing to do with the case. Tell me if I can assist you in any way with your pursuit of Captain Egorov's killer."

"Do you still have his body? His clothing?"

"No. His remains were cremated and are being returned to the motherland by convoy. We found nothing of interest on his person; apparently the child found the only relevant evidence. Do you have it?"

"No. Inspector Scutt at Scotland Yard does. Do you want to see it?"

"I don't wish to cause unnecessary trouble for his family, so it does not need to figure in my report to the Foreign Ministry. But perhaps it will help the investigation. I shall call on the inspector this afternoon. Now, if there is nothing else . . . ?"

"Just a few more questions," I said. Sidorov seemed to have switched gears, from the charming, tea-sipping commissar to suddenly giving me the bum's rush. "Have you gone through Egorov's paperwork? I assume he submitted reports on his activities."

"Of course, but that information is restricted, as I am sure you understand."

"But did you find anything that might shed light on his murder?"

"Lieutenant Boyle, that is what Scotland Yard is supposedly for. And now the Americans have assigned you as well. I hope our Allies will treat Captain Egorov's death with the same importance they would if he had been an English lord."

"Can you tell me what the business at High Wycombe with the Eighth Air Force was all about?"

"No. If you have to ask that question, you already have been told by your own people that it is top secret. Now, what is your other question?"

"Did Captain Egorov's duties bring him in contact with the Polish Government in Exile?"

"We no longer have relations with the so-called Polish government in London."

"That doesn't answer my question."

"It will have to do. This interview is concluded." Sidorov rose and wordlessly escorted me out of the building, all trace of friendliness gone. On the steps, I turned to thank him, but all I saw was the door closing and, out of the corner of my eye, the scarlet Soviet banner snapping in the breeze, like a whip.

CHAPTER ■ NINE

I HOOFED IT to the Notting Hill Gate, trying to figure out what Sidorov's angle was. Had he pumped me for information, then given me the bum's rush when he was done? Or did he have an appointment with his boss, or maybe his tailor? Or someone involved in murder and theft?

I turned before I got to the gate and walked slowly back toward the embassy. As soon as I got within sight of the two front sentries, I stopped and leaned against the trunk of a tree, staying out of their line of vision while watching for anyone leaving the building. I tried to look harmless, just a guy waiting for his date, but this wasn't the kind of neighborhood where you hung out on a street corner. Nearly every mansion had a shiny brass plaque declaring it some nation's sovereign ground. I waited for a bobby or a guy in a dark suit to roust me, but before anybody got the chance, I saw what I was looking for. Captain Kiril Sidorov, thankfully walking in the opposite direction, his overcoat as bright as a blue jay's among the brown, khaki, and dark blue that flowed along the sidewalk.

I followed, keeping the bobbing steel blue service cap in sight. He turned off the road and into Kensington Gardens, walking briskly past the palace with its black iron gates decorated in gold leaf. I wondered if he thought about the czar and his family, all those children gunned down in the name of the people. Probably as much as the czar ever thought about children starving in Russian villages.

He took the bridge over the Serpentine and stopped to admire the view. I had to remind myself that Sidorov was NKVD, and that surveillance was second nature to him. He had picked this route because it gave him a clear field of vision to spot a tail. I kept my head down and tried to blend in with the crowd of uniforms parading through the park. I took a chance and stayed on the opposite bank, walking along Rotten Row, keeping my eye on him across the narrow body of water.

I almost lost him crossing the street at Hyde Park Corner, when he waited until the last second before dashing across. Luckily, a double-decker bus stalled and I darted between slow-moving vehicles, managing to keep Sidorov in sight. He took a side street and emerged in Belgrave Square, where he sat on a bench and casually looked around, as if he were enjoying the winter sunshine. I didn't think he had spotted me or even suspected a tail. But it did tell me he wasn't out for an afternoon stroll. He was on his way to a meet, and I had to wonder if it had anything to do with my visit and Egorov's murder. Or maybe the Poles, or the Eighth Air Force, or who the hell knew. I didn't have a clue, except for the feeling in my gut that something was wrong with what Sidorov had told me. I had no idea what it was, but his sudden brusque switch hadn't felt right.

Sidorov got up, circled the small park, spun on his heel, and turned back the way he had come, almost colliding with a woman wearing a blue scarf tied about her head, her hands stuffed in the pockets of her plain beige coat, and her eyes cast down to the pavement as she plowed through the crowd. He put out one hand to steady her, then knelt to pick up the pocketbook she had dropped. He gave her a quick, almost courtly bow before moving on. He had a way about him, a confidence that flowed with every step he took, whether trying to spot a tail or playing the gallant with a woman on a busy London street.

He walked quickly for a few more blocks before entering Victoria Station. The narrow streets in the Belgravia district twisted and turned, hiding what was at the end of each passageway, but I was certain I was within spitting distance of the Rubens Hotel. I waited for a crowd to bunch up at the entrance to the station and mixed in with them. Sidorov was nowhere to be seen. I bought a newspaper and pretended to read, holding it up in front of my face and peering over the top. I stood in a ticket line, scanning the cavernous room, until it came to my turn, and I strolled away, searching for that distinctive coat. At the far end of the room, a giant sign advertised Aspinall's Enamel, sold everywhere in London. Beneath the sign was an entrance marked REFRESHMENTS, and I went in, looking for steel blue.

I saw it. The flash of a sleeve in a café, as Sidorov hung up his coat. He took a seat at a little table, his back to the wall, so he could see the station through the large plate-glass window. It was a snug place, no more than ten tables, built to offer a quick bite and a cup of tea between trains. It was packed with travelers, their suitcases and duffel bags making movement difficult. Sidorov sat alone, his eyes darting, his body still. I moved behind a pillar and took out my newspaper, allowing myself a glance up every few seconds. I was at the edge of his field of vision, one of a hundred GIs killing time in a busy station. I didn't think he'd made me.

A squad of British Tommies marched past, two abreast, their sergeant barking at them to look lively. They blocked my view and by the time they'd gone, there was another man sitting at the table with Sidarov. He faced away from me, and all I could make out was his dark hair slicked back and the gray cloth coat he wore. A waitress brought Sidorov his tea, but his companion waved her away, the gesture betraying his worry, as if he didn't want her listening, and couldn't wait to finish the conversation. In about two minutes, he pulled a fedora hat down low over his eyes, stuffed his hands into his coat pockets, and made a beeline for the exit. I glanced at Sidorov, sitting with his cup of tea in front of him, as he lit a cigarette. I wondered if he'd drink the English tea, but I couldn't hang around to find out.

I followed the fedora. It was a lot easier than tailing Sidorov. Out the main entrance, up Buckingham Palace Road a couple of blocks, before disappearing down an alleyway adjacent to the Rubens Hotel. As I turned the corner I heard a door slam shut. Three steps led up to an enclosed landing. Above the door the sign read STAFF ENTRANCE. I tried the handle and it opened. Inside, in a narrow hallway with coat hooks along the wall, Sidorov's pal had hung up his fedora and was pulling off his coat. He had a surprised look on his narrow, thin face. His eyebrows shot up in a questioning look, and he seemed on the verge of telling me I'd come in the wrong door, but he held back, uncertain of what I was there for.

"Here, let me help you," I said, grabbing him by the collar. I snapped his head against the wall, enough to let him know I meant business. Then I took one wrist and pulled it up behind his back and propelled him down the hall.

"Ow! Let go of me, you crazy Yank! Ow! That hurts! I'll scream for the police, I swear I will." He began squirming and kicking at my feet, but I pulled up on his wrist some more, and he stopped.

"Let's call the police. I'm sure that they'll be interested in apprehending a spy."

"I'm no spy! What, are you drunk? Let go of me."

"Not a spy? You might be right. I mean, the Russians are our Allies, so it's not like spying for the Germans. But the Poles are guests in this hotel, and I'm sure your employer will have something to say about that. What's your job here?"

"What's it to you? You're a Yank." I slammed his head into the wall again, to keep him focused.

"Ow! Stop that!"

"Are you all right, Eddie?" A small voice came from a door, held open a few inches. A girl in a maid's uniform gazed at Eddie and what I hoped was a good-sized bruise on his forehead.

"Yeah, yeah, just a misunderstanding, Sheila. I'll be there in a minute," Eddie said. I let his wrist go and put my arm on his shoulder, to show her we were just a couple of pals roughhousing. I figured it also put Eddie in my debt, since I didn't make him look bad in front of the young lady. I smiled at her, but she kept her eyes on Eddie, trying to figure out what was happening. She was good-looking, with thick, dark hair pulled back behind her ears, brown eyes, and a small mouth that hung open for a few seconds in surprise until she recovered.

"I'll see you later then, after our shift," she said, and shut the door. I tightened my grip on Eddie's shoulder and gave him the hard stare.

"I've got a whole bunch of options here, Eddie, and you basically have none. I could tell the manager you've been selling out the guests, and then you'd be out of a job. Or I could tell the Poles, and they'll cut your tongue out. Or I'll tell Sidorov you've been giving him phony information, and he'll slit your throat."

"Who's Sidorov?" Eddie said. He was beginning to shake, and his voice had a desperate quiver to it. "I haven't done anything wrong, honest."

"The Russian you just met in Victoria Station. He probably gave you a different name."

"Oh, Jesus," Eddie said, his voice breaking. "It was just some easy money, you know. Nothing was supposed to go wrong. What are you going to do with me?" His lower lip was shaky, and his eyes were watering up. I didn't want a blubbering mess on my hands, so I soothed him a bit.

"Listen, Eddie. I think **we can work** something out. I have a friend on the Polish staff. Do you **know** Lieutenant Kazimierz?"

"The baron, you mean? Small fellow?"

"That'd be him. He might be interested in hearing about the Russian. He might even see his way clear to paying you to keep meeting with him."

"How about I just stop, and we all part company as friends?" Eddie offered.

"Sorry, Eddie. It doesn't work that way. Either we talk to Kaz or I throw you to the wolves." Eddie had that look in his eye, the look I'd seen a hundred times before. A guy in a dead-end job, or with no job, sees a way to make a quick buck. At first it works like a charm, but then something goes wrong. The fact that you can count on something to go wrong escapes these chumps. Then when it does, they get the look that Eddie was giving me. A beseeching, haunted look. The look of a guy who is hoping you'll set things right, when the whole thing was his fault in the first place. The look of a guy who will never learn.

"OK, if you say so," Eddie said.

"You can trust me, Eddie. The name is Billy." I stuck out my hand and we shook. Eddie might never learn, but I'd learned fast. A chump is a chump, but the best chump is *your* chump.

Within twenty minutes we were in a room with Kaz and Captain Valerian Radecki. I couldn't leave Eddie in place as Sidorov's spy, so I explained to both of them what I'd seen, and suggested they might want to use Eddie to funnel phony information to the Russians. It gave me a headache trying to figure out which side I was on, so I'd gone with helping Kaz.

"Edward Miller," Valerian said, leafing through Eddie's billfold as he paced behind him. "Why are you not in the army, Edward Miller?"

"I tried to sign up. Punctured eardrum, they said. What are you going to do with me?"

"Eddie," Kaz said, leaning on the table, leaning into Eddie and his nervous eyes. "We should be asking what you were going to do with us. Betray us? To the Russians?"

"It didn't seem that serious, sir, honest. Just some harmless information, about who came and went, what the gossip was, that sort of thing."

"But the money was good," Valerian said. "More than a tip for your cooperation, correct?"

"Yes, it was." Eddie stared at the table. He was afraid of Valerian, who somehow managed to give the impression of easy violence lurking beneath the surface.

"What did he ask you about today?" Kaz said.

"About that fellow, the real nervous one. Tadeusz Tucholski. Lately that's all he's been asking about. Where does he live, who sees him, what does he talk about, that sort of thing."

"What did you tell him about Tadeusz?" Kaz said. I watched a nervous glance pass between him and Valerian.

"Only what I've seen—that you, in particular, are working with him on something. It looked to me like you were writing a book, taking down what he was saying."

"Did you overhear anything?" Kaz said, in a slow, patient voice that I knew was holding back fury.

"No, never. I only talked to him once, when I brought up a meal. You'd left the room, and as I laid out the food, I asked him how he liked London. He said it was very pleasant, that's all. Really, those are the only words I ever heard him speak. Honestly."

"Very well," Valerian said. "We believe you. We want you to continue to see this Russian as he wishes. But we will provide the information you are to give him. Do you understand?"

"Is this like being a double agent?"

"Yes, exactly, Edward Miller of 420 Penford Street in Camberwell," Valerian said, tossing Eddie his billfold. "Except this is not the moving pictures. If you perform well, we will pay you. If not, we will kill you."

"And forget you ever saw me, Eddie," I said.

"I wish I could," he said, holding his head in his hands.

"THANK YOU, BILLY," Kaz said when we were alone in the hotel lounge bar. "You didn't have to do that, I know."

"It would've been hard to ignore," I said. "Once I saw Sidorov meeting with that guy so close to the hotel, I knew it would involve you. I couldn't let it go."

"I hope we can turn this to our advantage," Kaz said, lowering his voice. "The Russians are about to issue their own report on Katyn, now that they've had their own so-called experts examine the site. If they know we have an eyewitness, they may take action against him."

"What kind of action?"

"What do you think?" Kaz said, finishing off the last of his lunch. "But I believe Eddie will soon tell them that our eyewitness confessed to being a fake. A deserter, a criminal who hoped to benefit financially, but grew afraid of unwanted attention. How does that sound?"

"Flimsy. Say he fell in love with his nurse, and she convinced him to tell the truth. The story needs a woman's touch; it will make his change of heart more convincing. Tell me something, Kaz. Have you been aware of any other spies, or Russians following you around?"

"That's very good—the woman, I mean. No evidence of Russian spying, although I have to assume they are aware of our activities. Why do you ask?"

"Just curious," I said, draining my glass of ale, working at not meeting Kaz's eyes.

"I am glad you are my friend, Billy. I'd hate to think you were suspicious of me."

"You know me, Kaz. I'm suspicious of everyone." I tried to smile and make a joke of it. Kaz laughed, but I don't think he thought it funny. "Ever see this guy before?" I handed him the photo of Gennady Egorov.

"No, I haven't," Kaz said. "He doesn't look well. Who is he?"

"He was Captain Gennady Egorov, late of the Soviet Air Force. Or NKVD. Stationed here in London, shot in the back of the head a few nights ago. I'm supposed to look into it for the general."

"And you can't help but wonder if the Polish Government in Exile was mixed up in it, given our differences with the Russians?"

"It's a possibility that has to be explored, Kaz. It's the first thing anyone would think of. It was the first thing you brought up."

"It is how I've come to view the world. Through the eyes of thousands of murdered Poles. Through the eyes of Tadeusz. I want the world to know what they did, Billy. I want them to pay!" His voice had risen, and I laid my hand on his arm, quieting him with my touch. Heads had turned in our direction, but the other patrons soon went back to their drinks and dining.

"I know," I said. I also knew that the Russians were fighting the Germans in far greater numbers than we were, and would be for months.

The Poles were important, for historical as well as moral reasons. England had gone to war with Germany over the invasion of Poland, and the Polish people had suffered terribly since then. But the Russians had many, many divisions in the fight, and they were headed for Berlin, killing Germans as they went. The more they killed, the fewer would be facing us when we landed and made our own run at Adolf. Uncle Ike had taught me the mathematics of war, the horrible truth of the planned deaths of thousands. Some must die now so that more would live later. And it followed that some causes would be sacrificed, no matter how honorable, if doing so would lessen the final tally of dead, maimed, and lost. "I know," I repeated, unable to tell Kaz what it was I knew with such certainty.

"What will you do next?" Kaz said, after the silence between us had become awkward.

"I need to check in with Harding, and then try to find a London gangster named Archibald Chapman."

"Archie Chapman? What do you want with him?"

"You know him?"

"I know of him, and that's quite enough. He's head of an East End gang, and quite vicious. Unbalanced and unpredictable, they say. His gang has gone heavily into the black market since the war, but still runs a prostitution ring and deals in drugs."

"There may be a link between him and the dead Russian."

"I'm not surprised he's the one left standing."

"Happen to know where I can find him?"

"He lives in Shoreditch, but I wouldn't advise asking for his address. He is superstitious about air raids, though. He still sleeps every night in the Liverpool Street Underground."

"So I've heard. That's not far from where the body was found."

"Be very careful, Billy. He has bodyguards with him at all times."

"How do you know all this?"

"I have a friend who works for the *Sunday Dispatch*. He was going to write a series about the London underworld, and he told me about his plans since he knew I was interested in American gangsters. Some of Chapman's men paid him a visit and convinced him to move on to other projects."

"How? Did they beat him up?"

"No, *he* was not injured at all. They stopped him at night on Fleet

Street, outside his office. Two of them with some poor soul from the East End slums. They slit his throat right there on the sidewalk and told my friend that would happen to him if he ever wrote a single word about Archie Chapman."

"I assume he found other stories to write."

"Yes. No shortage of stories in wartime. I think it gives people license to tolerate things they ordinarily wouldn't. The black market is harmless in some respects, but shockingly criminal in others. You see your neighbor getting a bit of extra butter or meat, and you quite naturally want yours, too. No one ever thinks about all the theft and organized crime behind it. Not to mention all the riches you Americans brought with you. It seems never ending, all the food, machinery, men, and supplies. Why not take your share, that's the common feeling."

"And men like Archie Chapman get rich while better men go off and get themselves killed," I said.

"Yes. Remember, he's feared, but also respected by some in the East End. He spreads a bit of his wealth throughout Shoreditch, so the locals tend to close ranks around him. Be cautious when you venture into the Underground, and don't go unarmed."

"You still carrying that little .32 automatic?"

"Of course. Do you want to borrow it?"

"No, but thanks," I said. "I have a .38 police special packed away, I'll bring that along. Not as conspicuous as a .45." I thought it was a good sign that Kaz offered his piece to me. A guy who'd popped a Russian in the head a few days ago would've gotten rid of it most likely. He sure wouldn't be eager to offer it to a cop, or whatever the hell I was. "One thing I forgot to ask, Kaz. You know anything about a Russian delegation visiting High Wycombe recently?"

"Eighth Air Force? No, why would they go there?"

"Just what I wanted to know. Big Mike has a date with a WAC from up there. He's picking her up tonight. Maybe she can tell him something."

"There is a Polish RAF squadron nearby at the Northolt base. I can ask them, although if they spotted any Russians I would've heard about the fight by now." He smiled grimly. It had been a joke, but it reinforced the truth about the feelings between Poles and Russians. Deadly.

CHAPTER TEN

I'D GONE BACK to the Dorchester, retrieved my Colt .38 police special from my duffel bag, donned a shoulder holster, and resisted the temptation to sit on the couch, put my feet up, have a drink, and think things through. It was tough since a suite at the Dorchester with Kaz's well-stocked bar had a lot more going for it than reporting to Colonel Harding then visiting a crime boss deep underground. It was tempting to goof off, get drunk, and forget about Kaz, dead Russians, and Diana risking her neck. But I knew the momentary respite would be followed by a hangover, and all the problems I was worried about would come flooding back, with a headache to boot.

So I told myself I was a first lieutenant now, and duty called. I was proud of my newfound sense of responsibility as I strode across St. James's Square and up the stairs at Norfolk House. Within minutes, I wished I'd stayed on the couch with a bottle.

"What have you found out?" Harding said, leaning back in his chair and drumming his fingertips on the arms. No preliminaries, no how are you, isn't it great to be back in London? Harding was permanently impatient, like a man late to someplace much better than this, his foot tapping in irritation at the forces holding him down—to this desk, this place, this city far from the fighting, where I knew he longed to be. I was part of what kept him here, if only by association, but I suffered for it just the same.

"Captain Kiril Sidorov is NKVD, as you thought. He's spying on the Poles, using a hotel employee to pass him information," I said.

"That's interesting. What does it have to do with Egorov's murder?"

"I don't know. The Russians are about to release their own report on Katyn, and I think they want to know if the Poles have anything up their sleeves. Could make for bad blood."

"OK," Harding said, lighting a Lucky and blowing smoke over the papers strewn on his desk. "What do the Poles have?" He said it casually, not meeting my eyes, as if he weren't really asking me to betray Kaz.

"More of the same," I said. "I'll stay on top of it."

"Who told you about Sidorov's inside man?"

"I followed him."

"You saw the meet?"

"Yeah. At Victoria Station. I trailed his contact to the hotel."

"And?"

"I told Kaz."

"Is the hotel guy still in one piece?" Harding didn't give anything away. Anger, satisfaction, joy, any of these could be lurking beneath the surface of his angular face.

"Yes. They'll put him to good use."

"You mean feeding misinformation to our Allies the Soviet Union. You remember them? The guys fighting millions of Nazis on the Russian front?"

"The Poles are our Allies, too, aren't they?"

"Listen up, Boyle. Your job is to find out who killed Captain Egorov. Stay out of any squabbles between the Poles and the Russians. Understood?" Harding ground out his cigarette in a cut-glass ashtray, oddly beautiful in its crystal clearness, even filled with gray ash. I thought the murder of thousands was more than a squabble, but I knew what to say.

"Yes, sir."

"Good. What else?"

I told him about the map that the kid had pinched from Egorov's corpse, about Archie Chapman and the possible black market connection. He nodded calmly, listening to my plan to seek out Chapman at the Liverpool Street Underground.

"Makes sense," he said. "That why you're packing that revolver?"

"Chapman is a hard case, from what I've heard. If he's responsible, he won't appreciate questions about Egorov." I shifted in my seat, trying to settle into my jacket so the bulge wouldn't show under my arm.

"What did you find out at High Wycombe? Big Mike said something about a fast getaway? I couldn't get much out of him, except a lot of talk about a WAC."

"That's Estelle. He's got a date with her tonight, and was headed back there this afternoon to pick her up. All part of the investigation, of course. She had a run-in with a Russian officer who broke up a conversation she was having with one of his pals. She identified him as Egorov." It occurred to me that Estelle's brief description of the Russian she had been talking to, that he spoke flawless English, fit Sidorov.

"What about the MPs?" Harding said.

"I ran into Bull Dawson up there, the guy who helped me out in Northern Ireland. He'd just been assigned to Eighth Air Force, so I decided to start with a friendly face. He gave me the heads-up that the MPs were looking for us."

"Because you were asking about Russians?"

"Yes. There's something odd going on. Bull had a big map in his office, showing targets in Europe. He had two places marked in Russia, well behind their lines. Mirgorod and Poltava. Are we going to bomb Russia, Colonel?"

"If we were, I doubt the Eighth would invite a delegation of Russian officers to their headquarters. Whatever it is, it sounds top secret. I'll see what I can find out. Let me know if Big Mike comes up with anything in his, ah, investigation. And meanwhile, you stay focused on Egorov." I was about to promise to be a good soldier and sell out Kaz and the London Poles when heavy footsteps in the outer office heralded Big Mike's return from High Wycombe.

"The bastards transferred her! She's gone, goddamn sonuvabitch!" Big Mike was not happy. He wasn't much on military protocol, and I knew he and Harding had some kind of odd understanding, born out of long hours together in cramped quarters, that allowed them to bicker like old friends. Even so, he had the sense to slow his forward momentum, remove his cap, and mutter, "Sir."

"Estelle?" I asked, although the answer was obvious.

"Damn right. They did the paperwork yesterday, right after we skedaddled. I went to see Bull and he filled me in. Orders from the top brass at Eighth Air Force. She was on a transport to Tangier by nightfall. Can you believe it?"

"You hit a nerve," Harding said.

"Yeah, but was it because of a top-secret air operation or the fact that she recognized Egorov?" I said, half to myself. Or was it that she had gotten close to Sidorov, even for a moment of harmless flirting? How would the Russians get that sort of pull with the U.S. Army Air Force?

"Can you get her back, Colonel?" Big Mike was still stuck on his missed date.

"Hell no, Big Mike," Harding said. "I'm only a light bird, not a miracle worker. Find a new girlfriend."

"Jeez, Colonel, she was a swell kid."

"She still is, Big Mike. She's not dead, she's on her way to Morocco."

"That ain't any kind of place for a gal like Estelle. Sir."

"Colonel, I'm heading over to Liverpool Street," I said, trying to cut off the argument over Estelle's fate.

"Report to me in the morning," he said. I left as fast as I could, their voices rising in unreasoning determination at my back. Outside, early winter night had descended, cloaking London in blacked-out darkness. The few vehicles on the street cruised slowly, their tires clinging to the curbside to guide them, as they laid on the horn at every intersection. I crossed Trafalgar Square, making my way through crowds of GIs looking spiffy and confident, and swaggering in small groups, with a sprinkling of other services and nationalities thrown in. Most of the females were with Americans, who were guaranteed to have ready cash, chocolate, and cigarettes.

Buildings were still sandbagged, great walls of them thrown up during the Blitz to protect homes and offices. Windows were decorated with tape in large white *X*s, precautions against shattered glass shards. I'd never seen an intact window after a bombing, so I guessed it was one of those things people did to help them believe they'd survive a stick of five hundred–pound bombs. Pieces of tape hung in tatters, neglected since the last raid months ago. Many of the sandbags had fallen, burst at the seams, the burlap weathered and rotting.

Working girls stood at corners, offering their services to anyone within earshot. Some were gaudily made-up, their red lipstick and rouge visible even in the city's darkness. Others tried to imitate them, but their threadbare coats, false smiles, and drawn faces gave them away. Bombed out, husbands dead, wounded, missing, or just gone, they offered the motions of sex to boys who could've been their kid brothers or sons. It would be a transaction, maybe fair, maybe not, but one that could satisfy only in the moment of release, or with the relief of cash and forgetfulness. I wanted to shake them by the shoulders, the women and the boys, but I didn't know what I'd tell them. Go home? Hers might not be more than a Tube station, and he might never see his again. I turned away, the crush of loneliness and desire heavy, the sadness of these couplings nothing I wished to witness. I scurried along the Strand, cries of *Hey, Yank* nipping at my heels, and I felt unaccountably afraid. For all these people gathered together tonight, for Estelle in Tangier, for Diana in disguise, for Kaz and Tadeusz, even Sidorov in all his icy mysteriousness. But not for myself, no. I was fine. I was between a Polish rock and a Russian hard place, lying to my boss, wishing I had a fistful of drinks, and looking to find a killer crime boss deep underground. I was doing just dandy.

Then the sirens sounded.

Everyone on the street stopped and looked to the sky. As if in answer, searchlights stabbed at the darkness, each one brilliant white at its base, fading into starlight and casting a reflective glow against upturned faces. The wail of the sirens rose and fell, rose and fell, the rhythmic pattern endlessly repeating. I didn't know which way to turn or where to go. Everybody seemed confused, dumbfounded by what had been a nightly routine short months ago.

I ran, heading for the Liverpool Street Underground. When the first explosions came, a woman screamed, holding her hands over her ears, as if the noise was what she feared most. But the sound was antiaircraft fire, coming from somewhere to the east, near the docks. Searchlights darted across the sky, followed by more gunfire, the explosive shells joined by tracer bullets in their deceptively graceful arcs as gunners sprayed the assigned quadrant of air, filling it with burning phosphorus and hot lead, hoping for that terrible symmetry, the geometry of death, as intersecting lines of fire and aircraft met, carrying the planes and men of the Luftwaffe to the ground, altering their course with a finality that only mathematics and bullets can ensure.

I ran along Fleet Street, gathering speed until a group spilled out of a pub, knocking me over, leaving me on my back in the gutter. The last of them sauntered amiably by, stopped and leaned down, his hands on his knees and his breath harsh with whiskey and smoke.

"So is this the real thing, or a drill, d'ya think?"

"Get to a shelter, pal," I said as I got up, wondering why he thought a Yank lying in the road might know one way or the other. I scanned the sky, watching for the searchlights to latch on to the bombers, but there was nothing but dancing spears of incandescence. A giant pair of spectacles gazed at me, eerily illuminated by the reflected light, holding me in its grip until I realized it was a store sign, a pince-nez suspended from curved iron grillwork. I wondered if the spectacles had witnessed that nameless East Ender get his throat slit as a warning to Kaz's friend, or if he had seen them in his last moments, the blank eyes of an uncaring, watchful God.

The sirens continued their wails, louder now, as I came closer to the docks. I caught a glimpse of St. Paul's just as the first bombs fell, the distant *crump, crump, crump* signaling the hits as they crept closer. I risked a glimpse up and saw, finally, the dark shape of a German bomber caught in the lights. I careened into another figure running in the opposite direction, and cursed myself for looking up. I saw a sign for a shelter and ignored it, passing the sandbagged Bank of England on Threadneedle Street as I turned north, close to Liverpool Street. I could make out the drone of aircraft over the howl of the sirens, and occasional explosions as bombs hit their mark, or at least detonated. The bombing seemed uncoordinated, as if the aircraft had been split up, each releasing its separate load, in a hurry to avoid the antiaircraft fire that was now growing in intensity.

"This way, please, to the shelter," an ARP warden said, as polite as if inviting me to tea. He stood in front of the twin brick towers marking the entrance, in blue coveralls. He was so coated in dust I could barely make out the white *W* on his soup-bowl helmet. He pushed his glasses up on the bridge of his nose with one hand and gestured with the other, beckoning the crowd into the Underground entrance with a calmness that the heightening sounds of sirens, bombs, and antiaircraft fire did not seem to penetrate. "Plenty of room. This way, please."

"Is this the shelter where I can find Archie Chapman?" I asked, stepping to his side so as not to interfere with his view and the flow of people entering the station.

"Yes, sir, you'll find him here, in one of the sidings. But why you would want to, I couldn't guess." He pushed his glasses up again. Freckles stood out beneath the coating of dust on his face. He glanced up, his practiced eye assessing the time we had left. He looked about sixteen. "Best get inside, sir," he said, before running down the street to help a woman holding a child in her arms and one by the hand. I took his advice and entered the Tube station, following the signs for shelters on the lower levels.

"I never thought they'd be back, the bastards," a woman said to her man as the escalator brought us down.

"I told ya, now didn't I? Told you we should've stayed in the shelters," he answered. "Now we got to make the best of it, instead of 'aving a couple of nice comfortable cots."

Now that solid rock was between us and the danger above, the mood among the crowd turned from panic to resigned petulance, at least among those who had lost their assigned places. At Liverpool Street, several chambers had been excavated for the expansion of Tube lines before the war. With that project abandoned, they had been turned into shelters, with cots, sanitary facilities, and a small canteen for the constant supply of tea that all Brits seemed to require. Tea was rationed, so I had no idea what they were brewing up, and didn't want to find out.

The station platforms were crowded and those who had grabbed blankets and other creature comforts were beginning to settle in, falling back into the habits of the Blitz. Others, like me, stood watching, unsure what to do next. A series of blasts exploded overhead, dull but not distant, the earth muffling the sound of bombs hitting directly above. I felt the vibration in my feet, and a thin line of grit spilled from the ceiling, showering the huddled crowd with dust. A woman shrieked, and the crowd of people contracted, men and women pulling each other closer, waiting for the next thud, fearing the walls would fall in on them. I felt it too, the sudden, grasping fear, and I wished I had someone to pull close. Diana would have been nice. The moment passed, leaving the platform quiet. All noise from aboveground vanished, the only sound below the escape of breath as voices and senses were regained.

I made my way to the siding, and fished a shilling out of my pocket as I looked for a likely guide. I spotted a kid a head taller than his four mates, the bunch of them weaving a path through the crowd, fast enough that I knew they were escaping from or headed to trouble.

"Hey," I said, catching his eye.

"Watcha want, Yank?" He was oblivious to the terror that gripped the adults all around him. He'd grown up with the Blitz, and this subterranean world looked to be a natural second home to him. He gave me the once-over, probably deciding I was ripe for the plucking.

"Where can I find Archie Chapman?" I asked.

"Why should we tell you then?"

"Because you're a good kid." I flipped him the shilling and took out a pack of chewing gum from my coat pocket. I gave that to one of his chums, who opened it up and spread the wealth.

"That I am, Yank. Not this first siding, but the next. Go on in and straight to the back. He's all set up like it's 'is own 'ouse. Don't mention we told ya, all right?"

"OK, kid, I won't. Wouldn't Archie like that?"

"Mr. Chapman don't like surprises," he said, and then they were off, vanishing into the crowd on the platform. I entered the second siding, which was as wide as the main chamber, with curved walls and an even floor: no rails or platform in this unfinished tunnel. Unlike the pandemonium outside, it was orderly, with people making themselves at home in their assigned bunks. Metal cots hung from the walls, with another row set up on the floor, leaving a narrow corridor leading to the end. These were the folks who'd come back every night to keep their places in the shelter, and most had a look of self-satisfaction about them. They'd probably been laughed at by their neighbors, but now that the Luftwaffe had returned, they all had *who's-laughing-now* smiles on their faces.

Near the end of the tunnel, a blanket hung on a line strung from wall to wall. In front of the blanket, a big guy in a brown leather jacket sat in an easy chair, reading a newspaper.

"End of the line for you, mate," he said, without looking up from his paper. "No visitors, this is a private area."

"I'm here to see Archie Chapman," I said.

"Mr. Chapman ain't receiving visitors. Beat it." He'd given me a quick glance, then back to his newspaper. His nose had been broken a couple of times, and his hands were thick, the knuckles swollen where he'd injured his tendons.

"You a boxer?" I asked.

"Used to be. Fought in the middleweight division for a while, but things didn't go my way. Now be a good Yank and turn yerself around." He turned the page of the newspaper. It was the *Dispatch*, and I wondered if he was one of Chapman's thugs who had slit that poor fellow's throat on Fleet Street. His boxer's knuckles didn't come from fighting in a match with boxing gloves. The swollen, ropy tendons were from repeated applications of bare knuckles to flesh and bone.

"Tell Mr. Chapman I'm here to see him about the dead Russian."

"Look, mate," he said, wearily folding his paper and getting up, "best for you to move along 'fore things get out of hand, know what I mean?" He wasn't as large as Big Mike, but he was bigger than me, and his arms strained against the leather as he folded them across his chest. I was trying to think of a snappy answer that wouldn't earn me a right hook when a figure stepped from behind the blanket.

"There are many thousands of dead Russians, so I understand. Which one exactly do you wish to talk to Mr. Chapman about?" This guy was tall and thin, dressed in a black overcoat, a black silk scarf at his neck. His dark hair was slightly receding and combed straight back, making his widow's peak a black arrow pointing between his eyes. His pronunciation was precise and proper, traces of the East End gone from his voice but not his eyes. Topper, maybe?

"The one found outside this shelter, last week, with a bullet in his head."

"What interest does an American have in a dead Russian, found on a London street?"

"A mutual interest," I said. I had no idea what that might be, but I was certain Archie Chapman's self-interest was my only hope.

The thin guy's eyes narrowed and his forehead creased as he decided his next move. He nodded to the boxer, who frisked me, quickly and expertly, stashing my .38 in his folded-up newspaper and handing my identification to his boss.

"Are you with the military police?"

"No. I'm with General Eisenhower's headquarters."

"You're a long way from Naples then, Lieutenant Boyle."

"I'm part of the advance party. The general will be in London soon."

"Ah, yes, the new Supreme Headquarters. Sounds grand. This way, please," he said, handing me my identification and ushering me into a room decorated with a carpet, chairs, table, and a cupboard. Two other guys, middle-management thugs by the look of them, sat at the table playing cards. It was cozy, for an underground bomb shelter. My escort parted another set of draped blankets, entered, and held them open for me. This room was even larger than the first, the carpet plusher. A small

electric heater provided warmth, aimed in the direction of a man with
starkly white hair brushed back from his own widow's peak. He sat in a
worn leather chair, a floor lamp to one side and a bookshelf to the other.
Beyond him was a real bed; no metal cot for Archie Chapman to rest his
bones on.

"What's this then?" Chapman said, closing the book he'd been reading with a fierce snap. A guy who didn't like surprises.

"A Lieutenant William Boyle to see you. About that Russian." I saw
a look pass between the men, full of silent meaning. It said there was an
advantage to my being here, one that was worth Chapman's time. The
elder Chapman, I should say. I could see the son in the father. Tall and
slim, sharp cheekbones, the same hair and widow's peak, whiter and
sparser on the father, but it was the same face. Hawklike, predatory.
Patient. A hunter who took what he wanted.

"Your son was kind enough to let me pass Tommy Farr out there," I
said, referring to the Welsh fighter who'd been beat by Joe Louis a few
years back.

"Ha! Good one, Lieutenant. Charlie's no Tommy Farr, although he
did have a few wins at Argyle Hall, a pretty good run for a while. Sit
down, and tell Topper and me what you want. Drinks, boy."

Topper poured three glasses of gin from a small bar. Not my favorite
drink, but with Topper and Archie for company, I was glad of it.

"To your health, Lieutenant Boyle," Archie said, raising his glass.

"And to yours." We drank. The gin tasted like pine needles soaked in
lighter fluid. "Nice setup you've got."

"All the comforts of home, Lieutenant, except that the goddamn
Boche can't blow us out of our beds deep down here. Now, why have you
come to visit me in my underground hideaway?"

"I work for General Eisenhower. He wants to be sure that the murder
of Captain Egorov is solved, and that it creates no difficulties for the
Allies."

"Egorov?" Topper said. "Is that the name of the fellow those boys
found?"

"Yes, Gennady Egorov. Did you know him?"

"No, I hardly know any Russians, much less Communists," Topper
said, shrugging, as he looked to his father.

"So you've come to us, Lieutenant Boyle, for what?" Archie leaned forward, studying my eyes, as if the answer might show there before I spoke it.

"Billy," I said, trying to ratchet down the intensity in the room. "Call me Billy. Everyone does."

"Well, Billy, then. Tell me what we can do for each other. What do you have to offer me?" Archie smiled, they way I imagined a cat would smile if it bothered to, contemplating a cornered mouse.

"They're calling Eisenhower's new HQ the Supreme Headquarters, Allied Expeditionary Force. That means everything for the invasion goes through us. All the supplies, all the food, all the gear. All the Scotch whiskey the generals and admirals can drink, all their fine boots and coats, penicillin, cigarettes, you name it." Archie's eyes flickered with interest, darted to his son, and then reverted to hooded sullenness.

"You're new to London then," Topper said. "Do you have your operation set up yet?"

"I just got here from Naples, but my boys came with me. We're getting things organized."

"Ah, Naples. I hear the Italian black market is thriving," Archie said, lifting his head as if he could see acres of supplies laid out for the taking. "But what is it you want from us? The killer? The vicious murderer of that innocent Russian boy?"

"Is he yours to hand over?"

"Of course he is. Whoever you want him to be. Dead or alive, with half a dozen witnesses who will swear they saw him do it, sold him the gun, and gave him the rope to bind Egorov's hands. Whatever you want, if you can pay the price."

"If I can't?"

"Then you've wasted Father's time," Topper said calmly. "And mine. We'd not be happy about that."

"Billy, this is a souvenir of my time in the trenches, fighting the Boche in the last war," Archie said. He picked up what looked like a short sword from beneath his chair. With remarkable swiftness he was up, unsheathing the blade from its scabbard. "My own bayonet, seventeen inches long, and still as sharp as the last time I gutted a Boche with it, or anyone else for that matter. Can you feel it?"

I could. He'd stepped around me, pressing the blade to my neck, and I wondered if it had been Archie and Topper that night on Fleet Street, never mind Charlie and his swollen knuckles. "Sure. My old man brought one back from France, too. He keeps his up in the attic." I felt the cold steel against my soft neck, pressed flat. A slight change of angle and pressure and the carpet would be a helluva mess.

"Did he now? Well, I say once you've learned how to use a tool, you don't let it rust." He moved away, rubbing his thumb gently along the blade before putting it back in the scabbard, and tucking it back under the seat. "Tell me, what led you to me? Of all the people you could ask about dead Russians in London, why did you decide to visit old Archie?"

"The map," I said. It was my only card, and I had to play it, weak hand that it was. I watched their faces, and saw the flash of surprise, too quick to hide. In a second their masks of languid cruelty returned, but it told me they hadn't known Egorov had it in his possession.

"A treasure map?" Topper said with a sneer, buying time to figure out what else I might know.

"Of sorts. The route of a supply truck, from farms up north straight to the Russian Embassy. Like the one that was hijacked a while back."

"Do tell," Archie said, settling back into his chair. "Topper, refills all round. One for the road, Billy. Come back when you have something specific to offer, and something specific to ask for."

"I'm after the murderer," I said.

"You may be," Archie said, "but it's nothing to us. The Russian was nothing to us, so how can we help you? If you have something of value on offer, then it may become something to us. Until then, all we'll do is have a drink and chat, get to know each other better."

"Cheers," I said when the glasses were full, resisting the urge to tell him I'd gotten to know the Chapman family well enough.

"To your father, and all the lads who didn't come back from that last blasted war, there were enough of them." He drank his gin down in one gulp, and Topper was ready with the bottle. "And now to you, Billy, in this war." We all drank again.

"You're not in the service?" I said to Topper as he filled my glass.

"For health concerns," Archie was quick to put in. "And I need my boy here, I depend on him, and so do many others."

"London's dangerous enough," I said, watching Topper sit back, clutching his drink, watching me with a stillness that reminded me of a hunter in a blind, quietly waiting for the right moment.

"True," Archie said. "I've seen hundreds of poor civilians killed within a stone's throw of my door. Life's risky."

I drank some more gin, thinking back to the night at Kirby's Tavern when my dad announced they had cinched the deal to get me on Uncle Ike's staff in D.C. He'd said exactly the same thing about life.

"No need to tempt fate," I said, recalling the next thing he'd said.

"Exactly! You never know where that bastard death might find you. Me, I served with the Royal Welch Fusiliers, three years in the trenches, never a scratch, none that could be seen, anyway. You ever heard of Siegfried Sassoon, boy?"

"He's some sort of poet, isn't he?"

"He was my captain! Served with him in the First Battalion. Mad Jack, we called him. A holy terror, a man made for night patrols and the knife. A right poof he was too, but no one cared about that, not with a killer the likes of him to lead us. Taught me how to slit a throat and how to appreciate a good bit of poetry; not many that can do both well, not like Mad Jack!" He knocked back his gin and before the glass was down, Topper had it filled. He refilled his and mine and we both drank, it seeming the only sensible thing to do.

"Oh, when one of his friends—his dear friends, you know—when one of them got killed, he'd be in an awful state. Terrible. Took its toll on him, it did, all those pals of his buying it. But he kept me alive, even though there were times I'd pray for a quick bullet. Do you know his poetry, boy? Likely not, likely not. I read it still, his war stuff, I mean, when the bombs fall. Makes me feel better, remembering where I've been, and survived. Now listen, and you'll know what I mean." He pushed his glass toward Topper, who added a splash and sat back.

He read from the book, poems about rotting corpses, mud, machine guns, and death. He read between slugs of gin, and his voice rose, until the book fell from his hands and he recited a final paragraph, his face turned upward, eyes searching the ceiling for ghosts, flares, or perhaps a glimpse of heaven.

Alone he staggered on until he found
Dawn's ghost that filtered down a shafted stair
To the dazed, muttering creatures underground
Who hear the boom of shells in muffled sound.

At last, with sweat of horror in his hair,
He climbed through darkness to the twilight air,
Unloading hell behind him step by step.

I sat in stunned and gin-soaked silence as he finished. The room beyond, and all the people in it, were quiet, hushed, as if in church at the end of a magnificent sermon. Archie's eyes were half open, but I knew he was somewhere else, somewhere beyond drunkenness and memory, someplace I never wanted to see, a place worse than hell, that place I'd glimpsed in my own father's eyes. The trenches.

I stood, glancing at the books on his shelf. All poetry, the big English poets—Blake, Wordsworth, and others I'd never heard of. Americans like Walt Whitman, Emily Dickinson, and Poe. But it was the volume of Sassoon that was dog-eared, scarred with bookmarks and notations, open on the floor. Topper rose and took me by the arm, guiding me out, into the open space.

"Don't come back, if you know what's good for you." He said it quietly, not a threat, more as a wishful entreaty, a desire for someone to escape the repeated misery of a father's wartime memories. Charlie returned my revolver, and I walked out of the siding, hardly aware of the faces gazing at me.

I made my way upward. The bombing had stopped, and as I came to the surface it seemed like bright daylight. I squinted against the light and saw it was a raging fire, enveloping a building farther down Liverpool Street. Fire engines pumped streams of water that disappeared into the inferno as I made my way around the wreckage that had spilled out into the street. Firemen snaked hoses around burning timbers as ambulances stood in the rosy, flickering light, their rear doors open, beckoning the injured. Beyond, bodies lay in a row where the sidewalk was clear, dust coating them a uniform gray, their corpses merging into a single lump of shattered flesh and torn clothing. It was the ARP warden I'd talked to on my way in, along with the mother and two small children he'd been helping.

I stumbled out into the street and broke into a run, not knowing where I was going.

CHAPTER ▪ ELEVEN

I'D DECIDED TO join Kaz on his early morning trot through Hyde Park. I wanted to sweat out the stink of gin and poetry that clung to my skin and clogged my brain like a foul nightmare. My head was thick with the smell of smoke I'd inhaled from the fires, the hangover I'd awoken with, and the confusion I felt as I tried to sort through what I'd learned.

I filled Kaz in on my trip to the shelter and the strange interview with Archie and Topper Chapman. Archie's alcohol-fired poetry reading, the sharp blade to my throat, Topper's warning, the home-away-from-home setup in the tunnel, it was all strange enough. But what I really didn't get was their entire lack of interest in Gennady Egorov.

"It doesn't make sense," I said, trying to draw in enough breath to speak and keep up with Kaz. "They were interested in doing business if I had something to offer, but they didn't give a hoot about Egorov."

"If the Russian had been their source of information, there would be nothing you could do to replace his services, at least in terms of hijacking Russian supplies. Why should they show any interest?"

"Because Archie didn't strike me as the kind of guy to let anyone get the best of him. Whoever killed Egorov hurt his business. That's not something any crime boss in Boston or London would let slide."

"Yes, I see," Kaz said. "He can't afford to appear weak."

"Which means that he already knows who did it, or that Egorov wasn't the primary source of his information."

"You mean someone else in the embassy?"

"Yeah. Or Archie already took care of things. Maybe the guy who pulled the trigger is floating facedown in the Thames right now."

"Perplexing indeed," Kaz said, raising his head to check the sky. "Cloudy today. Bad bombing weather."

"I could do without another night of that," I said. "Why do you think they came back?"

"The Germans? Because we didn't expect them."

"Archie Chapman did."

"From what you told me, Archie Chapman still expects the Boche to charge across No Man's Land. Do you think someone as crazy and blood-thirsty as he really reads all that poetry?"

"Yes, I do. He may be nuts, but he's not unintelligent, and he came under his captain's influence at an early age. He's been cultivating every-thing he learned in the trenches since then. Cruelty, killing, and the beauty of words. Maybe they balance each other out, who knows?"

"Maybe he's just crazy," Kaz said.

"Strange, coming from a guy as comfortable with books as he is with a gun."

"Poets are mad. Scholars are merely preoccupied."

"Mad Jack," I said. "That's what they called Sassoon, according to Archie."

"He went off his head after his brother was killed at Gallipoli," Kaz said. "Tried to get himself killed, I've heard, but ended up coming back alive each time he went out on a raid." We turned at the end of Rotten Row, slowing our pace a bit. I thought about Diana, and her need to confront death. Kaz looked solemn, and I knew he was thinking the same thing. Diana courting death, Daphne dead and gone.

"Sorry," he said.

"Me, too." I laid my hand on his shoulder as he wiped the sweat from his face, both of us breathing deeply in the cold morning air. "Kind of odd, isn't it, to think about a guy like Sassoon with Archie Chapman? What would they have had in common? Archie, from the East End, and Sassoon an educated officer?"

"He wrote a poem called 'Conscripts,'" Kaz said. "I don't recall all of it, but it spoke about the different kinds of men trained for combat. The educated, the sensitive, along with the rougher men, whom at first he disliked. Near the end, it went:

But the kind, common ones that I despised
(Hardly a man of them I'd count as friend),
What stubborn-hearted virtues they disguised!
They stood and played the hero to the end."

"So he admired a guy like Archie for staying alive," I said, "when his brother didn't?"

"Who knows?" Kaz said. "Who knows what a poet or a madman thinks? Or a killer like Chapman? I have enough trouble in this war without trying to ferret out the secrets of the last."

"I'm doing my best to keep you out of trouble, Kaz. Don't do anything to make that job harder."

"Thank you, Billy. You are a good friend."

I clapped Kaz on the shoulder and picked up my pace, trying not to get left behind. I remembered those words, spoken with a different accent, years ago. It had been Nuno Chagas, speaking to my dad. Nuno was a Portugee lobsterman who ran his boat out of Cohasset Harbor. He'd been a smuggler, bringing rum and whiskey in from offshore boats during Prohibition. He wasn't a hoodlum, just the son of an immigrant, a working stiff who did what he had to do when the Depression hit and lobster became a luxury many could do without. He and Dad, along with Uncle Frank, used to go out fishing every now and then. A few bottles found their way home, but it was a favor, not a payoff. One day Nuno had a problem. A big problem. He'd made his liquor runs for the Gustin Gang, run out of Southie by Frankie and Steve Wallace. The Wallaces weren't saints, but they were local Irish boys, and they robbed other thieves as much as they robbed anyone else. They were connected politically, and while they were arrested frequently, charges had a way of being dropped. I guess they were tolerated. Nuno had no beef with them, but a rival outfit was trying to elbow its way in, aiming at taking over the Boston liquor market. It wasn't the Italians, and no one could prove the rumor that it was Joe Kennedy, making a buck however he could. But that didn't matter. Goons from out of town were threatening guys like Nuno, and the Gustin Gang threatened right back. Each side wanted Nuno to work for them. Or else. . . . I was only a kid at the time, but I remember Nuno coming over to the house on Sunday, dressed in a suit that was worn to a shine. He'd thanked my father, and told him what a good friend he was.

Dad said, *My friend's troubles are my own*, and then Nuno stayed for Sunday dinner.

"My friend's troubles are my own," I said, and felt the presence of my old man, and the odd feeling of understanding what he'd meant, finally. The depth of it. This was more than words, it was the quiet opening of the heart, the indelible definition of friendship.

Kaz looked at the ground, strangely, just as Nuno had done. We walked in silence, everything necessary having been said. I never knew what Dad had done to fix things for Nuno, even when I asked him after I made rookie and wore the blue. Nuno got out of the business right after Frankie Wallace got himself gunned down by an Italian gang from North Boston, and if he missed the money, he seemed glad to be legit. I often wondered exactly what Dad had done, and if he'd ever spill the beans.

"Anything new about the Russians and Katyn?" I asked, after we stopped to stretch.

"Yes," Kaz said wearily. "The Russians will issue a report on Katyn soon. The bodies of those poor souls are being dug up once again. Only Russians are serving on their hand-picked commission; they're not even letting their own tame Polish Communists participate."

"No doubt what the verdict will be?"

"None at all. They will lie, and tell the world the Germans killed all those Polish officers. And the world will believe what it is told to believe."

"But you have evidence, you have Tadeusz."

"Tadeusz has not spoken a word since you met him," Kaz said. "Nothing."

"But the Red Cross saw all that evidence; the Germans brought them in. The letters and documents, all the dates ending in 1940. That has to count for something."

"The Russians will plant their own evidence, and their scientists will all swear it was dug up. The commission is headed by Dr. Nikolai Bordenko, head of the USSR Academy of Sciences. A very respectable figure. He will be believed."

"If he's so respectable, why would he put his name to a lie?"

"Billy, the Russians are as ruthless as the Nazis. His family would be killed or sent to a Siberian labor camp at best."

"Article 58," I said.

"What?"

"Sidorov told me. It makes it a crime in the Soviet Union to not report any activity against the state. It gives the NKVD a blank check to arrest anyone."

"Ah, I see," Kaz said. "If you refuse to do what you are told, and your family does not turn you in, they can be arrested."

"Nice and neat."

"Yes. Unfortunate that they will dig up those bodies again. It would save everyone a lot of trouble if they simply wrote their report and let them lie in peace."

I DIDN'T SEE any bomb damage on my way to New Scotland Yard, but gray smoke was visible to the east, from the area around St. Paul's and the dockyards farther down the river. It drifted lazily across the morning sky, marking the remnants of last night's sudden devastation. More bricks to stack in piles. More bodies laid out on the sidewalk.

"Boyle," Inspector Scutt said as I entered the detectives' chamber. "We wondered how you made out in the raid last night. You went to see Chapman, didn't you?"

"Yes, I had the pleasure," I said, sitting down in front of Scutt's desk.

"You were right in the thick of it then," Flack said as he joined us. "Jerry's a bit out of practice, but he managed to drop a few from the Surrey Docks up to Moorgate. Lucky for us a lot of them got nervous, or lost, and dropped their loads short. Tore up the countryside to the southeast, the bastards did, but better there than in the heart of London."

"Bomb alley, they call it," Scutt said. "The whole area from the coast, between Dover and Hastings, and straight up to London. Any German bomber that aborts or tangles with our fighters will drop their bombs and head for home. Between those random hits and actual targets in the area, it gets fairly nerve-racking down that way. My wife's family is from Folkestone, and I've heard plenty from them about it."

"Plus all the crashes, aircraft from both sides," Flack said. "There were more than twenty bombers shot down last night. If most of the aircrew got out, that means we have almost a hundred Germans on the ground right now. The Home Guard is spread all over the countryside looking for them. Hasn't been a dustup like this in months."

"I saw more than a dustup last night," I said, trying to keep my voice neutral. Flack seemed a bit too excited about the raid for my taste.

"Of course you did, Boyle," Scutt said, seeming to understand my reluctance to rejoice in the return of the Luftwaffe. "It's terrible, and at the same time, it brings us back to when we all stood together, Londoners and Englishmen alone, shoulder to shoulder. With all you Americans coming along, as grand as that is, sometimes I feel we've lost something."

"I heard it in the Tube station this morning," Flack said. "People talking to each other, saying we can stand up to it. Hard to explain, and I don't mean to sound callous, but it's almost like the war had passed us by. Civilians, in London, I mean. Now, it's back. Gives some meaning to all the difficulties. Rationing, homes destroyed, men scattered all across the world."

"All I saw last night was a lot of scared people, and corpses."

"It's been my experience, Boyle, that with the light of morning, those who find themselves alive put the best face on things they can," Scutt said. "I'd wager the most scared of the lot last night are shaking their fists against an empty sky this morning, cursing the bloody Germans. Human nature. Now, tell us about Chapman."

I did, leaving out much of the gin, and the knife at my throat, while focusing on his lack of interest in Egorov.

"You may be right in that Archie, or his boy Topper, have already taken care of business for themselves. We'll be on the lookout for any suspicious deaths, especially of anyone connected with the embassy," Flack said.

"Too bad you don't have anything you can really trade with," Scutt said, rubbing his chin. "Maybe some American supplies need to be sacrificed in the pursuit of justice."

"Good idea, guv," Flack said. "Boyle, maybe you can arrange for some coffee to go missing. Drop a bit off for us, eh?"

"It's not a bad idea," I said.

"I didn't really mean—"

"No, I mean going into business with Archie and Topper. If they know who really killed Egorov, that could be the key. Might be worth a truckload of Spam."

"Don't bother bringing that around," Flack said. "Worse than bully beef, that stuff."

"Whatever you use, Boyle," Scutt cut in, putting an end to a comparison of American and British canned meats, "it will have to come from your stores. The Met cannot provide supplies illegally. But we will assist in any way we can. Now we have some questions to put to you."

"OK," I said. I watched Scutt and Flack exchange glances. No more philosophical comments about Londoners at war, no more jokes about Spam and tinned beef. They had questions to put to me, and that was a shift. When a cop has something routine to ask another cop, he simply asks him. When a cop is about to interrogate someone, he tells him he has questions.

"Yesterday you were at the Rubens Hotel, correct?" Scutt began.

"Yes, I was visiting a friend."

"Do you usually enter the Rubens via the staff entrance?"

"What does that matter?"

"We have been informed that you accosted a member of the staff there."

"He was spying on my friend."

"Who is your friend," Flack said, studying a file Scutt had handed him, "and who was this Edward Miller spying for?"

"Lieutenant Baron Piotr Augustus Kazimierz," I said, giving them Kaz's name and title, thinking that might impress the royalty conscious. "He used to work on General Eisenhower's staff, and now he's with the Polish Government in Exile."

"Edward Miller?"

"He was being paid off by Kiril Sidorov, the Russian officer you met, to supply information on the Poles."

"We knew he was an informer, but not for whom. We have our own informants, but the data they provide only goes so far. What do you think Sidorov was after?"

"Information, of course, just like you." I didn't like how this was going.

"I think the stakes are a bit higher in this case," Scutt said. "This is more than routine gossip and information gathering, and you know it. You've been holding out on us, Boyle."

"About what?" I tried to sound irritated.

"About your friend, Lieutenant Kazimierz. His role in the controversy regarding the Kaytn Forest killings. That brings him in direct conflict with the Russians. Any reason you didn't mention that to us? To your brother officers, investigating the murder of an NKVD man on their own patch?" Scutt's voice had grown louder, and he leaned forward at the end, slamming his fist on the desk.

"Yes," I said, willing myself to speak calmly, letting a few seconds of silence creep between us. "Because he's my friend, and I'd trust him with my life."

"That's a fine answer," Scutt said, studying me as he leaned back into his chair. "One I might be satisfied with if not for the fact that Lieutenant Kazimierz goes about London armed with a .32-caliber pistol. The same caliber as the bullet that killed Egorov."

"That bullet was too damaged to measure accurately," I said, and regretted it instantly. I didn't want to sound like a lawyer. "Kaz carries that for protection, that's all."

"So far, it's been dangerous for one Russian, dead, and one Englishman, whom you apparently beat senseless."

"Sheila," I said, remembering the girl who had seen Eddie and me in the hallway. "She's your informant. She's the only one who saw me slap Eddie around. She must be sweet on him to claim I beat him senseless, not that he had much sense to begin with."

"Keep that to yourself, Boyle," Flack said in a low, angry voice. "Your friend bears watching, and so do you, as far as I can tell."

"You've been watching him already. If you thought he was responsible for killing Egorov, then you would have picked him up."

"No, we don't have enough at this point," Flack said. "We know he's armed with a weapon similar to the one used on Egorov. We know that he's made inflammatory statements about the Russians, but we don't know where he was that Friday night."

"Meaning you don't have someone watching him at the Dorchester," I said.

"Boyle, please understand this," Scutt said. "We are not watching any one individual. We employ informants to keep us updated on the comings and goings of the many foreigners we have in London. They are our allies, but they often don't see eye to eye with each other. The fact that Lieutenant Kazimierz goes about armed was just one detail in a routine report."

"Sheila didn't strike me as someone who could tell the difference between a .32 caliber and a blunderbuss. How did you find that out?"

"It was determined in the routine course of investigation," Scutt said. In other words, none of my business. They obviously had someone else inside. Or had they searched our rooms at the Dorchester?

"Are we working together, or are we not?" I said. "Either way is fine, I just want to know." I waited, watching Flack fume and Scutt consider. They were a good team, the experienced, calm inspector and the angry younger detective.

"We are still working together," Scutt said finally. "Detective Sergeant Flack will continue to monitor the Poles. Frankly, theirs is the only motive we have. If you believe your friend and his associates are not involved at all, then I suggest you pursue other leads."

"OK," I said. I had to agree with them, although I wouldn't do it out loud. "I'll try Chapman again. Tell me, does Eddie know that Sheila is working for you?"

"No, not according to her, anyway," Flack said. "She's been reporting to us for two months now, and she swears no one's the wiser. Anything else you've failed to tell us?"

"Just one thing I heard at High Wycombe. That the Russian delegation stopped coming right after they had a meeting there with some Royal Navy officers."

"What the hell does that mean?" Flack said.

"I have no idea. The Russians, the American Eighth Air Force, and the Royal Navy. The first two aren't talking, so I thought you might try your guys. Maybe ask our friend from MI5, Major Charles Cosgrove."

"Why don't you?" Flack said.

"Because the last time I saw him, I almost punched his fat face in."

"I think we will make the inquiry, Lieutenant Boyle," Scutt said. "For the sake of Allied unity."

CHAPTER ▪ TWELVE

IT WASN'T FAR from the Met to Norfolk House, but I wished it was farther so I'd have more time to work on my pitch to Colonel Harding. I didn't think he'd take kindly to my stealing U.S. Army supplies, no matter how good the cause, or the fact that I'd get paid for them, black market wholesale rate.

The sky was filled with low, dark clouds, just the thing to keep the Luftwaffe at bay. It would keep our bombers grounded as well, if the cloud cover extended over the Continent. How did our aircrew feel about that? Happy at another day of life on the ground, or wishing they could get in another mission toward the twenty-five they needed to be rotated home? All I knew for sure was that there must be a helluva lot of civilians all over Europe who prayed for lousy weather.

"How did it go last night?" Harding said, before I'd gotten my trench coat off.

"I survived the air raid."

"I can see that, Boyle. I mean with Chapman. You were headed to Liverpool Street when you left here yesterday."

"I can safely say he's a homicidal maniac," I said as I settled into an armchair across from Harding's desk. "He's set up at one end of the shelter like it was home sweet home, complete with bodyguards, a bedroom, and a pig sticker from the last war. But the one thing I thought he'd react to, he didn't."

"Egorov?"

"Right. If he had a hand in killing Egorov, I think he would've warned me off in no uncertain terms. But he hardly reacted. I'm betting that if Egorov was his main contact, he's already settled the score with whoever killed him. Or maybe he had nothing at all to do with it."

"It would be helpful to find out which," Harding said.

"There is a way, I think. Obviously, I didn't tell them I was an investigator. I hinted at a possible source of supplies. Black market stuff. Basically they told me to come back with something concrete or not to come back at all."

"So you want what?"

"Oh, I don't know," I said, trying to act like this was all Harding's idea. "A truckload of something. Nothing dangerous or too valuable. Booze, maybe?"

"A truckload of liquor is damned valuable, Boyle!"

"Yes, sir, but the thing is, we'll get paid for it."

"What the hell am I supposed to do, give the army a stack of pound notes as reimbursement?"

"OK, OK, liquor's a bad idea. But it wouldn't hurt to have some ready cash around the office for contingencies, would it?"

"What do you expect to get out of this transaction with Chapman?" Harding said, ignoring my attempt at entrepreneurship.

"The closer I get to him, the easier it'll be for me to find out if he had anything to do with Egorov's murder, or if he has any knowledge of it at all. He's not your average good citizen. If he witnessed a murder, the last thing he'd do would be to go to the police."

"So you want to get into the black market and return any money you make to the army?"

"Since I'll be stealing the army's supplies, it's only fair."

"I think it's worth a try. You won't be surprised to hear that Big Mike has made friends with the cooks in the mess hall downstairs. That's where he is now. You may need to spread some of that dough around, but try not to corrupt the entire kitchen staff."

"Thank you, Colonel," I said as I rose from my chair. "I assume I can refer to your verbal orders in case we run into trouble?"

"Hell no, Boyle. You get caught, you end up in the stockade. Who ever heard of a guy black marketeering who was following orders? Beat it."

I did. I found Big Mike in the mess hall, spooning sugar into a mug of coffee with three doughnuts at hand. I grabbed a mug and joined him.

"How you doing, Billy?" Big Mike said, with his usual lack of military formality. Even though he wore khaki instead of blue, he was still a cop at heart. He carried his shield with him everywhere, badge number 473, Detroit Police Department. You never knew when a flash of tin to a brother officer in a foreign land would come in handy, and with what I had in mind, we might need it.

"OK," I said. "I sort of have Harding's permission to pull off a heist, as long as we don't get caught. I need some army supplies to get in good with a local hood. Interested in a little petty larceny?"

"Could be, if you get Estelle back for me," he said, as half a doughnut disappeared.

"Come on, Big Mike, I don't have enough clout to make that happen."

"That's what Colonel Harding said, which is why I ain't speaking to him, except what's needed to conduct business. But you, you got an uncle in high places. You could make it happen."

"Big Mike, listen—"

"No, Billy, you listen. You get Estelle back from North Africa. Get her assigned here, in London. Otherwise, I ain't helping you, and I might even have to arrest you for whatever you're cooking up."

"You can't arrest anybody, Big Mike. You're not a cop or an MP."

"No, but there's MPs all around this joint. I want Estelle back."

"You really fell for her, huh?"

"Billy, I ain't never met a girl like her. Lookit me, I'm no Errol Flynn, I'm a big guy, kinda clumsy at times. Most girls make a joke, like I'm a sideshow strongman. But Estelle, she looked me in the eyes and that was that. We both knew, it's that simple. I can't bear to think of her alone in Tangier, wondering if I even cared enough to try and find her. You know what I mean?"

"Sure I do, Big Mike."

"Oh, yeah. Sorry, Billy, I didn't mean anything about Diana. That's different, she wants to go. You ain't leaving her all alone."

"OK, Big Mike. I'm in. How about I get to work on it after we—"

"No. Now. Go see Beetle and get Estelle back here. I'll wait."

"Jesus, Big Mike! Beetle will keep me waiting for hours and then have my ass for asking! It'll never work."

"No, he won't, and yes, it will."

"How can you say that? Can you read his mind? If you claim to know

Uncle Ike's chief of staff so well that you can guarantee it, why don't you ask him yourself?"

"I sort of did. I told him this morning that you would be stopping by to ask his assistance in getting a material witness brought back to London."

"What the hell were you doing talking to Beetle? The king would need an appointment to see him."

"I asked around and found out he used to hunt quail in Virginia. He has that cocker spaniel with him, you know, the one he got in North Africa. So I talked to a British captain who just came on board. He's the earl of something or other, and has a country place over near Cheltenham. I suggested to him that Beetle wouldn't mind an invite to kill birds with him. He liked the idea, so I went to see Beetle, and told him all about it. He said he felt like shooting something, and invited me to come along. Probably just to carry the shotguns, but still it was a nice gesture."

"Where did Estelle come in?"

"He asked how the investigation was going. Ike will be here in a few days, and he wanted to know if we'd have anything to report. I told him about Estelle getting transferred, and how it would be helpful to get her back here."

"I assume you didn't tell him she was the love of your life?"

"Hell no, Billy. I didn't make it out to be any big deal. Didn't want to overplay my hand. Beetle just said if you was having any trouble to let him know. So go let him know while he's in a good mood and thinking about blasting quail. Then we'll steal whatever you want."

I left Big Mike to wash down the third doughnut while I went upstairs. Luck was on my side; Mattie Pinette was the WAC on duty. She was a good friend from North Africa, and she'd heard about the quail hunt Big Mike had organized.

"We're all grateful, Billy," she said in a whisper. "Beetle needs a day off. Don't you worry. Estelle Gordon will be back in London as soon as we can get her on an aircraft. Is she a suspect in something? Is she dangerous?"

"She's a giant killer, Mattie."

Ten minutes later Big Mike—wearing a grin that wouldn't stop—and I were scouting out the back entrance to Norfolk House, along Charles Street, where the deliveries came in. It was a tight squeeze, and several vehicles were waiting in line, a plumber's truck and a jeep filled with typewriters jockeying for position near the double-wide rear doors.

"We can't touch the civilian stuff, and I doubt there's a market for typewriters," Big Mike said. "Want to stake the place out?"

"How about heading back to the kitchen, and we'll ask the cooks what they've got. We can tell them Beetle was asking for something special."

"Canned peaches," Big Mike said. "They're worth their weight in gold."

"Perfect," I said. We both went, and I played the snotty junior officer, ordering Big Mike around in front of the mess staff. We told the sergeant in charge that General Walter Bedell Smith was a sonuvabitch all day if he didn't get his canned peaches and that if there weren't any this afternoon he was going to get himself some new cooks.

These cooks and bakers worked hard, no doubt about it, but they also knew that duty at Norfolk House in London was preferable to cooking in some battalion kitchen out on maneuvers. They consulted clipboards, yelled into the telephone, searched shelves, and looked under counters, stirring up a cloud of flour in their haste and panic, until a kid wearing an apron bigger than he was triumphantly told us they'd be serving canned peaches in a couple of hours, and had enough coming in to keep Beetle in thick syrup for weeks. They were happy, I was happy, Big Mike was happy. But there would be no peaches tonight for the weary warriors of Norfolk House.

We waited on Charles Street, watching the traffic, wrapped in our trench coats and scarves, stomping our feet to keep warm. The weather was turning colder, the clouds still blanking out the sun, the pavement chill creeping up our boots. Finally, what we were waiting for showed up. One supply truck, driven by a corporal, with a PFC dead asleep in the passenger's seat. I stepped out in front of them as they turned off the street.

"Show me your orders!" I barked, imitating a combination of Beetle, Harding, and a rabid dog as I peered inside the truck cab. "How dare you show up to headquarters like this? You're both out of uniform. I ought to put you on report."

"Gee, Lieutenant," the PFC said, "we've been loading and unloading crates all day. We always wear our fatigues on work detail. These are uniforms, ain't they?"

"Looks like you've been rolling around in the dirt all day, soldier. Plus, no field scarf, and that wool cap isn't regulation wear without a steel helmet on top of it. If General Smith sees you, you'll lose what stripes you have. Pull the vehicle over then go inside, both of you. Wash up, make yourselves presentable, and then unload this stuff."

"But, Lieutenant, we can't leave this—"

"I'll sign for your shipment, Corporal, don't worry. And we'll wait right here. Now move!"

"I don't know, Lieutenant," he said, handing me the clipboard. I scrawled on the signature line and kept the clipboard.

"Trust me, I know. I used to be a captain. Then I showed up one day with mud on my trousers. Busted. Do yourself a favor—hustle inside, clean up, get back here on the double, and you might be all right. I can't wait all day."

"Yes, sir, Lieutenant," he said, getting out of the truck and reaching for the clipboard. "I'll take my receipt now."

"You're not putting those greasy fingers on my copy," I said, tossing the clipboard on the seat. "Clean those hands and then we'll finish the paperwork."

They both went off, shaking their heads, slightly unsure if they owed me thanks or if it was more of the usual chickenshit. Big Mike and I watched them go in, waited a couple of seconds in case they looked back, and jumped into the truck. I threw the clipboard out the window. They'd find it, signed, and maybe their story would be believed. I shoved the gear into reverse, backed into Charles Street, and took off, trying not to hit the statue of Florence Nightingale as I turned right onto Waterloo Place, watching the rearview mirror for cooks, bakers, MPs, or quartermaster troops on our tail.

"You got a can opener on you, Billy?" Big Mike asked. I didn't stop laughing until I realized I had to find a place in the heart of London to hide a three-quarter-ton U.S. Army truck, loaded with crates labeled PEACHES, CANNED, SYRUP, HEAVY.

Fortunately, Walter was on duty at the Dorchester, manning the front desk and unflappable as I told him we needed a place to park a truck for a few hours, out of sight. I hesitated to use the word *hide*, but he understood. He made a phone call and told me to head around the back of the hotel, between the two wings that extended from the rear of the hotel. I signaled Big Mike, who was circling the block, and he turned in, a Dorchester Rolls-Royce pulling in behind us, partially blocking the view from the side street. As long as the MPs didn't start searching fancy hotels for stolen peaches, we'd be OK. I untied the canvas cover at the rear and counted crates. Neatly stacked, there were four rows, four high, four deep. Sixty-four crates of canned peaches. I grabbed a pry bar from a tool kit bolted to the floor and popped the top of one crate, the thin pine giving way easily. Six industrial-sized cans in each crate, enough peaches to feed an army.

"Jeez, Billy, what do you think it's all worth?" Big Mike asked.

"I don't know," I said. "But we have some time to figure it out." I handed him the open crate, got down and secured the canvas tarp. We left the one crate with the Rolls driver, since it wouldn't do to carry contraband through the lobby, and told Walter to divvy it up as he saw fit. When I told him what it was, his eyes widened.

"I haven't seen peaches since, since, I can't remember when," Walter said. "There's four staff involved, Lieutenant, and one more coming on duty soon. Ah, are there sufficient supplies?"

"Six cans this high, Walter," I said, holding my hands about a foot apart. "I need to know what this stuff would cost on the black market. And don't worry, this is all in the course of an investigation. I'm working with Scotland Yard."

"Very well, Lieutenant. I shall make inquiries," he said in a whisper. "The sixth can will go to the chef, who should be able to find out."

"Thanks. We'll be out of here after dark." I swear I saw him lick his lips. He'd be a hero at home tonight.

I ordered room service, since it would be a late night, and Big Mike had gone without food for about four hours. As we worked on the lamb chops and boiled potatoes, we tried to figure out what to ask Chapman for the peaches.

"I know a carton of smokes goes for about twenty bucks," Big Mike said. "That's a lot because you can trade American cigarettes for just about anything."

"Yeah, but there's a built-in appeal for smokers, they gotta have them. Peaches, well, they taste good, but you can go without and not really be bothered."

"Maybe," Big Mike said. "They're a luxury. Some folks will pay top dollar for what everyone else can't have." There was a knock on the door and we both jumped, like a couple of heisters on the run. But it was only Walter.

"Our chef wishes to know how many of these cans you are looking to sell," he asked.

"Sixty-four," I said.

"He would pay five pounds each."

"Wow" was all I could say.

"Billy, remember it's sixty-three crates now, since we gave these guys one."

"You have sixty-three *crates*?" Walter asked, amazement registering in his normally cultured and calm voice.

"Yeah," I said. "Did you mean five pounds per crate?"

"Blimey, no," Walter said, dropping the high-society accent. "Five quid per can!"

CHAPTER · THIRTEEN

WE LEFT ANOTHER crate with Walter and his pals, just to let them know there were no hard feelings. I didn't know if the chef and Walter were in cahoots, planning to sell off the peaches at an even greater profit, or if it was all for the glory of the hotel's kitchen. I thought it might be the glory, the desire for the Dorchester to be seen as able to conjure up anything for their guests. The government limit of five shillings for any meal on the menu was still in effect, but that didn't mean the hotel couldn't charge separately for a dessert of peaches. The rumor of peaches alone would probably bring in droves of diners, all the Mayfair set ready to plunk down whatever it took for a delicacy out of reach for the common folk.

But we were headed to a different neighborhood, one where you didn't dress for dinner. Big Mike took Oxford Street and left the West End behind, the roadway changing to names that better suited the surroundings. Cheapside turned to Threadneedle Street, and that took us close to the Liverpool Tube Station.

"Pull in next to those trucks," I said. As I'd hoped, there were vehicles parked near the burned-out buildings a block away from the Underground. Work was still going on to clear the debris, and a couple of flatbed trucks and a van had been backed into the cleared space. Big Mike joined them and killed the engine. "You stay here, make sure no one noses around."

"I can't let you go in there alone, Billy," Big Mike said, but without a lot of enthusiasm. He knew our precious cargo might not last unguarded.

"Don't worry. I'll be back in no time at all with a buyer."

"Kinda interesting, isn't it?"

"What is?"

"Being a bad guy. I'm sitting here with a truckload of stolen goods, while you're looking to fence 'em. Who'da thought it?"

"Yeah. Makes you see the attraction. There's good money to be made."

"I'll take my PD pension any day. This is getting on my nerves. Hurry up, OK? I don't know what I'd say if a bobby comes along."

"Show him your badge and tell him about Detroit. That'll keep him from coming back." I shut the door before Big Mike could curse me out and pulled a crate from the back, wrapping it in a tarp. I carried it into the Tube station, thinking about the ARP warden the night before, staying at his post to help a mother and her children. Heroes and bums were everywhere, plenty of each on the homefront as well as the firing line.

The atmosphere was calmer down below, with a steady stream of East Enders carrying blankets, pillows, and bags to their places on the platform. The chances of another raid with all the cloud cover tonight were slim, but the place was filling up. Last night's terror was replaced by laughter and smiles of recognition as neighbors from above met each other below. A small group of girls was trying to sing the new song "A Lovely Way to Spend an Evening," but ended up giggling each time they got to the chorus.

The bunks in the siding were near to full, the soft murmur of conversation marking the more regular residents. Some read newspapers, others magazines and paperbacks. One man, old enough to have served in the last war, was reading *No Orchids for Miss Blandish*, a recent book that had caused a sensation in 1939 over its depictions of beatings, killings, torture, and rape. Odd, with one war behind him and another driving him underground, that he passed his time by turning the page from one act of brutality to another. Or maybe it made perfect sense. At least he wasn't deluding himself.

"Hi, Charlie," I said, as the boxer looked up from his newspaper. "I've got a present for Mr. Chapman."

"Let's have a look then," he said. I dropped the cover off the crate and watched him raise an eyebrow. "You can take that back, Topper'll see you. But hand the gun over first." I gave him my .38, and he folded the newspaper over it. I wondered how much they paid off the local constables, or if they were just too afraid to come down this way.

"Well, Boyle, I see you don't take advice," Topper said as I entered the room. The blankets to Archie's sanctum were drawn. "Can't say I didn't give fair warning." He was playing cards with two guys in brand-new suits. It was noticeable since nobody had a new suit in London, due to rationing and the desire of most people to do their bit. But not Topper and his pals. Elegant tailoring, silk shirts, patent-leather black shoes.

"All dressed up and nowhere to go?" I said, setting the crate down on their card table.

"Shut up, Yank," one of Topper's boys said, pulling the deck of cards away from the crate of canned peaches.

"You know, my dad always told me to make a good first impression when you meet new people," I said. "Because that sets the tone for every-thing that comes afterward."

"Ain't nothing coming afterward, Yank, so shut up before I get mad and do it for you."

"That's just what I'm talking about," I said, gazing at Topper across the table from me. The guy with the mouth was on my left, looking up at me. Topper made a show of studying his cards. The well-dressed thug on my right watched Topper, waiting for a sign. "This guy is going to give me a hard time every time I see him now, because of the lousy first impres-sion he has of me, letting him mouth off like that."

"So why don't—"

Before he could tell me what I should do about it, I grabbed him by the back of the head and snapped it down, smashing his face against the wooden crate. The pine wood and the cartilage in his nose cracked, and he started howling as blood christened his shirt. I didn't look at the other two. I knew I had to show disdain for whatever they might do. Charlie didn't stir, likely used to the sound of pain coming from behind the wall of blankets.

"Now," I said, still grasping his hair and holding his face back so I loomed over him, "wouldn't it have been better to start off politely, so we could've been pals?" He looked at Topper, waiting for him to have me dismembered. All Topper did was blow out a breath in mock boredom and toss his cards onto the table.

"Pals?" the tough guy said through the blood filling his nostrils, unable to follow what I was saying, stunned at the lack of support from his boss.

"Have some peaches," I said. Topper laughed.

I'd hoped for a chance to get their attention, beyond the gift of six cans of Uncle Sam's finest Georgia peaches. I needed to demonstrate that I was a tough guy, too, and the only way to do that with a bunch of crooks is to not let one of them give you any lip. That was one of the lessons Dad had taught me. Never take guff from a guy unless you're willing to take it every time you run into him.

"Stanley, get cleaned up. I'll get you a new shirt tomorrow," Topper said. He nodded to the other fellow, who stood, took the box from the table, cleaned up the cards, and stood behind me. "Thank you for the gift, Boyle."

"Lots more where that came from."

"I hope your delivery method improves. I won't let you get away with that again. But it was worth it to teach Stanley a lesson. He should think before he speaks."

"I don't intend on delivering these in person. If you're interested in acquiring more, I've got sixty cases to move. But the gift-giving season is over."

"Where are they?"

"Close, ready to unload."

"I don't intend to be drawn into a trap, Lieutenant Boyle. I appreciate this gift from the U.S. Army, but I have no interest in the black market."

"What's the clothing ration these days? Thirty-six coupons a year, right? You're each wearing about two-thirds of that."

"It pays to have friends, Lieutenant. In the same way it pays to not make enemies. It helps one get ahead."

"Five pounds per can," I said. "That's my price."

"What?"

"I'm making the offer to sell you army property. I don't know about the law here, but back in the States I'd have to wait for you to offer to buy if I wanted to entrap you."

"That's not what I meant. I must've misunderstood you. I thought you said five pounds per can."

"I did. You can't find peaches anywhere in England except on a U.S. Army base. They're priceless. You can sell them to fancy restaurants, rich folk, gangsters, anyone with a pocketful of cash. You could charge five pounds per peach, for crying out loud."

"Clive," Topper said, beckoning to the guy standing behind me. I tensed, waiting for a sap to my skull. "Open those cans. Take them around to the good people outside. Make sure they share them out, women and children first. Got it?"

"Yes, boss. You want any?"

"No. Leave a bowl for Dad, though. And yourself and Charlie, too."

"None for Stanley?" Topper shook his head, and Clive got to work with a can opener.

"I'll buy your sixty crates at four pounds each. That's two hundred and forty quid. My only offer."

"You going to give those away, too?"

"We're not a charitable institution," Topper said. "But these are all East Enders in here. Our folk. We take care of our own."

"And they take care of you."

"What's fair is fair," he said, as a chorus of cheers went up from the residents of the Chapman siding. "Take the two forty or take your leave."

"I want three hundred, and some information."

"Information has value, Billy, it's not something to be given away."

"OK, I'll knock fifty pounds off for the info. Two fifty, and you tell me what I need to know."

"My price is two forty, firm. Tell me what you need to know, and I'll tell you if that information is available and for sale. And for how much."

"Shouldn't we be talking to your father about this?"

"We will, once the terms are agreed. He's not one to haggle. What do you want to know?"

"I need to know who killed the Russian, Gennady Egorov. I don't care what business he may have been doing with you. If you had him killed, there's no reason for me to go to Scotland Yard, it's not my beef."

"You are seriously asking if I'm an accessory to murder? If I was, do you think I'd ever tell you? That's a foolish question."

"OK. Here's what I need to know. Was Egorov doing business with you, selling information about the shipment of supplies to the Soviet Embassy? If so, then I need to know if his death was in any way connected with that business, as opposed to a conflict with another party. No names, I just need to know the motive for his murder."

"This is for the investigation you mentioned, on behalf of General Eisenhower?"

"Yeah. If I can solve it, it'll mean a promotion. More pay, easier access to even more supplies. Listen, I don't give a hoot who killed him, I just need a story that will hold up. But if his death involves our business in any way, I need to know it so I can steer the investigation in another direction."

"All right," Topper said. "I think we may be able to come to an understanding. I need to discuss this with my father. We'll also need to make arrangements to get these crates delivered safely. We have a warehouse nearby. How long will it take for you to get everything here? You do have transportation, don't you? Our deal doesn't include a pickup."

"Five minutes," I said. "Everything's in a truck, close by."

"Good. Let me speak to him alone."

Topper and Archie talked for ten minutes or so, in hushed tones I couldn't make out. Then there was silence, and in a minute Topper came out. "Want a drink?" he said.

"No thanks," I said, not wanting to start up a repeat of the previous performance. "Is your father coming out?"

"No, he's not feeling well. But he did agree to two fifty, and we can tell you something about the Russian."

"Something?"

"Nothing held back. Do we have a deal?"

"Yes," I said. "Deal." I had no idea what the actual cost of the peaches was to the army, but I was sure two hundred and fifty pounds, illegal as it was, would cover it.

"The Russian was not ours. We had nothing to do with his killing."

"Topper, that may be true, but it's what I'd expect you to say."

"I understand, but there's something else. The map you mentioned, the one showing the route of the supply truck. That was for us. We were to receive it, but it never arrived."

"Do you think Egorov was the courier?"

"No, that's not how it was done. Truly, we have no connection to the man, nor do we know who killed him. But the fact that he had the map, it does point to his interference in a business arrangement."

"Which you won't reveal."

"Or ever acknowledge again."

"OK," I said. "Then let's finish the rest of the deal." I followed Topper out, and Charlie fell in behind us, promising to return my weapon when the transaction was complete. Topper stopped to chat along the way, as people thanked him for the peaches. He was especially popular with the young ladies, but the old ones liked him, too. Never underestimate the power of peaches in syrup when an island has been at war for four years. It was a happy group, and I had to stop three or four times to accept thanks as well, from those who'd seen me carry in the covered crate and put two and two together.

Once we made it aboveground, I led Topper to the bombed-out buildings, with Charlie at our heels. "Got the money on you?" I asked, wanting to sound like a legitimate bad guy.

"I do, and that's where it's staying," Topper said, wheeling to face me as I felt the muzzle of my own gun at my neck. "All set?" Topper yelled over his shoulder.

"That we are, boy," I heard Archie respond, a cackling laugh finishing his sentence. "Wasn't too hard either, even though this fellow is the size of a house."

Archie stepped out from between two trucks, advancing until his bayonet pointed straight at my chest. "Don't you play with me, Boyle. Either you're a thief or not. I don't like how you mix your business."

"Big Mike?" I said into the darkness.

"I'm OK, Billy. Except for the shotgun digging into my back. They got the drop on me."

"Amateurs," Archie said. "What pitiful amateurs. It gives honest crooks a bad name. First you ask too many damn questions, then you accept a pittance for these wonderful fruits of nature, then you tell Topper you've got the truck full no more than five minutes away. What did you expect, boy? You may as well have brought the whole load to my doorstep."

"If you need anything done, boss, I'd be happy to oblige." Stanley stepped from behind the truck, a scarf wrapped around his neck to hide the bloodstains. "Very happy," he added, his voice still nasal and stuffy.

"No need, no need. We'll take the truck and let these two fools find their own way back. But if you see them an hour from now, do whatever pleases you. And I might do the same!"

"Archie, you can't take the truck," I said, trying to sound reasonable.

"Oh no?" he said, waving the bayonet in a circle in front of my face. "I say I can do what I please. No man has stopped me, and yet many have tried. Why, in tires and engine parts alone, this vehicle is worth as much as the cargo. Now be glad you have your lives for one more day, and never come back to Shoreditch. And if you send coppers from the Met, there's no one down below who will ever admit to seeing you. You know that's the truth, don't you?"

"Yes," I said, feeling the complete fool. Archie had clearly been listening to my conversation with Topper, and snuck out just before we left, taking Stanley and Clive to hunt for the truck. There had to be a side passage from his room at the rear of the siding. "I do."

"And do you want to know why?" Archie whispered, leaning in close to my face, the tip of his bayonet lifting my chin until I had to look him in the eye. He lifted the blade and placed it flat against my lips, the point sharp against my nose. His voice rose with each line, echoing off the dark, black walls surrounding us.

To these I turn, in these I trust—
Brother Lead and Sister Steel.
To his blind power I make appeal,
I guard her beauty clean from rust.

He spins and burns and loves the air,
And splits a skull to win my praise;
But up the nobly marching days
She glitters naked, cold and fair.

Sweet Sister, grant your soldier this:
That in good fury he may feel
The body where he sets his heel
Quail from your downward darting kiss.

Keeping the blade on my lips, he leaned in closer, and kissed the cold steel. I felt the razor sharpness against my lips along with the unwelcome warmth of his, and someone's blood seeping between my teeth.

"'The Kiss,' by Siegfried Sassoon," Archie said, stepping back, as if at a formal recital. He bowed gracefully and pointed down the ruined road, back to the center of London. "Go."

"I didn't lie to you about the Russian," Topper said as we passed him by. "And I warned you not to come back, didn't I?"

CHAPTER ▪ FOURTEEN

I AWOKE TO thick, heavy splats of rain hitting the windows. For a couple of seconds I didn't remember what had happened last night, or realize that those two seconds were going to be the best part of my day.

The rain was murderously fierce, driving sideways against the glass, the dark, leaden London sky giving promise of a cold soaking and another postponed bombing run. Wordlessly, I joined Kaz in morning exercises, doing deep knee bends and stretches, trying to think of the next boneheaded move I could make. I'd told Kaz the whole story the night before, about how they'd sent Stanley out to stumble in front of the truck, as if he'd been mugged. Big Mike, being a public servant at heart, had gone to help, and ended up on the wrong end of a sawed-off. Then I showed up, we had the poetry reading, the Chapman gang drove off in our truck, and Big Mike and I hoofed it until we found a taxi, thankful that at least they hadn't taken the coins from our pockets. During the cab ride, I got angry with my dad for never telling me how he had handled the gangsters who were threatening Nuno. A few tips on dealing with the underworld would have come in handy.

I got out of the way as Kaz used a jump rope. I had to admit, I was pretty impressed with how he'd built himself up. He'd always had stamina but it had been that of the soul. Now his body was ready to keep up with his spirit and his intellect. Unfortunately, as smart as he was, he hadn't come up with an answer to my problems. I did knee curls with the weights, thinking through the list of my troubles with each slow repetition.

One, I was nowhere in terms of the Egorov case. I had no clue who killed him, or why. I had the word of honor from a guy who robbed me that he had nothing to do with it. Swell. Plus, the whole idea of a Russian officer working with the Chapman bunch didn't add up. No one in the Soviet Union was allowed to get rich, so what was he going to do with his loot?

Two, I'd stirred up a hornet's nest out at High Wycombe asking about Russians at the Eighth Air Force HQ. Something top secret was going on, based on those red strings from Bull's map, the squad of MPs who had been after me, and Estelle's sudden transfer after she talked with us. What it was, I had no idea, only a promise from Bull that he'd try to get in touch.

Three, there was no love lost between Kaz, his Polish buddies, and the Russians. I'd uncovered an informer, but that likely had nothing to do with the case. I still wasn't totally sure Kaz was innocent, and as I thought through the little I'd come up with, I realized he looked good for it. In the absence of any solid leads, my dad always said, go with what you got, no matter how slim. It at least gave the illusion of forward movement, and more often than not there was some truth embedded in your suspicions. Was that true of Kaz? I knew he could be ruthless, far more ruthless than his studious appearance would suggest. But Nuno was a hard case, too, and Dad hadn't given him up to the authorities or the Mob.

Four, I'd gotten myself in big trouble with the quartermaster corps, the military police, and, worst of all, Colonel Sam Harding. They'd be looking everywhere for that truck, and it wouldn't take anyone at Norfolk House with an ounce of sense to figure out who the fast-talking lieutenant and the giant corporal were. If I'd solved the case at the cost of a truck and goods, Harding might've backed me up. But to come up empty all around, no way.

Five. I needed a five. I kept up the reps, switching from one arm to the other, generating perspiration but no inspiration.

"What will you do, Billy?" Kaz said, rubbing his head with a towel.

"I'm not sure. I'd like to get in touch with Bull, but that might only set the dogs on me again. I guess I'll see if Inspector Scutt can help, then go fess up to Harding."

"Good luck. No matter how stern his visage, Sam Harding was always fair."

"Not so with your new boss, Major Horak?"

"No, sadly," Kaz said. "While he is my superior, he leaves much in the hands of Captain Radecki, who is far too impatient. A good soldier, but not a diplomat. Perhaps because he lives with pain every day."

"Is he still being hard on Tadeusz?"

"Yes, and I think it caused him to retreat into his mind forever. Radecki had threatened to turn him over to the Russians if he didn't speak. He meant to force the issue, but he has little understanding of the human mind. Now Tadeusz shows no response at all. The doctor says he needs to be sent to a hospital, where he can receive full-time care. He no longer speaks, barely eats, and spends most of his time sleeping."

"So the one surviving eyewitness to Katyn has everything locked up in his head, unable to get it out."

"It would have been merciful if the Russians had shot him that day, I regret to say. We've changed the story we are feeding the Russians through Eddie Miller. Since Tadeusz will now be safely out of the way, we are saying we have a witness, using much of his story as he told it."

"In hopes the Russians might do what?"

"We have no hopes for the Russians. It's the Americans and the British we need to influence. Hearing we have a witness may help open some minds. And perhaps Tadeusz will come out of his trance once he's had rest and quiet."

"Kaz, is there any possibility in your mind that someone from the Polish Army could have shot Egorov? Maybe someone who's heard Tadeusz tell his story? Hell, I know I'd be hard-pressed not to take some revenge if that happened to my own people."

"I know you have to ask, Billy, but no, there isn't. As for revenge, I have thought about it. I agree, it is difficult not to. But if I wished to take violent revenge against the Russians, why would I kill just one, way out in Shoreditch? It's not much of a statement."

"But there's the twine, and the execution just like at Katyn."

"True, but a bullet to the back of the head is not a purely Russian invention. And naturally the victim would be bound. It does make one think, but if I were to go to all that trouble, why kill him in the East End, where it could easily be mistaken for random violence? Why not dump his body in front of his own embassy, or at the palace, or on Fleet Street so the newspaper people would get the first look at it? It does not add up."

"You're right," I said. There was a knock at the door, and Kaz opened it for room service, delivering our morning coffee and toast. An envelope addressed to Kaz and a note on Dorchester stationery sat on a silver tray.

"The note is from the chef, and says with his compliments," Kaz said, a quizzical look on his face. I took the cover off one of the bowls on the cart.

"Peaches," I said. "Sixty-three crates, and this is what I end up with." I thought I wouldn't be able to eat them, but taste won out over remorse. "What's in the envelope?"

"I don't believe it," Kaz said. "A note from Captain Kiril Sidorov."

"What?"

"An invitation to the Soviet Embassy, tonight," Kaz said, as he handed me the elegantly lettered invitation on creamy card stock, topped with the emblem of the Union of Soviet Socialist Republics in full color, the red star over the globe, stamped with a golden hammer and sickle, a design leaving little doubt. Kaz read the note.

> Dear Lieutenant Kazimierz:
>
> Since relations between our two governments do not allow for an official invitation to be sent to you for tonight's cultural event, I have taken it upon myself to forward this personal invitation. Your most interesting colleague, Lieutenant Boyle, is also being invited, along with several other officers from Norfolk House. I sincerely hope you will attend and demonstrate that, in spite of the differences between us, we are united not only in our struggle against Fascism, but in the appreciation of fine opera.
>
> Yours,
> Kiril Sidorov, Captain, Red Army Air Force

"Opera?" I said, trying to keep what I knew was a childish whine out of my voice.

"Billy, I have been invited to the embassy of the government responsible for the deaths of tens of thousands of my countrymen, the regime that invaded Poland in collusion with the Nazis, and all you can think of is the ordeal of sitting through an opera?"

"Sorry, gut reaction. Why do you think Sidorov sent it, whatever it's for?"

"You tell me, you've met him."

"He's not what you'd expect. Relaxed, not all up in arms about the workers of the world. He obviously does his job well, but he doesn't present a serious front."

"You sound like you like the man."

"Actually, I was thinking that he reminds me of you in some ways. Educated, urbane, speaks English perfectly and, hey, he likes opera, too."

"There are some educated Russians," Kaz said, granting the possibility that Sidorov wasn't a swine. "The invitation says it's a new film of a Russian opera, not a live performance. *Ivan Susanin.* I've not heard of it."

"Are you going?"

"Why not? It will be interesting to meet the man who is spying on me. And someone will have to keep you awake. You won't be able to turn down an official invitation, you know."

"I could get lucky and get arrested."

"By Scotland Yard or the military police?"

"Funny," I said, as I drank my coffee. I resisted telling Kaz that he was the one who should worry about Scotland Yard, but now that I had MPs from High Wycombe to London looking for me, I had enough trouble keeping myself from behind bars. Anyway, there wasn't enough evidence to do more than question him, and he'd been through worse than that.

Something about how we were looking at it was off, and that's why it wasn't making sense to us.

I needed that number five. Number five would add up, I was sure.

I DECIDED TO head to the Met first, in case an unarmed bobby had captured the Chapman gang and rescued Uncle Sam's peaches. I took a cab, avoiding the worst of the downpour and arriving just as Inspector Scutt was shaking the water off his raincoat.

"Miserable weather today," he said. "DS Flack will be soaked to the bone, probably is already." He gestured to the chair opposite his desk as he settled in, glancing at the paperwork and messages waiting for him.

"What's he doing?"

"Out hunting Jerries," he said. "There's still a dozen unaccounted for from the raid the other night. Most give themselves up right away, glad to be alive and hoping not to get impaled by an angry farmer with a pitch-fork." He laughed, more to himself, as if remembering an unfortunate German who had met that fate. He lit his pipe, fussing with it the way pipe smokers did, tamping it down, filling the room with clouds of smoke until he was satisfied. "The Bromley station called for assistance, since the airfield at Biggin Hill is close by, and they've had reports of two or three Germans in the area. Flack is heading up the search down there."

"This rain ought to drive them in," I said. It was hard to imagine how the fliers could manage to evade capture this long, especially after the violence of being blown out of the sky, floating down in the dark, and landing in enemy territory, most likely alone.

"I'd guess it will, but the RAF wants them all caught, so they can stop worrying about some Fritz pinching an aircraft. That would be the only way off the island, and it would be an embarrassment for all, wouldn't it? At least they don't expect an old retread like me to tramp about the fields, that's something. Now, what news do you have?"

I gave him the short version of the truck heist, trying not to sound like a rookie.

"Well, there's some chance of finding the truck. Minus tires and engine. Peaches, you said? I couldn't even guarantee you'd get them back if I found them myself," Scutt said, winking to let me know he didn't mean it. I think.

"Yeah, I know. Any part of the vehicle would be appreciated. But there's more. Part of the deal, before it went sour, was for Topper to give me the inside story on the Russian. I think he kept that side of the bargain."

"He's an odd one, our Topper is," Scutt said, raising more smoke from his pipe. "Smart, I'll give him that. And protective of his father. I'll make no excuses for Archie Chapman, but he's not been right in the head since the war."

"He says he served with Siegfried Sassoon."

"True. I checked with the War Office the first time I heard Archie spout verse. They served together in the First Battalion, in Flanders. Did he recite for you?"

"Twice. Dead drunk first time, stone sober the second, as he robbed me."

"You're lucky to be alive. Archie Chapman could have slit your throat in front of a hundred East Enders, who'd all swear he was at their dinner table at the time. Some like him, most are afraid, and for good reason."

"Topper is different?"

"Cold, I'd say. Archie enjoys what he does. Topper does what is necessary. Without regard for the law, which makes him as bad as his old man, but I don't know if he has his heart in the family business. Don't rightly know if he has much of a heart, at that."

"Any idea why he's not in the service? He looks fit."

"Doctors can be bought, like anyone else. Maybe he has some sort of condition, maybe not. He did try to join up, at least."

"You sure?" I asked, remembering Archie cutting me off as I asked Topper why he wasn't serving.

"I remember it well. The army inquired about any criminal record, since he was known at the local recruiting office. We've never been able to charge him, so I had to say he was clean. I thought he was going off to war to follow in his father's footsteps, but a few weeks later, there he is, at Archie's side, conducting business as usual. Or better. He's got a talent for it."

"Evidently," I said. "I wonder how he got out after enlisting." My thoughts went back to my own army physical, and how Dad and Uncle Dan had hoped I would fail, to avoid the chance of serving altogether. After I'd passed, we'd hoisted a few pints at Kirby's, toasting to my health with an odd mixture of pride and wistfulness. The next step would be to pull some strings in D.C., with Mom's distant, somewhat obscure relative. Dad was certain he didn't want me to end up like his older brother Frank, buried in a French cemetery for helping the English fight a war. But there was something in his eyes, along with the certainty that he could pull this thing off—a sadness, perhaps, or a sorrowful joy, that I would not share his visions of the trenches, an experience that had made him the man he was. That was a good thing, but a thing that would always divide us.

"I said, Boyle, tell me what Topper told you about the Russian." Scutt spoke loudly, maybe for the second time, to bring me back from woolgathering.

"Topper said Egorov himself had no connection to them, and that they weren't responsible for the killing."

Scutt had the well-earned policeman's distrust of a criminal's protestation of innocence.

"But he did say the map *had* been for them. He as much as admitted they'd been behind the supply hijackings, and that there was a business arrangement with someone, probably at the Russian Embassy, although he never said so exactly."

"All to be denied if asked again."

"Yes, that was the deal. With everything else they did, without worrying about being caught, why would he lie about Egorov?"

"Murder means the rope, Lieutenant Boyle. Reason enough."

"Could be. Maybe he's trying to throw us off the track."

"We haven't much of a scent to pick up, much less be thrown off," Scutt said with a weary sigh.

"Excuse me, Inspector," a constable said, approaching Scutt and handing him a sheet of paper. "This just came in. A body was dug out of the rubble from the raid the other night, over on Tower Bridge Road. Looks suspicious, according to the report."

"Very well, I'll go take a look. Haven't had one of these in a while."

"One of what, Inspector?" I asked as he put on his raincoat.

"Murder, perhaps. Disguised as a bombing victim. Had quite a rash during the Blitz, as soon as people started getting the idea it would be a fine way to get rid of a body. Bash a fellow you don't like on the head, bury him in a bit of rubble from a bombed-out building, and as soon as he starts to smell, he's dug up and written off as done in by Herr Göring."

"What makes it suspicious?"

"Well, you take this fellow. About thirty years of age. No identification papers, and no one in the area knew him. Likely killed by a blow to the head. Now most people go about with their papers, and if you've seen a body after a ton of bricks falls on it, you'd know there would be other injuries. There are usually massive physical injuries. But only a crushed skull, and a stranger to boot? Unlikely."

"Good luck," I said. "And let me know if anything comes up about Sidorov. Something's not right there."

"I still wonder about your Polish friend, you know," Scutt said. His raised eyebrows invited a comment as we took the steps down to the main door.

"I talked with him," I said, and shared Kaz's thoughts about the placement of the body. "Not the best way to make a political statement."

"Perhaps not. Perhaps it was more personal than political. Or both. Lieutenant Kazimierz could have had words with Egorov, at some diplomatic function. Who knows?"

Not me. Scutt promised to alert the area constables to watch for the truck, but he was only going through the motions, the same sort of thing I'd said many a time when an automobile was stolen or a purse snatched, knowing it would only be dumb luck or a dumber crook that would see it returned.

THE RAIN HAD stopped, so I walked to Norfolk House, glad for the excuse to delay seeing Colonel Harding. Since he was regular U.S. Army, he was apt to look upon the truck and peaches as his personal property. Scutt could afford to chuckle about it, since I'd only gotten what I deserved. But Harding wasn't interested in failure, and except for break-fast, I had nothing to show for my gamble.

"Go on in, Billy, they're waiting for you," Big Mike said as I entered the office. He nodded to the open conference-room door, and winked. I wanted to ask him what he was so happy about, but Harding appeared at the door and told me to get in, pronto. He sounded mildly angry and agitated, but that was SOP with him. I had expected a full-bore lecture, maybe a demotion, but nothing like that was in the air.

"You know Colonel Dawson, I take it," Harding said, nodding toward Bull, who sat at the conference table, a large map spread out in front of him. "And Major Cosgrove."

"Sure. I mean, yes, sir."

"Boyle," Cosgrove said, nodding slightly, his eyes briefly darting up to meet mine. I didn't count Major Charles Cosgrove of MI5, the British Secret Service, among my friends. The feeling would have been mutual, except he was too much of a stiff upper lip to admit to the emotion neces-sary to say what he thought of me. There had been bad blood between us since he used me in one of his plots, back when I first arrived in London, and worse blood since the business in Northern Ireland a few weeks ago. He had a habit of manipulating people, and some of those people didn't live long enough to return the favor. I had, and someday I intended to.

"Good to see you, Billy," Colonel Bull Dawson said. Him I was glad to see. He looked spiffy in his Class A uniform, all decked out for a visit to HQ in London. His brass buttons gleamed, and the silver wings perched over his heart sparkled. His eyes, marked by crow's-feet from constant squinting into the sun at twenty-five thousand feet, flickered between Cosgrove and me. I could tell he sensed trouble, the way he could probably pick up on a Me-109 coming out of a cloud formation.

"Same here, Colonel," I said. "Unless there's a pack of MPs in the next room."

"That's what we're here to talk about, Boyle," Harding said, taking his seat at the head of the table. I sat next to Bull, and Harding gave him the nod.

"Ever since you hightailed out of High Wycombe, I've been asking around about you, Billy," Bull said. "You seemed like a stand-up guy in Northern Ireland, but I had to be sure. Everyone agrees, you get the job done. Some apparently wish you did it a bit more subtly, but I'm a guy who drops five thousand–pound bomb loads for a living, so subtle doesn't carry much weight with me. I've asked for the highest-level clearance for you on this matter. I briefed Colonel Harding this morning, with Major Cosgrove's permission."

"Major Cosgrove can call the shots on that?" I said.

"Yes, I can, Lieutenant Boyle, and it won't surprise you to know I do have concerns about your conduct. Still, it does make sense to bring you in on this, at least to minimize any damage you might inadvertently do. I already had to speak to Inspector Scutt and tell him to stop asking questions on your behalf. He asked me why the Russians had stopped going to High Wycombe, and over an open line! Lord knows what else you or he may blurt out."

"You mean like the flights to Poltava and Mirgorod?" I said, putting together the sum total of my knowledge to see if it would get a reaction from Cosgrove.

"This proves my point, Harding! Lieutenant Boyle should be confined to quarters until this matter is completed. And not a suite at the Dorchester, either!" Cosgrove turned beet red, puffing out his cheeks as he tried to control his anger. He was a big guy, around the waist anyway, and I almost worried about him blowing a fuse.

"That's Colonel Harding, Major" was the reply. The fact that Cosgrove worked for MI5 and could have shown up in an admiral's getup didn't matter. His cover was as a major, a rank low enough not to attract attention but high enough to get a decent table at a fancy restaurant. Harding outranked him and expected the military courtesies. "The fact that Lieutenant Boyle has figured out that much means we're right to brief him now. Bull, proceed."

"Billy," he began, playing the peacemaker. "Major Cosgrove is in charge of security for the Soviet personnel. This includes worrying about any potential threats from émigré anti-Communist groups in London. It's enough to make any sane man jumpy."

"OK," I said. "I understand. I only know about the two locations because I noticed they'd been marked on the map in your office. And of course I would've stumbled upon the Russian connection from the reaction when I asked about it. The transfer of Estelle Gordon was a tip-off that I was onto something."

"That was a bit heavy-handed," Bull said, working at not giving Cosgrove a look. "But we have to be sure word doesn't leak out about this. London is full of rumors, gossip, and informers. You sure you haven't heard anything else?"

"Nope. Well, except that the Royal Navy is in on it somehow."

"Good lord, the man's a menace," Cosgrove said, mainly to himself and the ceiling.

"Operation Frantic Joe," Bull said.

"Now simply called Operation Frantic," Cosgrove put in, as if reminding a child of a forgotten lesson.

"Right," Bull said. "The idea began as a response to Stalin's demand for a second front against the Germans. The Soviets wanted us to do something to take the pressure off them on the Eastern Front. We will, but on our schedule, not theirs. For now, we do have long-range bomber forces, and can put them to work pretty damn quick."

"Did Frantic Joe refer to Joe Stalin?" I asked.

"Yes, but it was thought to be more diplomatic to shorten it to Operation Frantic. We're going to set up Eighth Air Force airfields in the Soviet Union, flying shuttle missions back and forth between there and our bases in England. That's what they brought me back from Northern Ireland for, to plan optimal routes for our bombers."

"So we'll be hitting targets on the Eastern Front for the Russians?"

"Yes, plus our own strategic targets. You see, the plan has a dual purpose. It'll play havoc with the German air defenses. They won't know if we'll be flying back to the base we started at, or straight through the Reich. Right now, their air defenses try to intercept us on the way to the target, or on the way home. Once we're set up with the Russians, they'll have to spread themselves thin, since we can fly to bases in Italy as well."

"That's what the Russians were doing at High Wycombe," I said. "Planning for their end of Operation Frantic."

"Exactly. No one was supposed to know. Then you show up asking questions, and everyone gets nervous. So here we are. We need you inside the tent, Billy. Just keep your mouth shut about it."

"It is important that you solve the murder of Egorov," Cosgrove said. "We must know if that was a security breach, a personal matter, or simply a random crime. If word about Operation Frantic gets out, there will be hell to pay."

"I need to question the members of the delegation, to see if any of them know anything. I tried at the embassy and got the cold shoulder from Sidorov."

"He's NKVD, like Egorov was," Bull said. "They sat back and watched, hardly ever participated."

"Yeah. The question is, who's watching them? Can I have Big Mike in on this, Colonel Harding? And Kaz."

"Impossible," Cosgrove sputtered.

"Why?" Harding said.

"Kaz speaks Russian, and I trust him."

"He's Polish," Cosgrove said. "The Russians won't stand for it."

"How about he just listens? They ought to be used to that."

"I'll see if we can get him back from the Poles," Harding said. "But he'll have to remove the Poland shoulder patch. He'll be attached to SHAEF headquarters, so they won't have a basis for complaint."

"Never stopped the bloody Bolsheviks before," Cosgrove said. "Tomorrow the joint planning committee is moving operations down to Dover. Be prepared to join us, Boyle."

"Dover? Not High Wycombe?"

"That's where the Royal Navy comes in. Major Cosgrove decided that Red Air Force officers at Eighth Air Force HQ might lead people to put two and two together. So we're moving everyone down to Dover Castle, on the coast. It's a Royal Navy base, secure, with underground tunnels. Made to order."

"In case there are any spies about," Cosgrove explained, "we've put out word that we are giving the Russians a tour of the castle and of the defensive measures taken in the area, earlier in the war, when invasion was a real possibility. There will probably be a photograph in the newspapers of a Russian or two and some Home Guard chaps, that sort of thing."

"Perfect. I can interview them while the public relations stuff is going on."

"You'll have to cut them out of the herd, Billy," Bull said. "Those Russkies stick real close together. You can start tonight. We've been invited to the opera at their place."

"Russian opera," Cosgrove said. "Dreadful stuff."

"Major Cosgrove," I said, trying to sound respectful, "I'm investigating one of the London gangs that may have been involved with Egorov's death. Archie Chapman is the head guy."

"I've heard of him," Cosgrove said. "He runs a well-organized operation for a fellow who's off his rocker. Spreads a bit of the wealth around locally, which makes it difficult for the Met, I understand."

"Right. I'm interested in his son, Topper Chapman. Can I get a look at his file?"

"He's not in the army, so we wouldn't have a file on him," Cosgrove said.

"I mean the secret files you have access to. It may be important."

"Very well. I'll see what we have."

The meeting broke up and I hung back in the outer office until everyone was in the hall. Big Mike sat at his desk, the office chair creaking under his weight as he went through a stack of files.

"What gives?" I asked him. "Didn't you tell Harding about the truck?"

"Sure I did, Billy. I also told him about your idea to get it back. He liked it."

"My idea?"

"Well, I didn't want anything to mess up getting Estelle back here, so I figured we both had to come out looking good. I told him you wanted all the pubs and restaurants in Shoreditch placed off limits to U.S. personnel until the truck and shipment were returned."

"That's a stroke of genius, Big Mike. A lot of those joints must pay protection to Chapman. He'll have to give it up to protect his income."

"And his reputation. He can look like a hero on his home turf, getting us to lift the restriction. Plus he gets a few crates of peaches out of the deal. We only want fifty back."

"You make me sound like I'm one crafty lieutenant."

"That's a noncom's job, Billy," Big Mike said as he returned to the files and forms on his desk.

CHAPTER ▪ FIFTEEN

IT'S NOT EVERY pair of lieutenants who get their shoes shined regularly at the Dorchester, but I almost wished Kaz hadn't left our best patent leathers out for a workover. The smell of shoe polish was a reminder of home, so I didn't mind a go with a good brush. When I was a kid, it was my job to take Dad's shoes down cellar once a week and give them a spit shine. I'd sit on the wooden steps, with the door open behind me, listening to the sounds of the house. Mom cleaning up in the kitchen, my little brother Danny running around, and Dad fiddling with the radio. It felt like it would always be that way, that I'd never run out of weeks to put a shine to my father's shoes.

So I liked shining shoes, but I couldn't explain all that to Kaz. It would make me sound like I wasn't a tough guy. I sipped good Irish whiskey instead, hearing the *swoop swoosh* of the brush in my mind as it went back and forth over countless pairs of shoes, the aroma in the glass a poor substitute for mink oil, leather, black shoe polish, and the traces of my old man's sweat that I picked up on my fingers as I curled them inside each shoe, forcing out the folds and buffing them with all my might, desperate to do this job right, as if everything depended on a perfect shoe shine. I always complained, but I worked as hard as I could at it. Funny, the things you miss. Right now, I'd have given anything to have that shoe brush in my hand.

I watched Kaz knotting his tie in the mirror and felt ashamed of my homesickness. His family was dead, and his nation occupied by the Germans, with the Russians up at bat next. There was a lot of politics going on about Polish borders after the war, but reading between the lines I knew that the Soviets were going to bite off a big chunk for themselves and call the shots in what was left. I still had a home to go to. Kaz had nowhere to go, and no one to be with in England after the war. I wondered if he'd want to settle in Boston. Never mind that, I told myself. Make sure he doesn't hang first.

"Kaz, you need to see your tailor," I said, shaking off the melancholy. "You're busting the seams of that shirt."

"Do you think so, Billy? My collar feels tight also." He put on his dress uniform jacket, the one he'd had tailored. It did look a little tight in the shoulders. There was a barely discernible patch of darker fabric where the red Poland patch had been. Kaz had been glad to be released back into service with SHAEF, and had cut the stitching with no regrets.

"It's true," I said. "Those weights are working. You've got some real muscle."

Kaz beamed, proud of his new strength. I was glad of it, too. I knew I needed our morning workouts as well, to sweat out the alcohol I'd been dousing myself with. Some of it had been in the line of duty, but the rest was in the line of drowning my sorrows, worrying about Kaz and Diana, and feeling sorry for myself. I had to work at remembering I didn't have it half as bad as Kaz, or everyone else in this war who might get in the way of a bullet. I started to down the rest of my drink, and then thought about what we might encounter that night at the Soviet Embassy. If it shaped up anything like the Poles and their vodka and the Chapmans and their gin, I needed to save my energy. I set the glass down. Moderation was my middle name.

Shoes shined, ribbons and brass all in order, we put on trench coats and walked across Hyde Park to Bayswater Road, heading for the embassy. Clouds blew across the evening sky, and patches of stars shone through the breaks, glimmering on the still waters of the Serpentine.

"It could be bombing weather tonight," Kaz said, scanning the sky.

"You don't think it was an isolated raid?"

"No, I don't think so. Have you noticed the newspapers haven't reported it yet? They don't want it to appear as if it's a new phase of the Blitz, but it could be. If there's another attack, they'll probably report it as nothing more than a nuisance raid, to keep morale up. The Germans will likely report a thousand planes destroyed the London docks. If you want the truth in this war, the last place to look is in a newspaper."

"Where, then?" I asked.

"To people like Eddie Miller, and those who pay them."

"Who did you pay, Kaz, when you were with the Poles?"

"Ah, a gentleman does not kiss and tell, or reveal his sources. There are Eddie Millers everywhere."

"Are there Russian Eddies?"

"They proved quite difficult. There is a tremendous amount of fear, and of course they only go about in groups. It is hard to speak to a Russian alone."

"There was another guy in the room the whole time I was speaking to Sidorov."

"That is their system, which makes the killing of Egorov intriguing. Although the NKVD must be above the rules. I'm quite curious to meet this Captain Sidorov."

"You feel OK about going?"

"Yes, I don't think there will be overt hostility. As long as you don't fall asleep during the opera."

"Elbow me if I snore. Looks like quite a gathering ahead," I said, pointing to a line of cars parked in front of the embassy. British and American staff cars, black Rolls-Royces, and other private cars disgorged officers and ladies who made their way through a covered walkway into a formal side entrance. No burly guys in ill-fitting suits frisking these guests, just a Red Army officer with a clipboard.

"Lieutenants Kazimierz and Boyle, welcome, on behalf of the peace-loving people of the Union of Soviet Socialist Republics. I am Captain Rak Vatutin. Please, go in and enjoy some refreshments before the film starts. There will be a reception afterward."

"Thanks. How long is the film?" I asked.

"I have not seen it yet," Vatutin said. "But the opera is four acts with an epilogue. There is an intermission," he said with an apologetic smile.

We entered a large hallway filled with a mix of elegant evening gowns and dress uniforms. There were half a dozen colors, from the steel blue of the Red Air Force to the dark blues of three navies and the brown and khaki of Yanks, Brits, and Russians amidst a smattering of diplomats in tuxedos. I spotted Sidorov and he glided over, glad-handing as he went, the confident, genial host.

"Captain Kiril Sidorov at your service, Lieutenant Kazimierz. Thank you so much for coming. Lieutenant Boyle, it is good to see you again."

"Thanks for the invite, Captain. What's the occasion?"

"Simply a cultural event, to show the world that even in the midst of war against the Fascist aggressor, the Soviet Union still attends to the arts. We often screen new films as they make their way here from Moscow."

"You're a busy man," I said. "Aren't you in the middle of planning Operation Frantic?"

"Billy," Kaz said, "one does not bring up names directly, especially at an event like this."

"You Americans are so direct, aren't you?" Sidorov said. "Lieutenant Kazimierz is correct, and not simply about the social niceties. The walls have ears, as the ancient Greek said. So, I must say, I have no idea what you are talking about. Here, have some vodka." He signaled to a waiter, who brought a tray of tall, thin glasses over.

"To victory," Sidorov said.

"To victory and freedom," Kaz said. We drank, and three more glasses appeared.

"You must eat something," Sidorov said. "There are only a few minutes before we must be seated." He led us to a long table, where senior brass were feeding like locusts. "We call this *zukuski*, little bites. Things to eat while you drink vodka. Enjoy, please, and I will see you inside." He snapped his fingers, and Vatutin, fresh from clipboard duty, joined us. He guided us through a selection of pickled onions, caviar tarts, salmon pastry, beet salad, and half a dozen things I didn't recognize.

"Why do we rate all this attention?" I said as Vatutin went off in a search of a fresh tray of cold vodka. "Why do a couple of lieutenants get the royal treatment, in the midst of this high society?"

"Perhaps Sidorov took a liking to you," Kaz said. "I see what you mean about him. He is not as heavy-handed as most Russians, although he says all the right words."

"Think he believes them?"

"In their system, belief does not matter as much as obedience. If he has survived this long, and has been posted here, it is because he is trusted and connected."

"Family connections?"

"Not his family. We did manage to pick up a few tidbits of gossip about Kiril Sidorov. His parents died of typhus, and he was raised in a Soviet orphanage. From there he went straight into the Komsomol, the Communist youth organization. As soon as he was old enough, he began service with the NKVD border guards. Shortly before the war, he was transferred to internal security, courtesy of his wife's father." Kaz interrupted his story to wolf down another caviar tart.

"How do you know all this, and why didn't you tell me before?"

"Not every waiter and maid who works here is Russian," Kaz whispered. "The walls *do* have ears. I couldn't tell you before, but now I work for General Eisenhower, and I owe it to you to tell what I know, little that it is. No more than gossip, really."

"Gossip about Sidorov's wife? He mentioned that she worked in Moscow at the Propaganda Ministry."

"Yes, she does. The talk is that he married well. Her father is an official in the People's Commissariat for Justice, and that, combined with Sidorov's intelligence and his all-Soviet upbringing, marked him as a fast-rising Red star." Kaz stopped to smile at his own joke. "The posting here is undoubtedly a reward, and an indication that he is being groomed for higher service. He has a wife and child in Moscow, so they are fairly certain of his return."

"Fairly?"

"One never knows about a man's home life, or his inner life, so how could anything be certain?"

"I'm not certain of much, Kaz, except that you'll never get me to eat fish eggs."

"Here, comrades," Vatutin said, easing up to us with three glasses. "Ice cold vodka. One for the road, as you Americans say, yes?"

"Yes," Kaz said, raising his glass. "To Poland. First to fight."

"To Poland," Vatutin said, downing the vodka in one shot, and licking his lips, his drunkenness showing through the veil of diplomacy and courtesy. His eyes lingered on Kaz before his jovial mask returned. "Come, the film is about to start. I will take you to your seats."

I followed, feeling the warmth of the alcohol spread in my belly as a haze of dullness clouded my mind. Something told me to be careful, but I wasn't sure why or of what or whom. Vatutin led us into a ballroom with a screen set up at one end. Our seats were up front, not in the first two rows with the bigwigs, but in the third, where Sidorov waited, chatting with Colonel Harding and Major Cosgrove. I would have been more impressed if the film was *Casablanca*. Some pea-brain diplomat had decided that French officials might not like how Vichy was depicted in it, so it was held back from the movies they sent to North Africa, and I never got to see it. The lights dimmed, and the crowd settled into their seats, the conversations and rustles of finery fading as the *whir* of the projector and the first seconds of static and flickering images of Russian lettering filled the screen. It went dark, and the opening credits rolled by in the odd undecipherable script, the opening scene showing a medieval village, with an old white-bearded guy center stage. Ivan Susanin, my guess. Everybody sang for a while, and then some soldiers marched in— the home team, from the reception they got. More singing. A girl, she looked to be Ivan's daughter, was evidently sweet on one of the soldiers. They went up to Ivan, and the guy went through the age-old ritual of asking for her hand. Ivan said no. He wasn't mad at the guy; he seemed to be explaining something to both of them. More singing and crying, until someone comes in with big news, and everyone celebrates. I think the kids can get married now. Scene fades to black.

Next, we're in a castle. The music is different, more harsh and primitive. I glance at Kaz, and there's a hard look on his face, as if he's angry at what he's seeing, so I don't bother to ask him what's going on. The guys in the castle are singing and dancing, whooping it up over something. I can tell these are the bad guys, by the sneers on their faces, dark, hooded eyes, and ominous lighting. Then the music kicks off into what sounds like a polka, and I know why Kaz has that look. The bad guys are Poles.

A messenger enters and sings out some news that gets everyone in an uproar. They pound fists on the table and look like they're getting ready for trouble. So does Kaz, and I wonder when the intermission is. Not yet. We go to a humble peasant cabin in the woods. Ivan Susanin, the old Russian woodsman, sings some more, and the screen fades to a shot of a young noble boy being presented with a crown. Then I get it. The boy is the new czar, and the Poles don't like it. Ivan is getting all weepy over the czar taking the throne, so it must be a big deal.

Ivan's family gathers around him—his son and daughter, plus the soldier she wants to marry. He gives them his blessing, which is pretty clear from the smiles on their faces. I think it's got something to do with the czar. Maybe no czar, no wedding? Ivan is crazy for the czar, that much is clear. They all sing more than is necessary, especially the son, until a troop of Poles burst on the scene. Bad guys again, with the sneers and leers. They point at Ivan and his family, and the image cuts away to the young czar, hidden in a monastery. Seems the Poles are on the trail of the czar. Maybe Ivan and company know where he is?

More singing, and I wonder how much they have to say. I'm following the plot and I don't understand a single word. Ivan takes his son aside and tells him something, in a singing stage whisper. The son scoots out the door, and I figure he's going to warn the boy czar. Then Ivan does some business with the Poles. Money changes hands, and as his daughter weeps, he leaves with them. What's he up to?

A single Russian word appeared on the screen that had to mean intermission, and I hoped the opera was more than half over. The projector pulled the film through and the screen went white as the lights came on. Coughs and rustling sounds filled the air as people got up. Kaz was rigid, his fists clenched on his knees.

"This is an insult." Each word loud, spit out between clenched teeth. "An insult!" Kaz stood, kicking his chair back into a couple of admirals who were making their way back to the booze.

"Lieutenant Kazimierz," Harding said. "At ease. We are guests here."

"You invited me here to see *this*?" Kaz said to Sidorov, pointing at the screen and ignoring Harding as he pushed by me to get closer to our host. "I did not recognize the name of this cleansed Soviet version, but this is *A Life for the Czar*, a fervent anti-Polish piece of propaganda."

"Lieutenant, this is the first authentic Russian opera. I thought someone with your refined tastes would find it interesting," Sidorov said, his hands outstretched at his sides, palms up, as if bewildered at Kaz's reaction, as a crowd gathered to listen. "Yes, the czarist elements have been revised somewhat, but it is still the same opera. Just a harmless entertainment."

"Interesting? Harmless? Only a Russian butcher would describe killing Poles as entertainment!" Kaz's face was red, and he pushed by Harding, advancing on Sidorov, who stood motionless, waiting.

"Hold, Lieutenant!" Cosgrove boomed out, his loud mouth used to good purpose for once. "Do not embarrass yourself or your uniform."

Kaz stood, trembling with rage, unwilling to push Cosgrove out of his way. "You'll pay for this, Sidorov. I'll see to that, God help me." He turned and stormed by me. As I started to follow, I felt Harding's hand on my shoulder.

"Stay here, Boyle. We don't want to antagonize the Russians any further. One walkout is enough. Sit."

"But, sir," I said, as I felt his hand push me back into my seat.

"Sit," he repeated. "No more food or drink. When the damn film is over, we clap and leave. I don't know what is going on here, but we're not going to give them grounds for an incident."

"What was that all about?" I was surprised to hear Inspector Scutt from behind us. He was dressed in a well-worn tuxedo with a winged-collar shirt that probably was the height of fashion around the turn of the century.

"Nothing but a bit of a huff between the eastern Europeans," Cosgrove said. "Temperamental, that lot. This all happened in the early 1600s, and it's still fresh in their memories."

"Lieutenant Kazimierz took exception to the story line," Harding said, glaring at Sidorov, who was deep in conversation with other guests.

"I'm surprised he was invited at all," Scutt said, "with the Russians and Poles at each other's throats about their border claims and the Katyn Forest affair."

"It was a personal invitation from Kiril Sidorov," I said. "You were invited as well, Inspector?"

"I didn't crash the party, if that's what you mean. Yes, I was, and since my wife enjoys the opera, I was glad to attend. Can't say I minded the food either. I haven't seen some of those things since before the war. Enjoy the rest of the film. Strange, very strange," he muttered to himself as he turned away, drawn to the call of the *zukuski*.

It was strange. Sidorov was a smart guy. He had to figure the opera would upset Kaz or any Pole. Did he see Kaz as a fellow intellectual, expecting him to rise above the propaganda and enjoy the music? The lights flickered, and the room soon filled again.

We start off in the woods, with the soldier—did he and the girl ever get married?—singing to his men. They seem to be following the old man and the Poles. He goes on for a while, and it seems to be a morale boost of some kind. Then the scene switches to Ivan's son, at the monastery, where he warns the Russians guarding the boy czar. He points into the woods, and I get it. The Poles are coming, the Poles are coming. They take the czar to safety, wherever that is.

Next we see Ivan, leading the Poles into the forest. Snow is blowing and they tramp farther and farther into the deep woods, where the trees are laden with snow, the branches twisted and hanging low to the ground. The Poles start to look frightened, and there is a lot of singing between them, but Ivan keeps pointing ahead, and suddenly it seems like I can understand. Just over that next hill, he's saying, we're almost there. Night falls, and the Poles hunker down, casting suspicious glances at the old man, who stands apart. Ivan sings a long aria, and he's got to be saying his good-byes, to his children, his czar, his life. He's led the Poles here, into the deep, dark forest, and they will never find their way out. Dawn comes, and as the Poles awake, a blizzard sets in along with the realization that they've been had. They break out the knives and kill Ivan Susanin.

Then comes the epilogue. We're in Moscow, Red Square by the look of the buildings. The boy czar made it there safely, and everyone sings his praises. Ivan's son and daughter and her husband look despondent. Maybe he found Ivan and the dead Poles? They have a conversation with some Russian troops, who lead them into the square. It looks like the people know what Ivan did, and the film closes with songs of triumph, the masses heralding their new boss and the hero of the hour.

The applause was loud and instantaneous. Harding and I clapped twice, out of diplomatic courtesy only, but I had to admit, it was a rousing ending. Good propaganda for the international opera crowd. The wily Russian defeating the invader, sacrificing himself for the greater good.

"Please give my apologies to your Polish friend, Lieutenant Boyle," Sidorov said as we passed him at the end of the row. "I meant no insult by inviting him here. I thought sharing a common love of the opera would be a way to bridge the gap between us."

"Do you know all the likes and dislikes of officers serving with the Polish government in London?" I asked. "Don't any others like the opera?"

"You are not a naive man, Lieutenant. Surely you can understand why I would extend the hand of friendship to Lieutenant Kazimierz. He is your friend, and you are General Eisenhower's nephew. And it is my business to know the likes and dislikes of important and influential people in London, even those of mere lieutenants. For instance," Sidorov said, leaning in to whisper in my ear, "I know you care very much for a certain young British woman, who at this moment may be at great risk behind enemy lines." Sidorov stood back and smiled, enjoying the look of astonishment on my face. Then he allowed himself to be swept up in the tide of guests leaving the ballroom, in search of cold vodka and luke-warm little bites.

"What did Sidorov say to you?" Harding asked as we walked out into the cold night air.

"He basically told me they have a spy in MI5," I said. "He knows about Diana."

"What about her?"

"That she and I are an item, and that she is at risk behind the lines."

"You and she aren't a secret, Boyle."

"But that she's a spy? He has to have inside information. But why tell me? It didn't sound like a threat in any way, it was said casually."

"It could be anything," Harding said. "They could have a sympathizer in MI5, or one of their own agents came into contact with her. Whichever, you stay out of it, and get down to Dover tomorrow. I'll inform Major Cosgrove first thing in the morning. We'll put Diana's file on a need-to-know basis. Meanwhile, you tell Lieutenant Kazimierz to take a week's leave. Tell him to lie low, go to the country, whatever. Got that?"

Before I could answer, the wail of sirens rose from all around us, and searchlights to the east, past Kensington Gardens and Hyde Park, switched on and stabbed at the darkness. The steady beat of antiaircraft fire filled the air along with tracers and explosive *crumps* as shells explod-ed in the sky.

"There, over the docks," Harding said, pointing. With the parks in front of us, we had a clear view toward the east, and we could see lines of explosions as bombs hit all around the river. This raid was better organized than the one the other night. Instead of scattered bombs, the Luftwaffe bombers were in tight formation, and their bomb loads fell as one, send-ing thundering explosions through the factories, warehouses, docks, and homes of the East End.

We walked through Hyde Park, watching the destruction at a dis-tance, feeling oddly safe and suicidal at the same time. One bomber went down in flames, lighting up a distant section of the city as it slammed into buildings on its final fiery assault. In the glare of the searchlights I spotted two parachutes, and wondered if the aircrew would survive the drop into a city, or be consumed by flames reaching into the sky. Within minutes the bombs stopped, but the desperate firing kept up, until it too faded away, leaving only the sounds of sirens and secondary explosions to echo across the wounded city. Flames glowed in the distance, muted by the smoke churned up and sent to drift on the wind, as if protecting our eyes from the brilliant immolation of flesh, steel, and stone.

CHAPTER SIXTEEN

KAZ WAS BACK at the hotel, sitting in the dark, in front of the windows that faced Hyde Park, the drapes wide open. The reflected glow of the fires from the East End gave the bare trees a desperate, terrified look, as if their branches were arms raised in horror, ready to scream and bolt from the cold, hard earth.

"You shouldn't sit in front of the glass," I said, settling for an air-raid warden's warning since I didn't know what else to say.

"The bombing is over. Only the fires remain." Kaz drained his glass, then poured himself more vodka. His uniform jacket was thrown over the back of the chair, his tie was loose, and his revolver sat on the table next to him. I joined him, resigned to more hard liquor, hoping it would either dull me into uncaring sleep or sharpen my mind, granting some insight into what was going on around me. I knew it was a foolish wish, and that nothing would come of it but a headache and regret. Still, I drank.

"Interesting night," I said.

"I lost control," Kaz said. "Once I recognized the opera, I knew he had invited me as a deliberate provocation. *A Life for the Czar* was the first Russian opera, but the Communists changed the title, I assume, so as not to give the czar top billing."

"Harding wants you to lie low for a while. Maybe leave London for a few days."

"That's all? I am surprised I haven't lost my commission."

"Maybe that's why he wants you to scram, before it comes to that."

"You know, Billy, it is a horrible thing to have your country occupied by the Nazis, with the only liberation it can look forward to coming from the Soviet Union. Poles are fighting and dying, but for what? The Americans and English turn a blind eye to the murders of thousands of Polish officers by the Russians, and meanwhile Stalin lays claim to a postwar border that annexes a third of Poland. Tell me, Billy, what have they died for—all the Poles in the RAF, the Royal Navy, and the infantry in Italy? To trade a Fascist master for a dictatorship of the proletariat? Tell me."

"Could you stand by and do nothing ? Not fight one dictator because of another?"

"No. I don't think so," Kaz said. He began to pour another glass, but set down the bottle. "Better to hope that something honorable will come out of this war than to sit on the sidelines."

"Yeah. There's always a chance."

"Spoken like a true American optimist. But you are also an Irish Catholic, so you know the odds of relying on the English Empire to solve another nation's problems are slim. I would guess that most Irish Republicans are pessimists by now, wouldn't you?"

"Maybe. But they do have their own nation, or most of it. And you don't win your freedom without being a bit of an optimist. Both Americans and Irish know something about that."

"Very well, Billy. I shall work to remain an optimist. Who knows?" He filled our glasses and we raised them high, the empty-headed toasting the unknown.

"Something very odd happened after you left," I said. "Sidorov dropped a heavy hint that he knew about Diana and her SOE mission. Said it was his business to know about people—meaning you and me— and that he even knew about my relationship with a young British woman on a mission behind enemy lines. No specifics, but he described the broad outline."

"What does that mean? Was it a threat?"

"No, that's what's odd. It felt more like a tip-off. The only way for Sidorov to know about Diana would be if he were in contact with a spy within MI5 or MI6."

"A spy, or a talkative secretary, or an officer being blackmailed. Perhaps he's trading information. Still, it is strange that he should tell you."

"There are plenty of Communists in Italy, right?"

"Certainly. France as well. They are maneuvering among the partisan groups for power after the war. Why?"

"Could Sidorov be in touch with them?"

"I don't know. It would take a sophisticated communications system. Or a courier to Switzerland, perhaps. Being neutral, travel would not be impossible."

"The Vatican is neutral, and I'm fairly certain that's where Diana is headed."

"It is possible. Vatican City is full of spies, along with Jews in hiding, Allied airmen shot down over Italy, and diplomats from many nations. I doubt there are any Communist partisans there, but they are definitely close by in Rome. If any high-level communications go through the Vatican, and if the Russians are involved, it might be monitored by their embassy here in London."

"Where Sidorov, as an NKVD man, would have access."

"Who could say no to him?"

I sat for a while longer, trying to put the pieces together, but nothing fit, nothing made sense. I was left with dread and fear, wondering at the unseen forces gathering around Diana. Had she been betrayed? Arrested and tortured? Or was she sleeping soundly, safe, oblivious to news of her mission being passed on to the Soviets? The eerie glow in the park faded, and the dark night took over, masking even the largest and tallest trees. I waited for sleep to find me.

KAZ WAS ALREADY up and out by the time I rolled out of the sack. I didn't mind missing the morning workout, so I got going before he came back and made me do push-ups. Crossing St. James's Square, I spotted a familiar truck parked in front of Norfolk House. The canvas covering was lashed down tight, but the two MPs guarding it told me what I already knew—that Big Mike's scheme had worked.

"Nice work," I told Big Mike as I entered the office. "That didn't take long."

"Nope. A driver parked it there right before dawn, and told the MP on duty to thank Lieutenant Boyle for the peaches. They left the fifty cases, just like we wanted."

"Good. That puts us out of Dutch with Harding?"

"Think so. He seemed satisfied. We probably have more to worry about from Chapman than the colonel. Speaking of the Chapmans, Major Cosgrove sent this over. You're to read it now, and I have to return it to him by noon."

It was the file on Topper Chapman. I sat down and opened it, going through the biographical information first. Topper was born in 1919, and his mother died in the influenza epidemic. That left him to be raised under the sole care of Archie Chapman, and I wondered how much poetry from the trenches Archie had subjected young Topper to. Topper had dropped out of school at age fourteen, as soon as he legally could. A report from his school noted he was highly intelligent but difficult to control. He was placed in a remand home for a month, awaiting charges on a series of burglaries, but the charges were dropped, and he was never arrested again. Not because he gave up a life of crime, but through fear and intimidation due to his father's growing criminal empire, based in Shoreditch and extending along the river to the Isle of Dogs, where the Chapmans had a running border dispute with a neighboring gang.

There were few entries from the 1930s, except to note that Topper's ascendency within the Chapman organization shielded him from scrutiny, as he assumed more of a management role. For 1940, there were two crucial events. In January, rationing was instituted in Great Britain. With that, the Chapman gang began working the black market, ranging far afield to raid farms north of London, stealing chickens and geese. They soon escalated to hijacking lorries. A few gang members were caught, but they took their punishment and no one turned on the Chapmans. It was wryly noted that all the gang members came from Shoreditch and had families there.

The other significant event came in June, after Dunkirk. Topper Chapman enlisted in the army. He had been exempt from conscription as a dockworker, which was deemed a reserve occupation, immune from the draft. I doubted Topper did a lick of work on the docks, but his father knew how to pull the right strings. He went through the physical exam and was ready to leave for training when a London doctor by the name of Edgar Carlisle submitted a letter stating that Topper Chapman had been under his care since he was a child, and that Topper suffered from a heart murmur and had had a serious bout of rheumatic fever at age ten, which rendered him unfit for military service.

So Topper was a would-be patriot. There had been an odd current between Archie and Topper when I'd asked about his not being in uniform. Health reasons, Archie had said. London's dangerous enough, Topper had said. Something told me he wasn't referring to bombs or the police. His own father, maybe? I got on the phone and called New Scotland Yard. Scutt wasn't in, but I got through to Detective Sergeant Flack.

"Do you know a Dr. Edgar Carlisle?" I asked.

"I know of him," Flack said. "Likes the good life. Doesn't mind sewing up the odd gangster and pocketing a nice fee for keeping a knife or gunshot wound quiet. Never been able to prove anything, but I'm sure he's not entirely straight."

"Would he falsify records? Lie about a medical condition to keep someone out of the service?"

"Hm. Not sure about that, Boyle. That means putting his name on a piece of paper. He's more careful than that."

"What if it were at the request of Archie Chapman?"

"Oh. Well then, as I said, Dr. Carlisle likes the good life, and you have to be alive to enjoy it."

"OK, thanks, that's a help."

"Wait, Boyle, don't hang up. I was about to call you. Inspector Scutt wants you to meet him at the Rubens Hotel. There's been a murder there."

"Who?"

"We don't know yet, the call just came in. Somebody's been stabbed is all I know. Inspector Scutt thought you might want to know."

"Thanks, I'll be right there." My heart was pounding and my stomach felt like it had hit the floor. I didn't know what to worry about, Kaz being the victim or the killer. I gave the file back to Big Mike and hustled over to the Rubens.

I found Inspector Scutt standing on the sidewalk, watching the traffic on Buckingham Palace Road. He had his hands in his pockets and was rocking slowly on his heels, the practiced, efficient motion of a cop who has spent plenty of time waiting on hard pavement. The wind was up and there was a hard bite of cold in the air, damp and clammy from the river, overlaid with the smell of smoke from last night's fires.

"There you are, Lieutenant Boyle," Scutt said, his eyes narrowing as he studied me. "Thought you'd want to see this. Just in time, too. We've finished with the crime scene, and they're about to take the body away."

"Who is it?" I asked, following him down the narrow alleyway that I knew led to the staff door. He didn't answer. Beyond the stairs to the entrance a pair of legs was barely visible. Scutt gestured and I moved forward, in front of the body. Lying on the brickwork, with a knife driven deep into his chest, was Eddie Miller. His eyes were wide open, the mouth gaping in amazement, either at the shock of being stabbed or in surprise at the person who stabbed him. Or both. There wasn't much blood staining the white shirt he wore under his open overcoat. He'd died quickly.

"Was he on his way in or out of work?" I asked.

"He was at work, according to the manager. Why?"

"It's cold, and his jacket was open. Maybe he threw it on to come outside and sneak a smoke. Or grab a bite; there are crumbs scattered on the ground."

"Or to meet someone."

"What do you mean?" I knew what he was thinking. He had to mean Kaz. Kaz was my only link to the hotel. Why else would Scutt think I'd want to see Eddie dead in an alleyway? We both knew he was an informer, but other than that, what was important for me here?

"See this," Scutt said, and handed me a folded piece of paper. On it were the typewritten words MEET ME OUTSIDE, 8:00. "It was in his shirt pocket."

"No name," I said. "But he must've known who it was, don't you think? Otherwise why take it seriously?"

"Curiosity, perhaps, but I'm inclined to agree with you. He didn't confide in anyone, if the other staff are to be believed."

"Anything else on him?"

"Besides his billfold, a train ticket to Plymouth. First class, rather extravagant for a waiter."

"Any idea what's in Plymouth that would interest him?"

"No idea. He has family in Shoeburyness, a little town at the mouth of the Thames," Scutt said, consulting his notebook. "None of the hotel staff I talked with remembered him mentioning Plymouth. Tell me, did you know him well, Lieutenant Boyle?"

"I met him, when I came to visit Kaz," I said, close enough to the truth to satisfy a lawyer.

"So Lieutenant Kazimierz knew him personally?"

"Sure, he worked the Polish floor regularly. I imagine they all knew him, to some extent. Why the interest? Why did you call me here?"

"You share rooms with Lieutenant Kazimierz at the Dorchester, correct?"

"Yes, but what does—"

"Bear with me, Lieutenant. We sent someone over there earlier to find you both. Gent at the desk said he'd seen you leave, but not Kazimierz. He wasn't in his room. Any idea where he is?"

"He usually walks in the park, but very early. I don't know where he is now. After last night, Colonel Harding told him to lie low for a while, maybe leave London for a few days. He could have left this morning."

"Yes, last night. Very odd, wouldn't you say?"

"Well, I'm not much on opera, but I agree it was strange for Sidorov to invite him to that particular one."

"I'm not referring to that, Lieutenant Boyle. I'm referring to what Kazimierz said. He called Sidorov a butcher, and said he would pay, something along those lines, wasn't it?"

"Yeah. So?"

"Look at the knife. It's a bayonet, as you'll see. Don't touch it, but look at the marking." I knelt, peering at the shaft of the bayonet, keeping my hands on the ground to steady myself and not topple onto poor Eddie. I could see a symbol, an eagle, stamped into the metal. Next to it were the letters *W.P.*

"That's the Polish eagle," Scutt said. "And they tell me *W.P.* stands for Wojsko Polskie, Polish Army."

"What are you after, Inspector?"

"The truth, Lieutenant." Scutt nodded at the men standing by the body, ready to transport it to the morgue. "Let's step inside; it's too cold out here for these old bones."

We sat in two armchairs in the lobby, away from the flow of officers, staff, police, and guests. Scutt leaned forward and beckoned me closer. "You know of the Special Branch?"

"Yes. Started off as the Irish Special Branch, right?"

"It did, back when the Fenians were setting off bombs in London, in the 1880s, as if that might scare the Crown out of Ireland. Today, Special Branch specializes in intelligence gathering, foreign nationals, and coordinating with MI5 in particular. I called them after I got here and saw it was this Miller chap."

"Why?"

"Oh, a policeman's hunch. I've been doing this for decades, and I've got a sense for when things don't smell right. This didn't. With you nosing around, and after last night, it was just too much of a coincidence."

"What did Special Branch say?"

"I think you may know most of it, but as a professional courtesy, I won't put you on the spot. Edward Miller was not only a paid informer for the Soviets, but a member of the Communist Party. Had been, for the past six years."

"You didn't know that?"

"Not the bit about him being a card-carrying Bolshevik. I just learned that this morning. Now I'm telling you, because it points to your friend Lieutenant Kazimierz."

"Why, because he got steamed at Sidorov last night? You think he decided to murder the first Red he saw the next morning?"

"From all the talk of the Katyn Forest Massacre in the newspapers, I'd say he'd have had plenty of reason even before this morning."

"So would any Polish officer in this building. And listen, Kaz and Captain Radecki were paying Eddie to feed bad information to the Russians. Why would they kill him?" As I said that, I remembered what Radecki had said to Eddie. *If you perform well, we will pay you. If not, we will kill you.*

"Revenge, betrayal, there are many reasons for murder, all of them base. Come with me, I have something to show you," Scutt said, rising with a groan, slowly straightening his back. "I tell you, I can't wait for this war to be over, if only to get on with my retirement."

We entered what until the day before had been Kaz's office on the floor where the Polish Government in Exile was housed. A uniformed constable stood by Kaz's desk, as Major Stefan Horak approached Scutt, clearly agitated.

"I cannot believe this, Inspector. There must be some mistake," Horak said.

"What's going on?" I asked. Neither met my eyes.

"Look here, Lieutenant Boyle," Scutt said, taking control of the situation. "We searched Kazimierz's desk. He'd cleaned most everything out, but see what we found in the bottom drawer." He opened it and used his pen to push aside a few scraps of paper and an empty file. There, at the bottom, was a single bullet. A .32-caliber bullet, with fresh marks on the jacket nose where someone had filed an *X*, creating a homemade dumdum bullet.

"It appears Lieutenant Kazimierz forgot something," Scutt said.

"It only appears that someone placed this bullet in this drawer," I said. "He cleared everything out yesterday, didn't he? A dozen people could have put it there. Any rookie could tell you that."

"Perhaps," Scutt admitted. "We may learn something if there are any fingerprints on it, or on the bayonet."

"I must protest, Inspector," Major Horak said. "This is an open area; the desks are not guarded. Who knows who placed the bullet there?"

"True enough," Scutt said. "But why would anyone? Who here would want to frame Lieutenant Kazimierz for murder?"

"No one, of course," Horak said, and then stopped as the logic sunk in. If it wasn't a frame-up, then it *was* Kaz's bullet.

"When was he here last?" Scutt said.

"Yesterday," Horak said. "He came in midday to finish some paperwork, then he and Captain Radecki lunched downstairs. He came up to say good-bye to the staff, and departed."

"Then he couldn't have left the note for Eddie. It was found this morning."

"The staff changes their clothes here. Eddie was working the early shift this week. Eddie would be certain to find it this morning, as it appears he did. Lieutenant Kazimierz could have easily placed it in his pocket before he left yesterday."

"Have you questioned Sheila, on the hotel staff? She and Eddie seemed close."

"Sheila Carlson," Scutt said, consulting his notebook. "Today is her day off. We'll get to her soon enough. We're short staffed, with men rounding up more Germans each night. Nabbed half a dozen down in Croydon before dawn this morning." He sighed and pocketed his notebook, his heavy eyelids showing his exhaustion.

"Major Horak," I said. "Do you store weapons here?"

"No, only the sidearms we carry. The guards bring their weapons from the barracks."

"No rifles, no bayonets?"

"No. But come with me." Horak led us down the hall, to another, larger office, with Radecki's name on the door. It was spacious, by army standards. There was a table, and behind it a bookshelf held volumes in English and Polish. Framed pictures were arranged around a battered green helmet. "It's gone," Horak said.

"What is?"

"Valerian's bayonet. He is very proud of it, and the helmet. He was stationed with our border troops in the east and fought against the Russians. He escaped after all was lost, and is proud he never surrendered his weapons. They wouldn't let him travel through Romania with his rifle, but he did keep everything else. The bayonet has always been right here, with his helmet."

"Well, it found its way into Eddie Miller's chest," Scutt said, showing little care for Radecki's wartime exploits. "Where is this fellow now?"

"He is visiting Station Number Eight," Horak said, his discomfort visible as he looked away and spoke in a strangled whisper.

"What in blazes is Station Number Eight?" Scutt said, his anger rising. "And tell me where it is, for that matter!"

"I am afraid I can't, Inspector," Horak said. "I have my orders, which come in part from your own government. I can tell you Captain Radecki is on an assignment and I expect him back within the week."

"Is he here in London?"

"He has not left England. More than that, I simply am not allowed to say."

"You get in touch with him, and tell him Scotland Yard wants a word," Scutt said, and left the room, muttering loudly enough to be heard. "Not left England! Who the bloody hell has?"

"The inspector is not a happy man," Horak said.

"His feet hurt," I said. "Occupational hazard for policemen. Did Radecki and Kaz often lunch together? I didn't get the impression they were all that friendly."

"Lieutenant Kazimierz, you mean? It seems you Americans must shorten every name with more than two syllables. I'm sorry," he said, waving his hand as if to erase what he'd said. "No, they weren't especially friendly. They differed over the treatment of Tadeusz Tucholski, the young man you met."

"How so?"

"Captain Radecki pushed Tadeusz hard. He said it would be best for him to get everything out in the open. Lieutenant Kazimierz said Tadeusz needed time, and comforting."

"What did you think?"

"I think we have very little time. But we needed to strike a balance, and I fear Captain Radecki was too adamant and caused Tadeusz to retreat into himself. I had to agree when Lieutenant Kazimierz suggested a break. We've used the facility at St. Albans before. It's a sanatorium, run by the military, very secure. They specialize in treating shell shock. We hope it will help, but one never knows."

"What was it exactly that led you to decide to place him in a sanatorium?" I picked up the helmet displayed on Radecki's shelves. It was heavy, the brim a bit wider than ours. I put it back, staring at the shelves. I had no idea what I was looking for.

"Tadeusz slept more than usual," Horak said, tapping a Wills Four Aces cigarette down on the yellow tin case before lighting it. "He always slept after telling his story, but it began to happen more and more. Even when he was awake, he was lethargic in the extreme. You heard his last coherent words, Lieutenant Boyle."

"It must have been hard for him, reliving it on demand." I walked in back of Radecki's table, wondering what he and Kaz had talked about at lunch yesterday.

"Too hard, apparently," Horak said, blowing smoke up to the ceiling. "If you don't mind my asking, why does it matter to you?"

"I don't like the idea of Scutt considering Kaz as a suspect."

"Then you won't like what I am about to tell you. Captain Radecki spoke with your friend in this office before they went to lunch. I came in to say good-bye to Lieutenant Kazimierz, and saw Radecki showing him his souvenirs. The lieutenant was handling the bayonet, feeling the heft of it."

"So Kaz's fingerprints will be all over it."

"Unfortunately so," Horak said. "Unless the killer wiped them away, along with his own."

"He probably wore gloves. It's cold enough outside to not be noticed. What worries me is that it had to be someone who wouldn't have looked out of place in your offices, or elsewhere in the hotel. He had to have typed that note and left it for Eddie yesterday, and then taken the bayo-net, either last night or early this morning. When did Radecki leave?"

"Sometime late yesterday afternoon. He was gone when I returned here a little after five o'clock."

"So the bayonet could have been taken yesterday. You didn't see it?"

"I only saw that his office was empty."

"I suppose anyone could walk in there?"

"Once a person gains admittance to this floor, there are really no restrictions. Plus, we have hotel staff coming and going. Waiters, cleaning people, and so on."

"Eddie, of course. And Sheila Carlson?"

"Yes, she's been working on this floor for a month or so. Nice young girl."

"Do you mind if I use the telephone?" I asked, sitting at Radecki's table. Horak shrugged, ground out his cigarette, and told me to make myself comfortable. I did, and called Norfolk House to ask Harding if he'd send Big Mike over to pick me up and help look for Kaz. I had an idea he might pay a visit to Tadeusz, and that a drive up to St. Albans might turn him up. The switchboard put me on hold and, believing that idle hands are the devil's workshop, I let them pull open the drawers on Radecki's desk.

File folders full of papers typed in Polish. Notepads, none of the writing in English. A map of London, a pack of cigarettes, paper clips, a pencil stub. The usual office debris. The last drawer on the right held a first aid kit, along with a small glass bottle labeled TINCTURE OF OPIUM. LAUDANUM. Radecki probably had a spare with him, if his leg hurt as much as it seemed to. The doctor's name and address were on the label. H. T. Ruskin, Horseferry Street, about a ten-minute walk. Harding came on the line and I shut the drawer. He said Big Mike was available, and that he'd come right over.

I set the receiver down and tried to get my jumbled thoughts in order. Kaz was in trouble, or damn close to it. If I was right about his going to St. Albans, it would give me a chance to warn him of Scutt's suspicions. Nothing made sense about Eddie Miller's killing. If Sidorov figured out Eddie had turned on him, the smart money would bet on his playing along. Knowing Eddie was feeding him bad information could point him to the truth, or at least to its neighborhood. As for Kaz and any of the other Poles, Eddie was too valuable alive; there was no percentage in killing him. As for what I was supposed to be investigating, the murder of Gennady Egorov, the only loose thread I had to pull was Topper. He and his father didn't see eye to eye on his wish to serve king and country, and while I could appreciate the elder Chapman's desire to keep his offspring alive it also gave me something to exploit. If I could drive them apart, the truth might have a chance to slither out between them. There seemed to be a link between the truck hijackings and Egorov's murder. Somewhere in all this, there were connections that made sense, connections that would explain everything. I just couldn't see them yet.

I took the street map of London, figuring Radecki wouldn't need it while he was at Station Number Eight. I opened it up to see if by chance he'd marked the location with a nice big 8, but no dice. One street in Camberwell, south of the Thames, was marked. Penford Street, number 420. He had made a show of giving Eddie Miller the message that he knew where Eddie lived, reciting the address when he looked through Eddie's wallet. Was this simply a reminder, or had he planned on making a visit? Probably a reminder, I decided, since he could always talk to Eddie at the hotel. But if he needed to make good on his threat, a home visit would be more intimidating.

I stood, taking in the framed pictures Radecki kept on the shelves behind his desk. Family pictures—Valerian Radecki in civilian clothes with a pretty wife and two young children, the oldest no more than six. It looked like a picnic, blankets spread by a lake, smiling faces drenched in sunlight. Another was of Radecki in uniform, standing with an older man who was probably his father, in front of a small factory.

"All dead," Horak said. I hadn't heard him come in, intent on studying photographs of a happier time. "His father was killed when the Germans bombed Warsaw. He owned a steelworks, and was in the building when it took a direct hit."

"His wife and children?"

"Stuka dive-bombers. They were in a column of refugees, heading out of Warsaw, when the road was bombed and strafed. They and many others were killed."

"Senseless," I said, stunned once again at the scale of the losses endured.

"From a strictly military point of view, it is not senseless. Such attacks are designed to deny the enemy freedom of movement. If civilians cannot move, neither can troops. The road is left littered with burning hulks of automobiles and carts. Dead horses, dead civilians. Soldiers must dismount from their vehicles and walk around the carnage, demoralizing and weakening them. Is it not terrible, that we live in a time where such a horrible thing is done with purpose? Personally, I would prefer unthinking evil."

I didn't answer Horak. I left, descending the elegant staircase, passing under the crystal chandelier, pulling my coat on, and turning my collar up before I'd even gone outside, wishing I could shield myself from the ghosts and memories haunting the exiled and doomed Poles.

CHAPTER SEVENTEEN

"WHERE TO, BILLY?" Big Mike said as I got into the jeep.

"Camberwell, across the river. Take the Vauxhall Bridge."

"That where Kaz is?" Big Mike said as he turned left in front of Victoria Station.

"No. It's where Eddie Miller lived. He was the snitch for Sidorov."

"Past tense?"

"Yeah. Somebody put a Polish bayonet through his heart early this morning. It belonged to Valerian Radecki, one of the Polish officers Kaz worked with. Major Horak saw Kaz handling it yesterday."

"Fingerprints," Big Mike said, nodding his head as he drove, visualizing the frame with his inner cop's eye. "Who showed it to him, Radecki?"

"Yes, it was one of his souvenirs."

"Then it's going to have his prints, Kaz's, and the killer's. Or none."

"Right," I said, agreeing silently that Kaz was not the murderer.

"We trying to beat Scotland Yard to Eddie's house?"

"We might not have to try too hard," I said as we crossed the bridge, Big Ben visible downriver, its sharp spire silhouetted against white clouds drifting over the city. "Scutt says he's shorthanded. He had to send men out to hunt for Krauts."

"Harding said the docks took some scattered hits, but we shot down a dozen bombers, between flak and the night fighters," Big Mike said. "Not that you'd know from the newspapers. The Brits play their cards close in, know what I mean?"

"Yeah, I do," I said as I pointed out our next turn, onto Brixton Road. Big Mike had a point, and I wondered what connections I might be missing entirely. Connections between Major Cosgrove, MI5, and who else? The Poles, the Russians, the Chapman gang, or the local Communist Party?

Penford Street was one of several short side streets about a block from the railroad. A tall brick wall screened the view but not the noise as a freight train lumbered by. The street was neat and well kept, three-story row houses in uniform brown brick, white-painted trim, and the typical London door, lacquered in different colors. Eddie's was deep blue, and as we walked up the steps, it opened, and out came Sheila Carlson.

"Oh," she said, startled by the near collision. She seemed to be in a hurry, her eyes darting out to the street, in a rush to leave Eddie's house behind her. Her eyes took a second to settle down and focus on my face, and then they widened as she recognized me from the hotel.

"Oh no, please don't. Oh no, no," she muttered, as she took in my presence there and the towering form of Big Mike behind me. She thought she was looking at death itself. She put her hands on the door frame to steady herself, her face gone white, her mouth a gaping circle, little puffs of air escaping with each *oh, oh,* and none going in, like a gasping fish on dry land. I went to take her arm, which was a mistake.

"No!" she shouted, her voice finding anger as she swung her pocketbook, slamming me in the side of my face. I felt a sharp pain, a razor slice on my cheekbone, as a reinforced metal corner of the purse ripped at my skin. The bag flew out of her hand, opening and scattering all sorts of female accoutrements on the landing. Mixed in among the lipstick, compact, handkerchief, and change purse was a creamy white envelope from the Rubens Hotel, a thick wad of pound notes bulging out of it.

"Oh no," Sheila said again, a resigned sadness replacing the anger. Her hand went to her mouth to contain the sobs that were building. Her eyes were red, crusted with dried tears, and I knew there would be no more exclamations from her. Everything was lost now; she knew about Eddie, her bankroll was at my feet, and she was sure her neck was about to be broken by the Yank who'd slapped around her boyfriend, if not the giant standing behind him.

I felt a warm, thin trickle inch its way down my cheek. Big Mike knelt to gather the contents of the handbag, and handed me the handkerchief. "Hold this to your cheek, Billy. And you, lady, inside." He pointed to the interior, and she turned, seeming to understand from his tone that these might not be her last moments. She shuffled along with the certainty that they would not be among her best.

Big Mike introduced us, told her to sit on the couch, pushed me down into an armchair, and told both of us not to move. We didn't. He came back with a towel, bandages, and iodine, having raided the bathroom cabinet. Sheila dabbed at her eyes with a small lace handkerchief she took from her coat pocket. It was a plain utility coat, one of the government designs to reduce the use of rationed material. Sheila had tried to spice it up with a bright blue scarf, but drab was drab.

"Ow! Easy on the iodine, Big Mike." I jerked my head away.

"I'm sorry," Sheila said, in a timid voice.

"Me, too," I said. I looked around the room. It was furnished with the bare necessities—one floor lamp, the couch and chair, a radio, a side table, and a threadbare carpet. Dreary. A utility room. But a porcelain figure of a woman holding a vase was displayed on the side table. It was colorful, like Sheila's scarf. Light streamed in through the bow window next to the front door, beneath which a large green plant with pink flowers—an oleander—sat on a low table, soaking up the sun. It was evident someone was trying to brighten up the place. "Did you see who killed him?"

"No . . . how did you know?"

"You weren't at work. You're here, rushing out of Eddie's house with a wad of cash. Why else would you be on the lam? I don't think you were playing him for a sap, were you?"

"No, I...I loved him," she said, breathing a heavy sigh. I guessed all the tears had dried up, first replaced by a determination to get away with what she could, and now by the futility of it all. She was ready to open up. People who get drawn into things, things beyond their own imaginings, are lost without the person who had involved them in the first place. Sheila was lost, and while we weren't much, we were here, exuding uniformed authority, even as I winced over Big Mike's first aid.

"You found him dead in the alley, probably a little after eight o'clock," I said.

"Yes. It was awful. We were supposed to come back here, pack up, and leave. Eddie said he was going to be paid a bonus for his work, enough money to give us a new start."

"His work?"

"That's what he called it. He worked for our Allies, the Russians."

"Spying on our Allies, the Poles."

"It was all for the war effort, don't you see? To be sure nothing got in the way of victory, that's what Eddie said."

"What about your work?" I said.

"What do you mean?"

"You're an informant for Scotland Yard. You told them I beat Eddie senseless."

"I'm no informer, and you better not say so again," Sheila said, her lips compressed into a thin line of lipstick the color of blood. "Yes, I pass on the odd tidbit now and then, plenty of people do. They wouldn't pay if it wasn't important, now would they?"

"I can't argue with that logic, Sheila. Did you see anybody or anything this morning, when you found Eddie?"

"No, I saw that big knife sticking out of him and I knew he was dead. I didn't wait around for whoever did it to take notice of me."

"So no one saw you there?"

"No one from the hotel, if that's what you mean. But I couldn't take a chance, so I came back here, grabbed Eddie's wages—I mean our money—and walked straight into you two. It *is* our money, you know. We were going away together, going to get married," she said, her chin lifting her face into a profile of respectability.

"Where did Eddie get the money?"

"Some from the Russians, but they didn't pay very well. Eddie had been a Party member a few years back, and they expected him to do it for the cause."

"The rest?"

"He was being paid to keep a secret."

"He was blackmailing someone, you mean."

"It was part of his war work, he said. He'd found something out, and he said it was important. Eddie was smart like that, he could suss things out that no one else could."

"Did he tell you who?" I said, not pointing out the obvious fact that Eddie hadn't been smart enough to suss out a bayonet to the chest.

"No," she said hesitantly, shaking her head, as if to rid herself of a bad memory. "He didn't."

"Come on, Sheila," Big Mike said, moving closer and looking down on her. "You two were partners in blackmail. Engaged to be married. Are you trying to tell us Eddie didn't trust you?" He stood with his arms akimbo, the big bad cop.

"He did. Eddie was a good man, he looked out for me! Don't you dare suggest otherwise!"

"I bet he did," I said, mustering all the sincerity I could. "I'd guess he was protecting you, wasn't he? If you didn't know who it was, you couldn't be hurt."

"That's exactly what Eddie said." Sheila looked up to Big Mike, flicking her head toward me. "Your lieutenant understands. A gentleman wouldn't place his intended in harm's way. That's what Eddie called it. Harm's way, and he wanted me to stay out of it."

"Did he say anything about what he'd discovered? Not who, but what?"

"He'd give me a hint now and then. The way I had it figured, it was drugs."

"Somebody at the hotel was an addict? One of the Poles?"

"He never came out and said it, but I always felt it was more that the fellow was a supplier."

"Why?"

"Well," Sheila said, leaning in and speaking in a whisper, as if Eddie might be listening in the other room, "one afternoon Eddie was late. We used to meet at work, when we could, in one of the empty rooms. I was angry, since I had only a few minutes left before they noticed me gone. Right angry with him, actually. So he told me he'd had to run over to Horseferry Street, to pick up this fellow's drugs. I could tell right away he wished he hadn't said it, but he had. I said he must be a terrible dope fiend, and Eddie laughed and said it wasn't for him. That was all, he wouldn't speak another word about it."

"Horseferry Street? You're sure?"

"I'm positive. Now I'd like my money back, please, unless you two are thieves and intend to rob me."

"You could always go to the police," Big Mike said, "and tell them a couple of Yanks stole your blackmail money."

"You could go to hell, how about that?"

"Listen," I said. "This is evidence. I'm going to give it to Inspector Scutt at Scotland Yard. He'll decide how much, if any, you'll get back."

"It's gone then, all gone," Sheila said, tears rolling down her cheeks as she mourned the packet of pound notes. "Have some pity, will you? My man's dead, I'm alone, and a killer may be after me. What am I supposed to do?"

"Here," I said, pulling four of the large white five-pound notes from the envelope. "Lie low for a while."

"What? You think a few of them five jacks will get me far? You must be mad, both of you."

"Listen, sister," Big Mike said, squatting so he came face to face with her, "if it were up to me, I'd bring you and the money to Scotland Yard, and be glad to see you put in a cell. Lieutenant Boyle here is giving you your walking papers, and some ready cash besides. And you're complaining?"

"We had such grand plans," Sheila said, sniffling. "We were going to Shoeburyness together, today, as soon as he got home. It's a lovely little town, right on the seashore. Eddie was going to bring me around to meet his mum."

"I'm sorry for your loss, Sheila," I said, but I didn't mean it. Eddie's death saved her from being left behind, discarded at the last minute as he rode the train alone to Plymouth, almost two hundred miles in the opposite direction, far from London and Shoeburyness. She was just a chump, a girl Eddie used to fill his time while he accumulated his wages from blackmail and betrayal. I doubted she would've gotten even twenty pounds from him, so I figured she was ahead on the deal. A little cash, and a story that would undoubtedly turn into a tale of a secret agent killed in the line of duty, just as they were about to walk down the aisle. She had no idea how lucky she was.

We waited for Sheila to put some things into a bag. I walked around the apartment, looking for anything out of place, anything that could remotely be considered a clue. There was nothing except a few traces of female domesticity that Sheila had brought to the place. The plant with bright green leaves, a few of which lay in the sink, and the remnants of baking were left in the kitchen. Unwashed bowls and rotting apple peels stood in the sink. A cutting board with flour still dusted over it, next to gardening gloves left on the kitchen table. An empty container marked SUGAR lay on its side, a line of white granules sparkling on the counter. Two cake pans, large and small, sat soaking in the sink. With sugar rationed at three ounces a month, she must've been baking something special. Home life interrupted by murder.

Sheila came down the stairs and gave me the name and address of an aunt she was going to stay with, up in Birmingham, and I promised to give it to Inspector Scutt. I figured she was on the level, since she still hoped he'd see reason and hand over the wad of cash to her. I didn't disagree, since it would keep her there in case I needed to talk to her again.

Big Mike told her we'd give her a ride to Victoria Station, and we walked her to the jeep. A small dark blue sedan idled next to it, hemming us in. It was a Morris Ten, an old-fashioned, boxy-style vehicle with big front fenders and the headlights mounted on a bar attached to the grillwork, almost as an afterthought. A guy stepped out of the passenger's seat, his right hand in his coat pocket. Big Mike took Sheila by the arm and pushed her in back of him. I spotted the second guy, leaning against a car behind us, smoking a cigarette. He flicked it away and walked toward us, his hands showing.

"Just a moment, please," he said, looking at Sheila. I caught Big Mike's eye and turned to the guy who'd gotten out of the car. I pulled out my pistol, which was not exactly a quick draw as my overcoat was buttoned up. Big Mike had his .38 Colt police revolver leveled at the second guy before I cleared my holster.

"Hold it!" Big Mike said. "Hands where I can see them."

"You," I said, when I finally had my revolver centered on my guy. "Hand out of your pocket, slowly." I heard Sheila crying, Big Mike pulling his hammer back, and my heart pounded. The street was quiet, a midday lull broken by tension and blue steel.

"I have a warrant card here," my guy said. "Police." I glanced at the other guy, who stood silently with his hands open. They were calm, almost serene. I wondered why. I wondered how I'd react if two British soldiers pulled weapons on me in Boston. Nothing like these guys, and British cops didn't carry guns, usually.

"Who sent you?"

"We've been looking for Miss Carlson there. Have a few questions for her." His hand was still in his pocket, holding a warrant card, or a gun?

"I didn't ask whom you've been looking for. Who sent you?"

"I don't like being asked with that weapon in my face. You're in enough trouble already, Lieutenant, drawing your weapon on members of the Metropolitan Police."

"It's not in your face. It's pointed at your chest. High, close to the heart. If it misses the heart, it'll shatter your spinal cord. Or hit one of the big veins in your neck. That's what I like about a high chest shot. So many things can put you down. Last time, who sent you?"

"Lieutenant Boyle—" I stepped to one side to get a clear shot at the Morris. I pulled the trigger and shot out a tire, the retort echoing harshly against the buildings. The only sound after that was the air hissing out of the flat.

"Billy?" Big Mike said.

"They're not cops," I said. "No one knew we were coming here. So how could they know my name?"

"Wilson," the guy facing Big Mike said. "Sit in the car, please." Wilson did, a look of shock still on his face. "Now, perhaps we can step inside and have a word."

"No dice," I said, moving next to Big Mike. I holstered my piece, and Big Mike put his away as well. "We talk out here, in the open. Who are you?"

"We have a mutual acquaintance. Major Cosgrove."

"Does MI5 carry identification?"

"Yes, but you've seen through us, so it really doesn't matter what's written on our warrant cards. We came here to speak to Miss Carlson, and thought it best to wait and see who came out with her."

"You didn't follow us here?"

"No, not at all. We have some questions for Miss Carlson, that's all. We are aware of your involvement, but this has nothing to do with you, Lieutenant Boyle, I assure you."

"Is it about Eddie?" Sheila asked, peeking from behind Big Mike's left arm.

"No, Miss Carlson. A tragedy, to be sure, but Scotland Yard has that investigation well in hand. I understand you, as well as Edward Miller, often worked on the Polish floor, as it was called, at the hotel."

"Yes, I did," Sheila said, stepping out from Big Mike's shadow. I could see her figuring the angles, calculating what there was for her in this, wondering if she could take over as a secret agent or whatever other role Eddie had sold her on. "Did you work with Eddie, if you know what I mean?"

"Not our department, Miss Carlson. But I wonder if you might know where Captain Valerian Radecki is at the moment. You and Mr. Miller were acquainted with him?"

"He and Eddie would chat now and then," Sheila said. "But I can't say he'd even know my name."

"You've no idea where he may be then?"

"None at all. Is there a way I can get in touch with you if I find something out, Mister—?"

"Brown. No need, Miss Carlson. Thank you for your time. We'll be in touch if we need you." He touched the brim of his hat and headed for the Morris. Big Mike took Sheila to the jeep and I followed Mr. Brown.

"Sorry about the tire," I said. "I didn't know who you guys really were."

"Hopefully it can be patched; there's a terrible shortage of tires, you know."

"Didn't you ask Major Horak where Radecki is?"

"Yes, but the problem is, he hasn't shown up there. Something about Station Number Eight, whatever that is. Horak wouldn't say any more, except that Radecki was overdue."

"Why do you want Radecki?"

"Routine, that's all. You know how paperwork is with government security agencies. Never ending. Some form Captain Radecki has to complete. Well, good to meet you, Lieutenant Boyle. I hadn't believed all of Cosgrove's stories about you, to tell you the truth, but now I do. Good day."

"Good day to you, Mr. Brown. And Mr. Wilson."

CHAPTER ▪ EIGHTEEN

"BROWN AND WILSON?" Big Mike said after we'd dropped Sheila off at Victoria Station and drove slowly down Victoria Street. "What's that, the English version of Smith and Jones?"

"Yeah, and about as subtle as a couple of G-men. You sure we don't have another tail?"

"Absolutely. Them two knuckleheads are probably still changing that tire, and no one else followed us. As long as Sheila gets on a train, she should be all right. Hey, Billy, how about lunch? I'm starved."

"Sure, if we can find a place to park," I said. We were only a block from the station, and the streets were clogged with parked cars, taxicabs, and trucks. I pointed to a J. Lyons tea shop on the corner, and Big Mike pulled over, right next to a no-parking sign. A constable walked toward us, shaking his head. Big Mike was out in a flash, his Detroit gold policeman's shield held in his hand. The bobby studied it for a second before laughing at something Big Mike said. They shook hands, Big Mike crooked his thumb in my direction, and they laughed again.

"All set, Billy," he said as we entered the restaurant.

"Should I ask what you said about me?"

"No. There's nothing like a pain-in-the-ass officer to make one flatfoot sympathetic to another. He's watching the jeep for me."

"Great," I said. No matter the color of the uniform Big Mike was still a cop at heart. He ordered a tongue sandwich and lemon barley water, cold. Apparently there was a choice. I went with a ham sandwich and tea.

"What do you think Brown and Wilson were after, Billy?"

"I'd say they were genuinely surprised to see us, so I think they were looking for Radecki, following a lead."

"Maybe he's got a girlfriend somewhere."

"Maybe so, but why is MI5 looking for him? If it was about the murder, they'd let Scutt handle it, and keep themselves out of the picture." I lowered my voice, glancing around at the nearby diners. An RAF pilot stared at me from a poster, looking daring in his flight jacket, the caption warning that Careless Talk May Cost His Life. The tables were close together, and the waitresses, all dressed in black uniforms with red buttons and white collars, moved swiftly between them, tending to their customers and pouring steaming cups of tea. Too swiftly to pay much attention, I decided.

"You have any ideas?"

"Not really, but there was something that Sheila said that struck me. Radecki is taking laudanum for pain. He broke his leg on the way to England, and it wasn't set right."

"Is that what Eddie got for him on Horseferry Street?"

"Has to be. That's where his doctor is. I saw the name and address on one of his empty bottles." The food was delivered, and I winced as I always did when I saw someone take a bite out of a tongue sandwich.

"Why the hell would those clowns care if Radecki was dealing drugs on the side? That's not their turf," Big Mike said, smacking his lips after drinking down half his lemon barley water.

"They wouldn't," I said. "It's got to be something else."

"What else could it be? Maybe Eddie Miller swiped some of the stuff and double-crossed Radecki," Big Mike said, his mouth poised to take another bite.

"No, it has to be something that would get MI5 riled up," I said, looking down at my plate. "Cosgrove is involved in the investigation of Egorov's murder, so there has to be a connection there."

"How's that going, anyway?" Big Mike said out of the side of his mouth, the rest of it working on finishing what was left of the sandwich.

"I've got to get down to Dover and catch up with the Russians. I didn't expect to run into another corpse so soon." What *would* get MI5 all riled up, I wondered? Not drugs. Cosgrove had given no indication he had men investigating Egorov's murder either. So what were those two jokers after, and what did they have to do with Radecki? I sipped my tea, thinking back to my first meeting with him at the Rubens. What had that memo said, the one from the British Foreign Office?

His Majesty's Government have used their best efforts not to allow these German maneuvers to have even the semblance of success.

"What?" Big Mike said. I hadn't realized I'd spoken the words out loud.

"Even the semblance of success," I said, taking in the full meaning of those words. What agency would be charged with insuring that the truth wouldn't come out, that it would not have even the semblance of success at being believed?

"There's only one reason MI5 would be looking for Radecki," I said.

"He killed Egorov?" Big Mike said.

"No, it's got nothing to do with Egorov. Radecki killed Eddie, and he's going to kill someone else, to prevent even the semblance of success."

"TADEUSZ TUCHOLSKI," I said as Big Mike drove as fast as he could in the central London traffic, passing taxicabs and lorries along Edgeware Road, heading north. "The kid I told you about, who witnessed the Katyn Forest Massacre."

"You said he was a head case, and they had to send him to the loony bin."

"He's shell-shocked, that's for sure. But he's an eyewitness, and he's worth anything alive to the Poles, and worth as much dead to the Russians. I was too busy trying to link Egorov somehow; I didn't see the obvious connection. Horak even showed me a memo they'd intercepted from the British Foreign Office, saying they would never allow these claims to be successful."

"So the Foreign Office and MI5 take the side of the Russians," Big Mike said.

"They'd probably say it was all for the war effort, to defeat our common enemy, and they'd mean it, too."

"That's the problem with Poland," Big Mike said. "We've got one too many enemies, and not enough friends to go around."

"Some of those friends are questionable," I said. "My guess is that MI5 got to Radecki, and bribed or blackmailed him into keeping Tadeusz quiet. Horak told me that at first Radecki was too hard on Tadeusz, which made him retreat into his shell. That was Radecki's way of keeping him quiet, but he probably knew it wouldn't last, not with Kaz helping the kid day and night."

"So he started doping him."

"Yeah," I said, gripping the door as Big Mike veered out into traffic, laying on the horn, to pass a slow-moving staff car. "Horak mentioned that Radecki and Tad started getting along better a few weeks ago. I'd bet that was when Radecki began giving him the laudanum."

"You think the bad leg is phony?"

"No, probably not. But he said he reinjured it, falling on the stairs. That could have been his excuse to get the drugs. And knowing the condition Tad was in, Radecki would've become his best friend real fast. There's nothing like laudanum to help you forget, or at least not care if you remember. He must have told Tad to keep it a secret, or he wouldn't give him any more. The state Tad was in, he'd be sure to comply at first, and then be unable to stop later."

"You think Radecki was trying to kill him, or to keep him quiet?"

"Radecki must have been increasing the dose he gave him. Kaz told me that after Tad spoke to me, he never said another word. Maybe Radecki was caught off guard, and decided to hurry things up once I'd heard Tad's story."

"But it backfired on him," Big Mike said, hitting the accelerator as we cleared the most congested part of the road. "They sent the kid off to a hospital, where he couldn't get at him."

"Right. So he goes off to this Station Number Eight, but I'd bet anything he's making a side visit to St. Albans first."

"To give Tadeusz a fatal fix. Eddie must've stumbled onto all this, and he was blackmailing Radecki."

"Could be. Or maybe he was in on it with him. Picking up the drugs, watching Tad when Radecki wasn't there. Maybe the money was his MI5 pay, not blackmail money."

"War work," Big Mike said, shaking his head in disgust. "With Tadeusz gone, Radecki didn't need him anymore."

"A loose end. Radecki had it all planned, having lunch with Kaz, making sure Kaz's fingerprints ended up on his bayonet. He eliminates the one person who knows what's going on, pins it on Kaz, and then takes care of Tad."

"There's one thing that doesn't make sense, Billy," Big Mike said, drumming his fingers on the steering wheel. I could see his forehead crease as he worked at adding things up. "Why were Brown and Wilson looking for him, if he was doing what they wanted?"

"Good question. Maybe Cosgrove or one of his bosses has a conscience."

"They cover up a massacre of thousands, and you think maybe one of them has a crisis of conscience at the last minute?"

"This may be different for them. Eddie's blood is on their hands. Tadeusz's may be also, and this is happening here, in London, not in some distant, dark wood."

"Maybe they prefer Polish blood on Russian hands," Big Mike said. His finger tapping stopped, and his knuckles showed white as he gripped the wheel. We were in the country now, winter fields bordered by small trees and shrubs spread out over the gently sloping landscape. White, fluffy clouds decorated the horizon, and the sun shone brightly over our shoulders. It was beautiful, and I tried to imagine thousands of Englishmen from these villages and farms, gathered up, bound, and shot in the head, then buried in mass graves in the forests at the edge of the farmland. Or Americans, from the city of Boston or the dairy farms of western Massachusetts. How expedient would it be then, to sacrifice justice for the sake of the war effort? How simple to forgo revenge when the rotting corpses were your brothers, husbands, fathers, and friends? Or if their names were Robert, James, Peter, John, or Daniel, instead of Jerzy, Czeslaw, Stanislaw, Zygmunt, or Wincenty?

"Big Mike, how do you say Michael in Polish?"

"Mieczyslaw. Why?"

"Just curious," I said as a sign for Bricket Wood came up. "We're getting closer. Take this right."

"OK, Boleslaw," Big Mike said, giving me a quick glance as he downshifted and took the narrow road. "Don't ask me why, but that's Polish for William."

CHAPTER ▪ NINETEEN

ST. ALBANS REST Home sat on a hill east of the village bearing the same name. It was hidden from view, nothing but a small white sign, the paint blistered and peeling, to point the way down a narrow country lane. We were stopped at a gatehouse manned by two fellows from the Home Guard. One of them looked about sixteen, and I wondered why he wasn't in school. The other had wisps of gray hair sticking out from under his helmet and a bulbous red nose that meant his other duty station was in the local pub. Still, they were armed and all business, checking our identification papers and asking whom we were visiting. The boy went inside the gatehouse while the old fellow watched us for signs of trouble. Through the open door I could see the kid showing our papers to a guy in a gray suit, who glanced at us. He was no local Home Guard; even in the dim interior of the gatehouse, I could make out the steely glint in his eyes as he assessed us. He nodded to the kid, and picked up the telephone.

We drove on a wood-lined gravel driveway, passing two Home Guard soldiers patrolling the grounds. One of them gave us a cheery wave. As we neared the house, a civilian cradling a shotgun in one arm, and holding two dogs on a short leash by the other hand, crossed in front of us.

"Are they trying to keep people in or out of this place?" Big Mike said.

"Both. Probably a lot of secrets locked up in the heads of patients here. Wouldn't do to have any of them wander off and start yakking with the locals." Around a corner the woods thinned out and a great, green lawn opened up, with a four-story, ivy-encrusted granite building set on the far side. Patients wrapped in blankets sat in chairs on the lawn, facing the sun. Nurses pushed some in wheelchairs, or held onto the elbows of others as they took slow, hesitant steps. Some were dull eyed, their vacant stares focused on some distant vision. Others moved in abrupt spurts of energy, their eyes searching us for signs of recognition, salvation, or threat.

"Who are these people?" Big Mike said as he parked the car, the scrunch of gravel beneath the tires harsh and sudden.

"People who fight in darkness," I said. Commandos, secret agents, assassins, and the innocent who had seen the unthinkable. Would Diana know any of them? Perhaps an SOE agent she'd trained with, who had escaped the Continent in body but not in spirit. I caught the eye of a young woman as she walked past the jeep, her nurse's arm wrapped around her waist. She stared straight through me. "Let's go," I said. I had a vision of Diana shuffling along, dead eyes wide open, as a shiver passed through me

We checked in with a nurse at a desk strategically placed opposite the main entrance. An orderly, dressed in white, unlocked the door behind her and pointed up the main staircase. "Third floor, first door on your left." This being England, that meant a climb up four floors, since the Brits start with the ground floor, and then begin counting.

At the top of the stairs we stopped and huffed and puffed for a second, catching our breath. Muffled voices came from the room to the left. I put my finger to my lips and we moved closer. I saw Big Mike put his hand in his pocket, where he kept his revolver, and I found my hand resting on the butt of my pistol in its shoulder holster, as we each took one side of the door. Leave it to a couple of cops to assume gunfire to come through a door in a quiet hospital in England.

"No." That was Kaz's voice, for certain.

"*On potrzebuje tego*," the other voice said.

"*Proszę, pozwalał mnie*," someone else said, in a small, weak voice.

"He's asking for something," Big Mike whispered as he put his hand on the doorknob. I took my hand off my revolver and nodded. He opened the door and I went in, stepping to the side to make room for Big Mike. We were both breathing heavily, from the rapid stair climbing and the expectation of something wrong, something that needed cunning and cold steel. What we found was unexpectedly calm.

Tadeusz sat in an armchair, dressed in the same white pajamas and bathrobe as all the other patients. His face looked hollow and paler than the last time I'd seen him, his eyes bloodshot and rimmed with tears. Seated next to him was Valerian Radecki, in the midst of a discussion with Kaz, who leaned against the empty bed. The room was well furnished, with drapes pulled back from tall windows on one wall, and framed paintings adorning another. The rug was thick, and only the faintest trace of disinfectant lingered in the air. Otherwise, it could have been a guest room at a country estate. A very well guarded estate.

"What are you doing here?" Kaz said, his eyebrows arching in surprise.

"Looking for both of you," I said, giving Radecki the once-over, checking for a bulge in his jacket. He didn't reach for a weapon, didn't protest his innocence. "A few steps ahead of MI5 and Scotland Yard."

"Please wait outside," Radecki said, oblivious to the implications of what I'd said. "We are discussing a matter internal to the Polish government."

"That's the point," Kaz said, ignoring us and jumping back into the argument. "Tadeusz has information that is vital to the Polish government, and to the Polish nation. To our future."

"But can't you see that means nothing if he completely falls apart? He needs this simply to keep from going mad," Radecki said.

"What you say is madness," Kaz spat back. "Who will believe a drug addict? His word will be useless if the Russians find out. Or the press, for that matter."

"I am not an addict," Tadeusz said, but neither Kaz nor Radecki responded. Big Mike gave me a questioning glance, and I returned it with a quick, silent mouthed *no*. Neither was responding in the way I thought they would, and Radecki certainly wasn't acting like a guilty killer.

"I am glad you came to visit, both of you, but it would be best if you left us for the moment," Kaz said. "This is a decision we must make alone."

"Whether or not to keep Tad drugged up?"

"Please, Lieutenant Boyle," Radecki said. "It is none of your concern."

"Really? Is this what you've been giving Tad, the same stuff you use?" I picked up a bottle of pills from a side table next to Radecki, where it sat next to a tin of biscuits. The bottle was the same as the one I'd found in his desk. How easy would it be to add poison, or simply overdose Tad?

"It's the only thing that helps. Please," Tadeusz said as he reached out a trembling hand. Radecki took the hand in his and patted it.

"Not yet, my friend. Lieutenant Kazimierz must first agree. It is only right."

"I thought you two didn't get along," I said, trying to take in what was playing out here. Radecki wasn't acting like a guy who'd knifed Eddie this morning and then come here with MI5-inspired murder on his mind. And Kaz damn well had no clue Scotland Yard was looking for him either.

"We didn't," Radecki said, giving Tadeusz's hand a squeeze before letting it go. "But not because I disliked this brave young man. Rather, because I thought it best for him, and the government, if he would make a public declaration of what he saw at Katyn. But I was wrong. I saw how these terrible memories affected him, and I came to understand he had been wounded as terribly as a soldier struck by machine-gun fire. He needed rest, in a safe place, before he could face any scrutiny. So I withdrew, and Lieutenant Kazimierz took over."

"I'm afraid I had little success," Kaz said.

"You both helped me," Tadeusz said, "as much as you could. I'm sorry I haven't . . . I cannot . . ." Tears flowed from his eyes, but his face was calm, with no sign of anguish.

"You started giving him your laudanum," I said.

"Yes," said Radecki. "Our plan had been to coax Tadeusz along until he could speak for himself in front of strangers. Major Horak insisted it be done without drugs, so there would be no question of his stability, or willingness to speak the truth."

"But you thought otherwise."

"Yes, and I acted alone. Lieutenant Kazimierz didn't find out until he arrived here, an hour before I did."

"I'm sorry," Tadeusz said. "They won't give me anything here to let me sleep, orders from Major Horak. I can't close my eyes, because the dreams come again and again. And I can't leave them open, either. I stare at the wall, and I see all those men, their faces, staring back at me. Why didn't they kill me with them? I wish I were with them; anything would be better than this."

"Did you have an overdose," I said, "after I met you? Kaz told me you didn't speak at all after that."

"No, it was nothing like that. Valerian gave me a dose every night, to help me sleep. He did that night, and it worked as usual. I could drift to sleep, and hardly remember anything, or care. But the next day, Major Horak said he wanted me to speak to your General Eisenhower, if it could be arranged. It frightened me, it still does. I found I couldn't answer him, couldn't speak to anybody, couldn't communicate in any way."

"I believe his mind found a way out," Radecki said.

"Perhaps," Tadeusz said. "This morning, though, I could speak."

"I'm sorry," Kaz said to him. "But we must talk about that again. General Eisenhower will be in London soon, and we need to influence him. There are many Poles in America, and if he reports what you tell him, they will have to demand the truth!"

"I can't do all that. I can't."

"It will be just as you spoke with Billy. Not a lot of people."

"I don't think I'm able. Will you let Captain Radecki give me the laudanum?"

"Wait," I said. "There is a part of this that is my business."

"What part?" Radecki said.

"The part about Eddie Miller being murdered early this morning. With your bayonet through his heart."

"Eddie?" Tadeusz said. "Who would kill Eddie? He was so kind to me."

"He was an informer for the Russians."

"Oh no," Tadeusz said, thrusting his head back, as if to get away from the thought. "Oh no."

"We just found out," Kaz said, trying to calm him. "We were using him to send bad information to the Soviets. There was never any danger."

"Not from the Soviets. But what about MI5?" I said.

"You can't be serious," Radecki said.

"I'm not saying they killed Eddie. But Scotland Yard thinks Kaz did. That's one reason we're here, to warn you."

"What's the other?" Kaz asked.

"To find out if Captain Radecki did, and if he intends to harm Tad." As I spoke, Big Mike edged toward the door, blocking any route out.

"How dare you!" Radecki said, rising from his chair and advancing on me. "You accuse me? Are you an idiot? We were using Miller, he was valuable to us."

"Maybe he outlived his usefulness. To you."

"What do you mean, Billy?" Kaz said as Tadeusz looked at me and back to Radecki, as if trying to figure out whom he could trust.

"You were the ones who told me about the British government preventing the truth about Katyn coming out. Think about it. What agency would carry out that mission? MI5. How would they do it? Get someone on the inside. Bribe them, or hire them, to get the job done. For Allied unity. Get rid of the evidence. Get rid of Tadeusz."

"Absurd," Radecki said.

"No, it isn't. You thought you had time to kill him, with an accidental overdose, probably. But you hadn't counted on his being transferred out here, so you had to act fast. You killed your accomplice to keep him quiet, and tried to pin it on Kaz, to get him out of the way. He's the only other person Tad trusts, and who might have noticed anything. Two birds with one stone, pretty smart."

"My accomplice? That pathetic waiter?"

"Sure. He knew all about the drugs. He made the pickup for you at your doctor's office on Horseferry Road. That way no one would notice how often you went there."

"You fool!" Radecki said, his fist raised in anger. "Miller never went to get the laudanum. Sheila Carlson did. I couldn't take the time, and the walk only made my leg ache like the devil, so I paid her to go. I called the damn doctor to let him know, he'll confirm it."

"Sheila?" I felt a horrible sensation in my stomach, the dropping away of everything I had thought was true. What did it mean? "Sheila?"

"She was very nice to me," Tadeusz said. "She always stopped by to chat. A very pretty girl. Did she do something wrong?"

"She lied," I said. "About something she had no reason to lie about, unless she was covering something up."

"Or laying the blame on a dead man," Big Mike said from his post at the door.

"Why did you and Kaz have lunch together yesterday?" I said to Radecki, trying to keep the threads of my theory from unraveling. "And how did you get him to handle your bayonet? His fingerprints are probably all over it."

"I invited him in order to find out if and when he would visit Tadeusz, so I could get here first. But my train was delayed at Radlett, and as you can see, I was late. As for the bayonet, it was Lieutenant Kazimierz who asked about it."

"It's true, Billy," Kaz said. "I sensed he was interested in when I would visit, but I didn't know why. To change the subject, I asked him about the bayonet he kept on his shelf. I picked it up out of mere curiosity."

"No one was blackmailing you?" I asked Radecki.

"Of course not. Over what?"

"Drugging Tad, I had thought. Did Sheila know you'd been giving him your laudanum?"

"Not that I know of, no. Although I do remember her knocking on Tadeusz's door one day, just as I was bringing him some. It's possible she overheard."

"Did she ask about Tadeusz recently?"

"Why, yes, she did," Radecki said. "Yesterday. I told her I planned to visit him today, if I could get away."

"Please," Tadeusz said. "Why can't I have the laudanum now?" No one answered his pleas.

"Sheila," I said, thinking out loud, and not taking in the desperate measure in Tad's voice. "If she lied about getting the drugs, the only reason could be to divert suspicion from her, onto Eddie."

"And Eddie's dead," Big Mike said to Radecki, "by your bayonet. She made it look like there's a connection between you two and the drugs."

"Oh no," Tad moaned, but we were too busy trying to add things up to comfort him.

"Maybe we were right about Eddie outliving his usefulness," I said. "But wrong about whom he'd been useful to."

"No, I don't believe it," Tadeusz said, shaking his head vigorously. "She was so nice. So was Eddie. He was funny, I liked it when he visited."

"What did you talk about with them?"

"Nothing special. That is what was so pleasant. They'd ask me about Poland, where I went to school, but I didn't want to talk about the past. They wanted to know where I wished to live after the war, what my plans were. Sheila told me they'd take me to the shore at Shoeburyness, where Eddie's family lived, for a visit as soon as I was well."

"Let me guess," I said. "She wanted to know when that might be. When you'd be strong enough to travel, to go out and meet people."

"Yes, she did. She told me she'd write to Eddie's mother, to let her know when I'd be well enough. When Major Horak would be done with me." Understanding flashed across his face, the last words coming out slowly, as the terrible truth revealed itself. "She wanted to know how long before she had to kill me. I wish she had." Tad's voice trailed off, what was left of his spirit broken by this last betrayal.

"Dear God," Radecki said. "I nearly helped her do it."

"What?" I watched Radecki reach for the round tin of Ashbourne biscuits. He opened it, and instead of biscuits, it contained an apple cake, the top liberally sprinkled with cinnamon and sugar. It was about the right size for the large cake pan that was in the sink at Sheila's place.

"She gave me this, early this morning. After I'd told her the day before about visiting, she said she'd bake a cake to cheer Tadeusz up, and could she come by and give it to me. Perhaps it's been tampered with."

"Early this morning?"

"Yes, about seven o'clock."

"An hour before Eddie was knifed," Big Mike said. "And Sheila told us she hadn't seen anyone else at the hotel."

"Are you suggesting Sheila killed Miller with my bayonet?" Radecki demanded. "How could a slightly built girl take a man by surprise, and drive a large knife into his heart?"

"I don't know," I said. "Whoever did it got it right. There was very little blood; he died instantly."

"Is the cake poisoned?" Tadeusz said. He got up, pushing himself off the chair with both arms and shuffling slowly across the floor in his slippers. I took the tin from Radecki and sniffed.

"I don't know," I said. "Can't smell anything. Must be sweet, though, this is a lot of sugar, and the stuff's hard to come by." I broke a piece of cake off and sniffed, but got nothing. I resisted the temptation to lick my fingers and wiped the crumbs off on my sleeve.

"Around every corner, there is death," Tadeusz said. "Everywhere I go, death follows. Eddie is nice to me, and he is dead. Sheila is nice, and wants to kill me. Valerian, Piotr, you both try to help me, and what happens? You are framed for murder. I am a vessel for death." He paced the length of the room, passing Big Mike, then heading back, muttering to himself.

"Why don't you give him the laudanum?" I asked.

"No," Kaz said. "I am very sorry, but no. Tadeusz is a Polish soldier. He must do what is right, even at a cost to himself. We cannot take a chance with any more drugs."

I didn't care about other Polish soldiers; I just couldn't bear to see this kid suffer. I looked away from Kaz, knowing he was right, unwilling to meet his eyes. I stared at the floor, flushed with a sense of shame at what we were putting him through.

Crumbs. There were crumbs at my feet. Just as there had been on the ground where Eddie lay. I thought back to the kitchen at Penford Street in Camberwell. Why were there gardener's gloves on the counter? Why would anyone use more than a month's ration of sugar for a single cake?

"What does an oleander flower look like?" I said, bending down to feel the crumbs. They vanished into tiny pieces as I rubbed them between my fingers.

"They can be white or red," Kaz said. "They look a bit like propeller blades, I always thought. Five petals, I believe."

"With long, narrow, shiny green leaves?"

"Yes, why?"

"The plant at Sheila's place," Big Mike said.

"Yeah. I'm not much on flowers, but my dad once arrested a florist for murder. He used the sap from an oleander plant as poison. He found out that his wife was having an affair, and that the guy would come over while he was out making deliveries. He began to notice that his single malt Scotch was down about an inch or so every Wednesday, so he put two and two together and figured the guy was enjoying his liquor and his wife. So one Tuesday night, he takes the sap he'd harvested from his hothouse oleanders and adds it to the Scotch. Wednesday afternoon, he comes home expecting to find a dead body and a hysterical wife. Instead, he finds both of them dead. Gave himself up right away. Said his wife never drank a drop that he'd known of, but that she must've kept more than one secret from him."

"Oleander?" Tadeusz said. He'd come to a halt at one of the windows, leaning on the casement, his face resting on the wood frame.

"A flower," Radecki said. "Apparently very poisonous."

"It is," I said. "Fast acting, and very bitter. Which is why the florist added it to the whiskey, to disguise the taste. And why Sheila used so much sugar. She must've baked up something for Eddie, and he keeled over in the alleyway. Then all she had to do was kneel and drive the bayonet between his ribs."

"Is it a beautiful flower?" Tadeusz said, as he opened the handle on the window and took a deep breath of the fresh air.

"Beautiful and deadly," I said, thinking of Sheila and her earnest tears, her ingenuous and believable abandonment. *My man's dead, I'm alone, and a killer may be after me.* Just the right words to get a couple of flat-footed GIs to feel sorry for her, give her a few pounds and a ride to the train station. The air flowing into the room felt good, as if it were washing away the shock of how duplicitous even an innocent-looking young girl could be.

"How long would I have until you take me to see the general?" Tadeusz said to Kaz, without looking away from the open window.

"It will be in a week."

"I think not," Tadeusz said, hoisting himself onto the narrow sill, holding each open window with one hand. The hinges creaked, the breeze blew his white robe back, and for a second it looked as if he'd grown wings. Then he was gone.

CHAPTER ▪ TWENTY

IT HAD ONLY been four stories, but four was enough with a flag-stone terrace at the bottom of the drop. Tadeusz had put an end to his torture, and as much as I had wished he could see things through, I couldn't blame him. The only thing worse than being executed and buried in the Katyn Forest was to witness the executions and burials, then be thrown into a secret police prison, where fear and memories ate away at your mind until reality and sanity decayed beyond repair. Then to be sent back out into the world through a bureaucratic mistake, silent and withdrawn, adrift among people who wanted only to draw you out, stand you up, use you, and watch you relive the nightmare visions at their bidding. For the greater good.

Funny, but with all the sacrifices in this world for the greater good, I had to wonder where it had gotten to. That greater good. Just around the corner, like prosperity? Hoarded somewhere, stockpiled in a warehouse for after the war? Or had it been spent in payoffs, kickbacks, bribes, sweetheart deals, promotions for the incompetent but well connected? I don't remember seeing any greater good in Sicily, at Salerno, or along the Volturno River. Just death, snafus, and suffering. So good for you, Tadeusz.

All this ran through my head as I stood at attention in front of Colonel Harding's desk the next morning, Kaz and Big Mike a step behind me. I kept my mouth shut, which I had learned the hard way was the best defense when Harding had that look: lips compressed, jaw muscles clenched, the vein above his temple throbbing. It was like waiting for a hand grenade to go off.

"You," Harding said, pointing a finger at Kaz, "were supposed to be lying low somewhere."

"I—," Kaz began, drawing a dark look from Harding.

"When I want to hear from you, Lieutenant Kazimierz, I will let you know. You," Harding said, moving the accusing finger in my direction, "were supposed to be in Dover, talking to the Russians while they had their tour. And you, Corporal, were supposed to be driving him there. Instead, the three of you end up north of London, at a top-secret facility, standing by while a valuable asset jumps out a window. That wouldn't have had anything to do with your presence there, would it?"

"Tadeusz Tucholski," Kaz said. When Harding didn't snap at him, he continued. "That was his name. Tadeusz was very valuable, it is true. He was also very, very fragile. I don't think we understood how fragile. If we hadn't gone, he might not have killed himself, not that day. But some other day, certainly."

"It's true, Colonel," I said. We'd agreed that it didn't make any sense to reveal Radecki's use of his laudanum. He'd had the best of intentions, and it had nothing to do with what happened yesterday. Unless you counted the fact that we'd withheld it from Tadeusz. All around, a truth better not told.

"He was in real bad shape, Colonel," Big Mike said. "It's a wonder he held together this long."

"That may be, but it still doesn't tell me why you two went up there, when you should have been on your way to Dover."

"I came by here early yesterday morning, to read the file on Topper Chapman that Cosgrove had sent over. I called Scotland Yard to check something and heard that Scutt wanted me over at the Rubens, where a body had been found. It was Eddie Miller, the kid I saw with Sidorov. Apparently Kaz had been seen handling the murder weapon, a Polish Army bayonet, the day before, and Scutt was suspicious of him. Thought he might be taking his revenge on the Russians by killing one of their informers, something along those lines."

"Especially after that comment at the Russian Embassy," Harding said.

"Yes, sir," I said, eager to display the proper military courtesy, which sometimes had a calming effect on Harding. "We went to search Eddie's flat, and ran into a girl from the hotel, Sheila Carlson. She gave us a sob story about getting married to Eddie, and how she'd found Eddie's body but ran away because she thought the killer might be after her."

"But *she* was the killer?"

"Yes," I said, thankful that Big Mike must've filled him in last night. And now I knew what the smaller cake pan had been for. "She used poison, from an oleander plant. Left a note for Eddie, met him in the alley, gave him a piece of cake that he was probably happy to eat. That poison is fast acting, and in no time he was on the ground, with Sheila thrusting a blade into his heart. But first she'd given Captain Radecki a poisoned apple cake to take to Tadeusz."

"And you think MI5 put her up to it?" Harding said, in a tone of disbelief.

"We know she was an informant for Scotland Yard. And we know that the British government wants this Katyn Forest affair hushed up."

"We, Lieutenant Boyle? Do you mean SHAEF, Supreme Headquarters, Allied Expeditionary Force? General Eisenhower? How about FDR?"

"Sorry, sir. I mean Lieutenant Kazimierz."

"Suspect it, you mean," Harding said. I glanced at Kaz, unsure if I should mention the stolen memo.

"We—I mean the Polish Government in Exile—have a memo from the British Foreign Office, stating that the investigation into the Katyn Forest Massacre should not be allowed to succeed," Kaz said.

"Let's see it then" Harding said.

"It can't be released," Kaz said. "It would endanger the person who obtained it."

"Oh," Harding said, throwing up his hands. "So we have two lieutenants with absolutely no proof, accusing His Majesty's Government of murder."

"Two lieutenants and a corporal," Big Mike said. "And only MI5, not the whole shebang."

"Well, then, let's call in the press. The fact that there's three of you clinches it." He fumbled with a pack of Luckies, struck a match, and lit one. He threw the wooden matchstick in the general vicinity of an ashtray, but it missed and fell at my feet, trailing a thin line of gray smoke.

"I was worried about Kaz, Colonel Harding," I said as I leaned down to pick up the burned-out match. I laid it in the empty ashtray and couldn't get the image of Tadeusz at the window out of my mind. Harding swiveled in his chair and stared out the window, toward a small patch of St. James's Square, blowing blue smoke that curled against the window and came back at him.

"Understood, Boyle. And you lucked out, once again. The whole Home Guard tour for the Russians got put off by a couple of days. The Germans lost two bombers near Dover, the new Heinkel 177 type. Home Guard units from Maidstone to Dover have been out hunting for survivors. The RAF is eager to interrogate them, so it's top priority. Get down there today and see what you can find out. The Russian delegation is already at Dover Castle. Big Mike has the details. Now get going and don't stop until you hit Dover."

"Sir, I need to stop at Scotland Yard. I still have some evidence I need to deliver to Inspector Scutt."

"What kind of evidence?"

"An envelope full of money. What Sheila and Eddie had been supposedly saving up, from what she got from MI5 and what he got from the Russians. She had it on her when we ran into her at Eddie's place."

"How much money?"

"I haven't counted it, sir." I pulled the envelope from my jacket pocket, and Harding nodded in Big Mike's direction, so I handed it over. Maybe he thought Detroit cops were a less sticky-fingered bunch than their Boston brothers.

"Lieutenant Kazimierz, you stay away from Scotland Yard. I don't want you thrown in jail unless *I* order it. Big Mike, you are responsible for getting Boyle here to Dover today. Got it?"

"Sure, Sam," Big Mike said, heaving a sigh. He'd taken a seat on one of the chairs facing Harding's desk, counting out pound notes between licks of his thumb, while Kaz and I still stood ramrod straight. Harding looked at him, tapped his ashes, shook his head, and returned to his paperwork. Big Mike was a bluecoat down to his bones, and he'd never be a real soldier, not the spit-and-polish type anyway. Harding seemed to know it wasn't worth his breath trying to make him one, and I think part of him liked Big Mike's lack of proper military formality. It gave him a chance to let his guard down, to be human behind the closed doors of his office. Big Mike knew when to toe the line, but at any time he could tire of the whole thing, take a load off, and call the colonel by his first name. He did it with such sincere innocence that Harding never took offense. Or did Big Mike do it on purpose, to defuse a tense situation, and draw Harding's ire away from his intended victim? He finished counting, whistled, and gave the envelope back to me. "One thousand one hundred and ten pounds."

"That much?" I said. With everything that had happened, I hadn't given the envelope a second thought. Loose cash usually focused my attention, but it had been a helluva day.

"Yeah. You gave her the five-pound notes from the top, but the rest were all tens, twenties, and fifties. Over forty-four hundred bucks, Billy."

"That's a lot of dough. I don't think Eddie gave Sidorov anything worth half this much, and Sheila sure didn't get rich snitching for Scotland Yard."

"Maybe it was a down payment on an apple cake," Kaz said.

"You think that money came from MI5?" Harding said. "And stand at ease, both of you." Kaz shrugged, not wanting to get into another discussion of proof versus suspicions.

"Listen, Colonel," I said, leaning on his desk. "All we know for sure is that somebody paid Sheila to kill Tadeusz. There's no personal motive we know about, and no other explanation for her making a getaway with this much cash."

"You've spoiled her payday, Billy," Big Mike said. "If that was the down payment, she's got to get the rest of it quick, and disappear."

"We could make that difficult for her," Kaz said. "I called Major Horak last night, but he was unavailable. I decided not to leave a message about Tadeusz, and that I would tell him in person this morning."

"So no one else knows," Harding said.

"No. I spoke to the doctor at St. Albans, whom I'd met when we arranged for Tadeusz to be admitted. He will submit a written report, but I expect that since I was there in person, he has no need to inform anyone else directly. So I will go to the Rubens Hotel and tell Major Horak, and everyone else, that Tadeusz is much better and is ready to return."

"She's bound to have friends at the hotel who will pass that information on to her," I said.

"Lieutenant Kazimierz," Harding said, "are you prepared to lie to your superior officer?"

"Only since he is my *former* superior officer, Colonel."

"All right. Try to flush her out, as long as you stay clear of Scotland Yard, and as long as Big Mike gets Boyle to Dover by nightfall. Dismissed."

We went to the motor pool, where I had to sign out a jeep for an extended trip outside of London. Then we dropped Kaz off at the Rubens on our way to Scotland Yard, to spread the rumor of Tadeusz's impending and vocal return. Big Mike drove along the Embankment, where a cold breeze churned the fog rising from the Thames, creating an eerie, gray wall of nothingness. He parked the jeep as I grabbed my musette bag and went inside. I found Inspector Scutt at his desk, on the telephone, nodding his head and mumbling, *Yes, sir* and *No, sir* in a way that told me his boss was on the other end. Or his boss's boss.

"Tell me some good news, Lieutenant Boyle," he said as he hung up. He looked frail, and the bags under his eyes were dark and heavy. His face was creased with weariness, and white stubble on his cheeks told me he'd been on duty all night. "The Air Ministry is on the commissioner's back, and he in turn is on mine."

"Kraut aircrew, right?"

"Indeed. They're eager to chat with them about some new bomber we've shot down. I'd like to tell them to blast them all and be done with it. What are they going to do, fire me? I'd welcome it. Well, enough of my troubles. Sit down, and tell me yours."

"It's about this," I said, tossing the envelope full of cash onto his desk. "One thousand one hundred and ten pounds." Scutt looked at the envelope, staring at the embossed Rubens Hotel logo.

"What's this then?" His forehead narrowed, as if he didn't recognize cold, hard cash.

"Some small part of it is what you paid Sheila Carlson as an informant. Another part is what the Russians paid Eddie Miller for similar services, although I don't think it's much. It's the rest that interests me. My guess is that the lion's share came from MI5."

"For the moment I will ignore the reference to the Metropolitan Police paying informers. What exactly has MI5 to do with this, and why do you have their money?"

"It's not theirs anymore. It was Sheila Carlson's," I said. I recounted what had happened when Big Mike and I went to Eddie's place. How we came by the envelope, the visit from Brown and Wilson, and even how we'd been taken in by Sheila's poor-girl sob story, giving her cash and a ride to the railroad station on top of letting her go.

"Did you carry her bags to the train?" Scutt said, not even trying to hide his laughter.

"If you think that's funny, you'll find this hilarious," I said, pulling the biscuit tin out of the musette bag. I popped the lid to show him the crumbling apple cake. "Poisoned. Baked by Sheila as a gift for a Pole who saw too much before he got out of Russia. She even managed to have Captain Radecki deliver it."

"Are you quite certain?" Scutt sniffed the cake, careful not to touch anything.

"Have your lab boys check it out. She had an oleander plant, and there were cut-up leaves and stems in the kitchen."

"It appears no one ate any, thank goodness," Scutt said as he signaled to a constable. "Watkins, take this to the laboratory to be analyzed. Put a note on it that it may contain poison, and be damned careful with it, man."

I didn't tell Scutt that it had done its work, eaten or not. Tadeusz had seen too much death in his short life, and it was my bet that an apple cake was what finally pushed him over the edge. It was the shock of the unexpected; the domestic and comforting turned deadly and corrupt. *Everywhere I go, death follows.* I knew what he meant.

Scutt pulled a pipe from his desk drawer, along with a red tin of Old English pipe tobacco. He went through the pipe smoker's ritual, filling the bowl halfway, tamping it down, filling some more, tamping harder. He glanced at me a few times, as if to assure me he knew I was there, but he didn't say a word. He struck a wooden match, let the sulfur burn off for a second, and then passed the flame back and forth over the tobacco, drawing slowly until it gave off a glow and he exhaled the first draw.

"Now then," he said, giving me his full attention. "Time for us to talk."

"OK," I said.

"First, I'm pleased you turned over the money. A man with fewer scruples would have kept some of it, if not all."

"No, a man with only a few less scruples than me would have kept it all. I figure you know how much you paid Sheila, and probably what the Russians paid Eddie. And if you know about her working for MI5, well, then you'd have a good guess as to the whole amount."

"You'd make a smart criminal, Lieutenant Boyle. But in this case, you give me too much credit. Yes, she did pass on a few things to us, nothing important, really. I do know about this fellow Tadeusz Tucholski," he said, consulting a notebook. "Fairly important to the Poles and their cause, isn't he?"

"Very," I said.

"And Captain Radecki, he brought the cake with him when he went to visit St. Albans, yes?"

"You are well informed."

"A guess. Sheila Carlson did tell us about Mr. Tucholski's condition and where he'd been placed. That was the sort of thing she passed on to us and the Special Branch. She was good at picking up gossip, as well as the comings and goings of senior personnel. This is serious, certainly, but you should remember two things."

"Such as?"

"There's only been one murder other than that of Egorov. Edward Miller, with a knife to the chest. And I don't think Miss Carlson did that. Many women, when they kill, use poisons of one sort or another. Very few use the knife."

"I think she fed Eddie a piece of cake when she met him in the alleyway. Do you remember the crumbs at his feet? That would have taken effect very quickly, and put him on the ground. All she'd have had to do was press the bayonet in, using her own weight. There wouldn't have been a struggle."

"No, I don't recall seeing crumbs," Scutt said, riffling through a stack of files on his desk until he found the one he wanted. "But the constable who searched the place found the mess she'd left in the kitchen, and noted the plant materials. Garden gloves also. Careful girl, this Sheila."

"What's the other thing I should remember?"

"While I don't doubt Miss Carlson's capability with poison, I am not convinced she killed Edward Miller." He puffed, blew smoke, and inspected the pipe bowl. "Why? For this envelope? She had full access to his flat, she could have run away with it at any time. I still want to talk to Lieutenant Kazimierz about Miller's death."

"Kaz had nothing to do with it," I said.

"How do you know? Have you spoken to him about it?"

"I don't know where he is," I said, avoiding the question and Scutt's eyes at the same time.

"That is unfortunate. A Soviet official was beaten and nearly killed last night. Apparently, it was late, after that dreadful opera film. I'd like to know where Lieutenant Kazimierz went after he left the embassy. After he made his threats." Scutt eyed me, working his cheeks, sucking in smoke and blowing it out, leaving a haze hanging over the files and papers on his desk.

"He was back at the hotel when I got in," I said, remembering him sitting in the dark, liquor and pistol close by. "He was gone when I got up. Who took a beating?"

"Osip Nikolaevich Blotski, listed as an economic attaché, but certainly a security operative. Someone used a length of pipe on him, one blow from behind, then went to work on his legs. Both broken in several places."

"Where? Why did they wait so long to report it?" I wanted to say Kaz wouldn't have done such a thing, but I knew that was what any friend would say. Scutt was looking through cop's eyes, and I knew what that meant. Proof, not faith.

"Apparently Mr. Blotski went for a walk in Kensington Gardens after the opera, where he was set up by capitalist hooligans, or a rogue Polish émigré, or an economist of the Keynesian school."

"Pardon?"

"Please excuse my little joke. Keynes is a British economist. No reason you should know him, and I doubt our Russian economic attaché would either. He called for help, and another Russian, also out for a stroll, found him."

"Sounds fishy," I said.

"Indeed. But I saw the poor fellow a few hours ago, encased in a lower body cast, his head bandaged. They have him at the embassy. He was treated at a hospital and they brought him back before the plaster dried. His injuries are real, but I doubt they were inflicted in Kensington Gardens, as they told the story. We found no traces of blood or a struggle."

"He was probably somewhere he shouldn't have been. Or somewhere they didn't want to admit to."

"Yes, I agree. They took their time to get him under lock and key and come up with this story, cock and bull as it is."

"Did anything else happen? Any more delivery trucks hijacked, anything like that?"

"Deliveries for the embassy, you mean? No, nothing's been reported. They're angry enough about this beating, following on the murder of Egorov. The Soviet ambassador, Ivan Maisky, complained directly to the foreign minister. That's Anthony Eden, who has Churchill's ear. So I must investigate, and Lieutenant Kazimierz is needed for questioning on this matter and the death of Edward Miller."

"Are you seriously considering him a suspect?"

"I am seriously interested in speaking to him, Lieutenant Boyle. And I am growing increasingly interested in why he's become so hard to find."

"I'll tell him when I see him," I said as I stood, pushing the chair back with a harsh scrape. "And you ask MI5 what they paid Sheila Carlson to do."

"I'll ask them when I see them," Scutt said, giving me my own back. He drew on his pipe, but the fire had died out. He fussed with it as I walked away. Glancing back, I saw him nod to someone, the pipe stem pointed at my back.

CHAPTER TWENTY-ONE

"WE'VE GOT A tail," I said to Big Mike as he pulled the jeep into traffic. "Courtesy of Inspector Scutt."

"Any other good news?"

"Scutt wants to bring in Kaz for questioning," I said.

"He still likes Kaz for knifing Miller?"

"Yeah, and for beating a Russian within an inch of his life with a lead pipe, after the opera. No evidence, but it fits his theory of Kaz taking out his revenge on the Russians. Egorov, then Eddie, since he was their snitch, and then this guy Osip Nikolaevich Blotski."

"That doesn't sound like Kaz," Big Mike said. "The lead pipe, anyway."

"That's what I thought," I said. "Osip took one to the head, then they worked on his legs."

"Professional," Big Mike said, giving a quick glance to his rearview mirror.

"Yeah, right up Archie Chapman's alley. Spot our tail yet?"

"Pretty sure," Big Mike said. "Sedan three cars back, two guys wearing fedoras."

"Head over to St. James's Street," I said as we entered Trafalgar Square. Circling Nelson's Column, I was able to get a good look at the sedan. Two plainclothes men in a civilian vehicle stood out among the red buses, brown military vehicles, and black taxis. "Drop me off at MI5, I need to put some pressure on Cosgrove."

"Billy, Harding wants you down in Dover, and he wants me to get you there."

"Don't worry, we'll head out in an hour or so. If the tail stays with you, lose them and find Kaz at the Rubens. Pick me up in Berkeley Square. If our friends follow me, I'll lose them, so wait for me there. OK?"

"OK, but then straight to Dover. Right?"

"Right," I promised Big Mike as he pulled up in front of the nondescript entrance to MI5 headquarters. The fedora boys pulled over and watched me go in. It wouldn't be a problem shaking the tail. What I was more worried about was what to do with Kaz. I didn't want Scotland Yard finding and charging him, but I didn't think it would work out well if I brought him along to Dover, to question Russians.

The place looked like any office or government building, except for the lack of a sign or nameplate next to the door. I went through the identification routine with the receptionist as a stern-faced British Army sergeant eyed me from his post a few feet away. I asked to see Major Cosgrove, and she pointed to a row of chairs opposite her desk as she placed a call, speaking in hushed tones. I cooled my heels in the wide, carpeted hallway, watching officers in well-tailored uniforms from every service walk by, and a fair number of civilians as well. A busy place, everyone working hard at protecting the realm. I heard Cosgrove's name, and saw a man standing at the reception desk, a pipe clenched between his teeth as he doffed his raincoat. He was dark haired and square jawed, and he wore his pin-striped suit well.

"Kim Philby," he said to the receptionist as he showed his ID. "Major Cosgrove should have me listed for an appointment."

"Yes, Mr. Philby, I have you down. You can go right up," the receptionist said cheerily.

"I'll go up with him," I said, not wanting to wait for Cosgrove to finish gasbagging through some meeting.

"Not so fast, sir," said the sergeant. "Not until they call for you."

"Listen," I said, "I only need to talk to the major for a minute. He knows me, he won't mind."

"If he wouldn't mind, then why hasn't he called you up? Sir?"

"I can ring the major again and ask," the receptionist said helpfully, her hand on the telephone. "But he did say he'd be busy for quite a while."

"Never mind all that," Philby said. "I'll escort the lieutenant; I know the place well enough."

"All right, sir, if you say so," the sergeant said, his reluctance obvious. Whoever this guy was, he obviously had clout around here.

"Kim Philby," he said, extending his hand.

"Billy Boyle," I said as we climbed the staircase. "Thanks for rescuing me back there. Do you work with Major Cosgrove?"

"More of a liaison. I'm with MI6, the other side of the coin. We handle the overseas stuff, but we work closely with our brethren here. Your name is familiar, Lieutenant Boyle, Charles may have mentioned you. Aren't you looking into the murder of that Soviet fellow Egorov?"

"Yes, I am. That's why I'm here."

"I wish you luck, Lieutenant, for all our sakes. Murdered diplomats in the heart of London is something we could all do without. Whitehall is none too pleased, nor are the Soviets."

"I can imagine." I wondered if Philby would hang around when we got to Cosgrove's office. I had some dirty laundry to air, and it would only complicate things to have him listening in.

"Here we are," Philby said, opening a door and stepping in ahead of me. "Charles, I've brought you this American chap. Seemed harmless enough." He gave me a wink as he said it.

"Boyle," Cosgrove said. "What an unexpected surprise." He looked at me from his seat in a leather armchair, one of two facing a large, ornate desk, the wood polished to a ferocious gleam.

"Major Cosgrove," I said, a little confused at his friendly greeting, and what seemed like genuine surprise at seeing me. Then I saw the other person in the office, the man seated behind the desk. The one with the telephone at his elbow.

"Mr. Brown," I said.

"No, that's—," Philby began to say, then caught himself. "Sorry. Security, I quite understand. I can wait in the hall, if you like."

"No need, no need at all," Cosgrove said. "We're all friends here, right, Boyle?"

"Sure we are, Major. Friends and allies." Cosgrove was more jovial than I was used to, but it was forced, as if he was working to cover up something else. Or to send me a signal that things weren't what they seemed.

"What can I do for you then?" Cosgrove said, as if granting me a favor would be the high point of his day.

"For starters, you can tell me what MI5 was paying Sheila Carlson for, and if killing her lover and Tadeusz Tucholski was part of the contract."

"I may have to apologize for bringing Lieutenant Boyle up," Philby said, raising an eyebrow as he relit his pipe and settled into his chair, seeming to enjoy the tension in the room.

"Certainly you don't think we pay people to commit murder," Brown said. "Do you, Lieutenant Boyle?"

"I know one person on your payroll is a murderer, Mr. Brown. Edward Miller, late of the Rubens Hotel, was killed by Sheila Carlson. Nice combination of poison and bayonet."

"Gruesome," Philby said. "The other chap, the one with the Polish name, he's alive?"

"Alive and back in London, ready to speak his mind." I watched the three of them. Brown and Cosgrove exchanged glances, while Philby wrapped a smile around his pipe stem.

"It sounds like a domestic issue," Brown said. "More suited to Scotland Yard than MI5. Have you talked to them, Lieutenant Boyle?"

"Yes. They're on their way to pick up Miss Carlson right now. I imagine she'll sing quite a tune in exchange for escaping the gallows." It was a bluff, but you never know. I waited for a reaction, but got nothing. Cosgrove was quiet, and looked away from me, more interested in the carpet than the conversation. Strange, because he and I never got along, neither of us passing up the opportunity to show disdain for the other. He should have been lambasting me for what I was accusing him of. Instead, nothing. It had to be Brown. He was probably higher up than Cosgrove. I'd figured him for a heavy, but he was more than he appeared. Maybe he and Cosgrove didn't see eye to eye.

"I wouldn't be so sure," Brown said. He spoke with a certainty that couldn't be faked. It was the finality of the grave. "About her singing a tune, that is. But you're right about the gallows, she won't come to that end."

"She's dead?"

"Unfortunate," Brown said. "She got off the train at Slough. Last night, unfamiliar with the town, and with the blackout in effect, she walked in front of a truck."

"And how do you know all this? Last I saw you and your pal Wilson, you had a flat to fix."

"It's our business to know things, Lieutenant Boyle. We had people watching the trains, of course."

I began to see how everything fit. "You got what you were after on Penford Street when you asked Sheila if she knew where Radecki was, because you both knew he was going to visit Tadeusz. You just didn't know where he was."

"Really?"

"And when she told you she didn't know, her usefulness was at an end, and she'd become a liability. There was nothing she could do except implicate you. So you had people out looking for her, in case you missed her at Eddie's place."

"I don't know what you are talking about, Lieutenant," Brown said. "And I should have you brought up on charges for shooting up my vehicle."

"You shot at his car?" Philby said, more shocked at that than double-crossing murderers.

"One tire, that's all."

"Imagination and initiative," Philby said. "We could use you over at MI6. Perhaps an American with the Special Operations Executive would stir things up a bit."

"You run the SOE?" I asked, wondering what their meeting here was all about.

"Part of it, you might say. Never mind about that, Boyle, just idle conjecture. Probably best for you if you leave now," Philby said, blowing a stream of smoke as he spoke.

"Why?"

"Because I need to talk to these gentlemen about the Germans. Our actual enemies, you may recall. And I need to convince your Mr. Brown, as you know him, not to have you walk in front of a truck tonight. Best be careful, Boyle. Things are not always as they seem."

"As the head of Section Five well knows," said Brown, leaning back in his chair, his eyes on Cosgrove, daring him to speak. "Right, Charles?"

"Sometimes, they are worse than they seem," Cosgrove said, bringing his gaze up from the carpet. "Worse than one can imagine."

I left. I walked down the staircase, wondering what other strange conversations were taking place in the rooms I passed by, what death sentences were being handed out, what rationalizations were being made, and what burdens had suddenly become too much to bear. Outside, a fog had descended, the sky a solid, low gray, with swirls of yellowish brown hanging like a filthy veil from the barely visible rooftops. I crossed Piccadilly with care, the heavy traffic moving slowly but steadily, headlamps on, casting their gloomy, lost light into the fog. A real accident would be likely enough, never mind a surreptitious push into a crowded street. Had Sheila known she was being hunted, or had she still trusted her paymaster? Did she know her assailant, perhaps relaxing as he put his arm protectively around her waist as they waited at the side of the road? One good push, low in the back, is all it would take. If anyone saw it, he'd be gone in seconds, a nondescript man in a plain coat, a hat pulled down low over his face, making his way through the gathering crowd. Our "actual enemies" is what Philby had called the Germans, but at times I had to wonder. Even the worst of them wore a uniform that told you who they were.

Then I remembered. The Scotland Yard tail. I looked around for the sedan and the two fedoras, but in the narrow street, choked with fog, all I could see was the next lamppost. The gabfest with Cosgrove and his pals and this pea-souper had disoriented me. But the fog hadn't helped the guys following me either, since they were nowhere in sight. Maybe they'd decided it wasn't worth it and given up. Or maybe they were on foot, invisible a few yards behind me.

I turned a corner, hoping it was Albemarle Street, since that route would take me into Berkeley Square. I stopped and leaned against the brickwork, listening for signs of anyone following. A truck rumbled by slowly, the driver sounding his horn to warn those lost in the fog. Footsteps sounded, the *slap slap* of leather soles running on pavement echoing off the buildings. A woman carrying a shopping bag walked by me, visible only for a second before disappearing into the mist. A sharp, short whistle sounded, but I couldn't tell where it came from. I started walking toward the square, the cold and damp seeping into my bones as the sounds of running feet seemed to surround me. I heard them behind me, fading away in the opposite direction. Ahead of me, they drew nearer and slowed to a steady pace and stopped, as I tried to make out the vague outline of a figure in the fog. I stopped, and so did all the other sounds. I hoped I was only feeling jumpy, but I had the feeling there were more than two

Scotland Yard plainclothesmen out there. I stepped into a doorway, try-ing to melt into the fog and vanish.

I heard the throaty grumble of a motorcycle as it downshifted and came my way. The fog had kept most traffic off the roads, and the sound took on the sinister quality of a hunter seeking prey. The footsteps started up again, drawing closer from both directions. The same woman with the shopping bag walked by, this time halting and giving out the same sharp whistle that I'd heard before. She was definitely not wearing a fedora. Two men came up to me, one from each side. Stanley and Clive, Topper's henchmen.

"Boss wants a chat," Clive said. "Come on."

"I'm busy," I said, trying to make out if there were others hiding in the gloom.

"That's nice. Now hand over your pistol to Stanley and follow me. We're close to the Green Park Tube, we'll take that. Better underground than feeling our way through this mush."

"OK," I said, not seeing an alternative. I handed my piece over and asked Stanley how he was doing.

"Can't complain," he said. Since I'd just given him a weapon, I refrained from pointing out how I'd been right to slam his face when we'd first met, after he'd been so nasty to me. I'd told him then that if I hadn't, he'd have just kept being rotten. Now here he was, with me outnumbered and defenseless, and he was nice as pie. It felt good to be right about that, since I'd been so wrong about everything else.

CHAPTER ■ TWENTY-TWO

THEY'D BEEN ON me since I'd left the hotel that morning, Clive explained as we rode the Tube in the direction of Shoreditch.

"You didn't give us much of a chance, with that big bloke driving you around, stopping at Scotland Yard, then dropping in on MI5. A high-visibility mark, you are," he said as the train rolled out of the station.

"What about the two detectives who followed me?"

"Not much trouble at all, especially with this fog. Seems like both their rear tires went flat while they had their eyes glued on that door at St. James's Street. Lucky for us you left on foot. All we had to do was not lose you in this blasted fog. Not good for the lungs, you know, to be out running about in it."

"Who's the boss you mentioned? Topper or Archie?"

"There's only one boss, and best to keep your mouth shut about it for now. It's just a chat he wants, and no reason for trouble if you follow along like you're told. Got it?"

One goon had preceded Stanley and Clive as we boarded the train, and another followed us, making sure we had privacy at one end of the car. The odds were against me, and in an enclosed space to boot. It made me very agreeable. "Got it."

We rode in silence and took the escalator to the surface when we reached Liverpool Street, which meant that it was too early for Archie to have taken up residence underground. They led me through a twisting maze of streets, past dingy, low buildings that looked only marginally better off than the bombed-out ruins facing them. The thick, gray fog reeked of coal smoke from the chimneys on every building. They spewed gritty ash from low-grade, cheap coal. The gutters ran with stinking, greasy water, the runoff of cesspools and burned-out homes. A foghorn sounded from a freighter on the river, only a few blocks away, a low, mournful drone that seemed to come from the wounded city itself.

"Here," Clive said as he knocked on a door painted a bright red, the thick varnish shiny and garish in this neighborhood of boarded-up windows and ruin. He gave two short raps, waited a beat, then one final thump. The door opened, and a guy whose nose had been broken a few times but who wore a tuxedo well greeted us with a nod. Piano music tinkled idly from a room down the hall, as if a bored but accomplished musician was at the keys. Off the hall, in a sitting room, a fireplace glowed with coals, the warmth as welcome inside as the smoke was noxious in the street. Lush burgundy carpeting graced the hallway, and all the walls were painted a creamy white. It was a welcome contrast to the world outside, tucked away on a small side street in a seldom-traveled part of town. The perfect location for a whorehouse.

The muscle escort peeled off as Stanley and Clive led me down the hall, toward the music. The room was flanked at one end by a grand piano and at the other by a well-stocked bar. Between them sat Archie Chapman, looking comfortable in a leather armchair, as coffee was poured into his china cup by a stunningly beautiful woman in a black negligee. At the piano, a dark-haired woman in a red evening gown played with the keys while she smoked a cigarette in a long holder. Topper sat at the bar, and raised a glass in greeting.

"Peaches, my boy," Archie shouted. He was dressed in a three-piece suit, and his skin glowed as if he'd just stepped from a bath. It was a different look than his subterranean guise. "Good of you to come. Grand to see you again."

"Archie, the last time we met, you told me to never set foot in Shoreditch. Why the hoodlum-engraved invitation?"

"Ha! Good one, Peaches. I meant to say never return without a proper invite. Welcome to the Eastcheap Gentleman's Club. It's where I come after a night underground. Refreshing."

"Nothing looks cheap. And where are the gentlemen?"

"Billy," Topper said from his post at the bar. "Have a seat and take the chip off your shoulder, will you? Don't let that business with the truck get under your skin."

"Smart advice that," Archie said. "We had a good go-round with the truck, me takin' it and you gettin' it back. Shows you learn fast, and know how to get what's yours without burning your bridges. And that you have connections, to get the Shoreditch pubs declared off-limits. Impressive that. So listen to Topper and have some coffee. The real thing. American. Gisèle, more coffee, *s'il vous plaît*."

"*Oui*, Archie," she said with a smile that left her eyes dead.

"I own this establishment, Peaches," Archie continued, pausing to sip his coffee. "And you might be surprised at how many senior American officers partake of the delights here. Maybe some you know. Plenty of high-class toffs as well, military and politico. We even let in enlisted men one night a week. Supply sergeants get a special rate."

"So business is good?"

"Very good. We did well before, but since the war, with the Americans flooding in and so much talent coming from the Continent, it's all we can do to keep the place off the map."

"The Continent?"

"All of our girls are from Europe, Billy," Topper said. "When the war started, a lot of refugees came over, and many young girls were looking for work. Your average Englishman who uses our club wants something a bit different. He doesn't want someone who reminds him of his wife or his maid. One of the odd consequences of the class structure. Continental girls are another species altogether. Frees the stodgy old men up, especially the ones with money."

"Now, your average American, he doesn't care. Most of 'em couldn't tell the difference between a countess and a scrubwoman," Archie said. "Right, Dalenka?"

"I've been both," the woman at the piano said, not turning her head. "I scrubbed floors for the money when I first came to England, and now I tell them I am a countess for the money. Both I've done on my knees, and I tell you, scrubbing floors is much harder. And yes, the Americans are a bit naive. Sometimes it is endearing. Usually it is boring." She blew smoke toward the ceiling.

"Dalenka is from Czechoslovakia," Archie said. "She runs the place for me. Very smart, she is. Speaks several languages, and has a head for numbers. She is truly a countess in my book." Archie looked almost smitten, but I knew it was for show, to bolster the morale of the talent.

Dalenka put her cigarette out, sat silently for a minute, and then began playing with both hands. She sat up straight, her long, arched fingers gliding smoothly over the ivories. Gisèle put a tray of coffee down and served me, the vacant smile unwavering. The music rose slowly, building and then fading, joyous at moments, but ending on a downward slide of sorrowful deep notes that lingered in the smoky air. Dalenka's hands remained poised on the keys where the last notes had been played. Even Archie was silent.

"What was that, Dalenka?" Topper asked in a whisper.

"A requiem by Anton Dvořák. A Czech composer. It was written as a funeral mass for soldiers." She shut the keyboard cover, swiveled around on the stool, and looked at us as if we were dead men. Without a word, she left the room, putting her arm around Gisèle, who was still smiling as tears rolled down her cheeks.

Archie nodded solemnly, acknowledging the unspoken truth that lingered where Dalenka had been. Staring at the open door, he spoke, in hushed tones.

> *A Wounded Deer—leaps highest—*
> *I've heard the Hunter tell—*
> *'Tis but the Ecstasy of death—*
> *And then the Brake is still!*

"Emily Dickinson," I said, stunned that I'd remembered. I wasn't much for school, or poetry, for that matter, but the sadness of that poem had stayed with me since I'd heard it in senior English class. The wounded dear, leaping for life, finding death.

"So you're not a complete philistine, Peaches. Yes, your fellow American, Miss Emily Dickinson. 'A Wounded Deer Leaps Highest,' she called it, and she must've known about wounds, that poor one."

"What about Dalenka?"

"She and her lover were involved with the Three Kings," Topper said. "They were leaders of the Czech Resistance. The Nazis got all of them in 1941. Dalenka and her boyfriend were couriers, carrying everything from explosives to messages from London in and out of Prague. One spring day in 1940, the Gestapo was waiting; someone had betrayed them. The boyfriend was killed in a gunfight, but Dalenka escaped. Lucky for her that he was killed, otherwise they would have made him talk. She had false papers that got her out through Yugoslavia, then on to Portugal and finally here."

"They all have stories," Archie said. "Not all of them are heroic, either. But you don't start off in Nazi-occupied Europe and end up in an East End bordello without a tale worth telling. Or not telling, as the case may be."

"What story am I here to be told?"

"We both now seem to be looking for Russians, Peaches. Topper told me you want to know who killed that Egorov fellow. Fair enough. It had nothing to do with us. You know about the business with the delivery trucks, you've seen the map. Again, you're smart enough to leave well enough alone there. Tells me you're focused on the killer, not on farm produce. Right?"

"Right."

"Just to get it out in the open. We're not at cross-purposes here. There's a certain Russian we want to find. Seeing as how you are thick with them, I figured you might be able to point us in the right direction."

"Does this have anything to do with Osip Nikolaevich Blotski?"

"Who the hell is that?" Archie demanded.

"No one," Topper said. "A message. One that was apparently not received."

"Oh, that," Archie said, scoffing. "Told you, boy, that wouldn't smoke him out."

"A Russian from the embassy owes you something, and you can't find him. You crippled an associate of his, and probably gave him a message to pass on. That didn't work, and you remembered my questions about Egorov, and thought I might be able to ferret him out?"

"See, Topper, I told you he had half a brain in his head! Yes, Peaches, that's it in a nutshell. Will you help us?"

"What's in it for me?"

"Well, there's the other half of that brain. Good for you, Peaches. What do we have for him, Topper?"

"Gisèle? Perhaps her and a friend?"

"No thanks, my dance card is full. Who is it you're looking for?"

"Peaches, we are asking so nicely here. Over coffee, after beautiful music. As we offer you the delights of the flesh. Why be obstinate then? We aren't going to offer up a name until we have a deal of some sort. A handshake will do, but there has to be something between us, not simply a gift to your curiosity."

I thought about it, and had to admit I was curious. Who were they after, and for what? I still thought there had to be a connection between Egorov, where he was killed, and the truck hijackings. I also wondered what a Russian from the embassy had that the Chapmans wanted so badly.

"I want a cut," I said, deciding to see where this took things.

"So do we," Topper said grimly. I think he meant my throat, not a percentage.

"Deal gone bad?"

"All is not yet lost," Archie said, with a stern look at his son. "There is a man who we had an arrangement with. We're not certain if he's done a runner. We are prepared to provide a finder's fee if you can assist us in locating him."

I recalled Scutt telling me that there had been no more truck hijackings recently, and I wondered if it had anything to do with the movement of Russian personnel to Dover. Did Archie think he'd been betrayed when his contact moved out, probably under secret orders? Maybe I could turn this to some benefit.

"I think I may know where he is," I said. "But I can't tell you."

"What do you want?" Archie said, moving out of his chair faster than I thought he could, leaning over me. "More money, or more of the blade? Either will do the job."

"I didn't say I wouldn't take a message," I said. "But it's a military secret. A group of them moved out a couple of days ago, for security reasons. So if your boy hasn't been in touch, it's because he can't get away."

"How far away, Billy?" Topper asked, taking his father by the arm and moving him back to his chair. "Take it easy, Dad, we'll work this out."

"Not far. I'm supposed to go there today, as a matter of fact."

"Is this on the up-and-up, Peaches? I'd hate to think you'd try to fool an old man."

"Why would I? There's no reason for me to make anything up. As you said, we each have our own concerns."

"There's that, yes," Archie said, nodding to himself. "What do you want for your cut?"

"Not money. If I need some help with the Egorov business, I'll come to you. For a favor, in exchange for the one I'll do for you."

"You'll deliver a message directly to this person for us?" Topper said, clarifying the terms of the deal.

"Yes, but not a lead-pipe message. I'll talk to him and let you know what he says as soon as I can get back. I'll probably be able to move more freely than the Russians." I felt a little twinge of guilt at being a messenger boy for Archie, but I thought it might help before this was over to have him owe me one. And anything I could learn about his operation wouldn't hurt either.

"All right," Archie said. He nodded to Topper to shut the door. Topper checked the hallway, then sat next to us. Archie nodded again, and he spoke in a low voice, keeping their secrets close.

"As you know, we've had a relationship with someone who provides us with the routes the delivery trucks take going to the Russian Embassy. We've had other dealings with him, and came to trust him, as far as that goes in this business. We were in negotiations for another exchange of information for cash. We made a down payment, and before we could complete the transaction, he dropped out of sight. The timing is right from what you just told us."

"Without betraying any military secrets, Peaches, what can you tell us that will lend a bit more credence to your tale?" Archie broke in, trying for more than I wanted to give.

"It is directly related to military planning, so I can't say anything else. I should get there tonight if the fog lifts."

"Go on then," Archie said to Topper.

"We need to be assured that plans are still set. We have not received the time and place. That's the message. We've done everything on our end; now we need to know. Time and place. He'll understand."

"And who is he?"

"Captain Rak Vatutin. Red Army chap."

The last and only time I'd seen Rak Vatutin, he was serving Kaz and me drinks at the Soviet Embassy. Had he been trying to get Kaz looped, in hopes he would make a fool of himself once he saw the film? There had been something nasty in Vatutin's look, a glimpse of viciousness behind the diplomatic facade and automatic smile. But that could have been the vodka or simply his nature. I needed to find out more about what Vatutin did at the embassy, and if he'd had access to the delivery routes. And the "time and place"—but for what?

I took the Underground back to Norfolk House, wondering about Harding's reaction when he saw that, once again, I hadn't made it to Dover. I'd learned a few things, though. Scotland Yard was still looking for Kaz; MI5 was in the murder business and had contracted with Sheila Carlson to kill Tad, and then turned on her to eliminate loose ends; MI6, represented by Kim Philby, didn't seem to care very much; and Major Cosgrove had acted suspiciously out of character. Did all this violate his sense of fair play? Maybe.

I'd also learned about the Eastcheap Gentleman's Club, where Archie had female refugees from all across Europe on offer, and that Archie and Topper had something big planned, and the top-secret move to Dover had sent them into a panic, thinking they'd been betrayed. Now I was the messenger boy, my job to find Rak Vatutin and ask him what was the time and place.

It was finally time to get to Dover. All I had to do was endure Harding's wrath, find Big Mike, and figure out what to do with Kaz while the heat died down. Then find Vatutin, figure out what the target was, and somewhere along the way find out what Egorov's death had to do with it all.

The only thing that was guaranteed was how steamed Harding would be, but I came up empty on that one. I found Big Mike at his desk, apologetic at not finding me in Berkeley Square. I told him I'd made my way back OK, filling him in on my bordello detour.

"Sam won't be back until late this afternoon," Big Mike said. "He's up at Bletchley Park, whatever that is. Something hush-hush. But you got someone waiting for you in his office. Cosgrove."

"Interesting. Where's Kaz?"

"I stashed him at a pub across from the Rubens. I figured he could watch for Sheila to show herself, if the fog lifts, while I waited for you."

I filled Big Mike in about Sheila, then opened the door to Harding's office. Cosgrove stood by the window, hands behind his back. He gave a quick glance in my direction, then brought his gaze back to the green square below.

"I thought we ought to talk, Boyle."

"Sure, Major," I said as I took a seat opposite Harding's desk. It gave me a side view of Cosgrove's face, the best I could do. "Strange bunch in your office this morning. I got the distinct impression you didn't see eye to eye."

"Yes. I thought the hail-fellow-well-met routine would tell you as much."

"It did. But why bother?"

"We've not seen eye to eye, either, Boyle, on several occasions. But I daresay our differences have been more of style. Perhaps belief also, but sincere belief on both our parts."

"Can't argue that. But the way you used me in our first encounter, that never set well with me. It was more than a difference in style."

"Damn it, Boyle, there are pawns in war, and when you first came here, that was how you were best used. And to good effect, I may add. You know what Churchill said, about the best way to protect truth in wartime? To attend her with a bodyguard of lies. You were part of that bodyguard. Sorry if that's difficult to accept, but there it is."

"OK, OK, I get it. It doesn't help to debate the past anyway. Why are you here?"

"Whatever our differences, I wanted you to know that I don't approve of the actions of the man you know as Mr. Brown. He's gone much too far. In the past, he's had a number of successes that have gone to his head and blinded his superiors to the utter ruthlessness of his methods."

"Did he approve of the plan to kill Tadeusz?"

"Yes. I found out about it too late to put a stop to it. I'm glad to hear it failed and the young man is doing well."

"Really? Even though your government wants the Katyn Forest Massacre to be blamed on the Germans?"

"Boyle," Cosgrove said, still unable to look me in the eye, "I will follow the orders of my government. If it is judged that it is in the best interest of Great Britain and the war effort that the deaths of those Poles be laid at the feet of the Germans, I say so be it. History can sort it all out when the war is won. But I will not sanction murder on English soil to improve our chance of success. I came here to tell you something else, though. Brown spoke of Sheila Carlson's being hit by a truck, you recall?"

"Yes."

"Apparently he was speaking of a plan, not an actual event. One of the problems with Brown is that he plays fast and loose with the truth, even among colleagues. He had sent one of his men to follow her and do the job."

"But he didn't?"

"No. She spotted him and gave him the slip at the first opportunity. Now she's nowhere to be found. I thought you'd want to know."

"Thank you," I said, trying to work out what that meant in the mix of death, theft, intrigue, and betrayal I was trying to unravel. "There's something I should tell you, too. Tadeusz is dead. I made up the story about his being alive in hopes it would get back to Sheila, and make her try again."

"She was successful then?"

"Indirectly." I told him the story of seeing Tad at St. Albans, and his reaction to hearing about Eddie and Sheila.

"The proverbial straw," Cosgrove said, shaking his head. "How odd that we both have news about life and death, quite opposite in the telling. I must admit, I would have preferred the original stories to this outcome. Sheila Carlson seems to lack any moral center. Pity about the young Pole, truly."

"His life was a nightmare. He said he wished he'd been killed with all the others."

"He actually witnessed it? In Katyn?"

"Yes," I said. "He told me the whole story. They pulled him out of line when they discovered they hadn't finished questioning him. About one minute before he would have joined the bodies in the pit."

"Dear God."

Silence descended between us. Cosgrove rested his hands on the windowsill, weariness suddenly overcoming him. I waited, listening to the sounds drift up from the street below. Life flowing by, as if all the murders and lies in this war were to be expected and endured as a matter of course.

"There's something else," I said.

"What?" Cosgrove said, finally turning to face me.

"Kiril Sidorov knows about Diana Seaton, and her mission."

"Impossible!"

"He didn't mention her name, or where she is, but he did say he knew there was a woman I cared about on a mission behind enemy lines. How could he know that?"

"Do you know where she's gone to?"

"I had Italy figured, probably Rome."

"She didn't tell you, did she?"

"No, she got angry when I asked. But I put a few clues together, and Rome seemed like a safe bet. Maybe the Vatican?"

"I shouldn't comment," Cosgrove said, in a way that confirmed I'd been right. "But if that were the case, Rome is filled with Communists. She may have come into contact with a cell, but I don't know why that information would be routed back to London."

"Would Kim Philby know? He seemed to be in charge of SOE."

"He is, for Spain and the rest of the Mediterranean. He definitely knows about all missions in the area. Sharp chap, but I wouldn't come at him directly with a question about a security breach. He's apt to have you thrown in a military prison while he looks into it. I will ask discreetly."

"Will you let me know what you find out? About Diana, I mean."

"Yes, I will. I won't be able to reveal details, but I can let you know if she's come to harm." It was my turn to look away. I'd heard more than I wanted to about Gestapo torture chambers, more than I wanted to believe. "Sorry, Boyle, that was clumsily said. I will tell you what I find."

"Thank you," I said, facing Cosgrove. This was difficult for him, I knew. He'd followed orders all his life, with a certainty that he served a good and righteous master. Now his master had upset everything he believed in, everything he counted on, and he found himself conspiring with the likes of me. It took courage and, for the first time, I saw the younger man in him. Or maybe I simply saw him for who he really was, without regard to age, uniform, or belief in the British Empire.

"Save your thanks. I may need them and more before all is said and done."

"One more thing, Major. Is there any kind of shipment headed for the Soviet Embassy, something more valuable than booze or food?"

"Why do you ask?" Cosgrove narrowed his eyes, studying me, as if I'd come up with a really smart comment. He looked surprised.

"Is that a yes?"

"I can't answer that question, Boyle, to say yes or no. Either would leave the impression I know of such a thing, one way or the other. But I would like to know what you suspect."

"Scotland Yard says hijackings are down, so maybe it's a rumor."

"*What* is just a rumor?" Cosgrove was angry now, and we were back on more comfortable ground.

"Just some loose talk. I'll let you know if it comes to anything. Have you heard of the Three Kings?"

"I assume you're not talking about a Christmas pageant, Boyle. If you mean the resistance group from Czechoslovakia, yes, I have. Last of the leaders was taken in 1941. Showed potential, as I recall. No sign from any of the survivors since, if there were any."

"There is one. She's here in London. Is that something Philby might be interested in?"

"Smart chap, Boyle; he may indeed. Could you produce this woman?"

"She runs a bordello for Archie Chapman. I know where she is. Producing her might be a bit difficult. She goes by Dalenka."

"Well, MI6 would have no trouble if it comes to that. Could be a Nazi plant, but that would be useful in its own way. I'm certain Philby will want to know more, and information about Miss Seaton will be a small price to pay in exchange. I'll see him later tonight, and will be able to speak to him alone."

"You mean without the mysterious Mr. Brown?"

"Indeed."

"Do you think he had anything to do with the killing of Egorov?" I asked, as I opened the office door for him. He put his weight on his cane, and frowned.

"Brown? No, I don't. Egorov's name never came up, and as you've seen, he is a bit of a braggart. I think if he had, he would've said something about it. I expect you'll solve that mystery, Boyle. You seem to have talent in that direction. Be certain to tell me anything you learn about threats concerning shipments to the Soviets. Good day."

I watched his rolling, limping gait as he left through the outer office. I'd had some strange conversations with the man, but this was the first one that had ended on a friendly note, which made it the oddest of them all.

"Let's get to that pub," I said to Big Mike.

"You're the boss, Billy."

A FIVE-MINUTE DRIVE took half an hour in the thick fog. Vehicles hugged the curb to stay on their side of the road, and the late afternoon looked more like dusk. The only good thing was that the Germans wouldn't be sending over bombers in this weather.

"Sheila Carlson could have walked in and out of the Rubens ten times," Kaz said from his seat next to a window at the Bag O'Nails Pub.

"She probably won't show herself in London," I said, explaining that Mr. Brown had ordered her killed, and how she'd slipped away.

"There's a man who doesn't like loose ends, and a woman who is very careful," Kaz said. "What do we do now?"

"Let's eat," Big Mike said. "It's early, but we have a long drive ahead of us."

"We can't get to Dover in this soup," I said.

"We should've left earlier, before it got this bad. Sam won't like it that we hung around here and got stuck. So we're leaving, after we eat."

"OK," I said, giving in to the lowest ranker at the table. No reason to argue with a corporal who has generals and colonels for pals and who could lift me three feet off the floor. Big Mike and I ordered ale, while Kaz stayed with Scotch. I really wanted vodka, God help me, but I resisted the hard stuff. Before long I was tucking into a plate of fish and chips. Kaz had chicken and turnips, while Big Mike indulged his taste for odd English dishes.

"Steak and kidney pie?" I said. "I didn't know they still served that in the twentieth century."

"It's good," Big Mike said. "Beefsteak, nice fluffy pastry, and the kidney tastes like liver. Sort of." He chewed a bit, and took a long swallow of ale.

"What have you been up to, Billy?" Kaz asked, after we were through eating.

"I found out Scutt is very interested in talking to you, which I think means throwing you in a cell on suspicion of murder. Apparently a Russian named Osip Nikolaevich Blotski was beat with a lead pipe last night, and nearly killed."

"Inspector Scutt thinks I am hunting Russians one by one, on the streets of London?"

"I'd say he's seeking a motive, and you've got the best claim to one, after that scene at the opera. Things got stranger after that. I went to see Cosgrove, to confront him about Sheila Carlson and watch his reaction. Who do I find him with but none other than a Mr. Brown. They had a meeting with a guy from MI6, Kim Philby."

"Then Mr. Brown must be more than an errand boy," Kaz said. "Cosgrove and Philby move in the higher ranks of intelligence circles."

"I got the distinct notion that Cosgrove was the junior of the three, and that he and Brown were on the outs. Brown as much as boasted he'd had Sheila killed, to keep her quiet." I described my visit to the Eastcheap Gentleman's Club, the message I was supposed to carry to Rak Vatutin, and the surprise visit from Cosgrove.

"So now we know who among the Russians was tipping off the Chapman gang," Kaz said. "And that you are aiding and abetting them in hijacking farm produce. That doesn't help clear me of suspicion, or help you solve the case."

"It might be more than produce or vodka this time. When I mentioned it to Cosgrove he nearly blew a fuse."

"What else could it be?" Kaz said. "Weapons? Drugs?"

"We're missing something," Big Mike said, setting down his empty glass.

"Obviously," I said.

"I mean about Sheila. We figured she killed Eddie for the cash, right? But Scutt was right, that she could've taken that anytime. So there had to be another reason."

"There could be many reasons," Kaz said. "A lover's quarrel, a falling-out among thieves."

"No, we gotta look at it with this new information: Brown wanted her dead, and she got away."

"What do you mean?" I asked, not seeing where Big Mike was going with this.

"OK," he said, holding up one finger. "Let's say she has no clue Brown is going to have her done in. She makes the cake, gives it to Radecki, and then figures it's a big payday. Eddie's at work. She could take off with their nest egg, and then get whatever Brown promised her once the job was done. Why kill Eddie?"

"Maybe he found out about the poisoned cake," I said. "Or who was paying her to do it."

"No, he was at work. She baked two cakes, and brought him a piece of one, which he ate. He couldn't have known about her taking off with their money." Big Mike held up a second finger. "Now let's figure she knew Brown was going to double-cross her. Same question applies. Why kill Eddie?"

"It doesn't help to repeat that we don't know why," Kaz said.

"No, that's not what he's saying," I broke in, watching Big Mike nod his head in approval as I caught up to him. "We're stuck in a rut thinking it had something to do with MI5 or Tad. It doesn't. There's another reason entirely. Eddie had to know something that truly threatened her. Working for MI5 is its own protection; if she had faith in Brown, she would have felt safe. Or, if she knew Brown was going to have her killed, that threat would have been her top priority."

"I see," Kaz said. "You're saying she murdered Eddie for a third reason, external to the case. And that perhaps she didn't know Brown had ordered her death. Perhaps she slipped away for that third reason."

"I knew you guys would get it sooner or later," Big Mike said. "Being officers, you were bound to. How about you buy the next round?"

"Aren't you driving us to Dover tonight?"

"In this pea soup? No way. I'll sleep on the couch in your fancy hotel, and we'll leave at first light. Sam will never know."

"You're the boss, Big Mike."

AFTER THE NEXT round, we decided to detour back to Eddie's place, figuring that we might have missed something the first time. Scotland Yard would have tossed the place by now, but maybe they were looking at things the way we had: that everything Sheila did was about her work for Brown and MI5. Even after a few drinks, three pairs of eyes might see something new. The fog was lifting, but navigating in the blackout made for a slow trip across the Thames and through the twisting side streets of Camberwell. A railroad bridge crossed the main thoroughfare, where a large antiaircraft gun lifted its steel nose into the foggy night. I could see the faint red glow of two cigarettes where the crew leaned against the railing, relaxing under the dark gray cover. Were they bored, I wondered, when the lonely quiet hours stretched out before them? Did they prefer the excitement, tinged with a chance of death, which a raid brought? As we drove under the bridge, one of them flipped his butt out into the night, the fiery sparks arcing into darkness. Odd, I thought, the choices that war presents us. The slow passage of time, or the thrill of dancing with death. Everyone wanted to live, but when the minutes and seconds crawled into the small hours of the morning, the speed and decisiveness of combat had an allure that it lacked in the daylight.

We found Penford Street and Eddie's place. The front door was locked tight, but the back door gave way easily after Big Mike worked his knife blade into the latch and put his weight behind it.

"Back doors are always easier," Big Mike said, as Kaz flipped on the light switch in the rear hallway. "Now, what exactly are we looking for?"

"Nothing," I said, walking into the kitchen and turning on the overhead light. "Don't look *for* anything. Look *at* what's here."

"Billy, perhaps my English is not up to the distinction," Kaz said. "What are you talking about?"

"The biggest mistake you can make in a search is to expect to find something that shouldn't be there. It can blind you to common objects that might mean something. Since we don't know what we're looking for, don't look too hard. Just look at what's here." I could almost hear my dad drumming that into my head, over and over again, back when he used to pull me in as a uniform to help at a crime scene. The overtime was nice, but what he was really doing was teaching me an advanced course in homicide investigation. The problem was, I thought I already knew it all, and his lectures left me bored. Now it seemed to be such a simple, obvious truth, to not look for anything when you were looking for something.

"This kitchen is a mess," Kaz said, keeping his opinion about the Boyle wisdom to himself.

"Pretty much like we left it," Big Mike said. "Looks like the Scotland Yard boys pulled out a few drawers and fished around, that's about it." He was right. The cut-up oleander was dried out, and flies buzzed around the spilled sugar. Dirty dishes were piled in the sink, and cooking utensils were scattered over the counter.

"There is a third reason," I said. "Sheila was never coming back to this place."

"Just because she's a lousy housekeeper?" Big Mike said. "I've seen plenty places worse than this dump."

"No. Because she left the evidence out where we could find it. The cut-up oleander. She didn't even try to hide it, or clean up the sugar. When's the last time you saw a Londoner waste sugar like that? I don't think she cared what anyone found here, which may also mean she's assumed another identity. Or had assumed one as Sheila Carlson. If we ever find her, I bet she'll be using another name."

"Yes," Kaz said. "It makes sense. The rest of the kitchen is neat and orderly. The disarray is all from her baking, and what looks like morning tea." He opened cupboards, revealing stacked dishes and cups, nothing fancy, but well kept. We went through the rest of the house, following the cursory search that Scutt's men had done. We checked pockets in the clothing that hung in the closet, looked on the underside of a chest of drawers, pulled records out of their jackets, leafed through books and magazines. Nothing. I sat at a desk, glancing at unpaid bills, advertisements, and an empty appointment calendar, the past and future now useless to Eddie Miller.

"Anything in the bathroom?" I asked Kaz as I wandered through the bedroom again.

"Men's toiletries. A few patent medicines."

"Sheila's stuff cleared out?"

"There is a bottle of cologne, nearly empty, but not much else." I looked around the bedroom. A small vanity was set between two narrow windows, hairbrushes and cosmetics lined up by the mirror.

"I think she hightailed it out of here with the cash and whatever she put in her purse," Big Mike said.

"Yeah, looks like. Is there anyplace we haven't searched?"

"We've covered every inch of this place," Big Mike said.

"Except," said Kaz, "for one thing. The dustbin. It was by the back door."

We hauled the garbage can into the back hall, and dumped the contents out onto newspapers spread on the floor. It didn't look or smell pretty. They'd dined on fish and chips not too long ago—Eddie's last supper maybe? The cut end of the small cake she'd fed to Eddie. Damp tea leaves, moldy crusts of bread, a broken glass, crumpled newspaper, and various indistinguishable globs made up the rest. With rationing, not much in England went into the dustbin.

"What's this?" Big Mike said, holding out a small stained and wet piece of paper. It was dark green, and looked as if it had been ripped in half. A number was at the top and bottom. It was hard to read, but the printed words said *Railway*, along with some smudged ink stains that had once been handwriting. I ran my fingers through the garbage again, thinking how often I heard that a detective's life must be glamorous.

"Here!" Kaz said, shaking out the newspapers. He held the other half, this one dry and intact. Southern Railway. Ticket number 4882. London to Shepherdswell, via Canterbury. Third class, round-trip.

"Who went to Shepherdswell, wherever the hell that is?" Big Mike said. "Eddie or Sheila?"

"Impossible to say, but the Southern Railway goes to the channel coast. Canterbury is southeast of here, so it should be a simple matter to find Shepherdswell along the line," Kaz said. "We could ask around. If it's a small town, someone may have noticed one of them."

"That's on the way to Dover, isn't it?" I said.

"Ah, the ever-elusive Dover. Yes, it is."

CHAPTER ▪ TWENTY-THREE

EARLY MORNING FOUND us on the road to Canterbury. We'd used the rear entrance of the Dorchester, since Inspector Scutt was on the lookout for Kaz. The blackout curtains had come in handy, and the kitchen had fixed us up with a thermos of coffee and cheese sandwiches for our predawn departure.

Crossing the River Medway at Rochester, we heard the heavy drone of engines behind us, and soon the sky was filled with B-17 bombers, hundreds of them, heading into the eastern dawn. It was a solid stream of aircraft, bomber squadrons forming up from bases all over southern England, coming together above us, painting the sky white with contrails and vibrating the air with their thousand-horsepower engines. Big Mike pulled the jeep over by the embankment, and we craned our necks to watch the air show.

"You're not from around here then." The voice came from the side-walk, where an elderly gent rested his hands on his cane, a playful smile on his face.

"Don't tell me you get used to this?" I asked him.

"You never get used to Jerry coming over, and he used to, you know, day and night. Hit the airfield outside of town and us, too, for good measure. Now, at least if I hear airplanes during the day, I know it's you Yanks flying them. Makes a fella feel good not to have to look up. Safe and secure, like."

"You take any hits recently, with the new raids?" I asked.

"No, just some fields plowed up with those Jerries what got shot down, and them releasing their bomb loads. Sometimes the Home Guard has to round up the aircrew, or collect the bodies. Seems like every airplane in this war flies over us, going or coming from bombing poor souls somewhere. Better them than us, that's what I say. But I'll tell you, boys, I will look up when them B-17s come home."

"Why?"

"Not all of them make it. I've seen one try to land, smoke spewing out from two engines. They crashed, poor lads. Tore up a barn, too. You've got to watch out in the afternoon, but morning time, I go for my walk, and enjoy the sound they make. Different at night, though. Could be our own Lancasters or Jerry coming over, can't really tell. Anyway, I hope your boys knock Adolf for a loop. Good day, lads." He tapped his fingers to his forehead in a salute of sorts, and continued his constitutional. As we pulled away, I looked back, and saw him give a quick glance skyward.

"That's what comes of living in Bomb Alley," Kaz said. "Good advice about the afternoon, though."

"I think he was laughing at us, the old coot," Big Mike said.

"What he's lived through, I'll let him have a chuckle," I said. "No way to live out your old age, with the Luftwaffe bombing your hometown, and then both sides crash-landing around you for the rest of the war."

We drove on, watching the contrails disappear off to our left, as I wondered what the formations would look like coming back, and what the old man would think and feel as he watched them. He looked like someone who'd worked all his life, and probably served in the last war. These should be his golden years, and instead of tending roses, he was walking under a cloud of bombers, looking over his shoulder every day for the debris of war to fall from the sky. There were all sorts of victims in this war, in every war, and for certain there were plenty of people who'd do anything to be in his shoes. Still, it bothered me. I thought of my own father, another veteran of the last war, and a guy who worked harder than anyone on the force. I always imagined him going fishing and chewing the fat with his pals at Kirby's after he retired. What specter would he glimpse over his shoulder?

The countryside opened up after Rochester—low, rolling hills, farmland with fields marked off by stone walls and shrubs. The ground was bare, plowed over after the fall harvest, except for the apple orchards, with their neat lines of trees, branches pruned and ready for the spring. It was a pleasant drive, until we came to a crossroads outside of Sittingbourne. A military convoy had the right of way, and we sat, watching the parade of heavy trucks cross the roadway.

"Perhaps we should tell stories," Kaz said, after ten minutes of monotony. "We are headed toward Canterbury, after all."

"So?" Big Mike said, looking at me. I shrugged.

"Geoffrey Chaucer? *The Canterbury Tales*? Surely they teach Chaucer in American schools?"

"Wouldn't know," Big Mike said. "I left after the eighth grade to work at a gas station, on account of my old man kicking the bucket. Maybe they mentioned him in the ninth grade."

"The name rings a bell," I said. "But I never paid a lot of attention in class. What are they? Stories about Canterbury?"

"Do you want to hear about him?" Kaz said, from his perch in the rear seat.

"We ain't going nowhere soon," Big Mike said, gesturing at the line of stationary traffic in front of us.

"Well," Kaz began, warming to the lesson and a willing audience, "Chaucer lived in the fourteenth century. He was originally from London, but the story goes that he was peripherally involved in a power struggle between a group of powerful barons and King Richard II. He and his friends backed the king, and the king lost. Chaucer's friends lost their heads, so he wisely retired to the countryside, in Kent."

"Those barons, they knock off the king?" Big Mike asked.

"No, they kept him as a figurehead, but eliminated all his advisers. The parliamentary session after they took over was called the Merciless Parliament, since the death sentence was imposed on all the nobles who had supported the king's cause. Chaucer had been a soldier and a diplomat for King Richard II, but he was not highly born and probably would have been left alone, but he took no chances."

"Smart guy," Big Mike said. "Like after a Mob war. The ones who come out on top watch for any threat, and eliminate it. So Chaucer went on the lam?"

"Not in hiding, just out of the way, until Richard regained control, insuring a royal position and pension."

"Exactly like a Mob war," Big Mike said, bridging the gap between centuries with his common-sense analysis. "What did he do, bring in some muscle from out of town?"

"Exactly," Kaz said. "The king's uncle, John of Gaunt, returned with his forces from a war in Spain."

"And they put Richard back in power, and Chaucer got his cut for staying loyal, and alive," Big Mike said.

"Yes, quite. He wrote one of the great works of the English language while living here in Kent, presumably near Canterbury. It begins with a group of travelers setting out on a pilgrimage from London to Canterbury, to visit the cathedral. It is a long walk, so they agree to tell stories on the way there and back. At the end of the trip, the person who has told the best story will have their dinner paid for by the others."

"I get it," I said. "Since we're on the road from London to Canterbury . . ."

"I'm in," Big Mike said. "Kaz, you tell us some of those old Chaucer stories, and we'll see how they stack up against our yarns." The traffic inched ahead then started to move and as quickly came to a stop. There was a chill in the air, even with the bright winter sun, and I buttoned my trench coat collar and nodded to Kaz to begin.

"One of my favorites is 'The Pardoner's Tale.' He tells the story of three men who are drinking heavily, mourning the death of a dear friend. The more they drink, the angrier they grow at death, whom they hold responsible. So they go out, searching for death, vowing to kill him. On the road, they meet an old man, who points to an ancient oak tree and tells them that is where they could find death. The three wait by the tree, and while there, discover eight bags of gold coins. The bags are heavy and they decide to wait until dark to remove the gold, or else someone will see them and steal their treasure. By now, all thoughts of killing death are forgotten. Growing hungry, they agree that one man should go to the village for food and wine. They draw straws and the youngest draws the short one. He leaves without complaint, trusting that his friends will not depart before nightfall. As soon as he is gone, his companions plot to kill him, reasoning that the gold will be best split two ways instead of three. The lad returns, with three bottles of wine and ample food, when he is set upon and killed. To celebrate, his killers drink the wine, not knowing that the boy had poisoned two of the bottles, intending to kill them. When darkness finally comes, all three are dead at the foot of the tree, having found death, just as the old man had foreseen."

"Good one," I said. "What've you got, Big Mike?"

"I remember a story about Joey Adamo, whose old man ran the Westside Gang in Detroit. This was before I joined the force, but the old-timers told the story over and over. Joey was a Sicilian orphan, and Angelo Adamo adopted him, since he and his wife couldn't have kids. He'd picked a kid from Sicily, so he'd be sure to get a real Siciliano, pure-blood. Anyway, he raises him like his own, and brings him up in the organization. Joey makes his bones during the Vitale Wars. Lots of touring cars with guns, the whole nine yards. The Adamo faction does OK, they come out on the winning side. Joey marries into the Zerilli family, another Mob family, and the girl's a real looker to boot. He's got everything: respect, honor, money, a beautiful wife, and pretty soon a healthy baby son. All because he was plucked from some orphanage by a nun, to be the son of a Detroit hoodlum." The traffic moved, almost up to twenty miles an hour now, and Big Mike shifted gears and continued. "But something went wrong."

"What?" Kaz said, leaning forward from the backseat.

"Guilt. Regret. He shoots a kid by accident, a bystander who takes a slug to the chest and dies in the hospital. He'd killed five men without missing a beat, but after killing an innocent kid, he can't pull the trigger, no matter what."

"What happens to him?"

"He runs. Steals twenty grand from his old man, and hightails it off across the border, into Canada, wife and kid in tow. Old man Zerilli takes it as a personal insult, and starts a shooting war, demanding his daughter and grandson be turned over to him, along with some of the Adamo territory."

"Can he really do that?" Kaz asked. "Barter human beings?"

"They're from the old country," Big Mike said, as if that explained everything. "Anyway, Angelo agrees to one out of the three, but Zerilli wants more than his daughter back. Things get worse, and both sides are hurting. A Mob war costs money, and there's less dough coming in for everyone. So Angelo sends some boys into Canada to track down Joey. They find him. Couple of days later, Zerilli's daughter is delivered to the old man, with all her luggage. She's fine, but there's a steamer truck with Joey inside, and he ain't."

"Angelo Adamo killed his own son?" Kaz said.

"Orders him killed. According to the rules he lives by, he doesn't really have any choice. He keeps his grandson and all of his territory. The kid must be almost thirty by now. He's in the family business as well."

"He works for the man who killed his father?" Kaz said.

"Yep. Works for him up until his twenty-first birthday, the day he shoots Angelo and his bodyguard, both in the head. Story is, he weeps as he does it, and old man Adamo smiles and nods his head, just before he gets his."

"Don't tell me," I said. "Everyone falls in and stays with the kid?"

"They do. Guess they figure the kid set things right, according to his lights, and shows the other families that he isn't one to mess with. Counts for a lot with that bunch. Zerilli ends up the big loser. About a month after she was returned, the daughter runs away. She grabs some jewels the old man had stashed for a rainy day, and is never seen again. So, Kaz, does that story stand up to Chaucer?"

"And to Shakespeare," Kaz said. "Billy? What do you have for us?"

I held onto my seat as Big Mike hit the accelerator, the traffic jam finally giving way. We cleared an intersection, the tail end of a convoy disappearing off to our right. As I was about to begin, the distant sound of aircraft engines rose up from due south, and within seconds it became a sputtering, growling noise, signaling a plane in big trouble.

"There!" Kaz said, pointing ahead to a black smudge in the sky, descending and trailing smoke. It was a B-17, probably hit by fighters or flak along the French coast and heading for home. A couple of trucks ahead of us pulled over to watch, and Big Mike gunned the engine, passing them and a couple of other vehicles that had slowed down. The B-17 was closer now, losing altitude and airspeed. It was off to our right, but parallel to the road, and I began to wonder if it was going to land on top of us. Two of the four engines trailed smoke, and a third suddenly sprouted yellow flames, as the smoke turned an oily black. I saw its flaps go down, and knew the pilot was trying for a belly landing. It was going to have to be in the plowed fields alongside the road, the flattest ground within sight. I hoped they'd jettisoned the bomb load in the channel and the crew had bailed out over land. The bomber seemed to drop straight down as it slowed, its huge wings wobbling back and forth as the pilot fought for what control he could get out of the damaged plane. Kaz and I stared, transfixed, but Big Mike took his opportunity and sped between the line of vehicles, as nearly everyone on the road stopped to watch.

A line of deuce-and-a-half trucks blocked our view for a few seconds, but we got around them in time to see the pilot raise the nose a bit, seconds before the aircraft touched down. It slid forward, gouging out a blackened trench as one of the propellers spun off. The plane smashed through a stone wall, spinning crazily across the field, like a giant child's toy. The B-17 swerved sideways before coming to a shuddering halt, its nose yards away from a row of oak trees edging a lane between the fields. We were close enough to see shredded metal where machine-gun or cannon fire had raked the wing and fuselage. Dozens of GIs ran over to help, spilling out of vehicles, swarming the aircraft, reaching to help any survivors out through the hatches. Smoke bloomed from the damaged engine and enveloped the rescuers. An ambulance pulled out of the traffic ahead of us, bumping over plowed fields, and disappeared into the thickening haze. We drove on in silence, stories forgotten.

An hour later, with images of death beneath gnarled oaks playing across my mind, we turned off the main road at a sign for Shepherdswell. We crossed the train tracks and parked at the station, not far from the Bricklayer's Arms. It was a pleasant-looking place, and we walked toward it, silently in agreement on the need for a drink. Shepherdswell was a sprawling little village with a main street of shops and homes all built in the same brickwork style, painted a uniform white. Narrow side streets led off into country lanes dotted with larger homes, bounded by farmers' fields showing husks of the last autumn crops, endless rows of withered stems, lined up like tombstones.

The Bricklayer's Arms was warm and welcoming, the publican quick with his pints, a sharp, crisp ale that bit through the dust in my mouth and the visions in my head. We drank, and didn't speak, the only sound a long sigh from Big Mike after he polished off his pint. He spoke for us all.

"Another?" the publican asked, appearing as soon as he noticed the empty glass.

"Sure," Big Mike said. "But maybe you can help us first. We're looking for a girl."

"What kind of establishment do you think this is?" He took a half step back, his eyes wide with amazement at this cheeky Yank.

"No, no," Kaz said. "What my friend means is we are searching for a specific young lady. We were supposed to deliver a gift to her, from her fiancé, but we lost the address. All we know is that she's visiting here, and wondered if you may have seen her. She came by train, and we thought with the pub so close to the station, she might have come in."

"Well, then, that's a different story. What's her name?"

"Sheila," Kaz said, leaving it unsaid that she might have used a different name. "Early twenties, dark hair, dark eyes. A pretty girl, not a movie star, but nice looking."

"Kind of a small, round mouth," I added. "A smart kid, too." She had to be.

"Visiting here in Shepherdswell?"

"Yes, that's what we were told," Kaz said.

"Humph. Sorry, can't help you there. Sounds a bit like Miss Pemble, but she's not visiting anyone, and not named Sheila either. Been here off and on for some time now."

"Miss Pemble?" Kaz said, inviting more comment.

"Aye. Margaret Pemble. She's a nurse. Rented a cottage out on Farrier Street a fortnight or more ago. She stayed here—we have a couple of rooms upstairs in case you gents need a place tonight—for a few days while she looked around. Nice young woman, I'd say a bit older than the girl you described."

"Much call for nurses around here?" I asked.

"No, not much. We have the village doctor, that's all we need. She's a private nurse, specializes in rehabilitation, she said. Needed a place with plenty of room downstairs, to care for a crippled flier who hired her on. Some rich bloke, I'd say, after a quiet place in the country instead of a crowded hospital ward. I'd do the same myself, if I had the money."

"So the place on Farrier Street, it's his then?" I asked.

"I guess so, not that it matters. She's the one doing everything, getting it all ready. He's had several operations on his face and legs. Can't walk much, that's what she's going to help him with. Don't know what's hidden under the bandages. Some of those pilots get burned something awful."

"Yeah, we just saw a B-17 belly-land in a field," Big Mike said. "It came in with three engines on fire. They were lucky to make it down in one piece."

"Aye, we've seen plenty of crashes here, since 1940. A Hurricane came down not a quarter mile away, poor bloke dead at the controls. The Home Guard lads have rounded up a few Jerries as well, most of them glad to give up after a night in the woods. We had a Polish pilot—one of your lot, Lieutenant—he had to bail out, in September 1940, I think, and it took a while for him to convince the constable he was one of ours. He had a thick accent, just like Miss Pemble's patient."

"He's a Polish flier?" Kaz asked.

"Aye, from the Kościuszko Squadron, so he told me. Famous lot, those boys. He was a bit hard to understand, with his accent and the bandages to boot, but I got that much."

"Perhaps I should stop and give him my regards," Kaz said. "Miss Pemble and he are at home?"

"No, they left for London this morning. I think she has to bring him back for treatments at the hospital. We don't see that much of them. She said it would be a while before he could stay full-time." He briskly took our orders for lunch, gave Kaz directions to Miss Pemble's cottage, and went off to pull Big Mike's next pint.

"I think we should take a look at this cottage," Kaz said in a low voice.

"What, you think Sheila Carlson is moonlighting as a nurse?" Big Mike said. "Sounds out of character."

"Why not, as long as we're here? She fits the description," Kaz said.

"Look, you're already wanted by Scotland Yard," I said. "You want the local constable to throw you in the hoosegow for breaking and entering, too?"

"Hoosegow?" Kaz said, unfamiliar with the term.

"Clink. Pokey, the big house," Big Mike said.

"Ah, the slammer," Kaz said. "We must be careful then. I am only looking for my wounded cousin, Luboslaw. I am distraught, am I not?"

"Not responsible for your actions," Big Mike said. "We tried to stop you."

"Sure, that's believable," I said.

After a lunch of bangers and mash in apple cider gravy—two helpings for Big Mike—we drove along Farrier Street, past three small cottages, until we came to Miss Pemble's, marked by a large weeping willow. We knocked at the front door, and were greeted by the silence of an empty house. Big Mike looked in the bay window, and shook his head. No one home. We went around back, and Big Mike worked his knife-blade magic on the rear door. Ten seconds and we were in.

"Poor Luboslaw," I said to Kaz. "He'll never know of your grief."

"You guys search the joint," Big Mike said. "I'll be on watch. If you hear me start up the jeep, it means someone's coming. Go out the back, lock up, and say you were just knocking at the door. OK?"

"OK." Kaz and I went through the rooms. Margaret Pemble's room was upstairs, and she had a lot more stuff than Sheila had had on her last time I saw her. A few dresses hung in the closet, nothing fancy. A chest of drawers held the usual feminine stuff, and her dressing table was decorated with perfumes and makeup. No wads of cash hidden under the mattress, no oleander plant being cultivated. Downstairs, we went through the meager belongings of her patient. A couple of worn suits. One RAF uniform, a leather flying jacket, shirts, and corduroy trousers.

A small table by the window was stacked with bandages and dressings, along with a few bottles of medicines. A pile of books, one in Polish, rested on the nightstand.

"Stefan Grabiński," Kaz said. "He's called the Polish Poe. *Demon ruchu. The Motion Demon.* Horror stories, not to my taste."

"There's horror enough," I said. I flipped the pages of the other two books. One was a paperback, *The Saint Goes On,* by Leslie Charteris. I'd read a few of his books, and knew they were fairly easy reads. Maybe he was trying to improve his English. The other was a thicker hardcover, *Selected Poems,* by W. B. Yeats. That was heavier going, and I flipped through the pages, wondering at his wide-ranging interests. It opened to a bookmark at "The Circus Animals' Desertion," a poem I'd not heard of.

"Ah, Yeats," Kaz said. "A famous Irish poet. Are you familiar with his work?"

"Not really. I don't get this poem about circus animals, that's for sure."

"The meaning is in the last lines," Kaz said, reciting them from memory.

> *Now that my ladder's gone*
> *I must lie down where all the ladders start*
> *In the foul rag and bone shop of the heart.*

"He wrote it near the end of his life, about trying to recapture the creativity of youth," Kaz said. "It speaks about returning to the elemental truths, I think."

"He has those lines underlined," I said, feeling easier talking about concrete truths.

"Poles have a deep understanding of poetry," Kaz said, taking the book from my hands. "He knows Latin, too, if this is in his hand. *Corpora dormiunt vigilant animae.*"

"What's that mean?" I asked, as Kaz showed me the inscription on the first page of the book.

"The bodies are asleep, the souls are awake."

"Interesting guy," I said. "Not that it matters."

The nightstand also held a fountain pen and three small pebbles. Souvenirs of Poland, maybe? We looked under the bed, behind the chest of drawers, and found nothing but dust balls. Magazines and a radio in the sitting room. Coal in the bucket by the fireplace. Well-stocked larder and a few bottles of vodka to ease the pain. Nothing suspicious, just a chilly rural cottage with a decent stock of booze, books, and bandages.

"See anything out of the ordinary?" I asked Kaz.

"Nothing. It has a temporary look, no personal effects, but that fits with what we were told."

We left, checking to be sure nothing was disturbed, and that we had locked the door behind us. The only evidence of our visit was a few scratches around the lock, where Big Mike had used his blade. Nothing a nurse or crippled pilot would notice.

"Waste of time," I said to Big Mike.

"Worth checking out," he said, like any good cop would. You never passed up a lead, no matter how slim. That's how cases were solved. We drove back to the main road, turning south for Dover, belly landings and wild-goose chases behind us.

CHAPTER · TWENTY-FOUR

WE LEFT KAZ at the Lord Nelson Inn, on Flying Horse Lane in Dover, not far from the docks that ran along the channel. Dover Castle loomed over the town from the heights to the east, an ancient gray fortress that had been called the Key to England since the days of Napoleon, maybe before. All three of us got rooms at the inn, since there wasn't much of a tourist trade these days. Flying Horse Lane looked like a nice little side street, except for the building directly across from the pub that had taken a direct hit. The Germans still fired their big artillery pieces across the channel, aiming at the castle and hitting everything around it in the process. The front of the three-story structure was nothing but a mass of bricks, tumbled into the street. Stairs jutted out into thin air, and wallpaper fluttered in the sea breeze where it had torn away from the collapsed wall. A few men in blue coveralls worked at stacking the bricks, which meant this had been a recent hit. I hoped what they said about lightning held true for artillery shells.

I'd told Kaz to stay put, in case Scotland Yard had a long tail on us. We had passed a bookstore about a block from the inn, and Kaz said he'd only need a few minutes there and he'd be set to hole up in his room. The newly painted sign over the store window read FRONTLINE BOOK SHOP, and I got the feeling that folks here were proud to be closer than anyone else in England to the enemy, less than twenty-two miles across the channel.

Big Mike gunned the jeep up the steep road as we tried to figure out where the entrance was. The castle was huge, the outer walls and battlements encircling the hill above the town. There was an inner circle of fortifications, with the actual castle in the center of that. It looked like something out of Robin Hood, and I half expected to see knights on horseback. Instead, we came to a stop at an antiaircraft emplacement, where the sergeant in charge told us to go back down the switchback road and find the military entrance at the base of the cliff. It was much less grand than the approach to the castle. We parked the jeep under camouflage netting and walked into a wide chamber cut into the limestone cliff. The air smelled damp and chalky, and I glanced back for a glimpse of blue sky before we turned a corner and lost sight of it. The duty officer checked our papers and directed us to the area assigned to the Eighth Air Force staff. The tunnels were well lit, clearly marked, and filled with a constant hum from the ventilation system. Offices and large rooms had been carved out on either side of the main chamber. It made the Underground Tube shelters in London look cramped.

"Billy, good to see you," boomed the voice of Colonel Bull Dawson. "How do you like our little hideaway?"

"Not bad, sir," I said as Bull pumped my hand in a crushing grip that came from long hours of holding onto the controls of a B-17 at thirty thousand feet. "Where do you have the Russians stashed?"

"Come on," he said. "You'll both want to see this." Bull led us down a narrow stairway, the stone worn in the center by centuries of martial footsteps. He pushed opened two metal doors and ushered us into a large, square room with a catwalk, about five feet high, on one side. The other wall was filled with detailed maps, taped together, forming a mosaic of England, France, Germany, Italy, all the way to the Soviet Union. The tables between the two walls held plotting boards, maps with airfields, antiaircraft defenses, dotted with symbols for fighters and bombers along routes that stretched from England to the Ukraine, with connections to Italy and back to England. American and Russian officers huddled in small groups, pointing at maps, pushing aircraft markers across plotting boards. At the far end of the room was a communications center, filled with switchboards, radios, teletypes, and signal repeating gear, tall metal boxes that reached to the end of the corridor.

"This is where they fought the Battle of Britain from, can you believe that?" Bull said. "That was before either Russia or America was in the war. Now we're planning Operation Frantic from the same rooms. Amazing."

"Yeah," I said, trying to sound enthused about the historical import of the whole thing, but my attention was on Captain Kiril Sidorov. He was up on the catwalk, walking back and forth, his hands clasped behind him, watching every Russian officer who talked with an American. His eyes danced over them all, looking for what, I wondered? Signs of disaffection? Desire for personal property? Preference for bourbon over vodka? By his side was Rak Vatutin, who had his eyes on me. Both of them wore sidearms, and I had the sense of being in a cell block, with those two as guards. Maybe the Russians were used to it, but I didn't like it one bit. I was tempted to shout out Topper's message to Vatutin, and see what his reaction would be. But I wasn't here to have fun, so I waved to him, just to enjoy seeing him turn away.

"You wanted to talk to the Russians, right?" Bull said. "Captain Sidorov agreed, as long as he could sit in."

"Who'll sit in when I interrogate him?"

"Look, Billy, you tread lightly here, understand? This is a major operation, and I don't need a loose cannon right now. Talk to these guys, fine, but don't call it an interrogation and get their Russian noses bent out of shape. They're easily offended. Like me. Got it?"

"Got it, Bull. When can I get started?"

"Right now. I'll take you to an empty office. Forget you ever saw all these maps. Big Mike, you need some grub?"

"Thanks, sir, but I'll stick with Billy," Big Mike said, with a glance toward the Russian hawks on the catwalk. He must've been concerned to pass up a chow line. Sidorov took notice of us and came down the steps.

"I see you found us, Lieutenant Boyle," Sidorov said. "I hope you do as well finding the killer of Comrade Egorov."

"I will, unless they move all of you somewhere else."

"I hope not. This was done quickly and with great secrecy, so I believe we are secure. We even have a good cover story, about being shown the local defenses against invasion. The Home Guard has given us tours, showing off their hidden bunkers and many devious devices. A true proletariat people's army, the English Home Guard. We've gazed across the channel through binoculars, of course, and the British have allowed us to assist in firing some of their large artillery pieces at the Nazi beach defenses. It makes for good relations between Allies. Our officers go out to the pubs and local events to spread the cover story, along with our American and English hosts."

"Always in pairs, right?"

"Of course, except for Captain Vatutin and myself. Our job is to attend functions where our officers are in attendance, to provide additional security, and to make sure the script is carefully followed. It is good for the populace to see Soviet uniforms as a matter of course, instead of as an exception."

"Security is pretty tight, Billy," Bull said. "So far the cover story is holding up with everyone who has come in contact with the Soviets. It was Captain Sidorov's idea, to have them out in the open. Pretty good one, too. Keeps them from going stir-crazy in here."

"As long as everyone sticks to the script," I said.

"That is what we are here for," Vatutin said, sidling up to us. "What is your purpose?"

"To talk to your men," I said. "They may be able to help put together a better picture of Gennady Egorov's activities before he was killed. To help find his murderer." I could sense Bull relaxing at my diplomatic language. I almost added something about capitalist gangsters, but then decided that might be too close to the truth.

"That is acceptable," Sidorov said. "Since Captain Vatutin is with us, why don't you start with him?" Vatutin tried to smile to show that he didn't mind, but it was hard for him, coming out more like a snarl. He smiled more readily when drunk, I recalled from our last meeting.

Bull walked us to a small room past the communications equipment, and shut the door with a clang. Big Mike stood against the door, as if daring either Russian to try and leave. I sat at a desk, empty except for a pad of paper and a pencil. Tools of the trade. Sidorov and Vatutin sat opposite me.

"How well did you know Gennady Egorov?" I said.

"Comrade Egorov was a fine man, an exemplary Communist," Vatutin said, darting his chin forward.

"Come, Rak," Sidorov said. "We don't need funeral orations here. Simply tell the lieutenant the truth. You know, the thing that actually happens?"

"Yes, I know the truth," Vatutin said. "But do these Americans deserve it?" Sidorov nodded, and Vatutin shrugged, as if the responsibility for uttering this precious commodity was no longer his. "Egorov was not well liked. Some might say he did his job too well."

"What was his job?"

Vatutin struggled with this, but continued after an encouraging nod from Sidorov. Whatever the ranks they wore on their uniforms, it was evident that in the NKVD Sidorov was the boss. "The same as ours, to act as security for the embassy, to gather information, and to be sure none of our own were seduced by the West. But he had no sense of balance, no ability to let even the slightest infraction go unnoticed."

"Do you let infractions go unnoticed?"

"Of course. People need to feel they are getting away with something once in a while. It helps them cope with being in a strange country. Letting off steam, you say, correct?"

"Yeah, we do. I have to say I'm surprised. I thought you Soviets were a tough bunch."

"There is another reason," Vatutin went on. "If you stop every infraction, then you can never tell who will go on to commit a more serious one. But Egorov didn't care about that, he cared only about looking good to our superiors. So he denounced anyone he could."

"What did that get him? Didn't your superiors know the kind of guy he was?"

"Yes. One who would do whatever he was told, without the slightest thought of anyone else."

"That was an advantage. Did he ever denounce you?"

"No. I gave him no cause," Vatutin said.

"Did you know where he was going the night he was killed?"

"He told both of us he was meeting a contact. That's all."

"Who else besides the three of you have that much freedom of movement, to go out alone?"

"The ambassador, but he would never go alone. Along with our immediate superior, we are the designated security."

"You mean NKVD?"

"That is unnecessary to go into," Sidorov said. "The three of us— Egorov, Vatutin, and I—were the operational security team."

"OK, but no one else, other than the three of you, could just stroll out alone?"

"According to the rules, that is correct. But in actual practice, it could be done," Vatutin said.

"Who is your superior?"

"No one at the moment," Vatutin said grudgingly. He looked at the wall, the floor, then at his hands.

"Osip Nikolaevich Blotski?" I asked. Vatutin's eyes shot up to meet mine. Bingo. From me he looked to Sidorov, who looked as if he'd never heard the name, which was damned odd, since old Osip had been beaten within an inch of his life the night of the opera. Seeing no reaction from Sidorov, Vatutin decided it was up to him.

"Yes," he said. "We worked under Comrade Nikolaevich."

"And now?"

"Captain Sidorov is in charge, until a replacement is named," Vatutin said.

"Congratulations," I said to Sidorov. "Who planned this move? Who knew about it in advance?"

"Comrade Nikolaevich had approved the transfer of the planning staff to Dover the day before he was attacked. It had been presented to the ambassador by the British Foreign Office, since it involved the relocation of a number of Soviet citizens. A delicate matter."

"So it was left to you to work out the details," I said to Sidorov. "The logistics, the deception plan?" He nodded.

"Why would Comrade Nikolaevich go out alone, at night?" I asked.

"That surprised me, I must admit," Vatutin said. "He did enjoy walking in the parks for exercise, but always during the day, with a companion."

"Any idea why he went that night?" Both men shook their heads, clueless.

"Was Egorov in charge of scheduling the shipments of produce to the embassy?" I said, trying a different tack. Vatutin sat, silent. "Was that your responsibility then?"

"No," he said.

"Whose was it? His?" I pointed at Sidorov. "Protecting your boss?"

"No."

"The ambassador's?"

Sidorov laughed, and nodded to Vatutin again.

"All right. It was Egorov's. We were forced to investigate him. He found out and was quite angry," Vatutin said.

"What did you find out?"

"Nothing. We followed him, but he never met with anyone suspicious."

"But he must have met with his contacts," I said.

"He told you, no one of a suspicious nature," Sidorov said. "This line of questioning must cease. We have a responsibility to protect our countrymen on duty in Great Britain. Our meeting with contacts to insure the continued safety of Soviet citizens is not part of this investigation."

"OK, I get it," I said. "So someone was tipping off a London gang, and you're sure it wasn't Egorov."

"No. As Comrade Vatutin said, we never saw him meet with anyone suspicious. The manner in which he was killed, and the map you found, both suggest he *was* involved. He was a careful man, so we would not expect to find evidence easily. It was his death that showed he was. And, remember, the hijackings stopped after his death."

"Right," I said. I wished Sidorov would leave so I could give Topper's message to Vatutin and watch his reaction. Time and place. Time and place for what? It sounded like another hijacking, but I wasn't sure. "Who took over that responsibility, after Egorov was killed?"

"I did," Sidorov said. Strange, I thought. Did Vatutin have access to the same information? Was he rifling through the boss's files, or did Sidorov delegate the details to him?

"Any valuable shipments coming up?" I asked. I kept my eyes on Vatutin, who betrayed nothing, shaking his head. I thought I saw Sidorov's eyes widen for a split second, but by the time I gave him my attention, his face was a mask.

"No, just the normal supplies, or have I forgotten something, Rak?"

"No, not at all," Vatutin said.

"OK, I can't think of anything else. Thank you for your time."

"You haven't noted anything," Sidorov said, tapping his finger on the blank paper.

"Yes, I have," I said, tapping the side of my head. Big Mike opened the door, and we all got up. I asked Sidorov if he would bring in the next officer, and got between him and Vatutin as we exited the room. As soon as he was a few paces ahead, I took Vatutin by the arm and pulled him close.

"Topper wants to know time and place," I whispered. He pushed me away with the kind of look you'd give a pervert. He hustled down the corridor, toward the safety of his comrades.

"What the hell did you say to him, Billy?"

"Just gave him a message, Big Mike. Do me a favor and follow him. Let me know whom he talks to." Big Mike went after him, his long strides closing the gap in no time.

A few minutes later, Sidorov brought in a Red Army major, an engineer in charge of working with the Eighth Air Force on preparing runways. He knew a little about tractors, less about English, and nothing about Egorov. There was a marked difference in Sidorov with this fellow, and the next. None of the urbane chatter about telling the truth, or admissions of letting infractions slide. It was all business, his stern voice translating my questions into Russian. I had no idea if the engineer was telling the truth, but I was sure he was too scared to lie. Same for the next few. After a colonel broke into a sweat that beaded up on his lip and dripped onto his tunic, I gave up.

"They're all frightened," I said to Sidorov, once we were alone.

"You must understand, Billy," he said, leaning back to light a cigarette. "To get a posting to Great Britain is no simple matter. It is an honor. It shows that the motherland trusts you to sample the delights of London, knowing you will return to her bosom. They are afraid that they will be recalled simply because they are associated with questionable activities."

"If London in wartime, with the bombs and rationing, is delightful, I'd hate to spend a month in Moscow."

"In the winter, I would agree. But in the spring, Moscow is beautiful. However, not every Russian is from Moscow. Many of these men are from the country, and their homes may still have dirt floors. Not the ones who came here through Party connections, but the ones who really earned it."

"I thought the Communist Party ran everything in Russia."

"Oh, it does. But people are people, and will manipulate the system. Egorov was one such man. He was posted here because his father is on the Central Committee. No other reason."

"How about you? What did you do to get your posting? Didn't you say you were brought up in an orphanage?"

"The state was my parent," Sidorov said, smiling. His lips moved, but his teeth were clenched. "How much more influence could you ask for? Now, it is getting late. We have three men attending a meeting of the local rugby club, and a social gathering at the Lord Nelson Inn. Captain Vatutin and I must make the rounds."

"We're staying at the Lord Nelson," I said, not mentioning Kaz. "Maybe I'll join you for a drink later."

"It would be my pleasure," Sidorov said as he left.

I sat alone, thinking about what a strange guy he was. Mysterious. Likable. Hard. Maybe cruel. He was keeping something back, but that was his job. But was it a state secret or a Sidorov secret? Or were they one and the same? I closed my eyes and tried to bring his face into focus, to recall his reaction when I'd asked about a valuable shipment. It was only in my peripheral vision, but I had seen the whites of his eyes grow large for a second. He knew something he wasn't telling, something that had caught him by surprise. It had wiped that smile off his face for a moment, the smile that wasn't a smile, any more than the clenched teeth of a skull wore a friendly grin.

CHAPTER TWENTY-FIVE

"GET BACK TO London," I said to Big Mike as we walked out of the tunnels and into the fading late afternoon light. "Ask Harding to find out if there's anything special being delivered to the Soviet Embassy. Not food or booze, something more valuable. Press Cosgrove on it if you can. I think he knows what's up."

"Why don't I call Sam? They got secure telephones here."

"No. If there's anything to this, no one's going to talk about it on the phone. Sidorov's eyes lit up when I asked about something valuable coming through. He denied it, but he reacted to something. Put that together with Egorov being murdered, Osip Nikolaevich Blotski almost making it to the workers' paradise, and I'll bet there's something on its way to that embassy worth killing for."

"OK. I'll call you as soon as I get anything," Big Mike said.

"Don't call the castle. Leave a vague message for me at the inn and then get back down here. We've got MI5 and MI6 mixed up in all this, and they're both probably listening in on the Russians, as well as each other."

"What are you going to do?"

"Probably drink too much vodka."

"Damn!" Big Mike said, taking a corner hard enough to almost give me a tumble. He didn't like missing a fun evening, but I thought I was doing him a favor. He let me off in front of the Lord Nelson, threading his way around the rubble that had spilled out into the street. Crews of workmen were raising clouds of dust cleaning and stacking bricks, while others piled charred timbers and shattered furniture onto a flatbed truck.

Some were putting away their tools and cleaning up at the end of their shifts. Only one fellow was idle, leaning against a doorway that had lost its door. He wore a gray raincoat and a muffler wrapped around his neck, not exactly the duds for cleaning collapsed brickwork. He took a last drag on his cigarette and flicked it in my direction, then pushed off without a look back. Scotland Yard? MI5? Local oddball? I thought about following him, but if it was either of the first two, he'd lose me in no time, and if it was the third, there was no percentage. Instead, I tramped up the three flights of narrow stairs, hoping the Germans across the channel wouldn't shell the town while we were up here.

I found Kaz in his room, sitting by the window, staring at the destroyed building across the street. Newspapers were strewn on the bed and all across the floor. The *Times*, the *Daily Mail*, the *Daily Express*. A bottle of vodka was at his elbow, one quarter empty, and no glass in sight. I didn't think the war was over, so I knew it wasn't a celebration.

"German guilt," Kaz said, in a harsh, snorting laugh.

"What are you talking about?"

"Look at the headlines. The report of the Soviet Special Commission on the Katyn Forest Massacre. The press is swallowing their fabrications whole. Look, the *Times* itself, it does nothing but quote the Russian report! German guilt, indeed. The Germans are guilty of so much, why not this, too? It is only the facts that stand in the way of that argument, Billy. But those facts are too inconvenient to appear in print." He took a swig from the bottle and slammed it down on the table.

I picked up the paper and read. The article was headed "Report of Russian Commission," with the words "German Guilt" quoted beneath it. Kaz was right—it was nothing but one long recitation of the Russian findings. It stated that the local populace confirmed that the Poles were shot by the Germans in 1941, after they were captured while working as POWs on construction projects. The fact that none of the local populace was available to be interviewed was not mentioned, nor the evidence that none of those Polish officers was alive after 1940. The émigré Poles in London were blamed for sowing discord among the Allies.

"Émigrés," Kaz said. "It makes us sound like traitors who left Poland of our own accord. But they refer to the Poles in Russia as the Union of Polish Patriots in the USSR. Why are they, too, not called émigrés in the *Times*?"

I didn't answer, but not because I didn't know. The fix was in. Poland was taking another knife in the back. I flipped through the pages and found more bad news. The Russians were refusing to discuss the Polish border with their allies, the London Poles included. They planned on taking eastern Poland for themselves, setting the new border at the Curzon Line, which was roughly the same border they'd established with the Nazis when they both invaded Poland.

"You see that the Polish Government in Exile has asked for talks with the Soviets, with the Americans and British as intermediaries," Kaz said. "The Soviets rejected the idea. The response from our Western allies is silence. Look through all these newspapers. All you will see is stories of the Russian offensives and General Eisenhower's arrival in London. It's all there; any fool can see it. Poland is too unimportant to come between these grand allies."

"You're not unimportant," I said to Kaz, sitting next to him. I took a swig from the bottle and let it burn down my throat.

"But I am right," he said.

"Maybe we can talk to Ike?"

"Billy, you are a good friend. But the general takes his orders from politicians. And you know how much he wishes to minimize casualties. Why would he alienate over six million Soviet troops fighting the Nazis right now? Eastern Poland will be taken over by the Soviet Union, and what land we have left will be ruled by Communist puppets. Ironic, isn't it? The war will end as it started. Poland betrayed and overrun."

He took a long swallow, as if the bottle held spring water.

"I am going out. They say from the cliffs, you can see the flashes of the big railway guns when the Germans fire them across the channel. That would be interesting," Kaz said, wobbling a bit as he stood.

"I'll go with you," I said.

"No, I will not be very good company. I need fresh air. Air from occupied France, perhaps, blown across the water. Do you think it smells differently than free air?" He put on his coat, stuffed his revolver in his pocket, and adjusted his cap.

"Kaz," I said, not knowing what he intended.

"Don't worry, Billy. There will be too few Poles left alive after the Germans and Russians get through with us. I will not add to the carnage." He smiled, a lopsided, scarred grin that made him look slightly insane and totally in control of himself at the same time. "Did you see the fellow watching the inn? Man with a muffler?"

"Yeah, I did. Who do you think it is?"

"I really do not care. But be careful. Good night, Billy."

I watched Kaz walk down the street, his greatcoat collar turned up against the cold wind. The workers were gone, the ruined building a gaping, stark reminder of all that might be lost in a moment. I went to my room, and thought about some shut-eye, but the vodka was warm in my gut, reminding me that lunch in Shepherdswell had been quite a while ago. I went down to the bar and ordered the local ale and Woolton pie, which was an invention of rationing, some sort of vegetable mixture topped with mashed potatoes and baked in a piecrust. It was named after the head of the Ministry of Food, which didn't inspire confidence, but it did taste better than it had a right to. Maybe it was because it was warm, and I was indoors, not in a jeep, or deep underground. Or in a nation occupied by Nazis or Communists.

"Care for some company, Peaches?" The harsh voice of Archie Chapman jolted me as I raised my glass. He didn't wait for an invitation, but sat down at my table. I looked back to the bar and saw Topper leaning against it. He touched his fingers to his forehead and gave me a little salute.

"What brings you to Dover?" I asked, trying to hide my surprise. Archie leaned back in his chair and unbuttoned his overcoat. It was a double-breasted tweed, and there looked to be plenty of room within the folds for a hidden bayonet. Topper brought a large whiskey to the table and set it in front of his father, and then returned to his post at the bar. Archie brought the glass to his mouth, and wrapped his lips around the rim, drinking down half the liquid.

"You, Peaches. You brought us to Dover. Courtesy of a fellow at your motor pool, who shared your destination with us. You know, sometimes I can't decide between violence and bribery. Both work so well, but each takes something out of you. Violence, it brings out the ugliness inside a man. And then regret, maybe. But bribery, that's hard-earned cash, gone! But it leaves everyone happier, don't you think?"

"What do you want?" I was in no mood for another philosophical discussion with Archie. He finished the rest of the whiskey and slammed the glass down for Topper to fetch another. He leaned in, his breath hot, woody, and sweet with alcohol, and stared, fixing me like a bird of prey. I couldn't look away, I couldn't move. Finally he leaned back, closed his eyes, and gave me an answer of sorts.

Here we will moor our lonely ship
And wander ever with woven hands,
Murmuring softly lip to lip,
Along the grass, along the sands,
Murmuring how far away are the unquiet lands.

"You know those unquiet lands, don't you, Peaches?" Archie said, after a look around the room to see who might have admired his fine voice. "Isn't it better to murmur softly, lip to lip?"

"All depends on what you're murmuring," I said.

"Ha! You don't understand. You probably don't even recognize your own Irish poet, William Butler Yeats. A fine fellow, for an Irishman."

Yeats. It sounded familiar. I was sure that's who had written the book of poetry we'd seen at the house in Shepherdswell. Kaz had read a few lines, and I struggled to remember, if only to show up this poetic maniac. "Yeats," I said. "He wrote one of my favorites."

Now that my ladder's gone
I must lie down where all the ladders start
In the foul rag and bone shop of the heart.

"By God, you do have a brain, Peaches. Who would have thought you cared for anything but chasing killers and thieves? I'm impressed, and glad you know something of your heritage, misguided as it may be. But enough talk of verse, it's time for straight prose. Did you deliver your lines?"

"Yes, this afternoon."

"To Vatutin, shut up in that great fortress?"

"Yes. Is that why you followed me?"

"What we set out to do is important, Peaches. When I shake on something, it gets done. No regrets, no looking back. Now, tell me, did you get a reply?"

"No. Actually, he looked confused."

"Good! Confusion to our enemies! Ha! Now if this works well, I will owe you for your troubles. Wait for the reply to come. Do those Russians ever leave the castle?"

"I'm not sure," I said, not wanting Archie running after Russians with bayonet drawn. "Maybe with an escort."

"We will watch, Peaches. We will wait and watch, only a short distance away, but unseen. Just around the corner like." With that, Archie winked, rose, and walked out.

"Thanks, Billy," Topper said, as he pushed off from the bar. "No hard feelings about following you down?"

"No, I should've thought about it. You wouldn't have been hard to spot in that line of military traffic."

"Don't count on it. We have a staff car of our own."

"Tell me, Topper," I said. "Do you still want to join up? Like when you first tried and your dad got you out?"

His eyes went hard, and his easy manner vanished. "You shut your mouth, Boyle. I don't take that talk from anyone."

"I was serious. I'm not questioning you. But others will, after the war. Like those who lost their men, all those Shoreditch boys who joined up and bought the farm. And the ones who come back, who know hard steel and killing, they'll look at you, too, and wonder if you deserve to lord it over them. Archie's a tough one, he's seen the elephant, they'll respect him. But how long does he have? How long before it's Topper Chapman running things? Hey, it may work out fine, they may think you were smart to stay a civilian. I know I wish I had."

Topper was rigid, his face red, lips compressed. I watched his hands, figuring there was a one-in-five chance he'd pull a knife or use his knuckles on me. Instead, he stuffed them into his pockets, and followed his father out the door. I let out a sigh. I didn't know where it might lead, but I thought this might be where I could drive a wedge between Archie and Topper. Threaten Topper with the loss of respect, and threaten Archie with the loss of his son. I didn't like it much, but it was all I had.

I got myself another ale and tried to figure what I had that added up. A drunken friend wandering the streets, feeling betrayed. A crazy criminal waiting for a message from a Russian. Something obviously valuable making its way to the Russian Embassy. A Russian traitor, feeding information to the Chapman gang. Or was "traitor" too strong a word?

A crooked Russian like Rak Vatutin, selling, not feeding, information. But what was he after? What could he take back with him to the Soviet Union that would convert to wealth in a Communist system? It still didn't make sense.

But I did have something new. Egorov had been in charge of the hijacked shipments, and he'd been a stickler for the rules. That meant either he was the stoolie, or someone else was and it was making him look bad. Based on what Vatutin and Sidorov had said, and how the other Russians had reacted to questions about him, my money was on the latter. Had Egorov gone after the tipster, and found out more than was healthy for him? Maybe Archie and his gang had eliminated him after all and tried to pin it on the Poles.

I took a drink, hoping the confused swirl of facts in my mind would settle into some sort of pattern. They didn't, but at least the ale tasted good. I set the glass down, and noticed the wet circles where the glass had sat on the wood tabletop. Some overlapped, some stood alone. That was the problem, figuring out which facts overlapped and which didn't. Was Sheila Carlson out of the picture? Was her circle gone, disappeared, dead? I set the glass down again. Egorov, dead. Again. Eddie Miller, dead. Two separate circles. Valerian Radecki, his circle overlapped Eddie's. Tadeusz Tucholski had his own circle, crowded by Sheila, Eddie, Kaz, and Radecki. Sheila Carlson's circle went down over Eddie's, Radecki's, and Kaz's. The glass went down for Sidorov, taking in Eddie and Egorov. I gave Vatutin a circle, linked to Egorov and Sidorov. It was getting messy, which didn't surprise me. Then the Chapman outfit got one, taking in Egorov, since he was found on their turf, and Vatutin. But that still didn't tell the whole story. Vatutin might be just the messenger. It could be any of the Russians, Sidorov or even someone back at the embassy, it was impossible to tell.

I wiped away the condensation with the palm of my hand, my suspicions damp and clammy on my skin. A group of three Russian airmen and a couple of Royal Navy officers entered, the pale blue Soviet Air Force uniforms contrasting with the deep blue of the British Navy. The Russians looked away when I glanced in their direction, probably uncomfortable after our earlier talks. What was it like, always wondering who was denouncing whom? How different was it in Soviet Russia or Nazi Germany? In both places, you had to appear purer than pure if you didn't want to end up at the end of a rope or against the wall. What choice did they have but to be suspicious?

I finished my ale and got up to leave. No sense ruining their party. I pulled on my coat and stepped outside, deciding to look for Kaz. I nearly collided with Sidorov, who was half turned, looking up at the night sky.

"Look," he said, pointing to the southwest, and I understood he meant to listen. The distant, insistent drone of engines came from a corner of the sky. He opened the door and spoke in rapid Russian, and soon we were all out in the street, watching and listening. The stars were hidden behind clouds to the east, but to the south and west the sky was clear.

"There!" someone shouted, his hand pointing to a barely visible twinkling, as the German bombers passed in front of stars, their engines growing louder and louder. The Russians were jabbering excitedly to each other as the antiaircraft batteries around the castle started up, first the 40mm Bofors guns streaming tracers skyward, followed by intense beams of searchlights stabbing at the sky, trying to get a fix on the direction of the bomber stream. Then the big guns, 3.75-inch antiaircraft cannon, began blasting the sky, sending up shells rigged to explode at various altitudes.

The searchlights caught first one, then two, planes, providing a target for the gunners. The aircraft were passing Dover at an angle, and I could see the tracers and explosions arc toward the northeast, following the German bombers as they headed toward the Thames and the London docks to the north. The firing continued for another minute, and then the guns went silent and the searchlights switched off, leaving us in stunned silence and darkness.

Sidorov grabbed my shoulder and pointed, saying something rapidly in Russian. It was an orange flame, flying through the night sky, going down, down to the ground, shot out of the sky by the Dover air defenses. Another smaller flame lost altitude but held its course, descending and growing larger as it disappeared over the northern horizon to the cheers of the crowd.

"That's two less for London to worry about, lads," one of the Royal Navy officers said.

"Aye," said a constable who'd joined the crowd. "But it'll be another long night for us and the Home Guard. The crew could've bailed out before she went over. They could be anywhere from the cliffs or as far up as Shepherdswell if they waited another minute."

"In Russia," one of the Soviets said, "you would not have to search. You would find only their corpses."

"Well, sir, this is England, so we must search," the constable said, before addressing two men in civilian clothes. "Bert, Tom, get your gear, we'll form up at town hall in thirty minutes. Good night, gentlemen," he said to us.

"Good night, Constable, and good luck with your search," Sidorov said, his politeness belying his earlier cold-blooded comments. "Come, Billy, let us toast the downing of the bombers and the search for prisoners," he said, clapping me on the shoulder like a brother in arms.

"OK," I said, figuring on one last drink, then I'd look for Kaz. Maybe I could get something out of Sidorov, if only I knew what questions to ask.

We sat in the corner, where Sidorov could keep an eye on his fellow Russians, watching for any lessening of Bolshevik fervor. He'd ordered ale with me at the bar, and as he tasted it, he grinned.

"Good English ale," he said. "Better than our Zhiguli."

"Is that a type of ale?"

"No, it is the only brand of beer we have. Soviet efficiency."

"I didn't know Russians were big beer drinkers," I said.

"We have a passion for vodka, it is true. Beer is what you drink when you've had too much vodka the night before. Or when you want to keep a clear head. But still, you drink." I thought how much that applied to me, since I'd started spending so much time with Poles and Russians.

"Is it true, what he said about searching for downed fliers in Russia?" I pointed to the men at the other table.

"After what the Germans did when they invaded, it is doubtful that any aircrew who survived parachuting would also survive an encounter with our people. Yes, it is likely that only their corpses would be found. Stripped naked, every item of clothing gone. Even if a peasant were willing to let a German live, he wouldn't let him be taken away wearing warm boots and a leather flying jacket."

"That constable must have sounded quaint to you."

"The English and the Americans, I believe, have many beers and ales. We have one. It makes the choice easy. Drink or do not drink. Just as we do not have the luxury of deciding how to deal with our enemies any more than with our thirst. Kill or be killed. Those are our choices."

"There's a difference between killing in combat and killing a prisoner for his boots."

"Ah, yes. A fine distinction. One made in a warm room, drinking excellent ale, with no security police listening. Except for myself, of course," Sidorov said with a disarming grin, leaning in closer, his voice low, his eyes burning into mine. "But in the Soviet Union, mercy given to the Fascist invader may be interpreted as disloyalty. So the living prisoner with his hands up, begging for his life, may be your death sentence. He could be a dagger aimed straight at your heart. What would you do, Billy? Take a chance and let him live, this man who dropped bombs on your village, who machine-gunned refugees on a crowded road? Have a man like me come and question you, to ask why you did not save the state the trouble of housing and feeding this criminal? To ask, are you perhaps sympathetic to the Fascists? Is that why did you not take his boots, his leather belt, his gloves, his coat? Why did you not at least beat him, comrade?"

"You sound like you've spoken those lines before," I said. It was all I could say. I was almost ready to confess.

"Every actor has his choice. To speak the lines or have no lines to speak. Do you see how easy life is in the Soviet Union? A multitude of choices is dizzying to the average Russian. It is why I must shepherd my flock, like a priest, to keep them holy."

"A priest also forgives and shows mercy."

"Another time, perhaps, there will be mercy. For now, the Soviet Union must be merciless to our enemies, wherever we find them. Does that shock you, Billy? Do you show mercy to criminals in your city?"

"Back home, we enforce the law. The same law for all."

"Ah, yes. The same law for all. With liberty and justice for all, is that not what you Americans pledge? Yet you keep your Negroes in ghettos, and hang them when they step out of line, do you not?"

"No, I don't. It happens, but it's against the law."

"So the police in your southern states, they apprehend the murderers of Negroes, and bring them to justice?"

"Listen, I don't make excuses for what's wrong in my country. Maybe you should do the same."

"Forgive me, Billy, I did not mean to offend. We are taught that your country is wild territory, with gangsters, capitalists, and racists oppressing the workers and peasants."

"We don't have peasants. We have poor folks. And we have our share of the rest, too. But right now I'm more concerned about who oppressed Gennady Egorov and why. What do you really think?"

"Between us? I would not repeat this in front of anyone else, but he was an arrogant idiot, and angered everyone he worked with. Half a dozen people would have gladly killed him, and more were glad to hear of his death. We must demand a public investigation, but no one but his father will care, and he is in Moscow."

"Of those half a dozen, how many would have thought of pinning it on the Poles?"

"All, I'd say. The crisis over the rightful Polish government and the Katyn affair has preoccupied us. It would be an obvious ruse."

"OK, since we're talking off the record, how about telling me about that shipment?"

"What shipment? More food?"

"No, not food. The big shipment, coming any day now, the really valuable one," I said, as if I knew more.

"Sorry, my friend, I don't know what you're talking about."

"What about Vatutin? Would he know anything about it?"

"Rak? Oh no, he's a good one for taking orders, but that's all. If I don't know about it, I can assure you he doesn't. Now excuse me, I need to meet him at the rugby club. Those lads can almost outdrink a Russian."

I watched Sidorov talk with the tableful of Russian and English officers before he left. He had a casual way about him that put westerners at ease. His style was suave, which made him likable, all laughs and handshakes. But his countrymen eyed him as he left, and they seemed to breathe a perceptible sigh of relief as the door closed on his back.

A few minutes later I was outside, too, buttoning the collar of my trench coat against the cold night air and the breeze off the channel. I would have seen Kaz if he'd come back to the inn, so I knew he was still out there. I thought he'd either walk along the water or head up above the cliffs to the castle. There weren't many places open in Dover. Most of the population—many women and most children—had been evacuated during the worst of the Blitz, so there was a shortage of functioning pubs and no other entertainment. I walked along the deserted promenade, watching for Kaz and wondering if any Luftwaffe aircrew were lurking nearby. If so, they probably were thanking their lucky stars they'd landed in England and not at the Russian front.

I came to the end of the promenade and walked along a street where the houses nestled in under the white cliffs. There were no lights and little moonlight, and I turned around, deciding Kaz could pass me on the other side of the street and I wouldn't be able to see him. I found a foot-path leading up to the castle, and pretty soon I wasn't feeling the cold at all. I trudged up, wishing I'd worn boots instead of my dress browns. Or maybe it was the three ales I'd had. Either way, by the time I got to the top, I was winded, cursing Kaz, certain he was climbing the steps at the inn to his warm bed right now.

I stopped to catch my breath and turned around, facing the channel. A wooden bench was thoughtfully set by the path to afford a view out over the water. I took advantage of it. Even in the pitch black, the view was beautiful. Starlight reflected off low waves and sparkled on the break-ers. I could make out one or two vehicles, light leaking from their black-out slits, making their way down the coast road. I heard footsteps ahead of me, and I turned from the view to follow, hoping it might be Kaz. I walked carefully by the cliff edge, toward a gate guarded by a couple of sentries silhouetted against the night sky. Beyond them, I could see the snout of an antiaircraft gun pointed toward France. I heard a noise close by, but it was too dark to make out anything except a low, dark shape on the side of the path.

"Who goes there?" It was one of the sentries, advancing with his bayoneted rifle.

"Help," a voice croaked weakly from my right before I could answer. It was Kaz. I moved closer, putting my hand on his shoulder. He was kneeling over a body. It was facedown on the ground, lying in that grace-less pose that only death can arrange.

"What's this then?" the sentry demanded, shining his flashlight on us. I squinted against the sudden light, but not before I noticed four things, none of them good. The body wore the pale blue greatcoat of a Soviet Air Force officer. As I leaned closer, I saw it was Rak Vatutin. The back of his head was a dark red mess, and Kaz's hand rested on a lichen-encrusted rock that had its share of the same. What's this then, indeed?

"Kaz?" I said, shielding my eyes from the light, while trying to see into his.

"Billy, I found him like this, not one minute ago."

"Then why do you have that rock in your hand?" I pointed to where his right hand rested on the ground, palm down on what looked like the murder weapon. Kaz pulled his hand away, his fingertips stained crimson, his eyes wide with disbelief and confusion. We stared at each other as the silence was broken by a whistle, a piercing, screeching sound as the sentry blew his whistle with all his might, sounding the alarm, too late to do any good.

CHAPTER ▪ TWENTY-SIX

"Now let's get this straight," Detective Sergeant Roy Flack said for the hundredth time. I took a drink of tea, wishing it was coffee. It had been hours since I found Kaz, and we'd spent every one of them in this room. Brick walls and arched ceiling, every brick painted a glossy pale yellow, the kind of paint job you get when you have plenty of free labor, officers with not much else to do, and an endless supply of government-issue paint.

"You became angry after reading the newspaper accounts of the Russian investigation of the Katyn affair," Flack said, reading from his notebook.

"Yes. And then quite inebriated," Kaz said. He looked pale, but that could have been the lighting. It was harsh, a row of light fixtures above the table where we sat, Kaz and I on one side, DS Flack on the other, and a constable at the door. There was a British soldier standing guard on the other side of that door. I hadn't tried to leave, because I didn't want to desert Kaz and because I wasn't sure if they'd let me.

"Inebriated, as you say," Flack noted. "You left your room as it was getting dark, about 5:00 p.m. Lieutenant Boyle observed this, right?"

"Right," I said. "Inebriated is too strong a term. Tipsy, maybe."

"Angry and tipsy," Flack said, raising his eyebrows. "Sounds like a vaudeville act. Were you going to meet someone, Lieutenant Kazimierz? Or look for someone?" It had been the same question, over and over again, since Flack arrived. The sentries had summoned their commanding officer, who sent for Sidorov and the local constable. Sidorov was nowhere to be found. The commanding officer and the constable both sensed more trouble from more quarters than either wanted any part of, and made a call to Scotland Yard. Flack had been the closest inspector, still coordinating the hunt for downed Germans south of London. He'd been awakened in the middle of the night and forced to drive over country lanes in the blackout to get to Dover. By the time he arrived, rain clouds had moved in, and he'd gotten soaked dashing in from his car. He wasn't much happier about being here than we were.

"No," Kaz said, shaking his head, as if willing the cobwebs to be cleared from Flack's single-track mind. "I left rather than make more of an ass of myself. I knew I'd had too much to drink, and that I was verging on self-pity. I thought the cold night air would do me good, and I'd heard that from a good height, you could see the muzzle flashes from the German railway guns, when they bring them out to shell Dover."

"You were determined to get yourself killed?" Flack suggested.

"Not at all. It may not have been my most splendid idea, but it was something I thought interesting. Better than drinking more vodka. So I climbed the path up the cliff and sat on a bench at the top. I watched the bombers fly over. It was really magnificent, if one could separate spectacle from reality. When the antiaircraft gun behind me opened up, I almost fell into the sea. I watched the two planes go down, and sat for a while longer."

"How long?" Flack said.

"I have no idea. I was lost in my own thoughts after the firing died down."

"What were you thinking about, Lieutenant?"

"My homeland. The likelihood that I will never see it again. What to do with my life. To whom I owe my loyalty. The woman I loved and lost. How beautiful the water looked under the starlight. The things one thinks about late at night, in wartime, under the stars, after death has flown overhead."

"And you say you saw no one until Lieutenant Boyle came along?"

"No, I did not say that, DS Flack. I said I saw the sentries at the gate, when the guns fired. They were far away, though, and I'm sure they didn't see me. And I saw the body, before I saw Billy."

"Ah, yes," Flack said, making a show of consulting his notebook.

"You had no idea that the murdered body of Rak Vatutin lay just a few yards from where you sat? You didn't see it when you looked toward the sentries?"

"No, it was pitch black, except for when the antiaircraft gun fired, and there was a bright explosive light, which lit the area around the gun. The sentries were only shadows."

"With all that shooting, and everyone looking up, it would have been a simple matter to bash a man's brains in," Flack said, his voice mild but his eyes unblinking, riveted on Kaz. "It must have been tempting to come upon a Russian in the dark."

"If Joseph Stalin had walked by, I would have given it some thought. But he was nowhere to be seen." The constable at the door laughed, but lost the smile as Flack turned to stare him down.

"Explain the blood on your hands then," Flack said.

"When I saw the body, I knelt down to get a closer look, to see if he was alive. I rested one hand on the ground and felt for a pulse with the other. I didn't even notice I'd put my hand on a stone, until Billy pointed it out. Inspector, if I wished to kill anyone, Russian or otherwise, I wouldn't do it within plain sight of sentries and a gun crew."

"But you said yourself, they didn't see you, that it was too dark."

"I mean, I wouldn't have taken that chance."

"Very well," DS Flack said. "Now, Lieutenant Boyle. We know what time you left the inn, based on witnesses there. Approximately fifteen minutes elapsed between then and when you found Lieutenant Kazimierz leaning over the body."

"Yes," I said. Never give an interrogator more words than you need to. Words are his weapon against you.

"You saw no other people in the area?"

"Not in the immediate area. I saw Archie and Topper Chapman at the inn. They were looking for someone."

"Who?"

"Vatutin. They'd asked me to deliver a message to him."

"Why would they do that?" Flack said, underlining something in his notebook.

"They'd lost contact with him after the Soviet group moved down here."

"What was the message?"

"They wanted to know the time and place. Of what, I don't know. Maybe it had to do with the hijackings. Maybe they killed him."

"It would be unlike the Chapmans to eliminate a useful conduit for information. And I doubt Vatutin would have been a threat. One word from Archie and his own people would have sent him to Siberia. Still, it may put an end to the hijacking investigation. One less thing to worry about."

"You don't think Archie capable of murdering Vatutin?"

"Capable?" Flack said. "Certainly. But I know how he works. He wouldn't show up outside of his own turf and commit murder. Too obvious, too visible. He'd hire it out. Easy enough to pay someone to watch for Vatutin and do away with him. But not while Archie is within spitting distance."

"That makes sense," I had to admit.

"Yes. Now tell me, did you ever witness an argument between Lieutenant Kazimierz and Captain Vatutin?"

"No."

"Nothing unpleasant at all?"

"No. We met him at the embassy. He gave us food and drink and was a cordial host."

"On the night of the opera, when Lieutenant Kazimierz threatened Captain Sidorov? Called him a butcher, and said he'd pay for what he'd done?"

"Is that what Inspector Scutt told you?" I knew I should have kept my answer to one word.

"He told me he'd be happy to never see another Russian opera. Now please answer my question."

"It was a deliberate provocation. Scutt must've told you about the opera."

"So it did happen, as I said?"

"Exactly as you said," Kaz said, seeing I was reluctant to admit the truth.

"And were you drunk—sorry, tipsy—that night as well?"

"No. Quite sober," Kaz said. "I did my drinking later."

"After the film, a Soviet diplomat was beaten within an inch of his life as he walked in the park. Can you tell me anything about that?"

"No. I went back to the Dorchester and stayed there."

"I can vouch for that," I said.

"You can say with certainty that he never left? Would you have heard him leave? I understand the rooms you occupy are quite spacious." Flack sat with his pencil poised over a blank page.

"I didn't stay up all night watching him," I said. "What, do you think he went out in the middle of the night on the chance he'd find a Russian taking a midnight stroll?"

"What I think, Lieutenant Boyle, is that all this started with one murdered Russian. Murdered in such a way as to suggest Polish involvement. Then threats against Captain Sidorov, followed by the savage beating of another Russian, and a second murder right here. Eddie Miller, found stabbed outside the Rubens, after you, Lieutenant Boyle, discover he is working for the Russians and tell Lieutenant Kazimierz. To top it all off, Captain Sidorov has now completely disappeared; he's not in his quarters or any of the pubs. Three, maybe four people come to harm, and Lieutenant Kazimierz has been involved, to one degree or another, with each one. Inspector Scutt tells me the Soviet ambassador is throwing a fit, and so are the Foreign Office, and the home secretary. All that turmoil rolls right downhill to me, courtesy of Inspector Scutt. So rather than take a chance on this continuing any further, I hereby place you under arrest, Lieutenant Kazimierz, on suspicion of murder."

"You can't do that," I said, standing up.

"Sit down," Flack said, and I did, knowing he had to win this one. "I can and could do much more, being here at the invitation of the War Office. For now, it's suspicion. Be thankful for that much."

"Thankful?" Kaz said. "I'm under arrest for a crime I did not commit, and I should be thankful?"

"Yes. Since this crime took place in a secure military area, the Official Secrets Act applies. I could put you away for two years without trial if I didn't like an answer you gave me. So yes, be thankful."

"Billy," Kaz said. "You must find Sidorov. If they think I killed him too . . ." He put his head in his hands and was quiet. Flack nodded to the constable, who led Kaz out of the room.

"I had to do it," Flack said, after the door closed.

"Do you think he did it? Any of it?"

"He could have. Any one of them. The desire for revenge can be powerful."

"In the heat of the moment, yes. But four, or even three?"

"Not for me to say. All I know is that those in exalted positions are demanding the case be solved. An arrest is progress, and he's our only suspect."

"Yeah, the Poles make great sacrificial lambs. Can I go now?"

Flack sighed. "Of course," he said, nodding to the constable, who opened the door. His face held the weariness of cops everywhere who have heard it all. The protestations of innocence, the certainty that a friend, brother, lover could not possibly have done it. I felt the impossibility of communicating that to another human being who had not shared the terror, heartbreak, and friendship Kaz and I had. Flack had his job to do, and to him, Kaz was a legitimate suspect, and I could appreciate the logic in putting him on ice for a while. Still, I didn't feel like cutting him any slack.

"You done with the crime scene?" I asked.

"Yes. I'm waiting for the preliminary medical report now. Take a look, not that there is much to see. That path is well trodden, and between the rains, the sentry, the two of you, the constable, and the victim, there's not much in the way of discernible footprints."

Flack was right. The path was hard-packed dirt, soaked from last night's rain. The grass around it had been heavily trampled. A deep rust-colored stain showed where the head had lain. The stone was gone, but there were plenty like it strewn about. A five-foot stone wall, one of many encircling the castle and the outer buildings, had been hit by a bomb or a shell. Shattered stones were scattered about, and it would have been a simple thing for someone behind Vatutin to reach down, scoop one up, and smash him in the head. He might never have heard it coming.

"Billy," Bull Dawson called out as he strode toward me. "I just heard. What the hell is going on?"

"Rak Vatutin was murdered last night. Right here," I said, pointing to the matted grass and bloodstain. "Scotland Yard thinks Kaz did it."

"Your Polish buddy? Did he?"

"No. I found him here, kneeling beside the corpse. He'd found him a minute before me. But the British government is getting nervous about Russians being found dead or beaten on their turf, so they grabbed the best suspect they had."

"Jesus, Billy, it's not just the British. I've got a passel of Soviets here who want to call Operation Frantic off. They all think they're next, and I can't blame them. With Vatutin dead and Sidorov vanished, they have no secret police to watch them, and I think it makes them more nervous than being watched."

"Have you contacted their embassy?"

"Had to go through the chain of command. Right up to Ike. It's in all the papers, he just got back from the States this morning. Some poor bastard's probably briefing him on the situation right now. It'll be up to him to decide what to do next. I hope he can salvage this; we've put a lot into it."

"Jesus Christ on the mountain," I said.

"Pardon?"

"Ike's favorite curse," I said. I'd bet dollars to doughnuts that Colonel Harding was hearing it right now. I wondered what Big Mike had found out in London. "Did any of the Russians have an idea where Sidorov is?"

"Dead, they all figure. Like Vatutin. And Egorov. What do you think?"

"I think I need to get some sleep," I said. "I've been up all night, I'm tired and hungry, and can't think beyond a cup of coffee. I'll be at the Lord Nelson Inn. Let me know if Sidorov turns up, OK? Maybe he made a lady friend last night."

"He should be so lucky," Bull said.

I walked to the inn, knowing I had a lot of work in front of me, and although it felt like I was letting Kaz down, I knew I had to get some food and at least a few hours' shut-eye, otherwise I'd fall asleep at the wheel. Of course, that assumed I knew where to drive and what to do next. It also assumed I had a vehicle, I realized. I needed to get hold of Big Mike fast.

I walked along the promenade, where the night before I had searched for Kaz. The sun was at my back and the wind in my face as I passed a couple arm in arm, as if they were on holiday and not in a town under shell fire from occupied France. Both in civilian clothes, they were all smiles, the war a mere distraction. Could civilians under bombardment and artillery fire block out the war, and find time for themselves? In uniform, the war and the service were all consuming. The army dictated where I went, what I did, how I dressed, and whom I spent time with. I had almost gotten used to it, and forgotten what it must be like to take a break, enjoy an interlude from the day-to-day grind.

How long before Diana and I would enjoy a day like that, in civvies or khaki? Weeks? Months? Never?

Get a grip, I told myself, as I left the couple behind, arm in arm, gazing out over the channel. It was their time to be moony, not mine. Kaz was under arrest, and I needed a plan. I breathed in the crisp air, trying to force oxygen into my lungs and eventually my brain. I needed to think clearly, and the all-night session with Flack had worn me down. My eyes felt gritty and my legs heavy and clumsy as I opened the door to the inn.

Breakfast was being served and I made that my first priority. I sat at the same table I had last night and thought about the circles of condensation from my glass. Some connected, some separate. Vatutin's murder was another circle. If Kaz hadn't killed him, who had, and why? How did it all fit together? Or rather, which circles fit and which stood alone?

Tadeusz Tucholski, Sheila Carlson, Gennady Egorov, Rak Vatutin, Osip Nikolaevich Blotski, Archie Chapman, Valerian Radecki, Kiril Sidorov, and now Kaz. Mr. Brown, Cosgrove, Kim Philby, and all the invisible intelligence agents circling around the Russians and Poles as they fought their diplomatic war within a war.

I visualized another circle, one for the mysterious shipment that Archie was after, but I couldn't keep all the circles straight, my eyelids heavy with weariness as I finished breakfast. Ideas swirled through my mind as I took the stairs to my room, disjointed images from the past few days. The bomber belly-landing in the field; Archie with his bayonet and poetry; the pebbles on the nightstand in Shepherdswell; Topper in the bordello with Dalenka; the look of incomprehension on Vatutin's face as I gave him the message. I was missing something, something that I'd thought of, or had to do, I wasn't sure. I barely got my jacket, shoulder holster, and shoes off before I fell into bed, fatigue driving my head into the pillow.

I couldn't tell if I was awake and thinking, or asleep and dreaming. The same images floated through my mind. Topper gave me a message, but it wasn't Dalenka playing the piano, it was Diana. Vatutin was in the room, too, looking confused. Topper got angry, with me, I think, and then they were all gone, except for Dalenka, who had taken Diana's place at the piano. Why was Topper mad? Where was Diana?

Then I was on the road to Canterbury, but I was walking, and I was with Kiril Sidorov. We were escaping the Merciless Parliament, although I didn't know if they were after him or me or both of us. Sidorov was telling me about Joey Adamo, the Detroit hood in Big Mike's story, the guy who was adopted and ran out on his old man, only to end up in a steamer trunk. He thought it was funny, and I asked him why he was laughing. He said, Did you ever think it might not have been Joey in the trunk?

The next moment I was walking on a long, circular path in a garden. There was a fountain in the middle, with flowers and hedges all around. Other paths emptied into the garden, but at an angle so you couldn't see them until you had walked past. Suddenly, it all made perfect sense. There was only one circle, and all the other paths flowed into it. The circle wasn't only about this investigation, it was about everything: life, love, war, birth, and death. You kept walking, and sooner or later everything would come to you. Everything was in the circle, and it never ended. Every path led into it, and if you waited long enough, you would see everyone you'd ever known. People were coming down the other paths, but I couldn't recognize them. Shouldn't I see someone I knew? I looked for Diana, I looked for my parents, running, darting in between the strangers who were filling the circle, but I couldn't find anyone I knew. Part of me knew I was dreaming, but most of me was afraid this was heaven, or maybe hell.

Then I was on the promenade, watching the couple I'd seen earlier, except I knew the guy had to be Joey Adamo. He was walking with a beautiful woman on his arm. She wore jewels, and winked at me.

I thought I saw Diana, finally, ahead of me. I pushed through the growing crowd and grabbed her by the arm. But her hair had turned black, and it wasn't Diana at all. It was Dalenka again, wearing a plain beige coat with a blue scarf. She looked perplexed, but stopped and took my hand in hers. We stood silently for a while, as people brushed by us, scurrying around the great circle, before she spoke. "What are you holding?"

I opened the palm of my hand, and saw two small pebbles.

"Stones," I said.

"Why are they in your hand, Billy?" Dalenka asked me, then turned and melted into the crowd. I looked at my hand again, and it was empty.

CHAPTER TWENTY-SEVEN

THE POUNDING ON my door was real, not a dream. It was either a battering ram or Big Mike back from London. I groaned, remembering that I had meant to call him or check for messages last night. I rolled out of bed and opened the door.

"Billy where have you been? Jeez, you look like hell. I left messages last night, and called the castle this morning before I left."

"What time is it?"

"Quarter to eleven. Why are you sleeping in?"

"Because I spent all night with Kaz while Inspector Flack interrogated him," I said, rubbing the grit from my eyes. "Rak Vatutin was found with his head bashed in, and Kaz leaning over him."

"Did he do it?" Big Mike asked matter-of-factly.

"No, but Flack still arrested him. They need someone to feed to the dogs, or at least keep them at bay. The Russians and the British government are demanding the Egorov case be wrapped up, and more bodies don't help. I got in after dawn and plain forgot to check at the desk. What did you find out?"

"It's gold," Big Mike said, his voice excited and his eyes wide as he delivered the big news.

"What is?"

"The shipment. It's gold. Russian gold. Payment for arms and vehicles we sold them."

"That's Lend-Lease. The Russians don't have to pay for it."

"Right. Lend-Lease took effect in October 1941. But we'd been selling them trucks and planes since June '41. According to Sam, anyway."

"And they had to cough up real dough for those first four months?"

"Yep, gold bullion, no less. This shipment is the last installment. It came on a destroyer from Murmansk, escorting a convoy home to Scapa Flow. Comes to half a million dollars' worth."

"Russian gold," I said to myself. "Time and place."

"Sam said the Russians insisted on making the pickup from the dock in Scotland. Then they'll drive it to their embassy and in a couple of days make a big show of handing it over to the American ambassador."

"When," I said, nearly frantic as I washed up. "When is all this happening?"

"Now," Big Mike said, looking at his wristwatch. "They were scheduled to unload the cargo at 0900 this morning. The Russians should be on the road by now."

"With an escort, I hope?"

"Not much of one. One car and one truck, with a few guards inside. Sam said they insisted on running the operation themselves, and wanted to keep a low profile."

"How did Harding know all this? Is he in on it?"

"No. Cosgrove made the calls and came up with the answers. He got us in to see a Russian lieutenant, Andrei Belov, who was in charge while his boss was away. Cosgrove must've pulled some strings; the kid didn't hold out on us."

"Who's his boss? Vatutin?"

"No. Our pal Kiril Sidorov. Andrei said he's been trying to contact him by telephone all morning."

"Something tells me Sidorov isn't going to return the call." I threw cold water on my face, rinsing away shaving cream and a little blood from where I'd nicked myself. Slow down, I told myself. You're forgetting something. What is it? The dream. I'd had a bunch of crazy dreams, and I struggled to remember, as they seemed to evaporate in the face of daylight. I stared at my reflection, then closed my eyes. The dream had explained everything, or so it had seemed at the time.

"Circles," I said out loud.

"What?" Big Mike said from the next room.

"Circles. There's only one circle, and everything connects to it."

"Are you OK, Billy?" Big Mike leaned on the bathroom door, studying me, his eyebrows knitted in worry.

"Yeah, it was just a dream. I'd been trying to figure out how things were connected in this investigation, and in my dream, everything was connected in one big circle. Kind of hard to explain, but it all made sense, like I'd solved the case."

"Yeah, well if dreams were horses, beggars would ride. Or is that wishes?"

"Wishes, I think," I said as I knotted my field scarf. Diana had been in my dream, but sometimes it had been Dalenka. One of them had told me something.

"Where to now?" Big Mike said.

"The castle," I said, trying one last time to remember the dream before it was gone for good. "See if Sidorov turned up." Sidorov. He'd been in the dream, too, on the road to Canterbury. "Big Mike, did they ever positively identify Joey Adamo?"

"The guy in the trunk?"

"Yeah."

"Jeez, Billy, I don't know. He was chopped up in pieces, from what I heard. They didn't call Homicide, that's for sure. Zerilli let Angelo Adamo have the body back, so I guess he was satisfied."

My dad was a big believer in the subconscious. He always said the answers to most questions were lying around in plain sight, like the jumbled pieces of a jigsaw puzzle. According to him, the hardest job was to see *all* the pieces, to understand them, without worrying about how they fit, especially the ones that didn't make sense. If things don't fit a pattern, most people ignore them. But a good cop notices everything, then lets his subconscious work it out.

I'm pretty sure that sometimes, sitting in his armchair and staring out the window, Dad was taking it easy. Or when his eyes closed and his head went back, he might have been taking a nap. But once in a while, late in the evening, or after Sunday dinner, he'd jump up, pace a few times around the living room, tapping his index finger against his lips. He might shake his head *no* once or twice and stop the pacing, but then there would come the snap of the fingers, as if all the pieces had fallen into place.

I was close, but I was stuck at the head-shaking stage. I knew I had to look at this as one case in which all the parties were connected. I didn't know how, but I trusted my subconscious wouldn't steer me in the wrong direction. I hoped I could listen to it as well as Dad listened to his.

"Let's go," I said, grabbing my trench coat.

BIG MIKE TOOK the steep hairpin turns up to the castle like a race-car driver. He had to brake at the last turn for a column of soldiers and a couple of constables. I recognized one of them from last night, the fellow who'd organized the Home Guard search for Germans. I told Big Mike to stop.

"Constable," I said. "Any luck?"

"Don't know if I'd call it luck, sir. We found one Jerry, straightaway. Gave himself up peaceably enough. But then that Russian fellow got himself lost, and we spent the whole night and most of the morning searching for him."

"What Russian?" I asked.

"Captain Sidorov," he said. "He asked if he could join us as we were forming up. I saw no harm in it." There was a defensive tone in his voice, as if he expected me to blame him for something.

"Where is he now? Didn't you find him?"

"Well, he got himself killed, sir. You were with him last night, weren't you? Were you a friend of his? I'm very sorry."

I didn't know what to say. I stared at the constable as the weary Home Guard men stood around our idling jeep, obviously wanting to get home. They were wet and mud soaked, having gone out without rain gear, not knowing that they'd be gone long enough to get caught in a channel squall.

"I knew him" was the best I could say. I remembered I'd seen a pack of unopened Luckies in the glove box, so I got them out and passed them around, which brightened spirits considerably. "Tell me what happened."

"The captain got lost, after we sent two of the lads back with the prisoner. We kept on with the search, figuring we had a good chance of finding him as well as the rest of the Jerries."

"How did you know there'd be more?"

"It was a Heinkel 111 that was shot down. Crew of four, and they all bailed out. Searchlight crew saw 'em, had 'em in their beam all the way down. It promised to be an easy night, if they all came in like that first lad."

"Sidorov?" I said, trying to get him back on track.

"Right you are. Then the rain started up, and we figured he must've looked for shelter."

"Showed him the place meself, just the other day," one of the Home Guard said. He wore corporal's stripes and looked about fifty years old, thin and wiry, strong in spite of his gray whiskers. "I was with his group on the tour we gave, showing them Russians around our invasion defenses and all."

"Showed him what?"

"The bunker. He must've gone in to get out of the rain. It's supposed to be locked, but maybe we left it open by accident after the tour. Or if he had a knife, he could have pried it open." Nods greeted his assertion, the sad sort of nod that gives off a silent *tsk tsk*.

"What the hell happened?"

"The bunker was stocked with about one hundred No. 76 Special Incendiary Grenades," the corporal said. "Sounds impressive, but they're nothing more than pint glass bottles, filled with phosphorus and benzene. The mixture ignites when it comes into contact with the air."

"Don't tell me one broke," I said.

"He must've tripped in the dark and knocked a case down. The bottles are stored in wooden crates, half filled with sawdust. If just one went, it would have set them all off," the corporal said. "Horrible, it was. The sky lit up with the flames, and we all took off at a run, but it was already too late. A concrete bunker with one small door and three firing slits, well, that makes for one intense fire when a hundred of them incendiaries go up."

"You found his body inside?"

"What there was left of it, we did. He must've tried to get out, since we found him half out the door. If it wasn't for his cap, in that bright blue color, we wouldn't have known. It must have blown off his head from the force of the explosion. A small mercy, but quick at least. There were bits and pieces of his uniform left, a few you could see were that same color. And his pistol."

"What condition was that in?" I asked, thinking about how small a mercy indeed.

"Take a look yourself," the constable said, handing me a blackened piece of metal that had a resemblance to a revolver at least. The wooden

grip was gone, and the cylinder was misshapen from the rounds explod-
ing within it. The stamp of the Soviet star was still visible on one side. I
handed it back to the constable and wiped the black from my hands,
trying to put things together, listening to that small voice at the back of
my head that was warning me about something, something about the
dream I'd had.

"What kind of ammunition does that take?" I asked, aware of the
eyes on me. The men were almost finished with their cigarettes and were
losing interest in my question. "Anyone know?"

"That's a Nagant M1895, Lieutenant," the corporal said. "Fires a
7.62mm round. There were some on his belt as well, but they all
cooked off."

"I bet," I said. "Is that pretty much the same size as a .32-caliber
bullet?"

"A little larger, but close. Why do you ask, sir?"

"Just curious," I said. "Did you recover any of the slugs?"

"No reason to look for them, was there?" The constable was looking
at me a bit strangely now. "In any case, the heat was so intense in that
enclosed space, they probably melted past recognizing. What's your point,
if you don't mind me asking, Lieutenant?"

"I was a police detective, before the war. Makes me suspicious of
everything," I said, thinking of Dad sitting in his armchair, waiting for
the answers to come. "So, you ran to the fire, found there was nothing
you could do, and went on with your search, right?"

"I posted two of the lads at the bunker, and then we continued, yes."

I tried to imagine the scene and work backward. Sidorov blindly
stumbling into a bunker he knew to be filled with unstable incendiary
grenades did not fit well into my vision of the events. Then it came to
me, and I had to resist the temptation to snap my fingers.

"And you found only two of the three remaining German fliers,
right?"

"Why, yes, how did you know?"

"It came to me in a dream."

CHAPTER · TWENTY-EIGHT

I FOUND A Russian officer wearing a Nagant revolver, and asked for one of his bullets. He evidently didn't believe in reverse Lend-Lease, since it cost me a five-pound note. I'd sent Big Mike to make a call to Harding and then find Bull and see if Inspector Flack was still around. I waited in the same room where Flack had interrogated Kaz and me, playing with the 7.62mm bullet, rolling it around my fingers.

Big Mike had pestered me to tell him what I was cooking up, but I told him to wait a few minutes so I could think it through and explain it to everyone together. I had most of the pieces put together, and could guess at the rest. Proving them would be harder, but right now what I wanted was to throw as much doubt on Kaz as Vatutin's killer as I could. I knew that was going to be an uphill fight as soon as Flack came into the room.

"This had better be good, Boyle," Flack said, standing across from me, arms akimbo. "I've been on the telephone explaining to the Foreign Office how come two Soviet officers have been killed within hours of each other. And that was after explaining it to the commissioner, ten minutes after I explained it to Detective Inspector Scutt. So I am in no mood to waste time with you."

Bull and Big Mike sat. I gestured to the remaining chair and tapped the table with my Russian bullet, waiting for Flack to sit. He had a right to complain. I didn't envy his role as messenger when the news was all bad and he was the messenger delivering it up the chain of command. Finally, he sat.

"I want to start at the beginning, as much as I can. This began with Gennady Egorov found bound and shot in a manner suggestive of the Polish bodies found at Katyn. A map showing the route of a Russian supply truck was discovered on him, hinting at his involvement with recent hijackings. Plus, he was found on Archie Chapman's turf."

"Correct," said Flack.

"In the course of that investigation, I stumbled onto an informant for Captain Kiril Sidorov. Eddie Miller, of the Rubens Hotel, who provided Sidorov with information on the Polish Government in Exile. Then Eddie was found dead. You suspect Kaz, but I think Eddie was poisoned, then stabbed, by Sheila Carlson."

"We've been over all this," Flack said, drumming his fingers on the table.

"We know that Egorov was shot with a dumdum bullet. You recovered fragments that indicated a .32-caliber slug."

"Which fits the weapon Lieutenant Kazimierz carries," Flack said. "Remember, we also found a dumdum round in his desk, with the neatly filed X on top."

"Yes, so convenient. All you were missing was a big red sign that said, 'Look Here.' Tell me, does Kaz strike you as stupid?"

"No, he does not. But anyone can make a mistake."

"Sure. But think for a minute. If Kaz didn't kill Egorov, who put the bullet there?"

"Eddie Miller, perhaps. He was working for Sidorov."

"OK, same question. Did Eddie strike you as stupid?"

"From what I heard, he was not the brightest fellow. Gullible, certainly."

"The kind of guy to be entrusted with a key piece of incriminating evidence, to frame Kaz?"

"We'll never know, will we? Please come to the point, Boyle."

We were interrupted by an orderly with a pot of coffee and a tray of cups. It was perfect timing. The coffee smelled good, and as Flack dumped in a healthy spoonful of sugar, I knew he'd stay as long as the coffee lasted.

"Two things have bothered me about this case. First, Sheila Carlson. We know she worked for MI5, for an operative known as Mr. Brown. Mr. Brown seems to have gone to extremes for king and country, and

Sheila was happy to oblige, plotting to kill Tadeusz Tucholski with a poisoned cake. She might as well have, too. Everyone else was connected to each other: Sidorov, Egorov, Kaz, Radecki, Vatutin, Tad, Archie, and Topper. They all had a connection, no matter how slim."

"Sheila was connected to Eddie," Flack said. "She lived and worked with him."

"Exactly," I said. "And she killed him as well."

"So you say," Flack said, sipping his coffee. "Brown seems to have gone too far, even by MI5 standards. Cosgrove told me he's been reined in, transferred elsewhere."

"Good. And I hope you had the contents of Eddie's stomach tested," I said.

"As a matter of course, yes, but I haven't heard anything yet. It is not a priority with everything else we have on our plate: murdered Russians and German aircrews running about."

"Sheila was the one person who stood alone, after she killed Eddie. Eddie was the only one who knew her, who might have an idea of where she'd gone. Even Brown and his MI5 henchmen couldn't find her. Think about that," I said, leaning over the table, staring into Flack's eyes, willing him to see it as I did. "She needs her identity card and her ration card. How hard should it be for MI5 to find someone in England these days?"

"Your point?"

"She killed Eddie for a reason. To eliminate anyone who knew anything about her. If she was simply an MI5 agent, why would she worry about that?"

"Lucky for her she did," said Big Mike.

"Right, but how was she to know Mr. Brown had gone off the reservation and needed to get rid of her?"

"So she had another reason," said Bull, looking to Flack as if to coach him. Flack was silent.

"Yes. And that reason connects to the other thing that bothered me. The information on the truck hijackings had to come from within the Russian Embassy. They laid out the routes for the delivery trucks. But what was in it for whoever did it?"

"Money, of course," Flack said as Big Mike poured him more coffee. I made a mental note to get him promoted to sergeant.

"Sure, maybe for the produce and booze. A little extra to spend in

London. But what good are dollars or pounds back in the Soviet Union? He couldn't bring them in and deposit them in a bank."

"If I had to go back to Russia, I should be glad of extra money while I was in London," Flack said.

"But what if you didn't have to go back?" I asked, and watched Flack think that one through.

"We are Allies with the Soviet Union, Boyle. We couldn't let one of their officers defect. What is the point, anyway? We have three dead Russians; no one is defecting!"

"No. You have two. Egorov and Vatutin, both murdered by Kiril Sidorov. With help from his lover, Sheila Carlson." I sat back and took a sip of coffee. It was good.

"What?" Flack and Big Mike said at the same time.

"Sheila was working both sides of the fence. Maybe Sidorov recruited her through Eddie, but I don't think Eddie knew. She was working for MI5 and saw no reason not to supplement her income. But it went further than that. Maybe they fell for each other, or maybe it's all about the money."

"What money?" Flack said. "They can't have earned a fortune from tipping off the Chapman gang." I knew I had him interested at last. He wasn't sarcastic, he was working the problem.

"That was just for expenses. They needed it for forged identity papers and ration cards. There have been cases of papers stolen from bodies recovered after the bombings. I bet some of those match the descriptions of Sheila and Sidorov. Part of their deal with Archie Chapman. The real payoff was information about the gold shipment." I told him about the half million in gold coming from Scotland.

"And you're certain about Sheila and Sidorov?" Flack said.

"Certain enough," I said. "I remembered that Sheila had been wearing a beige utility coat and a blue scarf when we first met her. When I was tailing Sidorov, before he met with Eddie, I saw him bump into a woman wearing the same coat with a blue scarf over her head. She dropped her pocketbook and he picked it up. I bet they were close to the end of their game, and using spy craft to be certain no one saw them together. But they had to have a way of communicating. Passing notes on a busy sidewalk would do the trick." I didn't mention I'd remembered the coat and scarf in my dream, and that it had been Dalenka wearing them.

"That's something to chew on," Flack said. "Have you alerted anyone about the gold shipment?"

"Yes, my boss, Colonel Harding. He's sending an escort of a couple of armored cars."

"Archie will be cross," Flack said, a smile creeping up on his face. "What put you on to this?"

"I had a deal with Archie. I knew I'd need Chapman's help, so I agreed to deliver a message. Topper told me to tell Vatutin 'time and place,' that he'd know what it meant. I thought it was only another supply shipment, and figured it was worth it to get in with them. I think I made a mistake, one that may have cost Vatutin his life. I said Topper wanted to know 'time and place.'"

"How did that make any difference?" Bull asked.

"Vatutin was a trip wire. He worked for Sidorov, and Sidorov knew anything that was said to him would be reported. Sure enough, Vatutin ran right over to Sidorov when I delivered the message. I'm beginning to think mentioning Topper was not meant as part of the message, and that was too much information to let Vatutin live with."

"'Time and place' alone might have done the same," Flack said. "Vatutin might have put two and two together if the gold shipment had been hit. I wouldn't worry, Boyle. But I meant the whole scheme; how did you put all that together?"

"Chaucer and Joey Adamo," I said. "Chaucer fled to Canterbury to get away from the Merciless Parliament. Joey Adamo was a Detroit hood who escaped the Mob by fleeing to Canada, where his death was likely faked. Last night, Sidorov said it was necessary for his government to be merciless, and that set me thinking." I didn't mention the thinking had gone on in my dreams. "And then I remembered what he had told me about Article 58 of the Soviet Criminal Code. It makes the nonreporting of counterrevolutionary activities by family members punishable by a stretch in a Siberian labor camp, at best."

"Chaucer, as in *The Canterbury Tales*?" Flack asked.

"Yeah. He escaped to the country to save his neck."

"I know about Chaucer, man! It's a bit flimsy, don't you think?"

"I'm not saying it's evidence, but it fits. Sidorov has a wife and daughter. If he defected, they'd be punished."

"How could they?" Big Mike said.

"It doesn't matter. It's how they control people."

"Wait a minute," Flack said, holding up his hand. "Sidorov couldn't have known a German plane would be shot down last night. Are you claiming he killed one of the Germans, and put the body in the bunker? It's too fantastic."

"No, it's not," Bull said. "If Billy's right, then we put a huge crimp in their plans by moving the Russian personnel down here. Except for controlled outings, they've been virtually incommunicado. Telephone calls are monitored; this is a highly sensitive installation."

"Yeah," chimed in Big Mike. "They were all ready to go. Sidorov set up the route for the gold shipment, and made sure the guard would be on the light side, under the guise of not attracting too much attention. Sheila got rid of Eddie and gave Mr. Brown the slip. Chapman arranged for an identity swap with a couple of dead bodies on ice. And then, out of the blue, Sidorov was sent down here."

"Right. Archie was desperate to contact him. Sidorov was certainly feeling the same way. Archie followed me down here, and probably made contact."

"Couldn't Sidorov have left with Chapman?" Flack said.

"Would you trust Archie, after he paid you and got what he wanted?"

"Valid point," Flack said. "So Sidorov sees his chance. He knows about the bunker from his Home Guard tour. He volunteers to join the search party, in hopes of finding a German from the downed aircraft. Intending to kill him, and change clothes."

"Or one of the Home Guard, or even a constable. If any of them disappeared, and it looked like Sidorov's body had been burned in the fire, suspicion would fall on them. It would be enough to allow Sidorov to disappear, and to get around Article 58. He'd be mourned as a hero back home."

"You're right, it would look like one of them murdered Sidorov, and fled. That would have bought him time and confusion."

"The German could have been already dead, killed bailing out. Or he may have given himself up, and Sidorov led him to the bunker. You should have the body examined. There could be a bullet."

"There is," Flack said. "I had it looked at by a doctor here. I learned my lesson with the last dead Russian. But it could have been from the rounds going off in the fire."

"OK," Bull said. "I'm Sidorov. I've just changed clothes with a Kraut flier. That's a problem right there. Big, heavy flight boots. Flight jacket and pants with big map pockets on the thighs. He's going to have trouble getting around without being noticed."

"Right. I'll have the local constables canvas the area. If you're not wrong, Boyle, we'll find a report of missing laundry and a stolen bicycle close by," Flack said, pulling a notebook from his pocket. That was a good sign. What he said next wasn't. "You don't know where this bunker is, do you?"

"Not exactly. Close?"

"About a twenty-minute walk north, set into the woods near a cross-road. Lieutenant Kazimierz could have followed Sidorov and the Home Guard, perhaps even caught him unawares when he was separated from the group. Then he takes him to the bunker, and stages it to look like an accident. He would have had ample time to make it back to the castle and bash Vatutin in the head. If you hadn't come along, he might have gotten away with it."

"We have to find Sidorov," I said, more to myself than anyone else. If Scotland Yard got it in their mind that Kaz was the killer, and if that took off the political heat, then I knew what was likely to happen. If the killings stopped, Kaz was as good as convicted. And hanged.

"Or the fourth German crewman," Flack said, rising from his chair. "Either will prove a point. I'll have the Home Guard out again and alert the constables."

Suddenly I felt exhausted, my failure to fully convince Flack weighing hard. I stared at the table, trying to think of what else to say. There was nothing left, my arguments as empty as my hands.

My hands. I had dreamed about my hands. What was it? Diana, or Dalenka, or whoever the hell it was, had asked me something. The pebbles.

Why are they in your hand?

Of course. This time, I did snap my fingers.

CHAPTER ∙ TWENTY-NINE

FAKING A LIMP is hard. You can do it if you really focus on it, but if you slip up, you're done for. To pull it off, try walking around with pebbles in your shoe. You limp. You have to. That's what the mystery woman's question meant. The pebbles went in a shoe, not a hand. They weren't souvenirs of Poland; they were stones to put in Sidorov's shoe, to establish his identity as a bandaged, crippled Polish pilot. He and Sheila had visited Shepherdswell several times, laying the groundwork for their getaway. They probably planned to hole up there for a while, after Sidorov pulled off the switch with whatever body Archie provided. After the gold shipment was knocked off, of course. Then, with phony identities established, they could move away when the heat died down, Sidorov healed and rich. Free of the Merciless Parliament.

Operation Frantic had thrown a monkey wrench into things. But both Archie and Sidorov were determined to get what they wanted, and were daring enough for the job. Archie and Topper setting me up with that message, and tailing us in a staff car, provided the perfect camouflage. As did Sidorov's move, joining the Home Guard search, ready to kill again for a body to be consumed in flames.

We'd left Flack to organize the search. He was calling out the Home Guard, telling them they were after the remaining German, which worked for me, since Sidorov was wearing his clothes. Unless he'd already stolen other duds. That's what I would have done, I thought, as Big Mike barreled the jeep north on the open road. Lots of military traffic headed for the coast, but the left lane going north was clear.

I would've looked for a barn or outbuilding, hoping for some work clothes hung on a peg. One of those boilersuits, maybe. A commonplace blue one-piece outfit would be perfect to cover the Luftwaffe uniform, even the flying boots. Then a bicycle, on back roads, to Shepherdswell.

"But then what?" I said, not realizing I'd spoken out loud.

"Huh?" Big Mike said as he downshifted and passed a couple of trucks. I held onto my hat with one hand and onto the seat with the other. Even with the canvas top up, the wind whipped around inside and almost blew my service cap out. Big Mike's driving threatened to do the same with the rest of me.

"If they don't find Sidorov on the road, I don't think they'll find him at the house," I said, shouting to be heard above the wind and road noise.

"Why not?"

"He's most likely out of contact with Sheila. If anybody local saw him enter the house, they'd think he was a thief. Even if he got in, people would expect her to be there to care for him. If she's not there, he probably has to hide out somewhere and wait. Somewhere close."

"We broke in," Big Mike said. "No one called the cops or came at us with a shotgun."

"We didn't have much at stake. We could've talked our way out of trouble, if it came to that. But Sidorov is wearing a German uniform, and he has everything to lose."

"OK," Big Mike said. "He needs to hide out somewhere safe, until they can meet up. Wonder if they have a contingency plan?"

"They're both in the spy business. It would make sense." I thought about it for a while. Big Mike was dead-on. Sidorov was NKVD, Sheila was MI5. Between them, they'd know the ins and outs of the trade. "There'd have to be two contingency plans, at least. One for getting together if something unexpected happened to either of them, like the move to Dover. And another in case of total disaster, like one of them being found out. That would be a whole different kettle of fish."

"Right now, they're probably working under Plan A," Big Mike said. "If they go to Plan B, we'll never find them."

"Jesus, I hope Flack doesn't ring up the Shepherdswell constable and tell him to walk up and down Farrier Street until he sees a Russian dressed up as a German."

"He didn't strike me as thick-headed," Big Mike said. "Stubborn, for sure. You know the type—arrest and conviction, that's what counts. Some guys prefer a tidy closed case to a messy open one." He laid on the horn, passing three trucks this time, and didn't slow down.

WE MADE IT back to Norfolk House in record time, and found Cosgrove in with Colonel Harding. We gathered around his desk, bringing them up to speed.

"I've been in touch with Scotland Yard," Cosgrove said. "They are skeptical of your theory, but have agreed to watch Shepherdswell carefully. Meanwhile, they have brought murder charges against Lieutenant Kazimierz. The death of Captain Sidorov, if that indeed is his body, tipped the scales against him, I'm afraid."

"What exactly are they doing in Shepherdswell?" I asked, now very afraid for Kaz.

"They've sent a man down to stay at the pub, posing as a businessman. He has photos of both Sheila Carlson and Sidorov."

"That's it?"

"I've arranged for two WACs to visit Shepherdswell," Harding said. "They have a three-day pass, and I figured they wouldn't raise much suspicion. They can walk around like tourists. Mary Stevens, from the typing pool, and Estelle Gordon."

"Estelle? She's back?" Big Mike piped up. "Sir?"

"Yes, she came in after you two left for Dover. I figured it would give her something worthwhile to do."

"Well, OK, I guess she can take care of herself," Big Mike said grudgingly.

"Any other ideas, Boyle?" Harding said. "This whole thing is heating up. The Russians are screaming, accusing the Poles, the Poles are screaming about the Katyn cover-up, and both sides are screaming about post-war borders. We need to wrap this up, quickly and quietly."

"The only thing I can think of is to try Archie Chapman, and see if he can tell us anything. It had to be his gang that supplied Sidorov and Sheila with false papers and maybe even a stolen car. He might save us a lot of time."

"The same Chapman who you just cheated out of a truckload of

Russian gold?" Cosgrove said. "I think he'd be more in the mood to slit your throat than to help you."

"I agree," I said. "That's why I need you to do me a favor." After I told Cosgrove what I needed, he left and Harding told Big Mike to grab some chow. He got no argument.

"Ike's back," Harding said, after everyone had left. "Came in from the States yesterday. He wants to see you." He ushered me into Uncle Ike's office, one floor up.

"William," Uncle Ike said, setting down the telephone. "How are you?"

"Holding my own, General," I said, unaware of how much Uncle Ike knew about what had been going on. "How was your visit home?"

"It was great to see Mamie again. She sends her best wishes, by the way. Unfortunately, I spent more time with politicians than I did on leave. Sit down, William." Uncle Ike sat on a couch, and I took the armchair opposite. He nodded to Harding, who left the room. "I'm sorry to hear about this affair with Lieutenant Kazimierz. I wanted you to know I called the commissioner at Scotland Yard and asked for him to be released into my custody. He said no."

"I'm not surprised. They seem to think Kaz is the answer to their prayers."

"That's dangerously close to the truth, William." Uncle Ike lit a cigarette and blew smoke toward the ceiling. "This is a tightrope we're walking. On one side is our moral obligation to our Polish allies. Not to mention millions of Polish-American voters; FDR isn't one to forget that. On the other side, there are the hundreds of Red Army divisions fighting the Germans right now."

"Did you discuss this with the president?"

"What would be the point, William? If we openly side with the Poles, we cause a break in relations with our Soviet allies, just as we are beginning to plan the invasion. Do you have any idea what our casualties would be if the Soviets halted their offensive, even for a few weeks? The Germans could move a dozen more divisions into France."

"But we can't side with the Russians on this, can we?" Uncle Ike smoked for a minute, staring at the carpet, the view out the window, anything but my gaze.

"No, you're right. We can't and won't openly side with the Russians against the Poles."

"Which leaves nothing."

"Yes. We have offered to act as intermediaries, which the Russians have roundly and loudly rejected. So we wait for both sides to come to their senses, which may never happen. This entire matter may be settled by Russian tanks entering Warsaw, but don't you ever repeat that, William."

"Yes, sir."

"But I'll be damned if we let Lieutenant Kazimierz be Scotland Yard's scapegoat, and don't repeat that either. You find whoever is responsible for these murders, and get Kaz back to work for me. Can you do that, William?"

"Yes, Uncle Ike. I can. I will."

"Good, good. Do you need anything?"

"I've got Major Cosgrove organizing something that should help. I'll let you know if I need a company of Rangers to bust Kaz out." Uncle Ike smiled and draped his arm over my shoulder as he led me to the door.

"I wouldn't mind leading them myself," he said.

THE SOUND OF a dozen pairs of boots running down the stairs in the enclosed space of the Liverpool Street Underground set up an echo that signaled lethal intent, which was the general idea. We tromped into Archie's domain bristling with arms. The ten Royal Marines had Sten guns, and Big Mike carried a Winchester M12 shotgun. I satisfied myself with a .45 automatic at my side and a piece of paper in my hand. No one had a round chambered, but Archie and his boys wouldn't know that. We were going to give them something else to think about.

It was pelting rain outside, and with little chance of a Luftwaffe raid, the population in the shelter was light, only those diehards who coveted their regular bunks. Plus Archie and Topper. We'd waited until we saw them go down for the night, gave them twenty minutes to get settled, then came on like gangbusters. Two jeeps and a truck, with an armed guard left to watch over our little convoy. Can't fool me twice.

"Topper Chapman!" I bellowed as we stormed into Archie's shelter. It was tight going with the cots and bunks, but people scattered fast to let us through. First up was Charlie, the ex-boxer who stood guard at the entrance to Archie's blanketed retreat.

"Out of our way, Charlie. You don't have enough newspaper for all the iron we brought."

"This ain't right," Charlie said, holding his ground. "You all stop where you are."

"Billy, hold this," Big Mike said, handing me the shotgun. He put up his fists, and Charlie did the same, despite the fact that Big Mike stood a foot taller than he did. Big Mike pulled back his right fist, and Charlie moved his arms to block the punch, but Big Mike jabbed him in the stomach with his left, a quick punch that sent Charlie to his knees, gasping. I handed Big Mike the shotgun, and we all stepped around Charlie, who'd done his duty and lost only his wind.

"Topper Chapman!" I said again, and heard the scamper of feet as more residents of the shelter fled the scene. "Time to serve king and country."

"What's this then?" Clive said, open mouthed, as he peered out at us from behind the makeshift wall. Stanley pushed Clive forward, his hand in his jacket pocket. He took it out slowly, and empty, as he watched Big Mike's shotgun aimed straight at his chest.

"Down! Down on the floor!" The Royal Marine sergeant shouted, and with the snouts of several Sten guns to guide them, Stanley and Clive were spread-eagled in ten seconds. Two more marines pulled down the hanging blankets, and Archie Chapman was revealed, sitting in his chair, reading a book, *Poems from the Trenches*. He carefully placed a bookmark between the pages, then calmly watched the proceedings. Topper sat in a hard-backed chair, his legs crossed nonchalantly, a drink in his hand. The Chapmans were a couple of cool customers.

"Come in, Peaches," Archie said. "I've been hoping to see you."

"I came to see Topper. To give him this," I said, holding up the piece of paper. "His enlistment has been reinstated. Turns out your Dr. Carlisle has lost his medical license, which invalidates his diagnosis of whatever phony condition he cooked up for you."

"Bollocks!" Archie cried, throwing his book down. "You can't do this, Yank."

"I'm just the messenger," I said, handing Archie the paperwork. "These gentlemen are here to carry out the lawful order of your own government."

"You can't be serious," Topper said, but he knew I was. It was just something to say. He drained his drink, stood, and nodded to his father.

"Come, Mr. Chapman," the Royal Marine sergeant said, addressing

Topper. "Everything's in order. Let's get to the barracks and get you kit-ted out." He took Topper by the arm and as they left, I thought I saw a glimpse of what—excitement?—on Topper's face. Joy, maybe. The Royal Marines had to be an improvement over life with Archie.

The place cleared out quickly. Two marines remained at the entrance to the shelter to keep the denizens out. Big Mike took a few steps back and cradled the shotgun in his arms. I took Topper's chair, pulled it close to Archie, and sat.

"No poem for the occasion?" I asked. Archie frowned, a bitter, deep frown that pulled down the corners of his mouth as if he were caught on a fishhook. He looked at the paper, the stamp of the Crown, and the legalisms that had taken his son away.

"You want praise for this maneuver of yours, Peaches? I think one of your own, an Irishman, put it best."

> *You say, as I have often given tongue*
> *In praise of what another's said or sung,*
> *'Twere politic to do the like by these;*
> *But was there ever dog that praised his fleas?*

"That's Yeats, but I doubt you know it. This maneuver is a fleabite. I'll have Topper back in the time it takes to buy a politician, which is to say by dawn. What do you want with him? Have you taken him as a bargaining chip?"

"I'd like some insurance against taking a bayonet over that business with the Russian gold," I said.

"So that was your doing? I thought perhaps. What a surprise that was. Armored cars, machine guns, not what we expected. A great fortune lost. And such a loss does build resentment, so you're wise to have Topper at hand, at least for as long as you're down here."

"Think carefully, Archie. Think about what it takes to get a doctor's license revoked. Think about what pull it takes to get Topper into the service, without a question asked about his record. They weren't picky, right after Dunkirk. But now, criminal associations should keep a guy like Topper out. But there it is, in black and white. The Royal Marines, no less. Maybe a commando unit. Think about that."

He did. His mouth went slack for a moment, then he clamped it shut.

He reached for a bottle of gin, a couple of glasses, and poured. He downed his before I got mine to my lips.

"Pass me that book," he said, pointing to the volume he'd thrown to the floor. I did. "You won't believe what I was reading when you burst in here. Isaac Rosenberg. Jewish lad, died at the Somme. Would have been a great poet, perhaps, had he lived. I was in the middle of 'On Receiving News of the War.' Listen."

> *In all men's hearts it is.*
> *Some spirit old*
> *Hath turned with malign kiss*
> *Our lives to mould.*

> *Red fangs have torn His face.*
> *God's blood is shed.*
> *He mourns from His lone place*
> *His children dead.*

"What do you think of that, Peaches?"

"I think you did everything a father could do," I said. "I know my dad did, but I'm still here. Fate has a hand to play as well."

"You could be right," Archie said, letting the book drop to the floor. "So what do you want? It must be more than safe passage through Shoreditch should you come visiting."

"I want everything you know about Kiril Sidorov and Sheila Carlson." His eyebrows rose, a sign of admiration.

"So you've put those two together, have you? Regular lovebirds."

"I didn't know if it was love or money," I said.

"The course of true love runs a lot more smoothly cushioned by cash. Still, they seem to be dedicated to each other. I'm giving no evidence here, understand. We're just having a chat."

"About two people we both know," I said, gulping gin.

"And this chat will give the good doctor his medical license back? And Topper back to me?"

"Yes," I said, "if I'm satisfied." I wanted to tell him to let Topper go, but I was a military detective, not a social worker.

"I don't know, Peaches," Archie said, staring into his empty glass.

"I can get another sawbones anytime. And maybe Topper should serve. He told me the other day how it might be hard for him to hold his head up high after the war. That some in the neighborhood might think badly of him."

"Really?" I cursed myself for giving Topper that line to get him steamed.

"Really. If he's thinking that way, then he's weak and needs toughening. Once you start caring what others think of you, then you start living by their rules. Might as well get a proper job."

"I know some fellows in Boston who'd agree with you. They'd also agree that you should make that decision, not have it made for you."

"You're leavin' me with only bad choices, Peaches. I don't like selling out a client. It isn't good for business."

"Listen, Archie. Once we pick these two up, there's going to be no public trial, no testimony. This is wartime, and they're spies, pure and simple. If they're not hung they'll be thrown in a deep, dark hole far away from here. MI5 is backing me on this, and they'll back you, too, if you want."

"You're an interesting one, Peaches. A mere lieutenant who haunts the streets and tunnels of London, but who also can have Shoreditch declared off-limits, bring a squad of Royal Marines along as your own muscle, ruin my doctor's practice, and at the same time cavort with the likes of MI5. They've shed their share of Irish blood, haven't they? Don't you feel hatred for them? Who are you really, Peaches?"

"A mere lieutenant," I said. "Who understands what family means." Archie sighed, and refilled our glasses. We drank some more, but that sigh told me everything I needed to know. I relaxed, and Archie filled in the details, his mind clear even as his belly filled with gin. Names on fake identity papers and ration books. Make and model of the stolen car, plus stolen license plates. Dates and amounts of payments. Details on the split Sidorov would have received if the gold shipment had been taken. It was impressive.

Sidorov had controlled security for the gold shipment, and had talked his superiors into the low-profile approach. Egorov had been suspicious from the get-go, and Sidorov thought he had gotten too close, so one night he led Egorov to Liverpool Street and gave him the Polish treatment, down to the hands tied with twine. He planted the map on him to draw suspicion toward Egorov as a victim of thugs, Poles, or both.

Sidorov had traded information about the earlier produce shipment with Archie, to establish his bona fides and to put his hands on enough money to purchase the phony papers and rent the cottage in Shepherdswell, disguised as a crippled RAF pilot. That way, he'd be ready to pull his disappearing act once the gold was snatched and Archie supplied a body.

"It was our good fortune Jerry came back," Archie said. "I've got a stiff on ice, didn't even have to kill the poor bastard. Concussion did him in. Sidorov had given me enough of his uniform gear over time that we got him all outfitted. Need a dead Russian, Peaches? Fire sale, you might say. Ha! Wasted effort, that was, with him going off to Dover, and you spoiling our grand plans."

"It was clever, the way you used a staff car to tail me," I said, wanting to steer the conversation away from my monkey wrenching and on to how brilliant Archie was. "You didn't have any other way to contact Sidorov?" I said it casually as I filled my glass for what I hoped was the last time. I didn't want Archie to know how important this was. Otherwise, there'd be a price tag I might not be able to pay.

"Sure we did, Peaches. But we couldn't wait. There's a blind drop at the railway station in Shepherdswell. One or both of them was to check it every third day, five o'clock in the morning. It was a place to leave emergency messages, or to rendezvous if things went south. I didn't want to wait three more days."

"It had just been checked?"

"Aye. Sheila had been there the morning we last met, but my men told me she'd had no word from Sidorov. She was frantic, so they said, desperate for her cut. I thought we'd lost our opportunity, but with you willing to carry our message to Vatutin himself, it was easier to ride your coattails, so to speak."

"Cheers," I said, raising my glass and finishing off the gin. The stuff was beginning to grow on me. Now I knew where Sidorov would be in two days. No need to beat the countryside, just let him come to us, to the rendezvous with his lover at the station. It was more than I could ask for, but I had one more question.

"Did you give Sidorov a book of poetry?" I asked.

"Why, Peaches? Are you hurt I haven't given you a gift?"

"Just curious. Did you mark that passage, the one about the ladder?"

"I did give him the Yeats, yes. Marked it, no. I'm too careful with my books for that," Archie said, pouring himself another glass and smacking his lips as he drank. He leaned back in his chair, and we could have been sitting in a warm room by the fire, from all you could tell by the expression on his face.

"Did you write the Latin inscription?"

"Latin? No, I didn't go to no toff school to learn Latin! Didn't go to school much at all. What did it say?"

"The bodies are asleep, the souls are awake," I said. "That's what was written in Latin."

"I showed him Yeats, and pointed out the poem he should read. The book had no inscription when I gave it to him. I wouldn't chance some bright detective snooping around and finding my hand in Sidorov's book. But he had a need of poetry, that man."

"Why?"

"Oh, he's a tortured soul, did you not see that, Peaches? For all the brains you've got in that Yank head, couldn't you see into his heart? It was ruined, and this was his way back."

"His way back where?" Now I was confused.

"To himself, foolish boy! That's what he's escaping, don't you know? The Bolsheviks are bad enough, and worth fleeing, but he's running from something deeper and blacker, rooted in his very soul."

"What?"

"Haven't a clue, and don't give a goddamn. Ha! There you go. But mark my words, there's torment under that sharp mask he wears. I gave him the book so when he was free of Stalin and that bloody bunch, he'd understand. That there's no escaping the foul rag and bone shop of the heart. I know, Peaches. Believe me, I know."

"I'm sorry, Archie." I didn't know exactly for what, but I was. And for some reason, it was important for this half-mad criminal to know it.

"You must be a good son, Peaches," he said, clapping a friendly hand on my arm. I couldn't help but wonder what Dad would make of Archie. I was glad I'd never find out.

"Thanks," I said, and saw Archie grin as he stared past me.

"Now lookit those two. No sense of propriety, they should be fighting to the death! Ha!" Archie pointed to Big Mike and Charlie, who were sitting next to each other on a cot, the shotgun resting between them, as Big Mike lit up a Lucky for the ex-boxer.

"If Big Mike starts in about Detroit, he'll talk him to death," I said as I got up.

"Tell Charlie to come over and have a drink with me, willya? Then you go your way and I'll go mine, and neither of us will speak of who said what here tonight. Agreed?"

I agreed. Again, it seemed the only sensible thing to do.

CHAPTER ▪ THIRTY

WHEN IT CAME down to it, they gave up without a fuss. We had the station staked out all night, and spotted Sidorov in the shadows about four o'clock in the morning. He was watching for a trap, as I knew he'd be. So we kept our distance. There were two MPs in the locked station, along with a constable, sitting in the dark. Big Mike and I were in a windowed garage across from the station, the jeep ready to go. We had men stationed at every intersection, but we'd been careful not to have any military or police vehicles visible. Sheila was careful, too. She'd parked her automobile a few streets away and walked to the station, whistling a tune. Maybe it was a signal, or maybe she was looking forward to seeing her lover.

We knew Sidorov had been busy, stealing a motorbike outside of Dover, and there had been two reports of break-ins that matched his likely route to Shepherdswell. Clothes, blankets, and food. Odds were that he'd been living rough, waiting for the scheduled meet with Sheila. I watched him through my binoculars as he came out into the open. He was unshaven and dirty, but he'd gotten rid of the German uniform, and looked enough like a farm laborer not to attract undue attention.

They were pros, I had to hand it to them. They didn't immediately go to each other, but walked the perimeter of the platform in opposite directions, checking to see if anyone was around. When they satisfied themselves they were alone, they embraced. That was the signal. We wanted them both, and the moment Sidorov put his arms around Sheila Carlson and held her close, rocking in that way that people do when happiness overcomes them, the station doors burst open and the MPs took them. I opened the garage door and Big Mike floored it, getting us to the platform in five seconds. Detective Sergeant Flack, trailed by several constables, came out from another building to the sound of police whistles. Above it all, as Sheila Carlson was pulled away, her arms outstretched, fingertips clawing at emptiness, I could hear her wailing.

"Kiril! Kiril! Kiiirilll!"

Sidorov was silent, his eyes locked on to hers as they handcuffed him.

THAT HAD BEEN four hours ago. Now we were seated in an interview room at Scotland Yard. Detective Inspector Scutt, Detective Sergeant Flack, and me, across the table from Sidorov. Tea had been served. It was almost civilized. Sidorov had not spoken, except to say thank you for the tea, and more sugar, please. I had wanted to interrogate him in Shepherdswell, right in the station if need be. I wanted to get to him before the shock of his capture had time to wear off. But Scutt had ordered him taken to the Yard, and that was that. He'd been allowed to wash up, and now with his hair combed back and a teacup in his hand, he looked almost normal, in spite of the well-worn working clothes he had on.

"Captain Sidorov," Flack began, after a nod from Scutt. "You are facing very serious charges. Two murders and numerous crimes in connection with the hijacked trucks. We'd very much like to hear your side of the story."

"Murder? Whom have I murdered?" Sidorov said, manufacturing a surprised look on his face.

"You know very well, sir. Gennady Egorov and Rak Vatutin."

"They have been murdered, yes," Sidorov said. "But not by me."

"Perhaps we can simply start with what happened in Dover," Flack said. "The night you joined the Home Guard search party."

"I became separated from the group. Someone attacked me, hit me on the head, and after that, things are a bit vague. I have a memory of someone removing my uniform. I have no idea at all how I came to be wearing these clothes."

"How did you get from Dover to Shepherdswell?"

"I don't recall. The blow to my head must have affected my memory," Sidorov said as he sipped his tea. He wasn't even bothering to lie very well.

"I should inform you, Captain Sidorov," Scutt said, "that while diplomatic immunity does apply to many crimes, a charge of murder is quite serious. Immunity may be waived. In any case, at a minimum we can hold you for trial. Since Great Britain and the Soviet Union are Allies, and two of the victims were Soviet citizens killed on English soil, I would imagine your government would want the matter decided here."

"That makes sense," Sidorov said. "But I am not worried."

"So your story is that you wandered the countryside for days, and just happened to stumble onto your accomplice, Sheila Carlson?" Flack said, continuing with the questioning.

"Ah, there you have me. I do confess to a crime of the heart. I was having an affair with Miss Carlson. We had arranged to meet in Shepherdswell, and as I found myself close to there, and my wits returning, I thought it best to meet her."

"Thank you, Captain Sidorov," Flack said. He opened a folder on the table in front of him. "Or should I say Lieutenant Stefan Kobos, on medical leave from the Kościuszko Squadron. Or perhaps William Barlett." Flack tossed identity papers onto the table.

"These men do bear a resemblance, I admit," Sidorov said, giving the photographs the slightest of glances. "Not a very good likeness, though."

"You don't seem to appreciate the gravity of the situation, Captain," Flack said.

"I would say it is you who do not. While working with our American friends on a most secret and important project, I volunteered my services to join in the search for German parachutists. While in the field, I was attacked, and wandered for days with no clear recollection of where I was or what I was doing. Finally, when I am recovered enough to keep an appointment with a young lady, I am handcuffed and brought here, treated as an enemy of the people. And what do you have for proof of these fantastic claims? Forged papers with pictures of a man who looks somewhat like me? Preposterous."

"We have Sheila," I said, keeping my voice quiet and low.

"Or should we call her Margaret Pemble?" Flack said, pulling her papers out of the folder. "Or Victoria Fraser?"

"It was smart," I said, "having a second set of identity papers, in case your first plan went south. And I liked the wounded Polish fighter-pilot routine, too, right down to the pebbles in your shoes to make your limp look authentic." I took three pebbles from my pocket and threw them onto the table.

"Stones? These little stones are more proof? This is laughable."

"Here's the deal," I said. "Sheila hasn't killed anyone, so Scotland Yard is not interested in her." Sidorov didn't know that we had proof of Sheila feeding Eddie the poisoned cake and knifing him, so I left that out. Flack had gotten the medical report on Eddie's stomach contents, which included the poison-laced cake. "But MI5 is. Her controller, Mr. Brown, is looking for her to tie up loose ends. We've got her, Kiril. We've got her cash and all her identity papers. We'll cut her loose without a shilling, and call MI5 ten minutes before we do it. What do you think she'll do, faced with that choice? Rat on you, or take her chances?"

"Take her chances," Sidorov said, finishing his tea. "May I go now?"

Scutt didn't let him go. Next we had a try at Sheila. Since Scutt had her for Eddie Miller's murder, he didn't think there was much he could bargain with. But she took a tough stance, saying everything she'd done had been at the order of MI5, and she stressed her role as an informant for Scotland Yard as well. It was smart. If they charged her and brought her to trial, her evidence would have to be repressed due to the Official Secrets Act. That would give any lawyer enough to call for a dismissal.

We went back to Sidorov and lied through our teeth. Sheila had given him up, she'd sworn out a statement, and we were going to send her to America with a new identity, to protect her from MI5 and Mr. Brown. It was a good yarn, but Sidorov only had one question.

"What's the magic number?" he'd said. Nothing else. We didn't know what he meant until we pulled the same routine with Sheila.

"What's the magic number?" she'd said.

"They have everything planned," I said to Scutt and Flack in their office. "Even the signal for when they have to give each other up. They figured we'd try this, so they have a code. If things got too hot and heavy and one of them was forced to give evidence, they'd give the number. That way the other knows it's for real."

"Then let's make things hot and heavy," Flack said, and outlined his plan. I liked it, and made a call to Cosgrove.

Two hours later, we stood in the main entrance to Scotland Yard. Sidorov was in cuffs, held by two constables. Opposite him was Sheila. Her eyes darted everywhere as she tried to work out what was happening. Her handcuffs were unlocked, and a woman constable guided her out the open door, keeping her a good five feet from Sidorov. They called to each other, but that was all they had time for. The constables turned Sidorov so he could see out onto the street. Standing on the sidewalk, at the bottom of the stone steps, was Mr. Brown. Two burly men stood on either side of him, their menacing glares focused on Sheila.

"Too bad," I said to Sidorov. "She seems like a real smart dame." Sheila was out on the steps now, and the constable closed the door behind her. There was nowhere for her to go except straight into the waiting arms of Mr. Brown and his thugs. She turned, and I could hear her words through the glass.

"Good-bye, Kiril." She was a killer, but she had grit. No screams, no begging for mercy. She descended the stairs, head held high.

"No," Sidorov said. "Get her back. I will confess. To everything."

HE DID. BASED on my agreement to make good on a new American identity for Sheila. I promised I would make that happen as soon as she was released by Scotland Yard. What Sidorov didn't know was that she was being formally charged with the murder of Eddie Miller at that very moment, so I wasn't worried about her being released anytime soon. Another thing Sidorov didn't know was that Mr. Brown had been sacked, and was being debriefed about his excesses by MI5. Cosgrove had called in a favor and gotten him delivered to the sidewalk in front of Scotland Yard for five minutes. The thugs were our thugs, not his. It was a con.

Kaz had been released, and emerged from a very long bath at the Dorchester yearning to breathe free and eat hearty. In the hotel dining room that night, we gathered to toast his freedom: Harding, Big Mike and Estelle, and even Cosgrove. Estelle had done well on her surveillance duties, and Harding had given her and Big Mike a two-day pass so he could show her around town. They were in seventh heaven, and even Harding was in a good mood. Cosgrove was friendly, and told stories of the Boer War in South Africa, where he'd served alongside Winston Churchill himself. Kaz and Big Mike drank too much vodka, but I stayed away from the stuff. There was champagne and fine wine, and I drank enough to enjoy the taste and avoid a hangover. Everyone was so happy. I thought of Diana, remembering holding her tight on the deck of the destroyer, with smiling, laughing people all around us.

I should have known.

CHAPTER ▪ THIRTY-ONE

THE SUMMONS HAD come around noon. I was in the office at Norfolk House, typing up my report. Harding told me Cosgrove had called, and that he'd pick me up at the front entrance, and to make sure my shoes were shined. He wasn't as talkative as he'd been at dinner the night before, so I didn't ask questions, spit shined my dress browns, and hoofed it to the street.

"Follow my lead," Cosgrove said when I got into the car. It was a short ride. The driver let us off at the rear of the Foreign Office, and we entered a sandbagged bunker at the side of the white steps that led up to the government buildings, set along the Thames. Royal Marine sentries snapped a salute to Cosgrove, who showed his papers and was escorted in, with me tagging along.

"He'll be down this way," Cosgrove said, navigating the narrow corridors and cramped rooms as if he knew them well.

"Who?" I said. "What's going on?"

"The prime minister called, Boyle. That's what's going on. Look sharp, you're about to meet Winston. Guaranteed to be an experience."

"Charles, good of you to come!" boomed a voice as we entered a room made small by desks, ventilation ducts, support beams, a wall-sized map of the world, and the unmistakable figure of Winston Churchill.

"At your service, Prime Minister," Cosgrove said.

"No need to be so formal, Charles. I just asked an old friend over for a chat. Come, let's go into the Cabinet Room, much quieter there." The Cabinet Room was empty except for a square table that took up most of the space. At one corner sat a tray of bottles and glasses. Whiskey, brandy, water. Until now, Churchill had ignored me, and I stood back, uncertain of what to expect.

"Winston," Cosgrove said with an easy familiarity that surprised me, in spite of the stories he'd told last night. "This is Lieutenant Boyle, the fellow you asked about."

"Lieutenant," Churchill said, "I hope you'll join two old warhorses in a drink. Whiskey and water, I should think. Never liked whiskey as a young man, until I went abroad. When I was a subaltern in India and there was a choice between dirty water and dirty water with some whiskey in it, I chose the latter. I have always, since that time, made a point of keeping in practice."

"Yes, sir" was all I could get out.

"Oh dear," said Churchill, "we've made you nervous, Lieutenant Boyle. I should have remembered. Charles and I were lieutenants together in South Africa, during the Second Boer War. We wouldn't have enjoyed being dragged in to drink with two old men, would we?"

"Depends on their liquor," Cosgrove said. Churchill laughed and passed the glasses around.

"Sit, gentlemen," Churchill said. He settled in and produced a cigar from his jacket pocket. He wore the familiar three-piece pin-striped suit, with a gold watch chain decorating the vest, and a polka-dot bow tie. He worked at lighting the cigar, took a drink, and smacked his lips. For a moment, he reminded me of Archie Chapman, the bon vivant gangster in his underground lair.

"I understand, Lieutenant Boyle, that you've solved the puzzle of these dead Russians. One of their own, I take it?"

"Yes, sir, in league with a woman. An Englishwoman. Apparently he recruited her as an informant, and they fell in love. Their plan was to get some money, new identities, and disappear."

"Leaving a corpse behind we'd think was Captain Sidorov," Cosgrove added. "Apparently he was decent enough to want to spare his family retribution."

"Stalin is cold and ruthless," Churchill said. "As is their entire system of government. This Sidorov then is not entirely without scruples?"

"He killed when his plan was threatened," I said. "But much of it centered around protecting his wife and daughter from Article 58, if you're familiar with that, sir."

"The law that would make his wife and child enemies of the people," Churchill said. "I wonder if it will still apply."

"I don't know, this is a criminal matter, not political," I said.

"It is all politics, Lieutenant. It was politics when he dressed up the first murder to be blamed on the Poles. It has been political, with ambassadors hounding me; Stalin—Stalin himself—demanding that our man in Moscow explain what is happening. You're aware of the Polish situation?"

"You mean the massacre at Katyn? Yes."

"The less said about that, the better. There's more to this than Katyn, Lieutenant. The Poles are agitating for their prewar borders after the fighting is over. But they took their eastern lands from the Russians in the 1920 war, so who can say which is right? Now the Poles in London want us to take sides, and the Americans, too. And at what danger to this grand alliance? Do the Poles ever think of that?"

"I imagine they think of freedom, sir."

"Sadly, Poland is occupied by the Nazis. Freedom cannot be thought of until we rid Europe of Hitler and his regime. That can only be done in conjunction with the Soviet Union. Stalin may be a beast, but he's a beast at war with the beast at our door."

Why I was here began to sink in. I drank my whiskey and water and kept my mouth shut.

"I've spoken with the commissioner," Churchill said. I knew who he meant: Sir Philip Game, commissioner of the Metropolitan Police.

"Sidorov is going free," I said.

"He will go home to the Soviet Union," Churchill said. "Hardly free. At this juncture, we cannot allow any potential for rupture in our relations with Stalin. He could see this as a sign of our taking sides between the Moscow Poles and the London Poles. Too much of this affair has been wrapped up with the Katyn matter. The murder of Egorov, the informants at the Rubens Hotel, the attempted murder of that poor Polish boy. The arrest of Lieutenant Kazimierz."

"You're very well informed, Prime Minister," I said. I knew it was hopeless to say anything else. In Churchill's mind, the release of one Russian killer was a small price to pay for insuring all those other Russians kept killing Germans.

"I'd like to be informed as to your attitude, young man. Charles tells me you have a sharp mind, but that you can be unorthodox. I need to know this matter will be settled. Prosecuting Sidorov and creating a breach with Stalin will not help the Poles, or us. Only the Nazis will benefit."

I told him he had nothing to worry about. After all, I was drinking his whiskey.

"SO WHAT'S THE plan?" I asked Cosgrove as we got back into his staff car. I really wanted to ask him about my sharp mind, but I kept my curiosity to myself.

"Sidorov is going home with the story he told. Attacked by a downed German flier while assisting the Home Guard. Found wandering days later, severe concussion. No reference to Sheila Carlson. It's been worked out privately with Ambassador Ivan Maisky."

"The Russian ambassador and you worked this out?"

"Sometimes it pays to find common ground. Ivan likes it here in London. The more smoothly things run, the longer before he's called home to Moscow."

"When is Sidorov going?"

"Today. Ivan has sent Sidorov's uniform and personal effects to me. The captain will wash, shave, and dress. Then on to the RAF field at Digby for a flight to Gibraltar, then Lisbon, where he will be met by representatives from the Soviet Embassy, and thence to Moscow. Where he will be greeted as a hero, most likely."

"What about Sheila?"

"Miss Carlson will face a lesser charge, in exchange for keeping quiet."

"How much lesser?"

"Possession of forged ration cards. She will serve time in prison until the end of the war."

"They're getting away with murder."

"Yes. I don't suppose it will help to tell you I don't like it either," Cosgrove said.

"It does, actually. Could I ask two more favors?"

"That one with Brown wasn't difficult. What are they?"

"I'd like to ride with Sidorov to Digby. No funny business, I promise you. Then, whenever you have one of those MI5 and MI6 powwows, I'd like to drop by. As soon as it can be arranged."

"No sidearm, and you may escort Sidorov to Digby. Along with my men, of course," Cosgrove said.

"Of course. And the meeting?"

"As you well know, Lieutenant Boyle, such meetings do not exist, since MI6 operates only outside of Great Britain."

"Of course. When will you *not* be meeting?"

"Tonight, at ten o'clock, no such meeting will take place at the same location at which the last meeting did not take place."

"I'll be there," I said. "Or I won't be, right?"

"Now you've got it."

SIDOROV WAS SURPRISED to see me when the car picked him up at Scotland Yard. He hid it quickly, covering his expression with a friendly grin. "Billy, have you come to see me off?"

"I thought you might like some company," I said, opening my jacket and raising my arms for Cosgrove's men to search me. "Nothing up my sleeve, guys." They didn't even smile. One of them sat up front with the driver, and Sidorov and I had the spacious backseat to ourselves.

"I shall miss London," he said, looking at the Thames as we drove by.

"Maybe you could come back, after the war."

"No. There is only one chance given to visit the West. I shall remain in Russia, with my wife and child."

"Do you love her?"

"My daughter, yes. But my wife? I will tell you the truth. Her father is a high Party member. I married her as much for that as for love."

"Why?"

"To have a chance at something better than the life of an orphaned peasant. But I got more than I bargained for in that exchange."

"What do you mean?"

"Her father took a liking to me. He has encouraged my career."

"What's wrong with that?" I asked. "That probably got you this posting."

"No, it got me my previous assignment. This posting was a reward, for a job well done."

"What did you do?" Sidorov didn't answer. Instead, he watched pubs, houses, and shops pass by as the car drove out of London. A few miles later I tried another angle. "Why did you warn me about Diana?"

"A harmless piece of information I had come by. Harmless if kept out of the wrong hands, of course. I thought you might not look upon me as a suspect if you thought I had information that would bear on her safety."

"*Is* she safe?"

"Billy, I have no reason to think otherwise. I do not know anything other than that she is working within the Vatican. It was reported to us, through our network in Rome, that a British SOE agent had made contact with a circle within the Vatican. When her name was confirmed, we cross-referenced our contact files, and there you were. She may be in great danger, or she may be across the Swiss border. I have no idea."

"You have a pretty extensive network. Here and in Rome."

"The English have a lot of foolish romantics, Billy. Some of them saw the Marxist state as the salvation of humanity. Trust me, those who think that way have never been there."

"You have spies in the government? MI5? MI6? How else could you have learned her name?" Again, miles of quiet slipped by, and I knew Sidorov would not give up this information. A hint, perhaps, but nothing more. I took a book from my pocket. "Here. I thought you'd want this." It was the copy of *Selected Poems* by W. B. Yeats, from the cottage in Shepherdswell. Sidorov took it and pressed the covers between his palms, as if it held the essence of all that he had lost.

"Thank you," he said. Then he did an odd thing. He tore out the first page of the book, where he'd written the Latin inscription. He stared at it for a moment, then rolled down his window, and let it fly out into the wind.

"*Corpora dormiunt vigilant animae,*" he said.

"The bodies are asleep, the souls are awake," I answered. "Why can't that go home with you?"

"Latin is the language of the church. By definition, reactionary. A small thing, to be sure, but others have been denounced for less. For nothing."

"I can see why you wanted to start a new life here," I said. "Don't worry, I'm not trying to get a confession out of you, the case has been closed. Winston Churchill told me himself."

"Really? I thought my own government would free me. I never dreamed Churchill would be the one."

"He doesn't want to upset the balance of things. With inconsequential matters like two murders in London or thousands in Katyn."

"I am sorry about those two deaths."

"What about the Poles at Katyn?"

"I was not responsible," Sidorov said. "Egorov and Vatutin were pigs. If they hadn't been in the secret police they would have found other ways to inflict pain. But still, I did not wish to kill them. It was unfortunate."

"Is it their souls that are awake?" I asked. My question brought more silence, and the final miles fell away until we entered the gate of the RAF airfield. We drove directly to a waiting Lancaster bomber, already turning over its four powerful engines.

"It appears the English can't wait to get me out of the country," Sidorov said. I asked the guys in the front seat to give us a minute, and they got out, leaving us alone in the car.

"Where did you see that Latin saying?" I asked Sidorov.

"It was inscribed in a stained-glass window, in a small Norman church not far from Shepherdswell. I saw it when Sheila and I were looking for a secluded house to rent. Why?"

"Just curious," I said. "What does it mean to you?"

"A reminder, to never forget a great sin."

"I'm surprised to find a religious NKVD man."

"It is not common, especially if you want to move up in the Party ranks. It may seem strange to you, but I've always been religious, ever since the orphanage. And yes, I know, I have an odd way of showing it."

"I won't argue that. Confession is supposed to be good for the soul," I said. "Anything you want to tell me before you go?"

"My sins are too great, Billy. The worst of it is, where I am going, they are not considered evil. It is almost comical, isn't it? I commit crimes in England, and they send me home to Russia, where my greater crimes were rewarded. I can't seem to be held to account."

"For what, Kiril?" I asked, almost in a whisper. He looked down at the floorboard, then laid a hand on my arm.

"I was at Katyn." The words hung heavy in the air, as if they held a terrible curse. "I was second in command at an NKVD prison near Smolensk. I had orders to bring a contingent of prisoners to the forest outside of Katyn. Not Polish POWs, but regular prisoners, some criminal, some political."

"For what?"

"The graves had already been dug. Pits, really, you couldn't even call them proper graves. Excavated by heavy machinery. With the Poles stacked up in them, they didn't need bulldozers, just muscle and shovels to cover the bodies. That was my job, to cover up the bodies. Much like everyone else is still doing."

"You saw it all?"

"Yes. I stayed as far away as I could, but it was unavoidable. They marched them in from the railroad, all day. Thousands of Poles. Thousands of pistol shots. And my prisoners would work through the night, covering the bodies."

"That was the assignment you carried out so well?"

"Only in part. After the last of the Poles were killed, they sent us into the forest one more time. They'd left one pit unfilled, for my prisoners. A small pit, to be sure, for one hundred men. It was hard labor for the guards, shooting them and then having to do the work of burying them. The prisoners went quietly, though. They'd seen so much killing, they seemed to accept it as inevitable."

"Had you known?"

"No, not until that last day. There was nothing I could do if I didn't want to end up in the pit myself. I used my pistol and a shovel that day, to show my men I was a proper comrade, ready to share their burden. I could not do otherwise, could not order men to murder and keep my own hands clean. That is what my father-in-law rewarded me for. My enthusiasm."

There was a sharp rap on the window. It was time for Sidorov to go.

"Good-bye, Captain" was all I could say.

"Farewell, Billy. I'm afraid the confession has not helped my soul, and only unfairly burdened yours. But you asked."

"I did," I said, as Sidorov opened the door.

"Do you know what is odd?" Sidorov said, one foot out the door. "At night, I still pray. When I am alone, I pray. As if anyone might answer."

The door slammed shut, and the Lancaster engines roared their desire to fly into the high, cold darkness. I stayed in the car and watched until the bomber was lost in the starry sky and silence cloaked the night. I knew then why Dad had never told me what he'd done to get Nuno out of trouble with the Mob. There are times when the wheels of justice have to go off course to set things right, and those times are best kept to yourself. I'd never ask again.

THIS TIME, AS I entered the headquarters of MI5, I didn't have to cool my heels in the foyer. I was expected, and a guard escorted me up to a small conference room, slightly larger than Cosgrove's office, where the previous meeting had been.

"Ah, Lieutenant Boyle," Cosgrove said warmly as I entered. There were eight men in the room, and they all closed their file folders as I came close. Folders with *Most Secret* stamped in red. "You know Kim Philby, of course. The others, well, you don't really need to know their names. Sit." There was a round of chuckles, and I took a seat next to Philby. Besides Cosgrove, his was the only face I recognized.

"Where's Mr. Brown tonight?" I asked.

"Mr. Brown has been reassigned. Mr. Smythe has taken over his responsibilities, should you need to discuss anything with him. Now, tell us, how did things go with Sidorov?"

"Fine," I said. "He's on his way to Lisbon now."

"Good," one of the unnamed men said. "We can do without any further difficulties. Well done."

"Tell me, Lieutenant Boyle," Philby said as he lit his pipe. "Why did you ask to attend this meeting? Are you looking for a different posting? MI6 is always looking for new talent."

"Thank you, sir, but no. I'd been curious if I could get Sidorov to agree to work for us—meaning the U.S. and Great Britain—thinking it would be useful to have someone on the inside in Moscow. I had a hunch he might go for it, but I needed more time. I decided to try and close the deal on the way to the airfield."

"Close the deal?" Philby asked, arching an eyebrow. "In what way?"

"Talking to him, trying to figure out what motivated him. It seemed clear that if he wanted so badly to get out of going back, he must not be a big fan of the workers' paradise. Turns out he hates his father-in-law, who's some NKVD bigwig. Not too fond of his wife, either. She's too much of a dedicated Communist for his taste. Apparently she works for the Propaganda Ministry and believes everything they publish. I finally got him to see it would be his best revenge, to use them against Stalin, as his cover."

"Remarkable," Cosgrove said.

"I also promised him a bankroll, if he ever managed to get out," I said.

"Money is not a problem," Philby said. "But how are we supposed to contact him?"

"*Corpora dormiunt vigilant animae,*" I said. "That's the password. He'll repeat it back in English."

"The bodies are asleep, the souls are awake," Cosgrove said, slowly translating the Latin. "Fitting."

"Excellent, Boyle," Philby said. The others nodded, making notes. "It will be especially useful after the war."

"And now as well," one of the others said. "The more we know about Stalin's postwar intentions, the better. We'll put a man in touch with him."

Philby rose to show me out. When we were in the hallway, with the door shut behind us, he leaned in close and spoke in a low voice. "I wanted to thank you for putting me onto Dalenka. We never knew a member of the Three Kings had survived, much less made it to London. She'll be very valuable."

"I'm glad," I said as I shook hands with Philby. I hoped working for MI6 would be an improvement over the Chapman gang.

I left them to their pipes and files, and walked back to the Dorchester. It was a starry night, but no bombers flew over London. The crowds were out, filling the sidewalks and taking in the sights. I imagined Diana looking up at the stars in Rome, and felt certain that, at least for now, she was safe, doing what she needed to do. Someday, we'd walk arm in arm again, perhaps in London, perhaps in some city not yet free of the Nazis.

I thought about the eight men I'd left in that room. From Sidorov's hints, I knew there was a spy in MI6. There was a good chance it was one of them, or somebody who worked for them or to whom they reported. That was why I'd wanted to ride with Sidorov, to give myself enough time with him to make my story plausible, and to leave no chance of its being checked. Also to give him a chance to convince me he didn't deserve to be set up. But that hadn't happened. Instead, he told me what I needed to do. To be the one who held him to account.

I didn't know who it might be, and had to trust that Cosgrove would investigate discreetly, as he said he would. But I didn't dare raise suspicions at this point; whoever it was, I wanted him to think he was safe and secure so he wouldn't hesitate to send on information about Sidorov.

I had no idea how these things worked. It might be as simple as a telephone call or as complicated as a coded message left at a blind drop. Maybe the information would be sent to Moscow by the diplomatic pouch, or by radio. It might take days or weeks, but I was certain that justice of a sort would soon find Kiril Sidorov, as the NKVD took him in the dark of the night, arrested him as a traitor and spy, and threw him into Lubyanka Prison, perhaps in the same cell where Tadeusz Tucholski had been held. Perhaps he'd have a trial, but it didn't matter. The verdict was already decided. Kiril Sidorov had betrayed his family and the Motherland. The executioner would become the victim.

Perhaps then, souls might sleep. His, at least.

AUTHOR'S NOTE

THE EVENTS DESCRIBED in this novel regarding the Katyn Forest Massacre are true. Based on written orders issued by NKVD head Lavrentiy Beria, and co-signed by Joseph Stalin and other members of the Soviet Politburo, approximately twenty-two thousand Polish officers, policemen, and other professionals held by the Soviets were executed at Katyn as well as at other locations in the Soviet Union. Since the first graves were uncovered at Katyn, the entire murderous affair became known by that name.

When evidence of the massacres emerged, the western response was focused on maintaining the alliance with the Soviets, whose offensives were grinding down the Germans in advance of the D-Day invasion of Europe. Winston Churchill privately agreed that the Soviets were responsible, but his public statements pointed to German guilt. *The Katyn Manifesto*, published in England in 1943, placed the blame for the massacre on the Soviets, based on information obtained from Poles who had been released from Russian prisons. The author, Geoffrey Potocki de Montalk, was arrested by Scotland Yard's Special Branch for his writings and imprisoned for the duration of the war.

The American government also participated in the Katyn cover-up. Navy Lieutenant Commander George Howard Earle III, President Roosevelt's special emissary to the Balkans in 1943, was ordered by FDR to compile information on the Katyn Massacre. Earle's conclusion in 1944 was that the Soviet Union was responsible. FDR rejected the report, stating that he was convinced Nazi Germany had committed the atrocities. When he ordered Earle's report suppressed, a frustrated Earle formally requested permission to publish his findings. FDR issued a written order to desist. To ensure his silence, Earle was reassigned and spent the rest of World War II in the Pacific on the island of American Samoa.

In 1990, the Prosecutor General's Office of the Russian Federation admitted Soviet responsibility for the killings, but declined to categorize them as war crimes or genocide, thereby sidestepping the possibility of charges being filed against surviving perpetrators.

When Billy arrives in London in January 1944, he witnesses the start of an actual German air offensive that became known as the Baby Blitz. The Luftwaffe had assembled a force of over five hundred aircraft and in January '44 began a series of mass attacks, the largest since 1941. The raids continued for three months, and although they came as a surprise to the British, they were not a success. The Luftwaffe loss of bombers was high, which contributed to their ineffectual response to D-Day in June 1944.

The Liverpool Underground shelter, minus Archie Chapman, was a well-organized shelter, with the facilities described. Many Londoners did continue to sleep in the Tube stations long after the original Blitz was over, and it is easy to imagine them snug in their bunks with satisfied smiles, as their neighbors made do with a cold floor.

Operation Frantic, a series of shuttle bombing raids, commenced in June 1944 to support Soviet offensives that coincided with the D-Day invasion of Normandy. It was originally conceived on a grand scale, but the Soviets resisted the idea of large American bases within their borders. The raids did complicate German defenses, but only a small contingent of U.S. personnel was ever stationed in the USSR.

The beautiful and haunted Dalenka is fictional, but the Three Kings was an underground Czechoslovakian anti-Nazi organization. Its members were all killed in action or executed.

Kim Philby was the true-life head of MI6 Section 6, responsible for all intelligence matters in the Mediterranean. He was also a Soviet agent, originally recruited by his Cambridge tutor, and operated successfully until his defection to the Soviet Union in 1963. During his senior tenure at MI6 during the Second World War and the Cold War, Philby betrayed numerous secrets to the Soviets, including the names of British and American agents who subsequently were tortured and executed. Philby believed he held the rank of colonel in the NKVD, and would be received as such when he ultimately was forced to defect to the Soviet Union. Instead, the NKVD ignored him for ten years, during which he descended into alcoholism. He betrayed even his loyal English wife, who had remained with him, as he seduced the wife of another British traitor, Donald Maclean. He died in 1988.

ACKNOWLEDGMENTS

WHILE IT IS true that writing is a solitary endeavor, the end result can be improved through the thoughtful efforts of others. Two people stand out for special acknowledgment of their contributions.

Laura Hruska, Soho Press publisher and editor, has taught me more than I thought there was to know about the fine art of editing. Like a master mechanic who tunes an engine before a race, the work of a superb editor such as Laura works imperceptibly to smoothly speed the story along.

Deborah Mandel, my wife and now fellow writer, has willingly endured many readings of each manuscript, giving me valuable suggestions for improvements and clarity along the way. Her loving and constant support is a blessing.

Copy of the NKVD memo from Beria, ordering the execution of Polish officers. Signed by Stalin and other members of the Soviet Politburo.

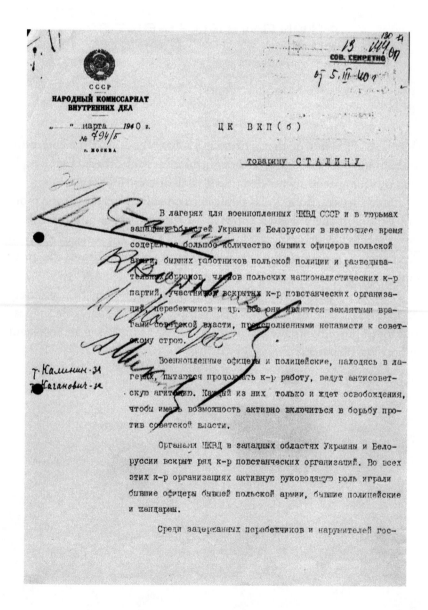